SECRET MISCHIEF

SECRET MISCHIEF

Robin Blake

SEVERN
HOUSE

First world edition published in Great Britain and the USA in 2021
by Severn House, an imprint of Canongate Books Ltd,
14 High Street, Edinburgh EH1 1TE.

Trade paperback edition first published in Great Britain and the USA in 2022
by Severn House, an imprint of Canongate Books Ltd.

severnhouse.com

British Library Cataloguing-in-Publication Data
A CIP catalogue record for this title is available from the British Library.

ISBN-13: 978-0-7278-9070-2 (cased)
ISBN-13: 978-1-78029-767-5 (trade paper)
ISBN-13: 978-1-4483-0505-6 (e-book)

All Severn House titles are printed on acid-free paper.

MIX
Paper from
responsible sources
FSC
www.fsc.org   FSC® C013056

Typeset by Palimpsest Book Production Ltd.,
Falkirk, Stirlingshire, Scotland.
Printed and bound in Great Britain by
TJ Books Limited, Padstow, Cornwall.

For my grandson
Freddie

'The secret mischiefs that I set abroach
I lay unto the grievous charge of others.'
William Shakespeare, *Richard III*

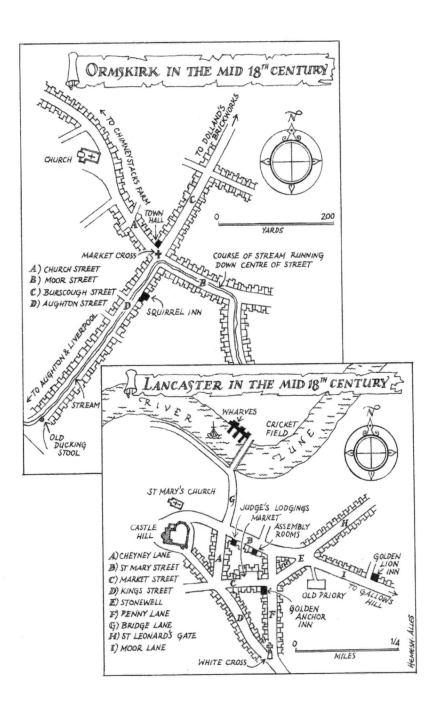

ORMSKIRK IN THE MID 18TH CENTURY

CHURCH

TO CHIMNEY STACKS FARM

TO DOLLAND'S BRICKWORKS

N

TOWN HALL

C

A

MARKET CROSS

0 — 200
YARDS

COURSE OF STREAM RUNNING
DOWN CENTRE OF STREET

A) CHURCH STREET
B) MOOR STREET
C) BURSCOUGH STREET
D) AUGHTON STREET

B

D

SQUIRREL INN

TO AUGHTON & LIVERPOOL

STREAM

OLD DUCKING STOOL

LANCASTER IN THE MID 18TH CENTURY

RIVER LUNE

WHARVES

CRICKET FIELD

N

ST MARY'S CHURCH

G

JUDGE'S LODGINGS
MARKET
ASSEMBLY ROOMS

CASTLE HILL

A

B

H

GOLDEN LION INN

E

I

TO GALLOWS HILL

A) CHEYNEY LANE
B) ST MARY STREET
C) MARKET STREET
D) KINGS STREET
E) STONEWELL
F) PENNY LANE
G) BRIDGE LANE
H) ST LEONARD'S GATE
I) MOOR LANE

C

OLD PRIORY

D

F

GOLDEN ANCHOR INN

0 — 1/4
MILES

WHITE CROSS

HEMESH ALLES

ONE

I t was on a breezy Monday in April 1746 that I received a letter from a townsman of Ormskirk. A violent slaying had occurred, my correspondent told me. 'The body still lies undisturbed where it fell here on my property, and is a sight that gives dole and grief as only the death of a member of the family can do. Please make haste to come and commence an inquest, for we would much like to know how it came about. Your servant, Richard Giggleswick.'

I left for the town the same morning, but first I sent a note to my young friend Dr Fidelis, asking him to stand by in readiness. In the past I'd been in his debt for his scientific examinations of bodies under inquest. I was sure on this occasion that if I asked him to come he would not dawdle, for I knew that there was a lady in Ormskirk to whom he was far from indifferent.

Ormskirk lies twenty miles to the south of my home at Preston. It is a small town at the cross of two coaching roads and with a battered old castle, formerly owned by the Earls of Derby, nearby. The ground on which it stands slopes, giving the whole town a tilted look. Indeed it has a long-held reputation for oddness. The most prominent example of this is the parish church, which always boasted both a thick square tower and, standing beside it, a pointed spire, as if its builders couldn't decide which they wanted most, and so had provided themselves with both. The spire fell down in 1731 but the town has been ever since determined to rebuild it, carefully preserving the stump until funds are there to put it up again. Riding around as I arrived I tried to call to mind some of the other quaint customs of the place. The town's ducking stool on Aughton Street was carefully maintained and was the site of some time-honoured ceremony each year, something like the ceremonious ducking of a goat. Or perhaps it was a duck. I seemed to recall, also, an annual bonfire on which a life-sized effigy of Old Mother Redcap made of gingerbread was burned. Ormskirk was noted for its gingerbread.

Enquiring of the landlord at the Squirrel, Ormskirk's coaching inn, I was told that Richard Giggleswick was a farmer with land that spread over thirty fertile acres. His house lay to the west, but close by the town.

'What type of man is Mr Giggleswick?'

'He is a good man, well liked.'

'Is he prosperous?'

'He seems so. Brings a lot of fruit and vegetables to market here. Sends much more to Liverpool.'

'Have you heard of a death at his house yesterday?'

'At Chimneystacks?'

'In the house, or perhaps on the land. A member of his family, I am led to believe.'

'A member of his family? No. We've not heard of such a thing.'

It surprised me that in a place where there had been a death – and perhaps a killing – the work of the day went on as usual. At my first sight of Farmer Giggleswick of Chimneystacks Farm he was driving a cartload of cabbages into the yard while shouting orders over his shoulder to various fellows who were at work forking over a midden. He was clearly no fireside farmer who left all the work to others. His boots were caked with muck and his clothing smelled of it.

'Are you Cragg?' he said.

I told him I was, and asked the name of the deceased that he had written to me about.

'It's Geoffrey. Come with me. I'll show you.'

A tall, lean man in middle age, he led me across the yard, which was bounded by his house on one side and a large well-appointed brick barn facing it, connected by a row of six neat stables. I noticed a small boy of eight or nine standing in the doorway of the farmhouse, holding the hand of a girl a few years older. They watched us with the expressionless curiosity often seen in children. I waved to them and the boy waved back.

'My son and daughter,' said Giggleswick. 'Sarah and Charles. With their mother snuffed out, they only have me to light their path. I constantly fear for them, Mr Cragg. A child has only its parents, after all. If I should die, what will happen to them?'

A narrow gap between stables and barn gave access to a second smaller dairy yard, very neat, which we also crossed. Outside this was a grassy field in which cows grazed and on the other side a range of low buildings beside a second field, this one churned up and muddy. A sharp pungency blown by the wind into our faces told me we were approaching the piggery.

There was a row of eight brick pig-houses facing the mud-field, each with a slated pitch roof, front door and extremely mucky little garden, contained and separated from the others by white iron fencing. In each of the first seven of these gardens a porker stood curiously eyeing us. The one at the end had a large square of sail-cloth covering something lying in the mud. Giggleswick pointed.

'There he is,' he said. 'There's Geoffrey's body, Mr Cragg.'

The mud was filthy and saturated and I was glad of my riding boots as I opened the gate and took a few squelching steps while the farmer remained outside the fence. He was looking constantly around, and with particular concern at the dense wood growing on the other side of the field faced by the piggery.

The sail-cloth was anchored by bricks all around its edge. I crouched and twitched it, catching a glimpse of pale pink skin beneath. Maybe a cheek, I thought, or part of a bare arm.

'And is Geoffrey your relation?' I said.

Giggleswick gave a humourless laugh.

'Give over.'

'Then who is he?'

'You will see,' he said. 'Look under the tarpaulin.'

'Will you not help me?'

He made no move to do so but kept his eye on the edge of the wood. I started to remove the anchoring bricks one by one until I was able to stand, pull the sail-cloth up and take a proper look beneath.

'Uh, Mr Giggleswick,' I said after a moment. 'I am a little dumbfounded.'

'Why is that, Mr Cragg?'

'This is not what I expected to find.'

'Why not?'

'Because it is the body of a pig, sir.'

'Why would it not be?' said the farmer. 'This is the piggery.'

'It is not the fact that it's a pig that puzzles me, Mr Giggleswick. It is for what reason you have called upon me.'

'Why, to look into his death! Geoffrey was my boar, and a highly potent one. Now he has been assassinated and I desire to find out who did it.'

I dropped the sail-cloth and slogged back to the gate. I let myself out.

'I think perhaps you misapprehend my job,' I said. 'I am the County Coroner. I look into the deaths of persons.'

Giggleswick pointed at the dead pig.

'Geoffrey was a person. He was a person of considerable character and importance on this farm.'

'It is a matter of legal definition. My task is limited to bodies that the law says are those of human beings. The law does not extend my powers in the animal direction.'

'Rubbish. Haven't you heard tell of pigs being wed by the rites of the Church? That happens. And when I were a young lad a sow killed a child here in Ormskirk. She were tried for murder by due process and duly hanged. So why cannot you, Mr Cragg, inquest into the death of this poor dead boar of mine?'

I couldn't help myself. I laughed.

'Only if you can prove Geoffrey was once a human being; that he committed a particularly heinous sin and was changed – or metamorphosed, shall we say? – by a power beyond our understanding.'

My repartee was prompted by what I'd been recently reading: the Roman poet Ovid and his vastly entertaining *Metamorphoses*, in whose stories such changes happen on every page.

'And if you cannot,' I added, 'then you have the consolation of two very fine sides of bacon.'

Giggleswick bristled with indignation at my tone.

'I am offended that you make a joke of this, sir. It was a murder just the same as if our Sarah or our Charlie were shot.'

I straightened my face.

'It's to your credit that you value your pigs highly, Mr Giggleswick. They are indeed lucky in their master. Geoffrey was shot, you say?'

'Yes, by someone lurking in them woods.'

'You saw it happen?'

'Aye, I was by. I was bringing his turnip-tops and swill. The ball went into his head. He gave not so much as a squeal, just fell

as dead as a sack of beets. Now I want this villain that shot him
to pay.'

'You do, and I am sorry. I suggest you make a count of your
enemies and ask the parish constable to catch the culprit.'

'Joseph Pickering? He is an idiot. A cold is all he'll ever catch.'

That was not unlikely, I thought, starting back towards the
farmyard where my horse was. Constables are often as feeble as
they are toothless. Giggleswick hastened to follow me.

'Whereas you, sir, have discovered more hidden murderers than
any man in these parts, I hear.'

'But I really cannot help in this case, Mr Giggleswick. You say
you are unhappy with my levity. Be glad that I do not take a more
serious view of this. Do you know, you have entirely wasted my
day? Be glad that I can see the amusing side.'

By the time I reached home in the evening the amusing side had
slipped out of my sight. I was cross and weary. Elizabeth, though,
laughed heartily when I told her the story of the day as we lay
that night in bed.

'Inquest a dead pig!' she said. 'That's what they're like in
Ormskirk. All sorts of tricks. Don't they have a crab tree that they
make mayor for the day?'

'That's a goat,' I said.

'Well, they've a crab tree that does something. It tells your
future, that's it. Did you happen to pass it by, my love?'

'I can tell you the future without any help from a crab tree, and
it is that I will be asleep in less than a minute. I am mortally tired.'

I kissed her and rolled over to fulfil my own prophecy.

The next morning Luke Fidelis called at the office. I heard him
admitted into the outer room by Robert Furzey my clerk and after
a short conversation he came laughing through to my inner room.

'Furzey has told me. You went to Ormskirk to view the body
of a porker. What was the verdict?'

'The pig was shot, its owner said. I didn't look very closely as
it was lying in almost liquid filth.'

'I am disappointed you never sent for me. Who shot it?'

'A cross-eyed hunter. A sausage-hater. How would I know? It
was a waste of my day.'

Fidelis was dressed for his rounds but he seemed in no hurry
to get on with them. He removed his wig and slung it on my wig-
stand, then sat down in one of my clients' chairs, which were
placed across the desk from my own.

'As you know I take a certain interest in the folk of Ormskirk.'

'Isn't it just one of them?'

'Well, yes, it is. But I am interested in knowing something
of the events of the place also, as it gives material for
conversation.'

'Is that why you visit the town? For conversation?'

'Of course it is. So who was the fellow with the dead pig?'

'Its owner.'

He snapped his fingers twice to simulate impatience.

'His name, please.'

'Richard Giggleswick.'

'And he farms?'

'Yes. His place is close to the west edge of the town. Quite
prosperous, I was told. Vegetables for the Liverpool market and
– as you've heard – pork.'

'Giggleswick. Giggleswick. No, the name means nothing.'

'Your, er, friend will know him I expect.'

Fidelis gave me a surprised look.

'Yes, I suppose that it's quite likely she will.'

'And you go there often. It is a small town. I expect the town
knows you quite well by now.'

Fidelis shook his head.

'I really doubt that. Now, I must be on my way. Shall we have
a bumper or two at the Turk's Head this evening?'

I agreed. It had been a week since we'd last drank together at
our favourite coffee house.

'Right,' said Fidelis retrieving his wig. 'Eight o'clock. But I
want no mention of her.'

'Whom do you mean?'

'*Her* – in Ormskirk. It's private. Agreed?'

The Turk's Head, unlike others in Preston, was a coffee house with
no politics. The proprietor Noah Plumtree did all he could to
encourage the spread of news, business discussions, philosophical
or antiquarian debate – even singing, card-play and arm-wrestling.

He encouraged anything but talk of Whig and Tory, which he held in abhorrence.

Tonight customers were circulating news of a ship that had foundered with all hands in a storm a few hours out of Liverpool, a bare-knuckle fight at Manchester that had gone sixty-five rounds, and a prodigious child at Kirkby Lonsdale who could do profound mathematical calculations instantaneously and all in her head. That was before customers got around to debating arguments taken out of the latest printing of *The Gentleman's Magazine*, and matters of local interest in the *The Preston Journal*.

This night a ropemaker by the name of Wagstaff was voluble on the subject of lotteries.

'Ask that child in Kirkby, gentlemen,' he was saying. 'The odds are grossly, impossibly unfavourable. But of course people prefer vain hope to mathematics. They would rather invest in dreams than in solid goods. I say Parliament should cease licensing all lotteries forthwith and save the people from themselves.'

Plumtree shouted a warning.

'No talk of Parliament in the house, IF you please, gentlemen. House rules.'

Wagstaff licked his thumb by way of ritual apology for his transgression but nothing would shut him up.

'The amount of disturbance on days when these lotteries are drawn is astounding. Rioting is usual. Violence against others is frequent and so is self-murder. Despair leading to incapable drunkenness is almost universal. And yet what do we hear? Our mayor is seeking to license one in Preston to build a hospital. But a lottery is the devil's instrument. Beware of it.'

Other customers, tired of Wagstaff's ranting, called out that a lottery was of no consequence, but a hospital was a different matter. Fidelis sipped his wine and listened carefully to all this. At the end he shook his head doubtfully.

'They may say that they want a hospital, and are sanguine about getting one by a lottery, but Wagstaff for all his shouting is quite right. Once the tickets go on sale and the prizes are published there will be a gambling frenzy and the object of the hospital will be quite forgotten in the excitement. The crazed gambler is devoid of moral conscience, Titus, because he – or she – is in blind pursuit of reward without merit.'

I am no gambler but Fidelis often played for stakes, and was liable to put his money down on all sorts of chances.

'Yet I have seen you seized by that excitement, Luke. I've seen you at the cockpit betting on fighting birds.'

'That's different. Seasoned gamblers understand the odds. People in general are fatally prone to the certainty that they will win – until the day of the draw, and of almost universal disappointment, followed by remorse, anguish and despair. No, Titus. Take gaming out of the cockpit and the racecourse and let it roam the streets – well, we may get a hospital, but it'll only be stuffed full of the distraught citizens whose greed and vain hopes paid for it.'

On my way home I was stopped in the dark by a wheedling voice coming from a recessed doorway. This had been the business premises of Thomas Jenks, Apothecary, but was now boarded across the windows, and the door had its brass knob and knocker removed.

'Will you spare a penny for an old fool?'

I knew the voice. It was that of Thomas Jenks himself. Two years had gone by since he had been ruined, first by his own drinking and then by the death of the wife whose stringency and thrift alone had kept him solvent. In his drunkenness he'd been making up his drugs in the wrong proportions, or with incorrect ingredients. Then a child died after taking one of his medicines for a light cold. Jenks's customers began to go elsewhere and soon enough his business failed. Jenks scraped together every coin he had, and then sold every piece of plate, and haunted the cockpit to recoup his losses. The result was predictable. He lost everything. I don't know where he slept, but he continued in business from the doorway of the same premises on Church Gate, though now the building itself was barred to him. The business he conducted was begging.

I sifted through the change in my pocket and peered into the dark space.

'Here,' I said, extending my palm holding tuppence into the darkness.

A hand grabbed the money.

'Thank you, sir. I'll eat tonight thanks to you.'

The voice was sibilant and trembling.

'Don't you mean you'll drink, Jenks?' I said, allowing a certain sternness into my voice.

'I might have a little celebration, Mr Cragg, and, if I do, I swear I'll give a toast in porter to your human compassion. You are a gentleman, sir.'

It is usually painful talking to beggars. Whatever the ostensible subject, the real one is always the contrast between their destitution, their hunger, their need, and your own comfort and security. Just calling me a gentleman seemed like a sly way of accusing me of not giving him enough. I handed over a third penny.

'Make sure you spend it on a pie, my friend,' I said. 'You cannot subsist on black beer alone, you know.'

TWO

Thursday
To the County Coroner, Preston, by Express:
    Sir, your presence is respectfully requested to attend a body here in Ormskirk for possible inquest. The place is Chimneystacks Farm on the edge of town, where I shall hope to make your acquaintance this day at your earliest convenience.
    Your servant, J. Pickering, Constable

So, Chimneystacks Farm again! It was only three days since my fool's errand to look at Giggleswick's dead boar. The letter had a postscript in a different, more childish hand. *Mr Cragg Please cum quick. It's me dad. Sarah.*

This time I thought of asking Luke Fidelis to accompany me, and I wrote him a note. The constable, however idiotic, surely knew enough not to invite me to view another of Giggleswick's dead pigs. And then there was Sarah's postscript: *It's me dad.*

Luke Fidelis answered my message by coming in person, and dressed for riding, so that we were ready to set off for Ormskirk immediately. This was the Liverpool road. It had been adopted

some time ago for turnpiking, but plans had come to nothing. Even
in its unimproved state, though, it was a good enough road and,
as our horses were fit, it was only two and a half hours later that
we rode into the yard of Chimneystacks Farm.

A sandy-haired man of around forty came out to greet us.

'I am Joe Pickering,' he said. 'I'm grateful you were able to
come so quickly.'

'What happened?'

'The farmer Mr Giggleswick's been shot yesterday night. It
looks deliberate.'

'And he's dead?'

'Oh yes, dead all right. Come in and see.'

The farmhouse was not in good order. Richard Giggleswick
may have kept a very clean and tidy farm, but evidently saw no
need to do the same in the house. I saw a sideboard with its legs
eaten by woodworm lurching drunkenly and the floors were
muddy and strewn with miscellaneous items: discarded boots,
rusty buckets, heaps of rags, cracked pots and broken chairs. In
the large kitchen-parlour a very old woman sat by the fire
mumbling to herself. The two children looking pale and big-eyed
were sitting at the table, the boy watching us warily, the girl
peeling potatoes.

'Are you Sarah?' I said.

'Yes,' she whispered, keeping her eyes fixed on the potato.

'I am Titus Cragg. You sent me a personal message, remember?
We shall have a talk in a little while.'

We went up a creaking oak stair to the bedrooms. Here the
disorder continued. The hangings were heavily moth-chewed. The
few carpets were ragged. Pictures hung cobwebbed and askew on
the walls. The windows let in limited light as the glass was so
caked in dirt and moss. The rangy body of Richard Giggleswick
was sprawled on the bed, eyes closed, mouth open, as if in some
drunken sleep.

'Did it happen in here?' I asked.

'No,' said Pickering. 'It were outside. The farm servants brought
him in. But he were already dead.'

'So they just spilled him on the bed like that? Have they no
respect?'

Fidelis and I, one on each side of the bed, straightened the body as best we could though it had stiffened and could not be arranged in a convincing attitude of repose.

'I will need to see those servants,' I told Pickering. 'Will you send for them, please?

Fidelis meanwhile was opening the front of the farmer's shirt to bare his chest. He immediately saw where the bullet had hit.

'It's found his heart,' he said. 'Looks like a perfect hunter's shot.'

Fidelis brought out various instruments from the bag of tricks he carried everywhere with him, and was ready to make a detailed examination. As he got started Pickering returned to say the two farm workers were waiting in the yard. I went down to them. As I passed through the kitchen the children and the old woman were sitting exactly as they had before.

A tall man in his thirties and a sturdy younger woman waited for me. They told me their names were Lance Brownjohn and Sally Glover.

'And are you both employed on the farm?'

They were.

'Living here?'

'I live here in the house,' said Sally. 'He lives in Ivy Cottage over by the road.'

'So will you tell me how Mr Giggleswick was found,' I said.

Lifting his eyebrows, Brownjohn jerked a thumb at the woman.

'Aye, I found him,' said Sally. 'I shouted for Lance and he came up next minute.'

'And what did you do then?'

'We carried him in the house.'

'Did you check to see if he was breathing?'

'He were never breathing,' said Brownjohn. 'His breathing days were over. I could see a bloody hole in his shirt by his heart. So we drew the conclusion and just carried him in. We put him on his bed and sent the boy running for Mr Pickering.'

'Where exactly was he lying when you found him, Sally?'

'Out near the piggery, just where the boar was killed, that's Geoffrey as was.'

'Will you show me?'

She led the way, into and across the dairy yard and over the pasture to the piggery. The occupants of the first seven sties were in their stinking little gardens as before, each regarding us with careful attention. Geoffrey's was empty.

Sally showed the place where the farmer's body had been lying, just in front of the fifth sty.

'Was there anything else here? A gun beside him, for instance?'

'No.'

'What time was it?'

'About half-six.'

'Yesterday evening?'

'Yes.'

'And what had Mr Giggleswick come here for?'

Brownjohn pointed to a barrow that stood nearby.

'Came with pigs' food. Turnips, scraps and that. Swill.'

'Was it his usual time for feeding the pigs?'

'His regular evening time, aye.'

'And had you seen him around the farm before you found him dead?'

'Yes,' said Sally. 'I saw him go in and out of the barn and the house two or three times. Then I saw him barrowing across the yard half an hour before I went to look for him.'

'And what made you go looking for him? Did you hear the shot? Either of you?'

'I heard nowt,' said Brownjohn. 'But about then I was sharpening a scythe. That's a noisy job.'

'Miss Glover?'

Sally shook her head.

'No, I'd been doing the evening milking and I took the churns down to the roadside for picking up. Happen it was then the gun was fired. I went looking for the master when I got back.'

'And why did you seek out Mr Giggleswick at that moment?'

'I thought one of the cows needed a look-at when I was milking. A bit poorly she was.'

'Do you think Mr Giggleswick came to the piggery alone?'

'Who else would've been with him?'

'Not the children?'

She shrugged.

'I doubt it. Sarah has that much to do in the house she'd no time to be trailing after her dad. Young Charlie? I don't know.'

'Who else works on the farm?'

'Just the Rudgeons, Big Jim and George,' said Brownjohn.

'Brothers?'

'Father and son. And George's boy Little Jim helps out running messages. They live in the next cottage to mine out on the road.'

'Where were the Rudgeons at the time of the shooting?'

Glover didn't know. She looked at Brownjohn.

'Working the fields,' he put in. 'A half-mile away or more.'

I pointed across the rough brown field at the wood.

'A half-mile beyond that wood?'

'Aye, that's where all Chimneystacks's land lies.'

'And when you first found the body, Sally, did you notice anything else, anything that was not usual?'

'No. I don't think so.'

'Did you see anyone or anything in that wood?'

'No, I didn't.'

'And can you think of any possible connection between the shooting of the pig Geoffrey and the shooting of Mr Giggleswick?'

'It might have been the same person shooting.'

'Quite so. If you have any more ideas on the subject, please come and tell me.'

I added that Sally, the first finder, would be needed to give evidence at the inquest, and told Brownjohn that I might want to call him too. Meanwhile, would he send Little Jim to fetch his father and grandfather in from the fields?

Sarah and I had our chat in the farmhouse's formal parlour, sitting on either side of an unlit fire. She was maybe twelve but in her misery looked even younger. First I explained carefully who I was, and ensured that she understood.

'Three days ago your father sent for me because his pig Geoffrey had been shot. I had to explain that as coroner I only enquire into human deaths. But now something has happened to Mr Giggleswick himself, something so terrible that it is proper for me to make enquiries. But of course I can only think there is some connection between the two shootings. Can you tell me what that is?'

'No, sir.'

'Had your father seemed worried about anything in recent days?'

'He is – was, I mean – always worried about something. Usually it was money or the weather.'

'Money? Can you tell me if your father had a man of business? A man who looked after money for him.'

'Yes, sir, that was Mr Parr from Liverpool.'

'Parr, you say? Ambrose Parr?'

'Yes, sir.'

'I have heard tell of him.'

'He must be a very great man of business, because when he came to visit me dad from Liverpool he drove in a fine carriage.'

I've mentioned the child looked miserable, but I would not say it was grief that made her so. She was not crying for her dead father, and was more frightened than grieved. Her next question told me why.

'What will become of me and Charlie, sir? And me grandma.'

It was much the same question that Giggleswick had posed to me two days before. So what caring father doesn't make provision against contingency?

'Your grandma?' I said. 'Is she the old lady in the kitchen?'

'Yes, sir. She's not compost mended, me dad said. She can do nowt for herself, not any more. Hardly says a word. Just sits by the fire. I can look after her but what about the farmwork? I can't take on that *and* me grandma. And Charlie's too young and needs looking after his self.'

'Your future all depends on your father's will, Sarah. He must have made provision for you and Charles in case of . . . In case of something like this happening. Don't you have uncles, aunts?'

'I don't know any.'

'Well, I believe your father's friend Mr Parr may. He is indeed a prominent attorney in Liverpool. If you would like to write a letter I'll see it goes straight to him. I would be surprised if he were not here to see you very soon, and give you counsel.'

I had a few more questions for the child. Had there been any visitors to the farm in the last few days? Had Giggleswick spent any time away from home? Had there been any change in the daily routine?'

She said no to each of these.

'And after Geoffrey the pig was shot, did your father say anything about who might have done that? Someone with a grudge against him, maybe?'

'Me dad didn't talk much to us kids, sir. He thought about the farm and not much else. We knew better than to ask him anything that he didn't choose to tell us.'

'He was strict with you?'

'Oh, he was stricter than any schoolmaster, was me dad.'

I caught a look in her eye, and it was an intelligent look. If I wasn't much mistaken young Sarah Giggleswick had a lively mind. Adulthood had come early for her now, but I felt sure she would find her way through and bring her brother along with her.

I heard voices outside the window, which looked into the garden, where there was a lawn, some flowerbeds and a mature elm tree. Luke Fidelis was walking there with Pickering. I excused myself and leaving Sarah went out to join them.

'You have made your examination, Luke?'

'I have made a preliminary one. Superficial, but suggestive.'

'In what way?'

'In the way of telling me that the killer was no mighty hunter. No champion marksman.'

'How do you make that out, Doctor?' said Pickering. 'The distance from the wood to the piggery's thirty yards at least. He would have to be a fair shot to get his man in the heart from that range.'

'He didn't, Joe. From that range he missed his target – twice.'

'Twice?' I said. 'How do you work that out?'

'First of all Richard Giggleswick had two gunshot wounds, Titus. The first one in the knee, very painful and enough to immobilize, but not fatal.'

'What about the shot through the heart?'

'That was from close range. My guess is that the knee wound was inflicted by a shot from long distance – from the wood on the other side of the field, in fact. Giggleswick went down, striking his head on something. Then the murderer re-loaded, walked across the field and put his second bullet into Giggleswick's chest from perhaps three yards. Not a difficult shot.'

'Why did the farmer not shout for help when he was wounded? He had the time.'

'I'm sure he did shout. I am supposing, with the wind blowing strongly from the east, and being a hundred and fifty yards from the house, that he couldn't be heard.'

'But you said the shooter missed the target twice.'

'Let's take another close look at the scene. Then I shall try to elucidate.'

At the piggery he was interested in the brick wall of the sty, and the metal fence which he looked at closely all the way along.

'Look here, Titus.'

He was pointing to a place in the fence in front of the late Geoffrey's sty, a place beneath the rail. A chip of paint on one of the uprights had come off and a scar of bright metal could be seen.

'This is recent – not yet rusty. The French have a word for it: ricochet. Without seeing the pig's corpse I am guessing, but I would say the bullet from the shot that killed the boar bounced off the rail and went straight into the animal's head.'

'The shooter was lucky to hit the mark, then.'

'No, the shooter was unlucky. He was not trying to kill the boar. He aimed at Giggleswick, but his piece shot low. Let's say he was trying to get Giggleswick in the heart. On Monday the bullet entirely missed him. Instead it hit the fence, perhaps two feet low. On Thursday it did hit Giggleswick, but in the leg – in other words at the same height from the ground as it had previously hit the fence. What does this tell us?'

'That the shot on Monday was a first attempt on Giggleswick's life, which failed. Yesterday the shooter came back for a second attempt, with the same gun.'

'Wonderfully summed up, Titus. The shot yesterday missed by about the same margin as it had on Monday, so it might well have been the same gun. But this time the target was felled with a crippling leg wound. The murderer simply had to get to close quarters to finish the job.'

'We had better have a look at the place where he took the first shot, then,' I said.

The wood on the other side of the field was thick and, in parts, near enough impenetrable. Approaching it we saw that it was separated from the field by a ditch and beyond that an old but effective wooden fence, made from parallel rails nailed to upright posts. The posts were about four feet high and spaced ten feet apart. The undergrowth was very thick along most of the wood's edge, but there were one or two places that were clearer at ground level. Here one could stand behind the fence and look across at the piggery in relative comfort, while being substantially concealed behind low branches and shrubs. Any one of these would have made ideal positions from which to shoot.

Crossing the ditch and walking along the fence on the field side, we looked into the first of these positions. It yielded no clue of any kind, and nor did the second. But the third was different. The grass underfoot was trodden down and there were lateral marks in the thin covering of green lichen on the wood of the fence's upper rail.

'It looks as if someone was standing on the other side there,' I said, 'and may have rested a weapon on this rail.'

'Not just rested but fired, I think,' said Fidelis. 'The top of the rail is strongly abraded in two places, do you see? And even the surface of the wood has been scarred. That is the effect of recoil.'

He put his finger on the rail, where the powdery coating of lichen had been removed across its width, as if by someone vigorously rubbing a stick back and forth. With sudden athleticism Fidelis vaulted over the fence. I left him and walked the remainder of the fence, but found no further marks that could have been made by resting a gun on it. I returned to Fidelis. He was crawling around on all fours with his face inches from the ground.

'I believe I can smell gunpowder very faintly,' he said. 'I would say there was a slight spillage when he loaded or more likely re-loaded, and doing so hurriedly. There's an indentation in the ground where he rested the gun butt.'

Back in the farmyard the Rudgeons awaited us. The old man was large and hale with an abundant white beard, while the younger was the wiry type, balding and sallow. I asked what conversations with their master they had had over the last few days.

'Every morning he gives us jobs for the day, like. Yest'day was no different. Blocked ditches out by Rook's Holt, he told us. Clear them out proper, he said. We were at it all day.'

'Did you come back to the farm when you'd finished?'

'No. It got dark. We just went home.'

'So you didn't know Mr Giggleswick was dead?'

'Not till we came in s'morning we didn't.'

'And had you noticed in the days beforehand any person or

people on the farm land, in any of the woods for instance, that shouldn't be there?'

Father and son looked at each other.

'Not a one.'

'And what about Mr Giggleswick himself? Did you find any change in his manner over the last few days, or weeks?'

They shook their heads gravely.

'No. It were always the same. He told us. We listened. No questions allowed. We just had to go and do it.'

'He was a demanding master?'

'You could say that.'

By now it was dinnertime and I felt the slight hollowness of hunger as I re-joined Fidelis and Pickering, who were smoking in the barn.

'I must go to the inn. There are letters to write and send. Constable, I mean to inquest this matter on Saturday. That will give me time enough to make enquiries, and for Furzey my clerk to get here.'

'You'll both come to dinner with us now, I hope,' said Pickering. 'The Squirrel's food's not bad, but my Caroline can do better. I've sent Little Jim with a note to tell her to expect you.'

At this moment Sarah ran into the barn with a folded paper in her hand, which she gravely presented to me.

'That's my letter asking for Mr Parr's help,' she said. 'Will you send it, Mr Cragg?'

'I'll do better,' I said. 'I'll take it to Liverpool myself.'

THREE

Pickering's trade was pottery and his shop, workshop and dwelling stood in one of the streets off the market. We went in through the shop and found it well-ordered and stocked with crocks of all kinds. I recalled Giggleswick's dismissal of the constable as an idiot, and how readily I had believed him. But I now saw that Pickering was a capable man whose business showed every sign of well-foundedness.

'Is the stock all of your own manufacture, Mr Pickering?'

'Oh yes. We can make anything you desire from egg cups to chamber pots. Caroline!'

A dark-haired, handsome woman came out from the dwelling apartment followed by three young children.

'Here's Mrs Pickering to greet you,' said her husband.

Caroline Pickering made a curtsy and invited us through to the table.

Although Mrs Pickering had had scant notice of our descent on her, the meal was ample and good. She laughed readily at my jokes and impressed me by her knowledge of literature. At a less cerebral level she impressed Fidelis too. He never picked his words so carefully as when in the presence of a pretty woman.

'We can inquest him on Saturday, can't we, Pickering?' I said.

'I've sent for my clerk Furzey on that assumption.'

'Aye, we'll have had enough time to drum up your jury by then.'

'And in the meantime we must set about finding the killer. But we are working in the dark. Knowing how he was killed isn't enough. We must know why. Nothing we've heard at Chimneystacks Farm suggests an answer – or not to me.'

'Nor me,' said Pickering. 'Giggleswick was a peaceable law-abiding fellow. He could be prickly, mind. But I can't see any reason why he would be purposely murdered.'

'Well, the murderer needs to be caught,' said Caroline. 'Suppose it's the start of a murder spree. They'll all be fretting in town till he's behind bars, whoever did this. But where on earth do you start looking?'

'We start with what we know about murder, Mrs Pickering,' I said. 'Love, money or pride: one of the three is almost invariably at the bottom of it, solely or in combination.'

'Well, Richard Giggleswick was a proud man, that's true.'

'However, was he in love, or in debt?'

'He was close, very private,' said Joe Pickering. 'So if he was in money trouble he wouldn't be telling. He'd talk even less about his heart.'

'What do you know about his past, Pickering?' I said. 'Was he born here in Ormskirk?'

'No, he came from Liverpool, though I don't know where he was born. He bought Chimneystacks Farm near twenty years ago.

We were led to believe he'd made a good profit on a merchant venture, which gave him the capital.'

'And he married?'

'Not immediately. He was prudent – or maybe choosy. His wife was local. She was a funny little woman, wasn't she, my dear?'

'Margery wasn't funny,' said Caroline. 'She was quiet. Her parents both died, leaving her to live with her grandfather until he died. Then she got work at Giggleswick's – an old story, this is. Soon enough she got into the master's bed, and then persuaded him to give her a ring.'

'Were they happy together?'

'Oh, quite probably. There was no public quarrelling, I can say that. Or talk of anything of the like indoors, either. As a wife she was capable enough to give him two children and run his house, before she was carried off with a fever, five years ago now. She was not the most popular woman in town, but nor did she have a lot of people taking against her.'

'And can much the same be said of Giggleswick?'

'Yes, but he had a strong will, mind. You wouldn't pitch your stall on his market-site, unless you wanted to hear the rough side of his tongue. He had views about anyone who he thinks doesn't play fair in business.'

'Well, I'm minded to go to Liverpool to see this fellow Parr, Giggleswick's man of business,' I said. 'If there is some reason in money why he was killed, Parr may assist us – and besides I have a letter for his attention. Luke, would you like to come too?'

'No, I . . . It happens I've an appointment. Since I am in Ormskirk it gives me a chance to see a patient who I don't visit as often as I should.'

He gave me a warning look. But I wasn't going to put his privacy in danger. I kept out of Fidelis's amours, them not being my business, and (more to the point as they were Ormskirkers) they were not the Pickering family's either. I just said, 'Then will you engage rooms at the Squirrel, Luke? I'll be back in time to sup with you.'

Ormskirk to Liverpool is a two hours' ride. I have been to that great port many times and yet I always have the same sense of excitement when I top the brow of the dale that overlooks the town, with its broad view of the Mersey estuary, the masts in the great harbour thick as bristles, and the quays and wharves stacked with goods. From here men criss-crossed the oceans. They took with them the produce of Lancashire and Cheshire and came back with the exotic stuff our nation had by now become used to as daily conveniences: sugar, coffee, tea, tobacco, silk, rum, spices, porcelain and lacquered China-goods. In Liverpool it seems as easy to make money as pie – until your ship sinks, your debts are called in. Then suddenly you're destitute.

Ambrose Parr's home and place of business was in a fine modern house a few minutes' walk from the port and the Exchange. It was a wealthy part of town. The paintwork and pavings were clean, and watchmen were employed to keep beggars and stray dogs off the streets.

I was greeted at the door by a footman in full livery who said that Mr Parr was at home and would perhaps be agreeable to seeing me. I sent in my printed card, word came back and I was ushered into the great man's presence.

Parr was approaching fifty with a taste for magnificence, both in his dress and his mode of living. He was sitting at ease in an armchair, drinking wine from a cut-glass goblet while, in the corner of the room, a harpsichord was being played by a small misshapen fellow. Parr as he listened kept time by tapping his opulently ringed fingers on his gold-threaded waistcoat, which stretched and strained across his expanse of chest and belly. Parr's breeches were of damasked silk and his buckles were of silver. He talked through his nose as if there were some precious obstruction at the back of his mouth.

'All right, all right,' he shouted at the musician. 'That will suffice. Leave us.'

The musician collected his sheets of music together, stuffed them into a cloth bag and trotted obediently out of the room.

'Music is the food of love, said Shakespeare,' Parr told me. 'And I do so agree with him. Have you ever considered that the musician is the very table-servant of Eros, Mr Cragg?'

'I sometimes think it is the other way, Mr Parr,' I said. 'But then I think, if love be the food of music, the scansion is ruined.'

Parr did not appear to consider this witty, or even that it was meant to be witty. He merely grunted and stood laboriously up, straddling his legs and propping his fists on his hips. He had sloping shoulders, large round eyes and a short neck with several fatty folds, giving something like the appearance of a frog in fine clothing.

'So you are Titus Cragg the county coroner. I have heard of you, sir. You are always finding murderers in unlikely places. You will take a glass of claret?'

A few minutes later I was sitting opposite the great lawyer drinking his wine and feeling the warmth of his fire as I told him my news from Ormskirk.

'Is Richard Giggleswick dead?' he said, when I came to the meat of it. He did not sound markedly grieved. This is a man in whom very little affects his feelings, I thought. And a man who guards against surprise.

'Yes,' I said. 'He was shot in the heart. Deliberately.'

For a moment Parr's face did not move. He regarded me with his mouth a little open. Then his lips stretched into a smile.

'Aha!' he cried. 'So you are in pursuit of yet another murderer, Mr Cragg. I congratulate you.'

'That would be premature. I have to name him first.'

'Murder will out, said the poet, did he not? But I wonder who Giggleswick fell foul of, finally. He was heading that way in recent years, you know.'

'Was he? My impression is that he was middling prosperous.'

'Oh no.'

Parr shook his head and his multiple chins wobbled like jellies.

'Oh no,' he repeated solemnly. 'Giggleswick was courting disaster. He had debts, he had obligations and he was overstretched.'

'You are his principal man of business? You know his affairs?'

'Intimately. He has always consulted me, and trusted me I think.'

'Have you known him very long?'

'Oh yes, we were boys together.'

'And later?'

'I tried to keep his financial affairs in order, despite much provocation on his part.'

'What then are the prospects for his children? I have talked with his daughter Sarah, who is very concerned about the future. I bring you this from her.'

I handed over Sarah Giggleswick's letter. Parr unfolded it and rapidly read it through.

'She wants to know what I can do for her security,' he said with a sigh. 'And the sad answer is, very little. The grandmother is alive so there is no need to make wardship arrangements.'

'The grandmother is feeble-minded. Are there no other relatives?'

'Giggleswick had a sister, married and living I believe in Wales. I doubt she is very prosperous, but she will I am sure know her duty.'

'Shall you not pay the children and their old grandmother a visit in person?'

Parr shook his head.

'It would not do. I was their father's attorney, not theirs. They cannot afford my fees. You may tell them that they will receive from me an account of the farm's finances and a list of creditors. And I'll make enquiries about the sale of the property so that they can pay the debts. I'll do that much for them.'

'Might Giggleswick's money troubles have any bearing on his death? I wonder if you know of any enemies he made. Or enemies of his family, perhaps. An old feud, or a grudge.'

'I know of nothing like that. His origins, like mine, and like many in Liverpool, are humble. We both came from across the river in Cheshire, but we left that county long ago. We were still boys, in fact.'

'What did Richard Giggleswick do when he came to Liverpool?'

'Scraped money together. There was plenty of work for anyone prepared to do it. Not very well paid, but if you kept at it and had your eye open for opportunities you could do well for yourself. In addition, Giggleswick had a certain liking for what you might call risky investments, but as it happened he had luck. He put the proceeds of all this into a Guinea voyage.'

'Slaves?'

'Yes, partly. And by the time he'd sold his share of the sugar and tobacco that the ship brought home he'd got back four times what he'd put in. It was highly satisfactory.'

'And he then bought the farm?'

'Yes. He decided to give up the irregular life. His father had been a farmer so he took it up himself. Then he married and all went well until his lady wife – well, strictly speaking she wasn't a lady, but never mind – until his wife got it into her head to die. Giggleswick never recovered. The silly man started gambling and speculating again. Very secretively of course but as his man of affairs I knew something of what he was doing.'

'So why was he killed?'

'I expect it was by someone he owed money to.'

'Ah, yes, I expect it was.'

But during my ride back to Ormskirk a voice in my head repeated a refrain, exactly matching the rhythm of the horse's hooves:

You won't kill a man that owes money to you.
You might murder one that you owe money to.

Fidelis had got me a comfortable room at the Squirrel. I had a bath-tub filled with hot water and enjoyed a long soak. I was just thinking of getting out, it being about ten at night, when Fidelis came in. His face looked pleased with himself.

'Don't get up, Titus. I have been speaking with a lady.'

'I know that,' I said.

'No, not that lady. My appointment there was . . . well, it did not occur.'

'Why not? Are you losing your touch, Luke?'

He smiled thinly. He did not like being teased.

'The lady was indisposed, so I returned to Chimneystacks Farm. I have interviewed Farmer Giggleswick's mother. I was hoping she would say something useful – and that she did, Titus.'

'Is it possible? Can she speak at all? My impression was that the woman is senile and away with basilisks and centaurs.'

'No, no, Titus. She is quite lucid if approached in the right way. I patted her hand and used my best beside-the-bed manners. They did the trick.'

'Did she say anything about her son going into debt? Ambrose Parr had quite a story of Giggleswick being addicted to specula- tion and possibly gaming.'

'Nothing like that. In his mother's eyes Giggleswick was a paragon, though she never liked Margery the wife.'

'Not unusual in a mother-in-law.'

'Old Mrs Giggleswick was not highly fluent. It took patience to retrieve and piece together the information from her scattered thinking. My impression was, however, that Giggleswick was

already more than a little worried about his own safety and that
of his family, which was only increased by the shooting of his
pig. When I asked why she simply said, "That damned paper is
somewhere about."'

'What paper?'

'I couldn't get her to be more particular. She just repeated "that
paper, about the house" and "that accursed paper".'

'What could it be? We must find it, must we not?'

'I will help you search, if you like.'

'Good. And as a matter of fact, a proper look at Giggleswick's
papers was already my plan for tomorrow. Hand me that towel,
if you please.'

The farm had a business room at the end of the stable block. The
walls were lined with shelved ledgers that recorded Giggleswick's
production year by year: how much was grown on what acreage,
notes on pests and diseases, and on marling, muck and other ways
of improving the soil. There were also lists of the various markets
where he sold the produce, and what the return was from each
and every market day. From these we quickly saw that potatoes
were the main stock in trade, accounting for almost half of the
farm's revenue. Other root vegetables and greens contributed
another quarter, with the rest being from the meat and dairy.

'This is a very different Richard Giggleswick from the man
portrayed to me by Ambrose Parr yesterday,' I said, turning the
pages. 'Parr spoke of a man growing more and more improvident,
owing money, and balancing on the edge of disaster. What we
have here are the business records of a man assiduous in agriculture
and careful in keeping track of his money.'

We also found that Giggleswick had future plans. In the drawers
of the sideboard lay a roll of architectural drawings labelled 'A
Salting-house', together with an inventory of materials needed and
costs expected.

'If he was going to salt his own pork, he may have had significant expansion in mind,' said Fidelis. 'He would need more
pig-houses for a start, maybe more land.'

'That doesn't look like a man about to be ruined.'

'No. It looks like a man who sees the chance of making more
money. Think of the market for salt pork in Liverpool. There must

be ten or a dozen ships a day sailing for deep waters with barrels of the stuff in their holds. If he were to start salting for himself, that is where he'd sell the meat.'

'And suppose some other rival pig-man got notice of this and feared the competition.'

'And was ready to kill over it? The rival would have to be unhinged, which I admit is possible.'

It was difficult to see how to push this line of enquiry forward, though, as the idea of salting meat at Chimneystacks Farm had gone no further than a few drawings and some building costs. I re-rolled the plans and replaced them.

'This cannot be the "damned paper" that old Ma Giggleswick spoke about. We need something that smacks more of the devil's work, Luke.'

We emptied the cupboards in the sideboard. We pulled out and upturned the drawers of a tallboy and rifled a chamber chest. We found much paper, but nothing that suggested it might be a 'damned paper'.

'One thing strikes me, Titus,' said Luke, after re-filling and re-inserting the last tallboy drawer. 'We've turned up nothing from your friend Ambrose Parr, yet Parr has been represented as Giggleswick's man of business. It's an anomaly. There ought to be documents from him.'

'Was everything kept at Parr's office?'

'Maybe. But even so, there would be correspondence. Just look around. Giggleswick was devoted to record-keeping. He would surely have kept any letters from his man of business.'

'Might he have burned Parr's letters?'

'He might, supposing he had reason to do so. If not, he's hidden them well.'

It was then that I saw something about one of the panels in the room. These lined the walls up to the level of a man's chest and were rectangular cream-painted panels, each as big as a quarto-size book. One of them, in the wall by the chimneybreast, seemed a little darker than the others. I went over to examine it.

'What's that?' said Fidelis joining me.

There was a pattern of faint smudges all over the panel, dirty finger marks. With my own finger ends I pressed the wood just at the place where the smudges seemed most numerous. The panel gave a little and, as I pressed harder, there came the sound of a catch being sprung.

'It stood to reason he would have one of these,' said Fidelis, a little put out that I, not he, had found the panel.

It opened like a small cupboard and revealed five bundles. Four were tied simply with ribbons, the last with string whose knots were secured with tags and wax. The first ribbon-tied bundle consisted of letters signed by Ambrose Parr which, on a rapid inspection, were concerned with purchases of land adjoining his own acres, made by Giggleswick eight years earlier. A second similar bundle dealt with a small number of government securities owned by Giggleswick. The third contained his will and the title deeds to the farm. It was the fourth that held the surprise. We broke the sealed knots and snipped the string.

'Yes,' I said, unfolding and reading through the large paper that was the main item. 'This may very well be the "damned paper" we've been looking for.'

'What is it, Titus?'

I showed him the heading written in large letters at the top of the page.

'A TONTINE FUND,' read Fidelis. 'I confess I don't know what that is.'

FOUR

The document was written out in legal hand and I could see that it was properly constituted. I could also see why old Ma Giggleswick might call it a 'damned paper'. I read it out aloud.

A TONTINE FUND
The principal being payable to the last
surviving signatory.

We the undersigned declare and attest that we have each severally and irrevocably paid Five Hundred Guineas

into the Fund, and that we agree jointly to renounce all
title to our several contributions both in ourselves and
in any of our descendants whatsoever unless and until
six of us be dead and one remain as the last and sole
survivor, whereupon that one shall be entitled to
ownership of the whole fund clear and without obli-
gation to any other person whatsoever.

Francis Dolland	Isaac Jones
Isabella Pettifer	John Bourke
Prenton Smisby	Richard Giggleswick
Thomas Hesketh	

I hereby attest that these are all true signatures and that
this is copy no 7 of the agreement.
Ambrose Parr
Attorney-at-Law

3rd March 1725

'I've never seen anything like it,' said Fidelis when he had taken
the paper and read these words through for himself. 'It is
extraordinary.'

'Not really,' I said. 'The idea has rather gone out now but these
Tontine agreements were quite fashionable twenty or thirty years
ago. I have never drawn one up, but I believe my father did some.
A Frenchman thought of it.'

Fidelis held up the paper.

'It seems crazy. Here you have a list of seven people, each with
a motive worth three and a half thousand guineas to get the other
six into their graves with dispatch.'

He wafted the paper in front of my face.

'In other words, Titus, it is a ready-made list of people who
may have shot Richard Giggleswick.'

'I agree, and there's not much time before the inquest in which
to find out which one it was. That document is dated 1725.
Giggleswick was then living in Liverpool.'

'Then that is where we must look.'

I took the document back, then folded and pocketed it.

'It's worth showing these names to Joe Pickering first. If any of these people are living closer to hand, he may know.'

We found Pickering in his workshop, moistening and kneading a lump of clay on his bench.

'Mr Giggleswick apart,' the constable told me when he had rinsed his hands and read the names signatory to the tontine, 'there are only two that might have connections around here. One could be the Thomas Hesketh who died – oh, a dozen years ago. He lived at Rufford Hall.'

'Tom Hesketh? Who used to be our Member of Parliament at Preston? How do you make out it's him?'

'It might not be. But I'm just saying it might.'

'Who is the other?'

'That's Dolland. Dolland's is a brickworks five miles out of town. The family is very well-breeched. Old Arthur Dolland is on the bench here.'

'And Francis Dolland is what?'

'She's his daughter, about the same age as Dick Giggleswick.'

'She? I thought it was a man.'

Looking again at the signatures I saw my error. In reading the name Frances I had mistaken the 'e' for an 'i'.

'Arthur Dolland has two children. The other is his son Perceval. The old man has handed over the running of the place to the two of them. He still tries to interfere from time to time but Frances is right firm with him, and keeps him out. She's got a clout in her that many a man couldn't fetch.'

'And Perceval?'

'An agreeable fellow. He takes part in society generally, such as hunting, going to balls, racing – all that. In theory he runs the business on even terms with his sister, but people that work there say it's her tells them what's what. Unlike Frances, Percy never married.'

'Frances is married?'

'She married her cousin, son of Arthur's brother Luke. She went with him to Manchester but soon came back again without her husband. The word is he didn't suit.'

'And you say the Dollands are rich.'

'Oh, very well off, and self-made by old Dolland. He is a

sheep-shearer's son from Yorkshire who started making bricks
with brother Luke on the other side of Manchester. With that
town growing so fast they wanted mountains of bricks, so the
Dollands did well. Then Arthur moved here and set up a second
brickworks to supply the builders of Liverpool. He's rough around
the edges but he educated manners into his children and they're
a class above now. Wait till you see the house – it is that of a
gentleman.'

'I'll go there this afternoon. I'll write a note to Mrs Dolland
telling her to expect me at three o'clock. Can you find me a
messenger?'

'You will come with me to the Dollands?' I said to Luke as we
finished our dinner at the inn.

'Certainly. I would be greatly interested.'

The Dollands' house was five miles to the north-east of Ormskirk,
and stood in its own grounds. Passing the gates we rode down an
avenue of young elms, with the house standing at the end. It was
a handsome residence on three floors. Beyond it and masked by a
band of trees were the smoking chimneys and workshops of the
brick-making business.

At the door I asked the footman for Frances Dolland and we
were ushered into a room immediately off the hall, a fine airy
salon occupying one corner of the building and with three high
windows. A lady of an age approaching fifty sat at a table reading
a fat ledger in which I could see multiple columns of figures. She
rose and picked up from a heap of papers what I could see was
my letter, glancing at it, then looking up with a cool smile.

'Good afternoon, Mr Cragg. From your note I understand that
you are the county coroner and have come in connection with the
death of poor Richard Giggleswick.'

'That is so,' I said.

'And who is this with you?' the lady said.

She inclined her head towards Luke Fidelis, who made a bow.

'Luke Fidelis, M.D., ma'am. At your service.'

She arched her eyebrows.

'Well, as it happens . . . Oh! But no! We must deal with this
other business first. How may I help you, Mr Cragg?'

'Because of the circumstances of Mr Giggleswick's sad death

I am forced to hold an inquest into it, and while running through some papers in his business room, I came upon a legal document which bears your signature, among others. Do you remember signing it?'

I passed the paper over to her and waited while she read it through.

'Well, of course I remember,' she said. 'I have my own copy of it somewhere. Quite a lot of money was at issue and we were a group of foolish young people.'

'Did you continue to see or correspond with them after the tontine was drawn up?'

'No. I saw very little of them after my marriage in 1726. Tom Hesketh occasionally. I've employed Ambrose Parr as my lawyer a few times over the years and he occasionally passed on news of the others.'

'Did you not see the other signatories at all?'

'Isaac Jones and I were cousins, on my mother's side. We lost him two years ago. He was a good man and I grieved.'

'But you didn't see much of him after you married?'

'We met at occasional family funerals and the like.'

'What about Thomas Hesketh? Was he, perhaps, the gentleman who lived at Rufford Hall?'

'Yes, he was. He has been dead these last eleven years. He was an avid sportsman and much seen in local society. He and I only met very accidentally, however, as I have never hunted or taken part in other sports, or social occasions.'

'And Richard Giggleswick – did you see him at all? At balls or assemblies.'

'As I indicated, I rarely attend balls and assemblies.'

'At church, then?'

'We would acknowledge each other but no more than that. The years of our friendship in Liverpool were long ago.'

'What were your circumstances, at that time in Liverpool?'

'As I mentioned we Dollands are related to the Jones family, not by blood, but through my late stepfather Mr Bellingham. Mrs Jones, Isaac's mother, was Mr Bellingham's sister and as I was a very contrary bundle as a girl and could not get on with my stepfather, I went to live with my aunt in Liverpool. That is how I was drawn into Isaac's group of friends.'

'But your marriage put an end to the association?'

She had a ramrod-straight back, but now she made it even straighter.

'I don't want to talk about my marriage. I have put it behind me. I have become a woman of business now. I manage the brick works with my brother.'

'Do you have children?'

'I do not.'

'Mrs Dolland, may I return to the other names on the tontine. You have told us that Mr Jones is deceased. May I ask how he died?'

'He fell sick and died. That is all I know.'

'What of the others?'

'I known nothing of them. You must enquire in Liverpool.'

'Mrs Dolland, this is – erm – a little delicate. The fact is that Richard Giggleswick was murdered. Isaac Jones and Thomas Hesketh are also deceased. It is possible that these deaths are consequent on the tontine to which you, like them, are a party.'

She grasped my drift immediately.

'You suggest I ought to be concerned for my safety?'

'Madam, it is a possibility, I put it no higher than that. But the fact is we do not know why Richard Giggleswick was shot and killed. And Isaac Jones's death too may not have been natural. Or even Thomas Hesketh's.'

Frances Dolland's face did not change. I was about to ask if she had herself had any near brushes with danger in recent days when the door opened and a servant appeared pulling a Bath chair with much effort into the room backwards, accompanied by a pronounced squeaking of its wheels. In it sat, or to be more exact sprawled, an enormously corpulent old man. I saw as he was swung around to face us that he had on a decayed full-bottomed wig and robes a little like those of a judge. I remembered Joe Pickering telling us that Arthur Dolland was on the magistrates' bench. From his attire one would have thought he was, or imagined he was, a judge of higher status.

'I must speak to the coroner,' he said between heaving breaths and pointing his ear trumpet at us as if it were a pistol. 'Clegg, is that your name?'

'It's Cragg, Mr Dolland. Titus Cragg.'

He struggled into a more upright posture and fixed me with his eyes as he might a prisoner in the dock.

'My daughter tells me you're conducting an inquest tomorrow. Is that right?'

'It is. Into the sad death of Richard Giggleswick, which occurred on Wednesday.'

The old man clapped his hands together in delight.

'That is prime news, sir. I won't myself attend – beneath my dignity, you know, to drop into another fellow's court. But I expect you to find me a murderer. A murderer at the very least, mind. Far too long since I had one up before me and there's nothing like a murderer to pack out the courtroom. I had a very good case of rape not six months back. And – ah yes! A very juicy bigamist came up . . . how long ago was it? Two or three years, possibly. Caused a great stir, as conjugal crimes often do. If I remember right we also had an arson in the same month, which is not as tremendous as bigamy of course, but dramatic enough. And I believe I am right in saying there was a killing in forty-two, but the fellow couldn't be got for anything worse than death by negligence. I detest a chance-medley death, or a manslaughter as some call it. Neither fish nor fowl. A man or woman that kills should be hung or, if not, patted on the back for doing the world a favour. What d'you say, Clegg? Will you bring me a man – or even better a woman – that we can properly hang?'

'That is not quite the object of the exercise, if I may say so,' I said.

Old Dolland raised the trumpet to his ear.

'What d'you say? *Sexual*, is it? Better and better.'

I tried to interrupt and put him right, but his flow was not to be stopped.

'Now that will always be the most popular of killings. Ha! My court will be stuffed and overflowing again. I've had poor audiences recently, very poor. There is little interest in petty larceny I fear, or public nuisance. And slander is hard to sell in any form, even combined with profanity. And as for poaching and horse-theft, well, nobody can be bothered with them at all. I might be lucky to get half a dozen in the court for a case like that. No, no. Give me an excellent murder, Mr Clegg, and I shall ever be in your debt.'

Mrs Dolland had been standing stiffly opposite her father, like a person waiting for a shower of rain to pass. Now old Dolland's spout of words ran dry at last. He sat looking from me to Fidelis, and from Fidelis to his daughter, and then back to me, as if wondering which one of us could give him what he wanted. The lady nodded sharply to the footman, who grasped the handles of the Bath chair and drew old Mr Dolland backwards out of the room, to which he offered no protest.

Frances Dolland closed the door after them and turned to Fidelis.

'When you said you were at my service, doctor, I thought you meant in a medical sense and then I thought of my father. He is on the whole well, though he has swelling in the legs and pain besides, and difficulty in walking. Perhaps you would be kind enough to examine him. Our own doctor is most loyal to us but he is I fear old-fashioned and his remedies have been of little use.'

Fidelis smiled and said that of course he would.

'How is old Dolland?' I asked Luke Fidelis as we rode back towards Ormskirk. 'To the layman's eye he seems hardly in the pink of health.'

We were on our way back to Ormskirk along a curious road laid with bricks – ones of Dolland manufacture, no doubt.

'He is seventy, Titus. In the book of life he's halfway through the final chapter. The inevitable might be delayed if he reduces his obesity, moderates his intake of port wine and takes exercise. I doubt he will do any of those things. When I told him that he spends too much time sitting, he said, "My dear sir, I am a magistrate. Sitting is what we must do."'

'He can still crack a joke then.'

'No. He is oblivious to humour. Just as he was when he demanded a murder from you. He brought to my mind a child that wants a sugar lump.'

'What, by the way, was your impression of Mrs Dolland?'

'A capable woman. Her manner is that of one used to getting what she wants. Has she got what she wants in the death of Richard Giggleswick? That's the question.'

He was right: that *was* the question.

FIVE

R iding fast, we cut the travelling time to Liverpool the next day by at least twenty minutes, and were both exhilarated as we walked our sweating horses down the street only half an hour before noon. Ambrose Parr kept us waiting. The same footman as I had already met showed us into a parlour just off the hall. The room did not look as if it was often used and was much smaller than the one in which I had previously met Parr. I listened to the sounds of the house and what struck me as strange was that, as far as we could hear, it contained no females, and no children. From somewhere further inside the building a man was shouting orders about fish and meat – kitchen matters. Nearer by we heard the chatter of a couple of boys passing through the hall and up the stairs.

Eventually Parr came in and shook my hand firmly and friendly.

'Pleased to see you again, sir. May I ask, as I forgot to do so yesterday – are you married?'

'Yes, Mr Parr, I am.'

'Oh good, very good, lucky man. And your – er – friend?'

'This is Dr Fidelis, who often assists me.'

'How d'you do?'

He shook hands with Fidelis just as he had done with me.

'And are *you* married, Doctor?'

'No, Mr Parr, I'm not.'

Parr leaned back and looked Fidelis up and down.

'I cannot see why not, sir. You are a perfectly presentable young man. Marriage is the only way to happiness you know, a fact that Mr Cragg in the full glory of his conjugation with Mrs Cragg must know full well.'

'Indeed I do, Mr Parr,' I said gravely. 'And it would give me and Dr Fidelis considerable pleasure to be able to present our compliments to Mrs Parr.'

'Oh, well, there is no Mrs Parr, sir. Hasn't been this last three years. It is terrible. The last Mrs Parr was only in the job eighteen months before removing her residence to the graveyard.'

'I condole with you. Were there other Mrs Parrs before her?'

'Oh yes, there were two of 'em – not at the same time, of course. But then . . .'

His face adopted a dreamy look.

'If only the laws allowed it, what a perfect blessing, do you not agree? To be allowed two, three, even four wives at the same time, as the Mahometans do. What bliss that would be. And yet now I have not even one, which is great misery, what with the temptations attending the bachelor state. I am looking, of course. I heard of a real possibility last week but, you know, she wouldn't have me no matter how often I said I loved her.'

He looked from my face to Fidelis's and back again.

'Do either of you know of any candidates at all? They need not be handsome. Just female. Female is the minimum requirement.'

But I had had enough of this foolery. I had made a copy of the list of signatories to the tontine, and this I now took from my pocket and handed to Parr.

'I wonder if you recognize these names, sir?'

Parr squinted at the list then went to the desk, picked up a pair of spectacles and looked through the list once more. He handed it back with a sigh.

'So! You've heard about the tontine, have you?'

'I found the document among Mr Giggleswick's papers and I am wondering why you didn't mention it yesterday when we spoke about him.'

'It has no relevance. You must understand the tontine is not interested in any one individual death. It only becomes active after six cumulative deaths. Had Giggleswick been the sixth person to die on that list, the tontine would be satisfied and the last person would come into the money. Then it would have relevance. I know, however, that he was not.'

'But can you not tell me how this tontine agreement came about in the first place?'

'I was one of a group of friends, still very young and making our way. And as for all young people the future hardly existed, reaction came a long time after action and consequence was of no consequence. We became fascinated by wagers of various kinds, an interest that culminated – that being the exact word – in our taking long odds on the death of the Tsar of Russia.'

'You bet on the death of Tsar Peter?'

'Oh yes, people often used to do that sort of thing – and still do, I believe. There is even talk now of making the practice illegal. But the Tsar died on the very day we had predicted, by which we cleared an incredible amount of money: four thousand guineas, to be exact. Split eight ways it gave us five hundred apiece.'

'Which equates to the amount each of the others sank into the tontine? Why did they do that?'

'Atonement, I think. They were awoken to the evil, as they thought it, of gambling on the lives of public men. I believe one of them had heard a sermon denouncing such bets. Talking about it together they decided they should deny themselves the immediate fruits of the wager. They hit on a tontine as a way to bet on life, rather than death, if you follow me. What happened to the money would be a matter of chance, you see. Or the intervention of God, if you prefer.'

'You never threw your five hundred into the pot. Why did you not participate?'

'Oh, I had better uses for the money. All this . . .'

He gestured at the room around us.

'What I now enjoy grew from that seed of five hundred guineas. I was not from a wealthy family and was starting out on my path as a lawyer.'

'You did not have the same scruples as the others?'

'As I say, I had a better use for the money. I confined myself to drawing up the instrument and witnessing their signing of it.'

'May we therefore run through the names? Perhaps you will be good enough to let me know which of them is alive. Oh! I should say we have already met Mrs Dolland.'

'A marvellous lady, is she not? I have had the honour of handling certain legal matters for her.'

'Thomas Hesketh, now. He was the late MP for Preston.'

'Yes, he was a most prominent figure but he died of a hunting accident in thirty-five. Did you know him at all, Mr Cragg?'

'At the grammar school in Preston. His family lived at Ribbleton Hall, and were very rich. He was our MP, much too young, but by then he wasn't living in Preston.'

'He took a ninety-nine-year lease at Rufford, or so I believe, off Mrs Bellingham, who'd lived there until her husband died. Bellingham, you know, had been a connection of the Dollands.'

'Tom was free-spender, was he not?'

'Oh yes. I do believe he hated money, so fast did he try to get rid of it. He had a good nature, though.'

'So, what of Mr Jones? I am aware that he also is deceased.'

'Jones died four years ago. He was a clockmaker, and a good one. A sad loss. His son continues the business.'

'The next is Isabella Pettifer. A lady.'

'Miss Pettifer, yes indeed!'

He reflected for a moment and a glassiness, or a dim kind of glint, came into his eyes.

'A fine woman, Cragg. Very fine. Never married, you know, though highly marriageable, as you might say.'

'Where does she live?'

'No longer in Liverpool but in the small village of Aughton, a few miles to the north of Liverpool.'

'And what are her circumstances?'

'She is comfortable. Her father always indulged her and when he died she was well provided for.'

'Do you see her at all?'

'I have received her instructions from time to time.'

'Legal instructions? What about?'

'You are a fellow lawyer, Cragg. You must know better than ask me about the affairs of a client.'

'Very well, let us move on. What of John Bourke?'

'Ah yes, Bourke! You couldn't help liking him, whatever your opinion of the Irish. He had a wonderful line in stories, and he danced so well, and sang. He was very musical. He took up the wine trade and as he never much prospered he left at last to go back to Ireland. We heard he had an accident and died before he could get there.'

'When was that?'

'Four or five years ago.'

'What accident was it?'

'I believe he drowned.'

'Very well. So what of the next name, Prenton Smisby?'

'Ah yes, poor Smisby. Another victim of the terrible curse of debt – and then drink. A hopeless case, I would say. When I first knew him I'd never have guessed his life would go so wrong. He appeared to our eyes an exceptionally clever man, particularly with figures. And he had a real desire to make himself successful. But you don't see each other clearly when you're young, do you? You can see the intellect but you miss so much of the shell that surrounds it.'

'What did you miss in these cases, Mr Parr?'

'The differences in character that determine success and failure in life. Look at me, or Mrs Dolland, and then look at poor Smisby, and poor Giggleswick. We thought we were *all* such fine fellows. But compare the cases now. Character, sir, that is the deciding factor in the end.'

'I would say from examining his paperwork that Mr Richard Giggleswick was a man of solid character, and by no means the ne'er-do-well you described to me yesterday.'

Parr wagged his finger warningly.

'You must not be misled by superficialities, Mr Cragg. The underlying facts are as I told you.'

Fidelis had been studying one of the seascapes on the parlour wall. Now he turned with a question of his own.

'So what of Smisby? Is he dead also?'

'Dead? No, no, my dear doctor. He's alive, but in gaol.'

'For what crime?'

'For the crime of debt, Doctor. And perhaps the crime of self-neglect. His case is really hopeless now, I fear.'

'So now,' I said, 'after twenty-one years, there are three surviving members of the tontine?'

'Yes.'

'Will you, in that case, give us Miss Pettifer's address? And that of Isaac Jones's shop, if you please?'

'I'm afraid, as I said, you will not find Mr Jones there.'

'I would like to speak with his son.'

Ambrose Parr sat at his desk and wrote addresses against the names of those three on my list. When he handed it back I saw he only had written 'DP' against Smisby's name.

'Where is the Debtors' Prison?' I said.

'You'll find it near Castle Square. A very dismal place.'

'It can hardly be otherwise, I suspect,' I said, re-folding the list of names and pocketing it. 'Thank you for your assistance, Mr Parr.'

'It is nothing at all, my dear sir,' Parr said ringing for the footman to show us out. 'Just let me know, will you, of any marriageable ladies you may come across in your travels.'

'There are three members of the tontine to investigate in or about Liverpool, Luke,' I said when we were outside. 'As we are pressed for time, we should divide the duties. Will you go to the clock-maker, while I find the Debtors' Prison? We may call on Miss Pettifer together on our way back to Ormskirk as I believe it is on our way.'

Fidelis knew the street in which Liverpool watch and clock makers clustered and walked there in five minutes. He soon found premises with the name of Isaac Jones above the door and inside a young man – twenty-one years old at most – sitting at a bench in the back of the shop, peering into the works of a bracket clock with an instrument poised in his fingers to make adjustments.

'Just one moment!' the lad called.

As in all clock shops, Fidelis stood surrounded not only by the many faces of time but by their constant sounds and motions, from the urgent tick of the pocket watch to the sonorous tock of the leisurely long-case grandfather. He looked from one to the next and found to the shop's credit every face showing exactly the same time.

'How do you do it?' he asked when the young man came to the counter, wiping his hands on a rag.

'Do what, sir?'

'Have every clock in here so well at your command. They all keep time exactly together.'

Fidelis checked his own watch, arching his eyebrows in surprise.

'Which I find my own watch lags eighteen minutes behind.'

'You must be from Preston, sir.'

'Yes. How on earth do you know that?'

'Different towns, different times. We in Liverpool set our time according to the latest machinery. Preston is about eighteen minutes behind us at the moment, while Chester lags by almost half an hour.'

'I expect time goes faster in Liverpool because of the busy place it is.'

The young man gave a patient smile.

'I cannot concur with that. If time were something stirred up by activity, like water or air, it could never be relied upon. It would be like a wild animal and must be tamed. I believe on the contrary that time is *our* master, and accordingly tames us. But what can I do for you, sir?'

'I have come to ask about your late father, Isaac.'

'My father-in-*law*,' he said. 'I have the honour of being husband to Isaac Jones's daughter. My name's Hugh Chingle.'

'Yet you have not exchanged the names over the door, Mr Chingle.'

'It would be a shame to waste Mr Jones's hard-won good name.'

'I am guessing you were the previous apprentice?'

'I was. When Mr Jones died it was . . .'

His eyes went sideways and up, as if checking they were not overheard from upstairs, and then lowered his voice.

'I suppose you could say we were both too young, but it was a question of marrying her or starting again with nothing, if you get my meaning. But what do you want to know about Isaac?'

'I am a doctor. It is a medical question. How did the decease of old Isaac occur?'

'Slowly. Sickness from within. He started getting thinner. Then weaker, until he looked like death itself. Then at last he went to bed and soon enough after that he was actually dead. I don't mind telling you, I loved the man. He taught me everything. I cried for a week.'

'What medical attention did he have?'

'Dr Fraser attended. He lives in the next street.'

'Did Dr Fraser make a diagnosis prior to death?'

'He talked of all sorts. I didn't take much notice. When a man is sick like that you just wait for the end. You don't want to know the ins and outs of what's wrong.'

Fidelis thanked the clockmaker and after a few more words about the excellence of his clocks left, making his way to the parallel street, where he enquired after Dr Fraser's house.

Fraser was at home. He was a young practitioner with up-to-date ideas so that he and Fidelis hit it off easily from the outset. He remembered Isaac Jones's case well.

'He had incurable cancer, which probably started in the stomach. There was nothing to be done.'

He went through the symptoms and signs as they'd developed in the course of the illness.

'He told me he had been feeling a stomach ache for months but never called me in. He just got powders from the apothecary. They did little good.'

'There are no powders for that disease.'

'No, such cases are usually hopeless from the first but of course no one appreciates that until later.'

After leaving Dr Fraser, Fidelis walked towards the dock and noticed a large warehouse with a sign saying it was that of Turnbull: Wine Importer. He went in and after walking past barrel after barrel, and hogshead after hogshead, of wine stacked from floor to ceiling, he was guided by the sound of laughter to the office. It was staffed by three very skinny clerks seated at writing desks, supervised by a bulkier older man with bright red cheeks. The supervisor had taken it upon himself to entertain his underlings.

'So here's a riddle for you,' he was saying as Fidelis came in. 'What does a poor woman say to a rich ugly man when he sneezes? She says marry me. Ha-ha! Marry me! Here's another. What's a good-luck charm? Big breasts. Ha-ha! You don't laugh, Simkin. What's the matter with you? Try this. What do you call a dog that eats shoes? Sole destroying. Ha-ha-harr! Why is a whale like an actor? Because they're both spouters. Ha-ha-harrgh! Ah! Yes, sir, how may we help you?'

'Are you Mr Turnbull?'

'Me, Turnbull? That's a good one. You won't find Mr Turnbull around here too often, not these days. Somewhere in the Newmarket area is more likely at this time of year. I have the honour of being his chief clerk, however. Name's Thomas Beckside. How may I help?'

'It is just a passing thought, prompted by the sign above your warehouse door. I used to know a man called John Bourke, who was also in the wine trade. I wonder if you knew him at all.'

Red-cheeks's cheery joke-telling visage turned grave in an instant.

'I'm sorry to say John Bourke's dead. He decided to take himself back to Ireland, with so many creditors on his tail here. Perhaps you were one of them?'

'No. I heard he'd died but I'm interested in why his business failed.'

'The word in the trade was, it was a question of nose.'

'Nose?'

'The capacity for discriminating good from bad. If you're in the trade without a nose, then you had better hire one. Bourke did no such thing. He fooled himself on the subject of nose. He thought he could rely on his own. But his nose was not adapted to discriminate between wines. He bought badly and sold insufficiently and soon acquired creditors.'

'Which is why he left Liverpool.'

'That is the substance of the case. He thought he could start again in Dublin. He had influential friends there, he said. But we heard he perished while being ferried across the Menai Strait on his way to Holyhead. The boat overturned and everybody who couldn't swim drowned. It is the most hellish narrow bit of water, that. It probably drowns as many as the Irish Sea itself does between Wales and Ireland.'

'Did you know Bourke yourself?'

'As a young man he ran around with Mr Turnbull, when my young master still applied himself to the trade.'

'And you yourself? Did you know him?'

'Not well. Remember he was a Teague. You can never cheer one of those up. I once said to him in a coffee house, what's the Irishman's idea of a light supper? A tallow candle. Ha-ha! You don't laugh, my friend? Nor did he. He hadn't got a nose for a jest, any more than for a good wine. The Irish don't. They're miserable bastards even when they're singing and playing jigs.'

SIX

'We eat the mice here, it's a firm tradition,' said Prenton Smisby, showing me his plate, which lay on the table under a grimy window. It was clean except for a few smears of brown gravy.

'I have just dined on one,' he went on. 'Mouse makes a rather delicate ragout, you know, if you can beg an onion and a bit of salt to give the cook.'

I had visited many clients inside verminous prisons, but never heard the vermin so highly spoken of.

'You are often hungry, I expect, Mr Smisby.'

'Oh, yes. All my own fault. I thought the business might go down to perdition, so I borrowed money and then it went down anyway. So here I am: down, out and with nothing to my name but debts, and nothing to eat but a mouse.'

Smisby was a wasted, crooked, pathetic figure in ragged though once gentlemanly clothes. He could stand upright only with the help of a staff. I gathered the sense of what he was saying with difficulty: his voice was wispy and his breathing laboured.

'What was your business, if I may ask?'

'Oh, ships, you know. Ships and cargoes. I once owned sixty per cent of a ship. I still do, but it's at the bottom of the sea, so not much use to me. Heh-heh! Well, I can still laugh. What brings you to visit a poor prisoner?'

'I have news that may be of interest in regard to your imprisonment,' I said. 'I am sorry to report that Mr Richard Giggleswick of Ormskirk is dead. He was your friend, I believe.'

A faraway squint came over his eyes. He was thinking.

'Dick Giggles?' he said at last. 'Is he dead? Yes I remember him of course. A dear friend in younger days. The times we had. Racing, the cockfights.'

He showed no sign that he appreciated he was now a little closer to pocketing 3,500 guineas and thereby buying his release from the gaol. I straight away led him to it.

'I found a document with Mr Giggleswick's signature on, and yours too, together with a few other names. It is a tontine agreement. Do you remember it?'

'A tontine?'

Smisby screwed up his eyes once more.

'I don't know. I mean . . . I do remember something of the sort back in . . . those days . . . of being young and having plenty. I drank a lot, too much really. My memory's gone soft since they sent me here, Mr, er, whatever your name is. See what I mean? I've only just been told your name and I've already lost it. Fogginess, you see? Just fogginess.'

'You say you do however recall *something* about a tontine. What exactly do you remember?'

'What do I remember? I don't know. I forget, you see, Heh-heh! I forget. I wonder what happened to all the money, though.'

'Do you know Mr Parr, Ambrose Parr? He is a lawyer. He drew up the tontine document.'

'Oh yes, I know Ambrose. Haven't seen him for . . . Lord knows, it's a long time. He won't be bothered with poor Smisby, not with poor Smisby in disgrace.'

'What about another name on the tontine – Miss Pettifer? Isabella.'

Smisby's face lit up.

'Isabella! Oh but she's an angel. My only friend, is Isabella. She sends me fruit and bread. A woman of charity and compassion. Yes, yes. A woman of charity and . . . who are we speaking of?'

'Isabella Pettifer.'

His face lit up all over again.

'Isabella! My true friend. My saviour on more than one occasion. There was that time when she . . . when she . . .'

His voice trailed away, then he said, 'Who did you tell me was dead?'

'Richard Giggleswick.'

'Dick Giggles – dead? How come? He's only a young lad, is Dick.'

'He was shot.'

'Was he shot?'

'Yes. And he was almost fifty years old, the same age as yourself.'

'Oh. I never thought . . . I mean, I didn't . . . he was such a young lad. Near fifty, was he? Isn't time the devil? Heh-heh!'

He stood there leaning heavily on his staff and staring down at the floor. I studied him. If his wits were not scattered, he was making a very skilful show of it. I bowed and bade him farewell – which he did not seem to hear – and then banged on the cell door for the warder to come and unlock it.

This person looked unlike a typical jailer. He was wiry, alert and clean shaven, with neither hams for shoulders, nor a broken nose. He had combed-up long oiled strands of hair from above his ears and laid them like black snakes across his bare scalp. His name was Muldoon.

'How much does Mr Smisby owe?' I asked as we walked back to the prison gate.

'Around six or seven hundred, I believe,' said Muldoon. 'Guineas, that is.'

'Has he no means at all?'

Muldoon shook his head.

'None. He is naught but a charity case in here, I can tell you. He lives by charity food and medicines sent in by a well-wisher.'

'He told me he'd had charity from Miss Pettifer but it seems they didn't meet. Did he have no visitors?'

Muldoon shook his head.

'Not unless you count mice and spiders,' he said.

'And would you say his wits are gone?'

'He has his good days, and his bad days. On good days he can talk wonderfully of Sir Isaac Newton and the search for perpetual motion. But on his bad ones Smisby's the worst for forgetfulness we've got in at the moment, though I've seen similar before. The debtor differs from the ordinary criminal in that particular. Their minds tend to go a-wambling, after a year or two in here.'

'Not helped by a diet of mouse and water.'

'He told you his dinner was mouse stew, did he?'

'Wasn't it?'

Muldoon took a ring of big keys that hung from his belt, selected one of the largest and unlocked the portal door in the oaken gate. He heaved it open and stepped aside to let me past.

'Well?' I said. 'Was it mouse or was it not?'

Muldoon smiled.

'Mrs Muldoon does all the cooking, sir,' he said.

Aughton was a village upon the road back to Ormskirk, and only a few miles short of that town. As we rode there Fidelis gave me the details of his doings in Liverpool.

'Jones had an internal cancer,' he said. 'I thought it likely from what the young fellow in the shop told me, but I went on to call on Fraser, the doctor who attended him, who put it beyond doubt. Isaac Jones died painfully but naturally. And by the way I have also confirmed what Parr told us about Bourke.'

He related his visit to the premises of Turnbull.

'No nose, you see,' he said in conclusion. 'A simple lack but, in Bourke's case, an expensive one. Now, what of the Debtors' Prison, and Prenton Smisby?'

'Another case of improvidence and loss. Disastrous loss.'

I passed the time telling him about my visit to the prison, and so we reached Aughton. The door of Miss Pettifer's residence, a decent house on three floors and set back from the road, was opened by a young housemaid holding a feather duster. She told us that Miss Pettifer was at home and let us in, then went to tell her mistress who we were. In the hall there were two maids polishing brass and another in the passage beyond, busy with a broom. After a minute, the first housemaid returned and we were shown into the parlour, where Isabella Pettifer sat beside the fire. She was a grey-haired, pale and thin woman with watery blue eyes. Although sat down, I could see her stature was exceptionally tall.

'Your house is a whirlwind of cleaning and sweeping, Miss Pettifer,' I said. 'Are you preparing to host some large celebration?'

'Celebration is a thing of my past, sir,' she said. 'I am almost an invalid and, besides, such things are worldly and ungodly, are they not? I cannot abide the ungodly and I choose to stay out of the world as far as possible. My staff are busy because I make sure they are busy. These are all fallen girls, you see. Liverpool is a town of the grossest temptations. I do what I can to put them on a better path. Hard work and Bible readings each evening, that is what I prescribe.'

She indicated that we sit and rang for tea.

'What brings you here?' she asked. 'You are a lawyer, I understand. Is it some legal business?'

Her voice was light, I might say weak.

'Yes, madam, it is,' I said. 'Tomorrow I hold an inquest into the unfortunate murder of Richard Giggleswick of Ormskirk. I believe you knew him.'

She put her hand to her heart and for a moment closed her eyes.

'Dick Giggleswick murdered, you say?'

The news had shocked her but after a moment she gathered herself and said:

'Can you tell me how it happened, please?'

I summarized the circumstances of Giggleswick's shooting and Miss Pettifer listened intently, saying nothing until I added the story of how only a few days earlier Giggleswick had summoned me from Preston to inquest the pig Geoffrey. She clapped her hands to her cheeks and bowed her head.

'Oh Dick! Foolish Dick! Dear, dear Dick!'

She started to weep. Fidelis and I exchanged glances in tacit agreement to let Miss Pettifer's grief run its course. After a long minute she was mopping her face with a large handkerchief contributed by Fidelis.

'Now, Mr Cragg, and kindly doctor,' she said giving back the handkerchief. 'I have shed my tears, and there will be no more. I knew he was dead of course, but these particulars are so grievous. How may I assist you in this business? I have really not seen Dick Giggleswick for many years, though he lives not far away.'

'It is regarding the tontine agreement. The one that Mr Giggleswick signed on the third of March 1725, along with yourself and five others.'

It was as if her face, previously open, had snapped shut.

'I regret that whole episode. I don't like to think of it.'

'How did it come about?'

'Is this material to Dick Giggleswick's murder?'

'It may be the very reason for it.'

'Truly? I must try, then. May I first repeat that, although Mr Giggleswick and I were once close friends, I have had no communication with him for twenty years or more?'

She closed her eyes to aid concentration, or to summon self-control, and after some seconds began to tell us.

'Until his business declined towards the end of his life my father was a convivial and active host and he specially enjoyed the company of younger people. He would fill our house with guests for music, dancing and wine every week or more. He was also indulgent towards me. I was his only child and as I got older, and as my mother had no taste for it, I would be my father's hostess. He didn't object if I drank and played at cards or even billiards with his young guests, and he gave me a generous allowance of money to spend in the town. I became especially friendly with a group who I blush to admit were very enthusiastic gamblers, always ready to put money, or some forfeit, up against chance.'

At this point tea was brought in. Fidelis and I said nothing as Isabella Pettifer poured in silence, and then continued her tale.

'Our biggest success in this field was towards the very end of 1724, when a ship trading with Russia came into Liverpool with news that the Tsar was gravely ill. Next we heard there was a scheme for gambling on his death. The fellow who organized this was inviting players to select any week in the course of the coming year, and if Tsar Peter died within that week he would pay them at odds of fifty-to-one. Furthermore, he offered an extra prize. Players were asked to select a single day during their chosen week, and if the death of the Tsar occurred on that day the return would be doubled. One of the weeks in February had not yet been selected, and we put our money on it. We also picked out a date at random within that week and each contributed five guineas. Some weeks later we read in the *London Gazette* that Peter the Great had died on the very day we had nominated.'

She lapsed into silence, drinking tea and thinking back.

'Your winnings must have seemed an incredible amount,' I suggested.

'Yes they did, and they were. What had happened sobered us all. Soon afterwards I heard a sermon preached on gaming and it changed all my ideas on the subject. It convinced me that the money we had won was poisoned, because it was the proceeds of a very vicious kind of play, based on wishing that somebody would die. The next time we all met, I set out to persuade the others that we must give this tainted money a new purpose. All except Ambrose Parr agreed.'

'That was creditable. Was it your idea to put all the money into a tontine?'

'Oh no. I had never heard of such a thing. It was Mr Smisby. He was so clever. He suggested it and then Tom Hesketh seized on it with great energy and decision, saying that the destiny of the money must be removed from human agency and be subject to chance. He much enjoyed that sort of thing, did Tom. A legal agreement would be made that the money would go to whomsoever of us survived all the others. We all agreed – all except for Ambrose Parr – that it was a fine and fitting idea. It meant that, as Tom and Mr Smisby both argued, we were betting on life rather than death. But I think the real attraction was that the destiny of our three and a half thousand guineas would be settled not now but at some unknown date in the future, and that we could therefore put it right out of our minds. So it was agreed and we seven signed according to Mr Smisby's plan, with Mr Parr's legal help.'

'And did you mind that Mr Parr did not take part, but kept his share of the money for himself?'

She shook her head.

'Why should I? It was his money and his decision.'

'Was he excluded from the group after that?'

'As far as I know the group itself dissolved. I can't be sure as I myself had resolved on a better path, no longer taking part in my father's *soirées*, no longer seeing the others at our house, and no longer meeting them in town. I had determined never to play at games of chance again and I feared that if I saw them I would. So I withdrew.'

'It must have been hard to give up your friendships.'

'It was the right thing to do.'

'Was it specially hard in the case of Richard Giggleswick?'

The question, quickly interjected, came from Luke Fidelis. She answered in a near whisper.

'Yes, sir. If you must know, it was.'

'And you see gaming now as an absolute evil?' I continued.

'Most certainly I do, Mr Cragg, and my belief is in line with what Mr John Wesley has to say in his sermons. But, you know, I have also seen for myself what gambling means. It pretends to be a cure when itself is the disease. But please will you tell me why all this is material to the sad loss of Richard Giggleswick? And why it concerns me. I only hope you've not come to tell me I am the last survivor of the wretched tontine.'

'No, madam,' I said. 'Mr Smisby and Mrs Dolland are living still.'

'Then why?'

'It is a question of murder, ma'am,' said Fidelis, a shade more suddenly than I would have liked. 'It may be that one of the signatories is bent on winning the tontine and will stop at nothing to do so.'

Once more she put her hands one over the other on her chest.

'Oh my! You mean I must fear assassination by Mr Smisby or Mrs Dolland?'

'If I were you,' I said, 'I would take all precautions, especially if you are approached by either of them. I understand you have been in touch with Mr Smisby in his confinement.'

Miss Pettifer had sniffed, blown her nose and put aside the tearfulness of earlier.

'Yes I have,' she said. 'My energy is not what it was, so I do not go to Liverpool very much. But I couldn't help but respond when he wrote to me a pathetic letter from the gaol, appealing to our youthful friendship. I thought of the subtle, clever young man that he had been and wondered what had happened to him. I was shocked to find he was incarcerated. A man in that terrible place, without support from family and friends, does not live long. Or if he lives he goes mad from insufficiency of food. So I have been sending him some.'

'That is charitable indeed, madam. And what of Frances Dolland?'

'No, I never see her. Now, as you don't appear to think that I might be Dick's murderer—'

'Certainly not,' I said hastily. 'Of course we don't.'

Smiling she picked up the teapot.

'In that case, would you like some more tea?'

Walking away from the house I said nothing at first. I wanted to hear Fidelis's response to Miss Pettifer, but he was deep in thought.

'What say you about that, Luke?' I said at last.

'Prenton Smisby was wrong,' he said. 'He argued that if the bet on the Tsar was bad because it hoped for a man's death, the tontine was good because it was a gamble on life. But a moment's thought will tell you that, in reality, it pits one life against six deaths.'

'But whether the tontine is immoral in theory is not the point. Four tontine deaths have already occurred in practice: two accidents, an illness and a murder. It is these we have to reckon with.'

'So which of them is a murderer? It is an interesting problem.'

'I find it hard to see Miss Pettifer in that role.'

'On the other hand there is oddity in someone who gives up gambling just after they've made a large gain: you would think it would happen after a ruinous loss.'

'Miss Pettifer reformed her life and is now a follower of Wesley. She saw the light, which shineth in the darkness.'

'Smisby never stopped speculating, it seems. He is a very difficult quantity to weigh up.'

'No. In many ways he is easier than she is. Smisby may once have been brilliant but, as Miss Pettifer herself implied, he now gives all the appearance of having lost his wits. Also, he is not free and he has no means.'

Fidelis smiled and rubbed his chin.

'As I said, my friend, it is a very interesting conundrum.'

SEVEN

In the evening Fidelis and I sat down to a supper of hotpot at the inn. The house had become lively after a crowd of townspeople came in to join the inn's residents for a Friday night of drinking. We sat in the quiet parlour, which was not that quiet as the public room next door was full of roaring and laughter.

'Perhaps this is nothing to do with the tontine,' I said. 'Are we poking our heads into the wrong rats' nest?'

'It is the only rats' nest we have,' said Fidelis, pronging a chunk of lamb on his fork and raising it to eye level for examination. 'It's too soon to give up the idea that the tontine is at the bottom of Giggleswick's murder.'

He introduced the piece of meat into his mouth and chewed reflectively.

'Very well. I would be grateful for your analysis of what we have learned so far.'

'Let's put the probabilities into proportion, Titus. There are three names left in the tontine. Smisby, now. He is the one with the strongest interest in gaining the tontine. The two ladies are comfortably off while he languishes in living hell. Do you know how much he owes, by the way?'

'The gaoler told me at least six hundred guineas.'

'So if Smisby did win the tontine he'd get out of debt and set himself up in comfort.'

'From his conversation he seems hardly to remember the tontine at all. Unless he is royally fooling me.'

'Then he might be royally fooling you, Titus. Consider this. Debtors' prisons are often lax and gaolers enjoy poor salaries. Did you form the impression that Smisby might raise a bribe? Perhaps he has been allowed out from time to time, in return for an inducement of that kind?'

'He has no money, Luke, no possessions. I found him eating the meat of a rodent, for God's sake! Enjoy your lamb and think of that for a moment. His case appears quite hopeless.'

Fidelis rapped the table for emphasis.

'But it's not hopeless, is it? The very existence of the tontine is his hope – indeed his two-to-one chance – that he can gain the prize.'

'You have not met him, Luke. He really cannot have shot Giggleswick, or his pig. And nor can either Miss Pettifer or Mrs Dolland, in my opinion.'

'Any of them might have employed someone to do it. Maybe Smisby told a fellow prisoner of the tontine, or a visitor, and they agreed to split the profits after the said accessory got rid of the other names – with Farmer Giggleswick heading the list.'

'I grant you that possibility,' I said. 'The most plausible accessory would be a fellow prisoner of Smisby's who, having learned of the tontine, made common cause with him.'

'Or it may be a visitor.'

'Muldoon the gaoler told me Smisby had none, but that someone brings him charity. Victuals.'

'Who is it?'

'As it happens it is Miss Isabella Pettifer.'

'Miss Pettifer, indeed!'

Fidelis returned to the contemplation of his food for a moment.

'Unfortunately,' he said, 'that lady is one of the two people Smisby cannot have conspired with to win the tontine. But she sends him food. Now, there's a singular fact that might reverse the equation.'

'In what sense, Luke?'

'Let's not forget that Smisby is not only a possible murderer, he is simultaneously a possible victim. In that regard it is interesting that she who sends Smisby victuals to keep him alive also has a pecuniary interest in Smisby's untimely death.'

'Well, I take the point, but can Isabella Pettifer truly be a murderess? She is respectable. She is religious. And she is comfortably settled.'

'Perhaps Smisby has told her that he'd rather die than have only mice and rats to eat for ever.'

I laughed.

'So she's helping him die, is she? Charity indeed. So what, then, of Mrs Dolland? Is there anything that points to the murderess in her, do you think?'

Another chunk of lamb stood poised on the end of Fidelis's fork.

'She is a woman who likes to get what she wants. She is used to commanding men, and she surely knows one end of a monetary agreement from another.'

The meat passed its inspection and went into Fidelis's mouth. He chewed for a while, then stated his conclusion.

'Yes. If her circumstances demanded it, I don't think she would jib at murder.'

For some time a crude musical band had been piping and fiddling beneath the hubbub in the next room. Now the laughter and conversation lessened as a baritone voice began to sing 'There Was a Lass of Islington'. Soon – apart from hoarse bursts of lewd laughter – the drinkers were almost hushed because not only was the voice rich and expressive but no one wanted to miss what you might call the ins and outs of the story, full of bawdy innuendo over the maid's ripe pears and the vintner's pipe and two butts.

We put down our forks, rose and slipped into the public room to listen. The singer, who was dressed in the uniform of an officer, was a handsome fellow though past his first youth. His great nose had a pronounced elbow to it, and was framed by a set of lush feathery whiskers. He was plainly much given to drink and I'd noticed him earlier standing in front of the fire, glass in hand and legs apart, giving an open-mouthed audience bloody tales of the French war, with himself in the hero's role.

The ballad ended with the lass getting the five pounds she'd demanded for her services from the scheming vintner. The crowd gave a raucous cheer and someone called for another song. The officer was all too willing. He had a quiet word with the musicians and announced the song in a booming voice.

'An old tune, ladies and gentlemen, but with words of my very own invention. It is called "The Seven Brave Gamesters".'

He had hardly got started with his song when I noticed Tom Pickering pushing through the throng towards us. He was carrying a bottle of wine. Nodding towards the door of the parlour, he ushered us back inside, where we sat down once more at our table. Fidelis and I resumed our meal while the constable filled our glasses. He jerked his thumb towards the public room, where the officer was still working his way through the song.

'That flash with the Roman nose has been staying here all week,' he said. 'What d'you make of him?'

Fidelis held his hand up and lay back in his chair with his head cocked to the side, listening to what was happening in the other room.

'He looks like a typical officer come home from the Dettingen campaign,' I said. 'All mouth and whiskers.'

Pickering laughed.

'Yes, so it seems. Sings well, though.'

We sat and heard the song out. I did not gather who the brave gamesters were, or what happened to them, but the thing skipped tunefully along and the performer got another cheer as it ended.

'I was drinking with him last night,' said Fidelis. 'His name is Captain Garland of the Welsh Fusiliers. Of course he's addicted to drink and boasting, but not more so than most soldiers. And he tells a damn good tale.'

Pickering had taken a paper from his pocket and attended to it throughout the music. He now rested it on his knee.

'What I meant by my question,' he said, 'was what do you think of him in relation to tomorrow's business?'

Fidelis gave Pickering a sharp look. If there was anything that annoyed him, it was to be accused of missing a vital thread.

'The inquest? How do you mean? How is he connected?'

'Well, Doctor and Mr Cragg, I ask you to consider this. That man is from a regiment of fusiliers.'

Fidelis's eyes flashed. He was no longer confused.

'Ah! I see it,' he said. 'I suppose—'

Pickering stopped him with a gesture.

'Just a moment, Doctor! The point is that not only can he shoot a gun, he possesses one. It's in his baggage. Priestley, the landlord here, has just allowed me a quick look inside his room, and there it was, sirs, there it was leaning against the wall. A bloody big long-barrelled musket, hunting-type.'

'That is interesting,' I said. 'It ought to be investigated.'

'I'm going further than that,' said Pickering. 'I'm arresting him.'

'For what?'

'For murder, of course.'

He held up the paper.

'The arrest warrant which I have just had signed by the magistrate Mr Arthur Dolland at his house. Did you meet Mr Dolland when you were there?'

'I did.'

'He's cock-a-hoop about this. He said if he could've stood up from his chair, he'd have done me a little dance. His very words. A little dance!'

'Are you quite sure this is the right course, Joe?' I said. 'Perhaps it's a bit too soon to draw conclusions about this gun.'

Pickering was not to be thwarted.

'No, I am quite convinced, Mr Cragg,' he said firmly. 'He'll get arrested and spend the night in the cell. Tomorrow he can give evidence at the inquest and we shall see just what he's been doing in our town. I'm only waiting for my assistants to come in. It's always a tricky business arresting soldiers. They are liable to fight back. Collar them when they're in a different room from their weapons, that's the best policy. It would've been ideal to have taken him in the middle of that song. What did he call it?'

'"The Seven Gamesters", his own composition,' said Fidelis. 'And you are quite right, constable. Get him under guard. Lock him up. I fancy Mr Dolland may have his murderer after all.'

'Luke!' I said in some amazement. 'What do you mean? We really know nothing about this man. Isn't it too early to draw these rapid conclusions?'

'Not if his choice of song is any indication. I think he knows all about the tontine. But why he should tell us all so is beyond me at the moment.'

'Tell us all? What are you saying, Luke?'

'I'm telling the constable to go ahead and do his duty.'

He smiled but would tell me no more. A few minutes later as we smoked our after-supper pipes Captain Garland was arrested. At first, far from resisting, he seemed amused, laughing and playing the fool. His companions laughed with him, until they realized Constable Pickering was in earnest. Then they cried out in the Captain's defence, but no one made any physical move to stop him being placed under restraint. As the shackles went on him, the Captain's own mood changed. He shouted angrily that he'd done nothing, and what the blazes was this about?

Pickering returned to us before the prisoner was escorted away.

'Do you wish to interview the Captain, Mr Cragg?'

'In the morning,' I said. 'When he is sober. But a word of warning, Constable. I insist that tomorrow's hearing be an inquest. I insist that it not be what I suspect you, and certainly Mr Arthur Dolland, would like it to be.'

'What is that, sir?'

'The criminal trial of Captain Garland.'

'That is how it may turn out though,' said the Constable. 'By the evidence given, so shall he be judged.'

He swivelled about and joined his small deputation of helpers – the rag-tag members of the Ormskirk Parish Watch no doubt – as they marched Garland out of the inn.

I felt oddly riled. I thought Constable Pickering's actions over-hasty and unnecessary – indeed, undesirable. They would be extremely liable to tilt the inquest and prejudice the jury.

Fidelis seemed unaffected by any such scruples.

'We must call Priestley,' he said, laying down his pipe. 'Before I retire for the night I would dearly like a tour of the Captain's room.'

'So would I,' I said. 'The fact that he has a gun is nothing remarkable. But we may find something else to pin him to this crime.'

'Exactly, Titus. There is more to this than the gun. There's also the song.'

What he meant by this I knew not and he didn't explain.

Priestley the landlord, a heavy, cumbersome man, was happy to do anything to assist the coroner. He took us up to the Captain's room himself, his breath twanging in his chest as he laboured up the stair.

'Did you notice the tin-whistler in the band, the one with the black beard?' he said as he led the way along the landing that lay outside the inn's guest-chambers. 'Name of Charles. That's the Captain's servant.'

'Is he indeed?' I said. 'Then I must talk to him. Would you fetch him up for me?'

Priestley unlocked Captain Garland's bedroom door and let us in.

'Right, sir,' he said. 'I'll go and get Charles for you now.'

The room was untidy. A wash-bowl stood on its stand, still containing cold and scummy shaving water. The Captain's box was on the bed, the lid thrown open and the clothing spilling out. I pulled out handfuls of shirts and underwear, breeches, tunics, stocks and stockings. There was nothing else. Fidelis meanwhile was fishing things out from under the bed. One of these was a book.

'Look at this, Titus,' he said.

The book was Thomas D'Urfey's song-book *Wit and Mirth, or Pills to Purge Melancholy*. Fidelis turned the pages for a moment and then began to sing.

'There was a Lass of Islington,
As I've heard many tell;
And she would to Fair London go,
Fine Apples and Pears to sell . . .'

He riffled the pages then held the book spine uppermost and shook it. Nothing fell out.

'I fancy the other tune that he sang must be in here, Titus,' he said. 'But he'd written new words to it. Where the devil are they?'

He knelt and looked under the bed once more, finally pulling out another volume.

'Ah-ha! This is his memorandum book.'

He turned a few pages.

'Good, very good. Just as I hoped, it's full of doggerel rhymes. Now, where's "The Seven Gamesters", I wonder. Yes! Here we are. The most recent entry, by God. I could only hear one word in three from the parlour but I was sure it would be to the point.'

'*What* point, Luke?' I said in some exasperation. 'What's the significance?'

But he was reading, with a frown and lips a little pursed. Then he handed the book over with a look on his face something like triumph.

'Of the greatest possible significance, I think. Read it for yourself and you'll agree that Joe Pickering did the right thing. Quiz Garland on those verses and see what he says.'

I read through the verses. And then I read them again.

'No!' I said in surprise. 'I don't believe it!'

I read again, this time aloud.

'*I'll give you seven gamesters, of friends they were the best, each made a bet that he would yet live longer than the rest . . .* Yes, yes, yes. *And then there were six . . . and then there were five . . . four . . .* and so on and so on until we have *One gamester happy with his lot, His fellows six have snuffed their wicks and he collects the pot.* It's hard to believe, Luke, but this, by God, is a song about a tontine.'

We now heard the clumping and wheezing of Priestley returning along the corridor.

'I'm sorry to tell you, gentlemen, but I have bad news,' he said when standing at last in the door.

He waited for our reaction.

'Well, out with it,' I said at last.

'The servant Charles has gone. He's scuddled off with his flute, or whistle, and nobody I spoke to has any idea where he's gone.'

'Then we must see if the watch can find him.'

EIGHT

I was out and about by seven next morning. Fidelis, who never rose early by choice, was not to be seen. I drank some chocolate and asked Priestley if the Captain's servant Charles had re-appeared. He had not. So I asked the whereabouts of the town gaol and, making my way there, I stopped a man with a tray to buy some muffins. Garland would be hungry for his breakfast.

The gaol had a single cell and a guard's room inside a small stone building with a conical roof. This stood opposite the Guild Hall where Ormskirk's government was carried out. I found Garland lying on the bench that served him for a bed groaning with a sore head and a dry mouth. He was calling for a drink. The guard, who told me his name was Parkinson, was refusing this on the grounds that the Captain had earlier called him a jackass. I negotiated a jug of water and the use of the guardroom for my interview with the Captain. Parkinson went to stand outside as I brought Garland, hampered by his irons, out of the cell.

'What brought you to Ormskirk, Captain?' I asked, after I had explained that I was enquiring into the death of Richard Giggleswick.

'I wonder why that is your business,' he said, taking a long draught straight from the jug.

'My business, later this morning, will be to establish who shot a respected farmer of this town with a hunting or military gun. You have such a gun, have you not?'

I'd handed him a muffin and he hungrily devoured it.

'Why should I not have a gun, sir?'

He pointed to the water jug.

'Have you nothing stronger for my nerves? Just a glass of rag-water or backstreet gin would tickle it.'

I shook my head and he put his head in his hands, scrubbing his fingers across his scalp.

'So, Captain, what is your regiment?'

'I've been in and out of different ones. I'm on half-pay at the moment, like a lot of us.'

'Have you been fighting the Scotch rebels?'

'No, the French. And I've spent time, too much time, on garrison in Ireland. A country ridden with vermin and Papists crossing themselves wherever you go.'

He spat.

'I hate 'em.'

'So what *does* bring you to Ormskirk?'

'Not to enjoy the shooting, I can assure you.'

'Then why?'

'I'm visiting. That is all.'

'Who do you know here?'

'I've met a lot of people at the Squirrel.'

'I know. I am also putting up there. I saw you last evening. You sang for the company.'

'It was a good party. I don't think I paid for a single drink. I'm paying now, though.'

'I am curious about the song you sang. "The Seven Gamesters".'

'A silly little ditty of my own devising. What of it?'

'What is it about?'

He looked at me incredulously.

'What's it about? It isn't about anything. It's a hoppet's ditty, man, a nonsense song.'

'Well, by my reading it's a tale of seven gamesters each of whom made a bet that he'd live longer than the rest.'

'Exactly so. They pop off one by one until there's only one left. It's what we used to call a counting-out song, d'you follow me? Little children dancing in a ring and dropping down, or out, until there's only one left. Did you never play at musical chairs?'

'Of course. But there is a kind of musical chairs that is a good deal more grown-up. A tontine. Do you know what that is?'

'Tontine. Tontine. No, I cannot honestly say I do. It sounds French. What is it?'

'It is a contract between people to subscribe to a fund that will pass to the last survivor amongst them. Recently Mr Richard Giggleswick was murdered in this town, and he was a signatory to such a contract. Do you know Mr Prenton Smisby?'

'Never heard of him.'

'Isabella Pettifer or Frances Dolland?'

'No, damn you. Who are these people?'

'Other signatories to the tontine.'

He peered at me through the gloom.

'Are you sure you can't obtain any strong drink, sir?'

I ignored the request.

'Tell me about your gun,' I said. 'When did you last fire it?'

'Not recently. I did a bit of shooting a while ago when I was staying with a comrade from the regiment.'

'Where was that?'

'In Ireland.'

'When did you come from Ireland?'

'Three months ago.'

'Where were you before you came to Ormskirk?'

'Liverpool.'

'What were you about on the evening of Wednesday last, and previously on the morning of Monday?'

He wafted his hand vaguely.

'Last Wednesday and the Monday before, you say? I'd have to think about that until I remember.'

'Take another muffin while you do,' I suggested.

He seized a second helping and, as he ate, I made him a short speech.

'Although my court is not a criminal court, its outcome is decided by a jury of local men. If those men should happen to find that you did shoot Farmer Giggleswick, you will be referred to the magistrate and sent to the assizes. To go on the stand and refuse to account for yourself at the time when the death under inquest occurred, or to lie about it under oath, will not help your cause.'

'I am an officer, sir, and this is a matter of honour.'

'I see. Is there a lady in the case, then?'

There was one more muffin. Garland, without replying, took it and ate it, more slowly and reflectively this time. I took a folded paper from my pocket.

'This is your summons. I will leave it with Mr Parkinson. It says you must appear before me this morning. Parkinson will bring you along. You have no choice.'

'What about these?'

Garland lifted his manacled wrists to show the heavy iron that linked them to his manacled ankles.

'You can't come to court like that. I'll ask Parkinson to remove them.'

I had gone to the stables to make sure my horse had been comfortable overnight. Coming out I met Luke Fidelis and Constable Pickering entering the yard from the street, with Pickering carrying a roll of sail-cloth about a yard long.

'I pictured you still groggily detaching yourself from the arms of Morpheus,' I said. 'Instead I find you've been out early.'

'Yes, Mr Pickering and I've been shooting.'

'Shooting? Did you bag anything?'

Fidelis laughed.

'You'll find out soon, I promise.'

Very well. I wouldn't enlighten him about my meeting with Captain Garland. *Quid pro quo.* Instead I spoke to Pickering.

'Is there any word of the whereabouts of the Captain's manservant?'

'I've had the watch out looking, Mr Cragg. They've not found him. If you ask me he's gone, whistled off. We won't see him again.'

We went through the Squirrel's large dining room towards the breakfasting room and found it already being cleared to make room for the inquest. After breakfast I went into the writing room and scribbled a few words about my doings to Elizabeth. 'I can't be sure in advance how the hearing will go,' I wrote in conclusion, 'but there is a man in custody and if he proves to be responsible for the shooting I'll be home tonight. Kiss Hector for me.'

Just as I finished, I heard the familiar voice behind me.

'Good morning, sir. Another of your murder mysteries, is it?'

It was Furzey, ever my doubting Thomas, who had ridden from Preston to be clerk of the inquest. I was glad to see his sardonic smile.

'You are just in time, Furzey,' I said. 'The inquest will start in fifteen minutes.'

The townspeople of Ormskirk turned out in numbers on this fresh April Saturday to learn what had happened to Richard Giggleswick. The jury was sworn and viewed the body, which had been locked up in a convenient potato store behind the inn. I showed them the two bullet wounds and the abrasions on the head, caused by his fall. Then we returned to the inn's dining room.

I quickly surveyed the room. I had asked for chairs to be reserved for the use of the Dollands, but they were unoccupied. I asked Pickering if they had been seen and he said not. Perhaps they were delayed, or staying away, but in light of the new evidence about the Captain and his gun, that might not matter now. I called for the evidence of the first finder: Sally Glover.

Sally gave her evidence in a clear voice. She described her job at Chimneystacks Farm as dairymaid who doubled as a housemaid. She had liked her master, though he was strict, and believed his future plans for the farm were good ones and would benefit them all. At my bidding she went on to tell us about the evening of the murder: how she had finished the milking and filled the churns to send to town. These she had put on a handcart and taken out to the road where the milkman would pick them up before dark. Then she had gone back and looked for Giggleswick.

'Why did you want to see him?'

'One of the cows had a hot nose. If she were poorly and I didn't tell him about it he'd be very angry. So I went out to the pigs thinking he was likely still there, being as he was nowhere about in the yard. That's when I found him lying on the ground.'

She gave a description of how and where he lay, and of how she ran for help to get the body inside.

'And do you have any idea who his murderer was?'

'No, sir.'

'Sally, before I let you go, will you tell us about something that happened at the piggery just two days earlier?'

'You mean when Geoffrey, Mr Giggleswick's prize stud boar, was shot?'

'I do.'

'Tell us, if you please, about this unfortunate incident.'

'Well, Geoffrey was in his pen, just outside his sty, and Mr Giggleswick, who always worked as his own pig-man, had begun a-feeding of him when there came a shot and the pig fell dead. We thought the shooter must have been hiding in the woods across the field. That is all I know.'

'What happened to the pig?'

'He went to the butcher's, of course.'

'Did you see the pig's body?'

'I did. He had a bullet hole in his head. The butcher told us later that he found the ball in Geoffrey's brain.'

'Did any of you who worked on the farm have any idea who could have done this?'

'No, sir. Except that . . .'

'Yes?'

'People are saying it must be the same as shot the master two days later.'

I let her down and called Doctor Fidelis.

'I examined the body of Mr Giggleswick in his bedroom,' he said. 'I understood it had been brought up from where it had been found, at the piggery. I quickly saw that he had been shot twice. One bullet, which I take to be the first to hit him, did so in the knee. It shattered the patella, the kneecap.'

'What effect would that injury have had?'

'It would have been crippling and extremely painful but not fatal. It made him fall down, whereby he hit his head a sore blow probably against the side of the pigsty.'

'But you found another bullet wound also?'

'Yes. This one went through the chest and into the heart. Death from this second shot would have been almost instantaneous.'

'Do you have any idea from where his fatal shot was fired?'

'If I am right, and the knee wound was from a long-range shot which knocked Mr Giggleswick to the ground, then I suggest the shot into his chest was fired while he lay there, from above and at close quarters.'

'By which you mean what sort of distance?'

'From two or three feet.'

'Did you recover the bullet?'

'I did. Here it is.'

He took a piece of misshapen lead from his waistcoat pocket and laid it on the table in front of me. I handed it to the jury foreman who passed it down the line while I continued my questioning.

'Now, Doctor, we have also heard about the incident on Monday last when the pig known as Geoffrey was killed at the same spot by a gunshot. I believe you have some thoughts on the matter.'

Fidelis explained from the evidence of the fence at the edge of the wood, and the fence in front of the pigsty, that shots were fired from a gun at a distance of about a hundred and fifty feet, and that this gun did not shoot straight.

'The shot that killed the pig on Monday,' he said, 'was aimed at Mr Giggleswick but its trajectory was low. I say it ricocheted or bounced off the fence and into the boar's head, killing it.'

'And what about the shot fired from the wood on Wednesday?'

'The first shot, the one from the wood, was also low, wounding Mr Giggleswick in the knee. I suggest the shooter then walked across the field and shot the victim dead in the way I've already described.'

'Leading to the conclusion that the same person made those shots on Monday and Wednesday?'

'I do not say that. But I do say the same gun was used.'

Joseph Pickering was next up.

'Mr Pickering,' I said, 'I understand you have a man in custody in connection with the death we are enquiring into.'

'Yes, Your Honour. I have a Captain Garland formerly of the Welsh Fusiliers.'

'Where and when did you arrest Captain Garland?'

'Here at this inn, sir, last night.'

'Why was that?'

'The Captain is not a resident of Ormskirk. He arrived on Saturday last and took a room here at the inn. On Monday the pig Geoffrey was shot dead. On Wednesday Mr Giggleswick was shot dead also, and in like manner. I was suspicious of Captain Garland and I asked Mr Priestley to show me the Captain's room while he was downstairs drinking. I found a musket there, along with powder and bullets. Here is one of the bullets.'

He took a bullet from his waistcoat pocket and passed it up to me.

'Please compare it to the one the doctor found in Mr Giggleswick's heart.'

I had that bullet on the table in front of me. Against the perfect globe of the unused ball, the murder bullet was deformed. I handed both bullets to the jury foreman and they were solemnly passed from juryman to juryman for inspection.

'One bullet looks much like another, Mr Pickering,' I said as this was going on. 'I wonder what conclusion you draw from the comparison.'

'Not all bullets are the same size and weight – in other words the same calibre, as the term is. But I have weighed these two bullets and they are the same.'

'That doesn't prove that Captain Garland's gun was the one used to kill Richard Giggleswick, does it?'

'No, but it proves that it might have been, as it is the same calibre as the gun used to kill him.'

'And that is all?'

'No. At the suggestion of Doctor Fidelis we made another experiment using the Captain's gun. He can explain it better than I can.'

'In that case,' I said, 'I believe we had better hear from Doctor Fidelis once more.'

Luke Fidelis came back to the witness chair, carrying with him a large piece of folded cloth.

'As I've already told the court,' he said, 'the first bullet fired at Mr Giggleswick on Wednesday evening hit him in the knee. Assuming the gunman was shooting to kill, that is a low shot. It is inaccurate by a matter of two or three feet. On Monday morning a similar shot was fired from a similar place. The bullet missed Mr Giggleswick by a few inches. It hit the fence of the pig enclosure and pinged off it, striking and killing the pig. Now the bullet hit the fence at knee height. Even if it had hit him it would not have been fatal. But the main point is that it showed the same inaccuracy as the gun fired two days later from the same position.'

'So you draw the conclusion that the same gun fired both shots.'

'I do. And as we have learned this morning it was indeed a gun of the same calibre as that later discovered in the room of Captain Garland. This made me wonder if Captain Garland's gun exhibits the same tendency to shoot low as the gun used in the murder. So earlier this morning Mr Pickering and I fired it at a target.'

He unfolded the piece of cloth and I beckoned two from the audience to come forward. They held the cloth up. It had drawn on it in charcoal the outline of a man. Fidelis showed us where he had marked an 'X' over the position of the heart.

'This is the mark I was aiming at, with the gun in a fixed position, at a range of a hundred and fifty feet, which is the distance between Mr Giggleswick's piggery and the edge of the wood. And this—'

He pointed at several holes in the cloth close to the knee of the target man.

'This is where the ball hit not just once but, as you can see, several times over as we repeated the trial. The consistency is remarkable.'

There were admiring murmurs among the audience.

'I have one difficulty, however,' I said. 'Is it not the case that the military musket is a highly inaccurate weapon? And is this not a military musket?'

'No, it is a little different. It is a sporting gun and therefore designed for accuracy. The barrel inside is grooved in such a way as to make the ball spin in the same direction as the line of its flight. This according to the science of ballistics will make it fly straighter.'

'But you have told us that this gun, in fact, fires inaccurately.'

'It is inaccurate, but to very much the same degree with each firing. A ball flies from the smooth-barrelled military musket every which-way at random. The inaccuracy of this gun is a quirk intrinsic to itself.'

I returned Constable Pickering to the witness chair.

'We have established that the gun found in Captain Garland's room shoots low. And we have heard the doctor's idea that the gun fired at Richard Giggleswick also shot low, and in just the same way. What conclusion do you draw?'

'That Captain Garland's musket killed Mr Giggleswick.'

'Then it only remains for me to call Captain Garland to give evidence.'

NINE

Furzey, sitting beside me, had written three or four pages of notes on the evidence so far. Now, while we waited for the Captain to be produced, he tapped me on the arm.

'I've said it before, but he's right dexterous is the doctor. Here, I forgot to give you this.'

He dropped a sealed letter on the table in front of me. It was addressed in the hand of my beloved Elizabeth. I quickly slid it into my pocket and said in a loud voice:

'I would like to get on. Is Captain Garland ready to give evidence?'

There was the sound of iron clanking on iron and the officer appeared at the back of the room, a wig-less, dishevelled figure. Two men knelt down beside him and began wrestling with the shackles on his ankles. After some difficulty he was freed at last and went to the witness chair stiff-backed, in the manner of a martyr to the stake. Nevertheless he spoke the oath in a ringing way that recalled his singing voice and when he sat I noticed how deliberately he relaxed in the chair, as if willing himself now to adopt a confident posture.

'You are an army officer, are you not?' I said.

He indicated his stained and rumpled uniform.

'As you see, sir. I have the honour of having served with the Welsh Fusiliers and elsewhere.'

'And now you are on half-pay?'

'Yes.'

'And prior to that you fought in the action at Dettingen, I believe.'

It was three years since our battle with the French, when the king had taken command of the British forces and later claimed it as his own personal victory.

'Certainly I did,' said Garland. 'We were in the first line. The French cavalry charged us with the reins in their teeth and pistols in both hands. Of course we sent them packing back to their mammies.'

'The nation thanks you, Captain. What was your service after the battle?'

'The Irish garrison. A filthy posting. I could tell you a thing or two—'

I held up my hand.

'If you would simply answer my questions I would be grateful. When did you return from Ireland?'

His testimony, delivered in gruff tones, closely followed the answers he had given me earlier at the gaol. His move to Liverpool, and then Ormskirk. Visiting someone whose name has no bearing here. Weeks since he'd fired the weapon found in his room. No knowledge of Giggleswick. Likewise the other names mentioned. Had no idea what a tontine was. Never heard of such a thing. He'd composed that song for the amusement of children and simple folk. Couldn't understand how it had anything to do with these proceedings. Hell of a dry throat. Yes a drink of water would be good, though something with a stronger kick would answer even better.

I asked that someone find the witness a draught of water and while it was fetched I looked over the jury. Some of them seemed to hold Captain Garland in awe, no doubt having heard his tales at the Squirrel of numerous reckless deeds in battle. But others, I conceived, were now regarding him with a sceptical eye. I fancied they saw him as another tongue-valiant fireside soldier, bluff as every officer believes he should be, but bluffing now for his life.

I leaned towards Furzey while the Captain drank.

'Is this truth or flim-flam do you think?' I murmured.

'He's lying, sir.'

'I am leaning the same way. But let's see. I've one more line of questions for him. I am going to offer him a way out and see if he takes it.'

The witness put the pot he'd been drinking from on the floor and raised his noble nose and bloodshot eyes in my direction.

'Now, Captain,' I said. 'Would you tell me about the companion who came here with you?'

Garland's face did not move for a tell-tale couple of seconds before he frowned and shook his head.

'I don't know who you mean.'

'I mean your manservant, Charles.'

'Oh, yes! Charles, my man. Of course.'

'So what is his surname?'

'Just so.'

This reply nonplussed me.

'I beg your pardon?' I said.

'That's it. His surname.'

'What is?'

'Watt is, Mr Coroner. He's Charles Watt.'

The room burst into laughter and Garland looked this way and that, pleased with himself. I waited for silence.

'Have you known him long?' I said.

'No. I engaged him just before I quit Dublin.'

'Did he come with good recommendation?'

Garland frowned and shook his head, a mere flick, as if this were the stupidest question he'd been asked for weeks.

'Recommendation?' he said. 'I was in Ireland, sir. You can't trust recommendations there. Nobody tells the truth. You have to go on intuition when you engage a servant in Ireland.'

'Did he turn out to be a good manservant?'

'He's not been very bad. And he plays the penny whistle fairly well, which I like him for.'

'And you haven't found him at all untrustworthy in your employ?'

I saw that beads of sweat had appeared on the Captain's brow.

'I do not give him a chance to be untrustworthy.'

'Then would you be surprised to learn he has absconded and there is no sign of him in any part of Ormskirk?

A buzz circulated around the room. The disappearance of someone, never mind who, is always a titillating occasion in the public ear.

'Well,' said the Captain, who had now developed a tic under his right eye, 'he has never come to attend me during my detention in that poxy pit you call a gaol. At just the time when I most needed him. So no, I am not surprised to hear that he's run away. All Teagues are cowards. Charles wouldn't face down a women's tea party.'

'Let us go back to before all this, before your arrest and so on. Might Charles Watt have got hold of your musket during your stay in this town, at times when perhaps you yourself were – er – otherwise engaged?'

'What the devil d'you mean by engaged? What d'you mean by *otherwise*?'

Several members of the public, and the jury, chuckled once more. I banged my fist on the table.

'Do not question me, sir! It is your answers I require.'

To have witnesses who relish their time in the chair is not unusual. Nor is it uncommon for the public to enjoy their humorous or incongruous answers. This case was different, though. The Captain was not having a happy time, indeed he was shifting with restless discomfort in the witness chair.

'Tell me this, please,' I went on. 'Would Charles Watt know how to use the weapon? Could he load it? Fire it and hit something? It's a simple question.'

'And I have no answer for you. I need a drink.'

He raised his head and looked around, appealing directly to the room.

'Is there anybody present as can spare a thirsty old soldier a nip of rum or brandy?'

I rapped the table with my knuckles.

'To proceed. It seems you're not on confidential terms with Charles Watt.'

'Of course I'm not. He's a servant.'

'Can you tell me where he might fly to, if he has indeed flown?'

'Ireland, I suppose.'

'And Watt never made any suggestion that he had business of his own in Ormskirk?'

Captain Garland was trembling now. He crossed his arms in an effort to conceal the fact. In answering me his earlier gruffness was lost as his voice thinned and wavered.

'Why would he? He only came here because I'd engaged him. There is nothing more to be said about Charles Watt. And nothing more to be said about the accursed gun.'

I looked around, letting this remark lie in the minds of the jury, and the audience, for several seconds. Then I looked back towards the witness.

'Captain Garland, I will shortly release you from that chair. But I must tell you your testimony has been less than candid in many respects.'

I was using the high register of speech on purpose. I was damned if a low-ranked officer was going to best me with his repartee in my own court.

'It has been least satisfactory in your refusal to tell the court why you travelled from Liverpool to Ormskirk in the first instance. It is a refusal on which the jury will certainly dwell during its deliberations. Do you therefore have anything further to say on the question?'

But the Captain's repartee, such as it was, had exhausted itself. I doubt he even listened to what I was saying for a sudden and emphatic change had now overwhelmed him. His body suffered a bout of wild agitation lasting a few seconds. Then the shakes left him and he sat up. He was attending to his legs. He began to make violent brushing movements down them with his hands as if insects were crawling all over them.

'Good God!' he said. 'Get them off me. Get them off!'

He was pouring sweat. His head went back, eyes casting about as his trembling intensified. Then with two or three violent jerks of his limbs he toppled off the witness chair and fell on the floor.

'Make way! Make way! He is in danger of a seizure.'

The voice was Fidelis's as he pushed through the standing crowd at the back of the room. As ever he had with him his medical bag. He raised his arm and called for the innkeeper.

'Will someone find Mr Priestley, and ask him to bring me a small glass of brandy? I mean *now*, if you please.'

The audience watched rapt as Fidelis knelt beside the writhing witness. He ripped open his stock and loosened his shirt, then pulled off his boots. He then supported his head with his hand. When the brandy arrived he pulled Garland up and presented the glass to his lips, on which a rime of froth had formed. As soon as the brandy hit the Captain's tongue he began to calm down. He swallowed once, and then again, whereupon Fidelis took the glass away.

'No! No! I need more.'

Garland's resonant voice had reduced to little better than a croak.

'That's enough for now,' said Fidelis sternly. 'Mr Priestley, please have two of your strongest porters carry the Captain to his bedroom, where I will attend him shortly.'

Two beefy men were called. They heaved the sick man up and on to the back of one of them, who carried him out of the room, followed by his fellow carrying the Captain's boots. While this was done I beckoned Fidelis towards me.

'What's just happened to him, Luke?'

'It is the result of his having nothing to drink since last night. I mean strong, intoxicating drink. The man is evidently in the habit of taking it continuously throughout his waking hours. In such cases, when the flow ceases, you see the result. His body is so inured to the drink that without it he goes violently mad. The only known way in which it can be alleviated is by the administration of more of the same. Have you additional questions for him? Shall you adjourn until he can come back to the chair?'

'No. I think his testimony has run its course. I believe I am going to put the question to the jury.'

I turned to Furzey.

'Are there any more due to give evidence that I have forgotten?'

'No, Mr Cragg,' said Furzey. 'The only other name on the roster is that of the absent Mrs Dolland.'

'Mrs Dolland's lack is regrettable.'

'But I venture that we have enough evidence. I venture that the Captain, drunk or sober, will go to the assize.'

'You are right. We'll get this business done with.'

Both the jury and the audience had by now fallen into vehement conversation on the degree to which Captain Garland's evidence could be trusted. I therefore rang my handbell and called the room to order. Fidelis left the inquest room as quietness gradually returned and I addressed the jury.

'You have heard a narrative account of how Mr Giggleswick was found near his piggery, and that he was dead. Dr Fidelis then told us of the farmer's wounds and of the way in which he received them, from which we understood that Richard Giggleswick was the victim of someone lurking in the woods a hundred and fifty feet across the field that fronts the pigstys. The piece used, according to Doctor Fidelis's account, shot low so that Mr Giggleswick was first of all wounded in the knee, which crippled him. The shooter then, it is assumed, crossed the field and administered the coup de grâce – as we might be tempted to miscall it – with a second shot directly into the man's heart. There is therefore no doubt in my mind, and there should be none in yours, that Mr Giggleswick was deliberately killed.

'Who, then, fired that shot? The only evidence we have is that of a musket with the same fault in its accuracy as the one used in the murder. This turned up in a guest-room at this very inn, a room occupied by Captain Garland whose evidence you have just heard and who owned the gun. The Captain denied having any knowledge of the crime. Although he was taken ill before I discharged him from the witness chair, I am satisfied that he would not have provided us with any more material facts.

'It is for you now to reach a verdict derived only from what you have heard here today. Mr Foreman, will you require a separate room in which to deliberate?'

Philip Chancellor, the foreman of the jury, said this would not be needed. The twelve men therefore huddled together and held a brief debate. After five minutes the foreman broke away from the group and came to me with a question.

'Mr Cragg, you didn't mention in your summary the servant, the man Watt. You asked if he could have used the gun when the Captain wasn't looking. But he never answered the question, did he? What should we make of that?'

'Well, we know very little about this servant. But as the Captain himself pointed out, Watt had no reason to kill someone in

Ormskirk, where he came only because he was in the Captain's service.'

'But he has run away since. Does that not signify?'

'It may signify no more than his fright at seeing his master taken up and put in gaol. It is regrettable, certainly. His evidence might have helped us better understand what happened. But we have no reason to think he was material.'

'Not the murderer, then.'

'No.'

Chancellor returned to his colleagues and another five minutes' discussion followed. Although the Captain had had his admirers beforehand, his strange behaviour in court, and his evasive answers to my questions, seemed now to have turned those votes against him. So it was not long before the foreman came back to me and said they were all agreed.

I brought the court back into session, stood the foreman up, and asked him to state whether the jury had reached a verdict on the manner in which Richard Giggleswick died.

'So we have, sir,' said Chancellor.

'And how do you find?'

'We find that Farmer Giggleswick was murdered by a ball from Captain Garland's hunting piece in his heart, and that the Captain himself fired the shot.'

'So your verdict is "murder by Captain Garland"?'

'It is that, sir.'

'Then I call this inquest concluded and you are discharged.'

The people of Ormskirk began to get up and go, talking animatedly. As far as they were concerned this was the ideal finding. One of theirs had been murdered, yet the deed was not to be pinned on another one of theirs. Instead it was the responsibility of an incomer who happened to be an inveterate sot, and whose downfall could be easily attributed only to his own base nature and gross habits.

While Furzey wrote the verdict out in proper style, to be signed by Philip Chancellor and myself, I sought out Constable Pickering, meaning to ask him if there had been any word from Mrs Dolland as to why she did not come. Before I could do so I saw the lady herself entering the room.

'Well, sir,' she said when she reached us. 'It appears I have wasted my time in coming here. It appears these proceedings began at ten, whereas I understood it would not be until the afternoon.

'You were told so?' I said.

'I asked the messenger that brought the constable's summons and it is what he told me. I thought I would be early but it seems I am too late.'

'It is a pity, madam, but a verdict has been reached nevertheless.'

'What verdict?'

'That Captain Garland did kill Richard Giggleswick by shooting him.'

'Captain Garland? I don't think I know the name. Who is he?'

At that very moment the Captain himself re-appeared, almost running into the room from the stairfoot in the hall. He was closely followed by Luke Fidelis.

'Damn you for a quack doctor,' Garland roared over his shoulder. 'There's nothing the matter with me that a flagon of wine or a bottle of brandy won't mend.'

He looked into the room and saw me first.

'Ah! Coroner Cragg! I'll have a word. I have been told of this disgraceful verdict, and I'll have you know—'

At this moment he caught sight of Mrs Dolland, and stopped short. A look of frozen panic came over his sweaty drink-puffed features.

'Good God!' he said.

Mrs Dolland fixed him with a disdainful Gorgon's stare.

'Peregrine,' she said. 'I thought I made it clear that I never, ever, wished to clap eyes on you again. The passage of time has not diminished that desire a single jot.'

'Mrs Dolland,' I said. 'Am I to understand that you know Captain Garland?'

She looked at me.

'Where is Captain Garland?'

'Why, here. This is him.'

She turned and took four steps until she was almost nose to nose with the Captain.

'No, it is not,' she said. 'This, sir, is Peregrine Dolland, to whom I have the misfortune of being married.'

TEN

That night, lying in my bed at home, I told Elizabeth the whole story of my investigations into Giggleswick's death, then of the inquest, the verdict and the surprising discovery that followed it. But it was the tontine that caught her interest, and one name in particular from the list of subscribers.

'Thomas Hesketh, Titus. Is it the same as was once Member of Parliament for Preston?'

'That he was, when you were a mere child. Tom and I were boys together at the grammar school. When Mr Fleetwood gave up the seat in twenty-three he fixed it for Tom to succeed him, though he was still not much more than a cherry-cheeked lad even then.'

'Was he a good MP?'

'Hardly. He never took to the parliamentary life and gave it up after four years. He much preferred sports, gambling and improving his house. And I do know that he loved the Pretender a good deal more than the German Georges.'

'And he died, didn't he?'

'He was only a little over thirty. A hunting accident at Rufford, where he lived near Ormskirk. He hadn't lived in Preston for years.'

'And it was this tontine that he was part of that caused the Ormskirk farmer to be murdered.'

'The tontine was created in Liverpool, but at least three of them had Ormskirk connections, Tom Hesketh being one. Tom was always a gambler. I well remember him at school. He would arrange beetle races, and offer odds on how many shaving cuts there would be on the master's face in the morning.'

'So do you think the man who murdered the farmer—'

'Captain Dolland who called himself Garland.'

'Yes, him. Might he have helped Mr Hesketh off his horse on the hunting field?'

'Who knows? It is perhaps too long ago. I mean why would there be such an interval of time – eleven years – between the two deaths? And in any event it must be difficult now to ascertain the facts of Hesketh's accident.'

'I'm thinking there is someone in this town who might know the facts, or some of them.'

'Who is that, my love?'

'Lady Derby. She was born Elizabeth Hesketh, was she not? I believe she was Thomas Hesketh's cousin.'

The Countess of Derby, the wife of Lancashire's most august and powerful nobleman, lived for much of the time with her husband at Patten House in Church Gate. She had become friendly with Elizabeth in recent times through their work on the Preston Ladies' Committee for the Relief of Starvation.

'That is quite true,' I said. 'But I cannot simply go over to Patten House and demand the truth behind cousin Thomas's demise. For one thing my work on the Giggleswick death is over now. Such questions would not be warranted.'

'So will this Captain swing for the killing?'

'He ought to. The fact of his being married to Mrs Dolland, who was part of the tontine, makes the case against him stronger because it supplies what had previously been lacking in the case: his motive. If Mrs Dolland were to become the last survivor of the tontine then her husband would be the real chief beneficiary, legally speaking. It would be him, not his wife, who would rake up the cash. He looks the kind of fellow who always needs money. But as I say all this is not for me now. It is a matter for the assizes, where the Captain must be committed for trial by the Ormskirk magistracy.'

'What did Mrs Dolland think of that?'

'I'm sure she was happy. She detests the man. She would give evidence if she could.'

'Perhaps she will.'

'No, she is not allowed to, as it happens. Spouses as far as the law is concerned are one person – or should I say *is* one person – and what's the sense in a person testifying against himself? Lawyers call it spousal privilege.'

She kissed me with a laugh.

'I hope you feel privileged, my love, where your spouse is concerned.'

I said that I felt extraordinarily so.

*   *   *

A few days later, over our breakfast, Elizabeth read me a note she had just received. It told her that Lady Derby would be calling at the house on business connected to the committee. Later in the morning, looking out through the window of my adjoining office, I saw her ladyship's stately approach to our front door and used my connecting door into the house to be in time to greet her.

In reality, Lady Derby was not a born aristocrat. The Hesketh family were solid Lancashire gentry, although from the wealthier end of the class. For centuries they had benefited from appropriating and enclosing common Lancashire land for their own profit, enabling them to inhabit large houses, sit in Parliament and help to rule the nation in their and their friends' own interest. Such is our system of government: who am I to question it?

The countess and I sat together in the parlour while Elizabeth went into the kitchen to make sure that a cup of chocolate was made in exactly the way her ladyship liked. I mentioned that I had been conducting an inquest in Ormskirk, a town I believed her ladyship knew well.

'Oh, yes,' she said. 'I passed my childhood in Rufford and Ormskirk.'

'Your cousin Thomas from Ribbleton Hall, did he visit you from Preston?'

'He did, often. We were of an age, and playmates.'

'I too was a playmate of his, Lady Derby. We were together at the grammar school. I remember he had, or so it seemed to the rest of us, unlimited pocket money.'

'Then you will also remember how terribly boyish and naughty he was. At times ungovernable.'

'The reason I mention him is that the deceased man whom I inquested at Ormskirk was a friend of your cousin's youth. His name was Richard Giggleswick.'

'Oh my Lord! Is he dead? Yes, I remember him, but not in Ormskirk. In Liverpool. I was schooled there, and I had two particular friends, Isabella Pettifer and Frances Dolland. Frances, dear Frances, she was very forthright. She later made a bad marriage to a cousin, so I heard. Isabella was a tiny bit brisk, a bit free, you know? Later she became very religious. It is often that way. A girl is given, and gives herself, too much licence and then quite suddenly she turns about and becomes a religious fanatic or a Methodist or something of the kind. Where was I? Oh yes, Dick Giggles, as we three called him. Ha-ha! We made fun of him but he was very handsome and agreeable, though painfully shy. Isabella in particular was a little giddy for him. But it came to nothing. We were so young.'

'Did you used to see Thomas in Liverpool?'

'Oh yes, Dick was one of a particular group of friends of Tom's, all merchants' sons, but very agreeable and amusing. We girls first met them at dancing classes, I believe. We were only about fourteen at the time. One was an extremely clever, a fellow called Prenton Smithby – was it? No, Smisby! An almost prodigious brain he had, though he was a very poor dancer.'

'Do you remember anyone else? There was a man from Ireland mentioned, Bourke.'

'Bourke? No, I don't think so. I don't remember that name. What on earth can you find of interest in my girlhood companions, Mr Cragg?'

'I am sorry to tell you that Richard Giggleswick was found by the inquest to have been murdered. It may have proceeded from certain connections he made in his youth.'

'Good heavens! That is shocking. Murdered by whom?'

'According to the inquest, by the husband of your friend Frances Dolland, Lady Derby.'

'No!'

'Yes. He is Captain Peregrine Dolland, who was calling himself Garland.'

'Peregrine Dolland was the cousin whom Frances was made to marry by her family, as I mentioned. But what a terrible thing!'

'Did you yourself know Captain Dolland?'

'Not at all. He lived over in Manchester, if I remember right, and he came along many years after I married my Edward. I was the first to wed of all of us and I believe after that the only one of them I would ever see was Tom, though in a different way, of course. Then poor Tom died. That was about a year before my Edward succeeded to the Derby title.'

'It was a riding accident, I believe.'

'It was hunting. No one saw it happen. He was detached from the main body of the hunt, as often happens you know, and was found in woodland with a broken neck after his horse came home without him. Ah, my dear Mrs Cragg. How kind of you to supervise in person the preparation of my chocolate.'

Elizabeth had come in with a tray and cups of chocolate. It was my cue to leave the ladies to the alleviation of poverty and return to the office.

'Furzey,' I said as I came in, 'I wonder if we can find out about an accidental death eleven years ago. I want to know if it was subject to inquest?'

'What sort of death, and where?' he said.

'Hunting accident. At Rufford, I think. The deceased was Thomas Hesketh of Rufford Hall.'

'The Jacobite? I remember him as member for Preston. The worst one we ever had. He fell off his horse, did he? That wouldn't normally be deemed questionable enough for inquest.'

'I know that. But most who die while riding are seen. This death was unwitnessed, and the dead man was an important local landowner. Under those circumstances old Coroner Mortimer might at least have enquired.'

Furzey sighed. He stopped writing and reached down a letter from the shelf above his desk.

'I might go and see if there is anything in the duchy legal records, I suppose. In the meantime, you may be interested in this from Ormskirk. It came in while you were slurping chocolate with the Quality.'

He handed me the letter and I saw it was from Joe Pickering.

Dear Mr Cragg,

You will be interested in what happened after the inquest into Richard Giggleswick. Old Arthur Dolland as you know is our high magistrate, a position that he dotes on. Well, in the matter of what to do about Captain Garland (i.e. Dolland) following the inquest verdict, the Old Man has ruled that there is no case of murder for the Captain to answer. Can you believe it? He has let his nephew (and son-in-law) off with a fine for his carelessness in keeping a loaded gun on enclosed premises, which is not an offence as far as I know. Old Dolland, much as he loves a murder, cannot stomach the idea that his brother's son might go to the gallows, so he invented a lesser crime to cover the more serious one, and then let him go. It is a scandal to justice but there the matter rests. Unless the man is referred by a justice of the peace he cannot go to the assize, and that will not happen now. The junior benchers here at Ormskirk do not go against Arthur as a rule, and are not likely to over this.

Yours respectfully, Joseph Pickering.

A scandal to justice indeed. Handing the letter to Furzey, I wondered what Arthur Dolland's daughter thought of the matter.

'Read it,' I said. 'It says that the Captain is at large again.'

Furzey glanced through it, then handed it back with an ironic laugh and resumed his writing.

'He must now think he's young Prince Hal in the play,' he said. 'Exempt from the law.'

'But the question is, will he go on with his campaign to win the tontine? There are now only Smisby and Miss Pettifer standing between him and three and a half thousand guineas.'

'He'd never. He wouldn't dare harm them, not now.'

'That depends on how much he might need money. And it might not take a great deal of effort to see them off: Miss Pettifer is almost an invalid, and Smisby isn't in the best of health.'

'The Captain's been branded a murderer, never mind what his uncle and father-in-law says. A reputation like that follows you around. He must be proper cunning to get away with that, while everything I've seen of him tells me the man's a complete numps.'

'Yes, Furzey, but being a numps he might think he *can* get away with it.'

Furzey's sigh was indicative of his thinking I was a numps.

'And are you serious about sending me off to look for an inquest into the death of Thomas Hesketh?' he said.

'If you please, Furzey.'

Furzey finished the line he was working on and dropped his pen in its stand.

'Very well, I'll go there now. Mind the office while I'm out.'

Sometimes I wondered who was the attorney and who the clerk.

An hour later I was absorbed in drafting a complicated trust document when Furzey returned.

'Here. I copied that from the register, signed by the late lamented coroner.'

He handed me a piece of paper, on which I read.

Thomas Hesketh of Rufford Hall dec. 15 April 1735. Inquisition post-mortem held 18 April 1735. Verdict, hunting accident.

   (signed) Jer: Mortimer Coroner for Duchy of Lancaster.

I looked at Furzey, on his way back to the copying he'd earlier paused.

'Is that all there is?' I said.

'What more did you expect to read?' said Furzey. 'What the foxes in the covert thought of it all? There are no additional details in the record.'

'We know there was a hearing at least. It's a pity about old Mortimer. I'm sure he could have told me more about Thomas Hesketh's death, and the evidence in the case. Now there's no one to ask.'

I pictured in my mind the old Duchy Coroner, who had died seven years back. My father had known him as a fellow student at the Inns of Court in the 1680s, and they'd continued as friends. Mortimer would visit us whenever he came to Preston. He had been highly effective in the Duchy post as, unlike many coroners (but like my father), he was diligent in his duties and stringent in matters of right evidence.

Furzey had scratched his way through another line of his copy before he put his head around the door once again.

'By the by, I may be able to obtain details of that inquest you mentioned.'

'Thomas Hesketh's? But old Jeremiah Mortimer is dead and gone.'

'His clerk isn't. He is living here in Preston with his daughter.'

Furzey disappeared back to his desk.

'What's his name?' I called out. 'Who's the daughter? I must go and see him.'

Jeremiah Mortimer's old clerk was called Linus Cotter. A widower, he lived in retirement with his daughter, whose husband John

Jackson was a button-maker. I found Jackson's house outside the Friar Gate Bar and standing next to his shop. The door of the shop was open and I strolled in.

'How do, Mr Jackson?'

'Very well, Mr Cragg,' he replied. 'Yourself?'

We got the formalities over, and I asked him about his father-in-law.

'Middling, you might say. He isn't as strong as he was and has arthritis pains in his hips and knees.'

'How old is he now?'

'Seventy-one next birthday.'

'I particularly hope he is not confused. Many are by that age.'

'He isn't, not very,' said Jackson. 'Why do you ask about Linus?'

'I have come to see him. Shall I go to your house front door?'

'No, no, come through the by door.'

Jackson had a door, as I did, connecting his place of work to his dwelling house. He led the way and I followed until we stood in his small parlour, a comfortable room with walls decorated by a set of unusual pictures. These were not out of the ordinary in the subjects they depicted: one showed a shepherd and two of his sheep, another the Tower of London, and a third a ship of the line. But taking a closer look I saw that they were formed by the sticking of coloured thread and buttons on a felt ground.

'These are most remarkable,' I said.

'They are all done by Linus,' said Jackson. 'It is his retirement pastime. I provide him with the buttons. It fills his time nicely.'

Jackson left me alone to fetch Linus Cotter, who appeared after a few minutes. He knew me immediately though I must confess I had quite forgotten his appearance.

'Mr Cragg! What a pleasant surprise. I hope you have not come to offer me employment, as I would have to disappoint you. I have quite lost my clerking skills.'

'No, Mr Cotter. Mr Furzey supplies all my needs at the office.'

'Ah! Yes, young Robert. He writes a very good hand.'

I mentioned the excellence of Cotter's pictures and we discussed his method of sticking the thread and buttons in place.

'I do not call myself an artist such as Mr Devis or Mr Hogarth,' Cotter said. 'I am a craftsman only but I do enjoy the work.'

'I believe I have seen them for sale in the Wednesday market,'
I said.

'Most likely, Mr Cragg. They are obtainable at the stall of Mr
Wainwright the printseller.'

Mrs Jackson came in with tea and a plate of spiced currant
cakes. An organized person, I thought, who was ready with something to offer even the least-expected visitor. She and her husband
then withdrew and Linus invited me to sit beside the fire. He sat
himself in the chair opposite.

I looked him over and felt reassured. He was dressed in a good
waistcoat over a clean linen shirt. His hair was clean too, and so
were his fingernails, and he was shaved. Linus Cotter was an old
man but he presented himself with care.

'So, how can I help you, Mr Cragg?' he asked once he had
poured me a cup of tea and pressed a cake upon me.

'It is a matter of an old inquest,' I said. 'Mr Mortimer's enquiry
into the death of Thomas Hesketh, who was previously Member
of Parliament here in Preston. Do you remember the case, Mr
Cotter? It was eleven years ago, in Orsmkirk.'

Cotter's face lit up.

'Oh yes,' he said. 'I remember it very well. Very well indeed,
and it was a peach.'

'There was an inquest?'

'Oh yes, there was indeed.'

'I'm afraid in that case I must tax your memory of it.'

He laughed delightedly and shook his finger from side to side.

'No, Mr Cragg. No, no. There's no need to tax my memory.'

He laid down his cup and stood up.

'If you would be good enough to wait here, I shall leave you
for a moment to go to my chamber.'

He left the room. I was looking again at the Tower of London
on the wall when he returned with a thick folio minute-book under
his arm. He placed it reverently in my hands.

'Mr Mortimer made me make a narrative record of all his more
interesting inquests. They are contained in this volume, which I
have preserved as a keepsake of my old employer. You may take
it away, Mr Cragg, if you solemnly undertake to return it intact.'

'Of course,' I said.

'You will find the hearing that interests you under the date the seventeenth of April 1735. Read it. You will find it is, as I mentioned, a peach, and a ripe one.'

ELEVEN

According to Linus Cotter's narration of events, the death of Thomas Hesketh took place on a wet spring day in 1735, at the tail end of that year's fox-hunting season. The pack of hounds were Hesketh's own, kept in the kennels that adjoined Rufford Hall. He himself was Master of Hounds. On this day many of the more prosperous local farmers turned out for what would be the last hunt until the autumn, as well as members of the gentry and professions. There were also some of Mr Hesketh's own house-guests from further afield.

After the hunt was over, and the riders had assembled for a parting glass of hot punch, it was found that the Master wasn't among them. Then his gelding came home, saddled but riderless. The huntsman, a Mr Rodgers, asked everyone to tell him their last sighting of Mr Hesketh, and with these collated it appeared that no one had seen him since the time when the hunt picked up a fox on the Twenty Acre Field, on the other side of Bentley's Hill.

A party of riders immediately set out to look for the Master. The Twenty Acre Field was bordered along one side by a jumpable brook and on the other bank of this a coppice, about a hundred and fifty yards deep. It was here in the thicket that the lifeless body of Thomas Hesketh was found by one of the hunt servants, a man named Leo Olivant.

As the first finder, Olivant was also the first witness to give evidence before Mr Mortimer. He said that he had been one of several men making a systematic search of the wood by entering at intervals along its length. He had found Mr Hesketh's body lying with head twisted unnaturally. It gave no sign of life. He called out. One of the riders who came in answer to his cries was the local physician, Doctor Tetley. He pronounced Hesketh dead.

Giving next evidence, Tetley said that in his opinion Hesketh had died from a broken neck, sustained in his fall from the horse.

However he also noted that Mr Hesketh's clothes, his shirt, waist-coat and jacket, were wet with blood around his lower ribs. Investigating this, he found a bullet wound in Mr Hesketh's side. It was not the fall from the horse, but this gunshot that forced Mr Mortimer to inquest into the death.

Further investigation of Mr Hesketh's clothing turned up a pistol in a pocket on the same side of the body as the bullet wound. Moreover the pistol had been discharged. Mr Mortimer asked Graves if this wound could have killed Hesketh before he hit the ground. No, said the doctor. It was a serious wound but it had not passed through the heart, or any vital organ. He thought the gun must have discharged itself when Hesketh hit the ground. Mortimer asked whether the doctor had seen any physical signs in Hesketh's body, such as a seizure or heart attack, to explain why he fell from his horse in the first place. The doctor had not.

Rodgers the huntsman was the next witness. Before the Master's disappearance, he had seen Mr Hesketh in company with other riders at various stages of the hunt. As they entered Twenty Acre Field, with the hounds finding no scent, Mr Hesketh had told Rodgers that he himself and one or two others would go into the coppice in order to flush out a fox, as he was sure there was one in there. He was correct as, shortly after the Master went in, a fox broke cover and the hunt was on. They had a long, semi-circular run that took them back to the slopes of Bentley's Hill before they killed. After that, as evening was near, they headed home to Rufford. Yes, Rodgers had noticed that the Master was absent at the kill but guessed his horse had gone lame and been walked home. He had at no time heard the sound of a pistol being fired.

Both Mr Smisby, a ship-owner, and Mr Bourke, a wine-merchant, were questioned, and both said they had ridden in company with Mr Hesketh at different times. They had both made forays into the coppice, as had Mr Hesketh, trying to flush out a fox. They confirmed that these moves were successful as a fox broke out and they had a long and exciting run. Neither man had heard a pistol shot.

Mortimer then questioned the groom who looked after Hesketh's horse. He was a gelding called Goliath, being an unusually large animal and on the high-mettled side. But the Master was a good rider and the groom did not think Goliath would have deliberately thrown him. There was one thing about Goliath, though. He had a particular aversion to rats. He had been cast in his box once and had become terrified by the rats that ran around him while he lay there. What does 'cast in his box' mean? That is when horses go down and try to roll in their stall and, the space being confined, sometimes get themselves in a position that they can't get up from. If this occurs at night they might thrash about for a long time and seriously injure themselves. On this occasion Goliath had hurt himself so badly on account of the rats that he couldn't be ridden for three months.

The groom suggested Goliath may have startled at the sight of a rat in the wood, and this had caused him to throw his rider. Mortimer was interested in this idea and returned both Smisby and Bourke to the witness chair to ask if they had seen any such small creatures in the wood. They said they'd seen rabbits but no rats, though because of the brook, water rats were naturally very likely.

Mortimer then proceeded to summarize the evidence. He accepted the idea that Goliath had thrown Mr Hesketh while in the wood, at around the time that the fox had broken out and caused the hounds and riders to give chase. It was likely that the fall had been caused by the horse sighting a water rat, or perhaps a rabbit that Goliath mistook for a rat. Mr Hesketh had gone down to the ground head-first and broken his neck. At the same time his pocket pistol had fired, causing him the non-fatal side wound.

After such a summary by the coroner the conclusion of the jury was foregone: Mr Hesketh had suffered an accidental death as a result of being thrown from his horse.

'There is something badly wrong with this, Titus,' said Luke Fidelis two days later, as he dropped the minute-book on to my table in the Turk's Head Coffee House. 'It's the wrong verdict.'

He sat down opposite me and poured himself a cup of coffee from the pot. I had already stuffed a pipe for him, and this I pushed across the table. I watched him as he lit a taper from the candle and applied the flame.

'Oh? What makes you so sure?'

I had lent him Cotter's book because I knew he was curious, as I was, about the lives and deaths of any of the names on the tontine. But I had not expected him to inquest the inquest.

'I'm sure of one thing,' said Fidelis drawing on his pipe and sending up plumes of smoke, 'that gun was fired before Thomas Hesketh died. If the injury had indeed been inflicted simultaneously with the broken neck – which Mortimer assumes it was – it would not have caused bleeding sufficient to soak through the man's shirt, waistcoat and coat.'

'Why is that?'

'When a neck breaks – I mean when it is severed – it causes immediate death. At the same instant the heart stops. No wound bleeds in any great quantity once the pulsion of the heart has stopped.'

'You say "when the neck is severed". Do you know it was? It may have been partially broken, with life continuing for some time after the fall. Hesketh was not found for some hours, remember. The poor fellow may have died slowly where he lay.'

Fidelis opened the book and found the page.

'This is why,' he said, and read from the book aloud. '"Mr Mortimer: And in what position was Mr Hesketh lying when you found him? Olivant: He was lying on his left side with his head twisted unnaturally so that it rested with his right cheek on the ground." There. Without seeing the body I can't be utterly sure, but the extreme twisting of the head tells me Hesketh's neck must almost certainly have been severed by his fall.'

'And therefore . . .?'

'And therefore he didn't fall from his horse because of a water rat. He fell because a pistol was fired and he was injured. The question then is, who shot him?'

'Come, come, Luke. Suppose the gun simply went off accidentally while Hesketh was still in the saddle. Hesketh was painfully injured, and at the same time his horse startled at the noise and reared. Hesketh was so shocked and pained by his wound, he was unseated and fell to his death.'

'What in that case made the gun fire?'

'It had a sensitive trigger. It was jolted and went off.'

'This won't do, Titus. The wound was in his side, so the gun would need to have pointed upwards inside the pocket. That is not a likely way to carry a loaded pistol. Besides, if the pistol was liable to go off in the way you describe, it would surely have done so earlier in the hunt when Hesketh was riding at full gallop. It would hardly be triggered while he was riding cautiously through a wood.'

Not for the first time in my life, I could not fault my friend's logic.

After this, my professional life in Preston was for some time unremarkable, even humdrum. But if legal life was dull, my family gave continual delight, not only in the company of my Elizabeth but also in watching the growth in body and mind of Hector. He was highly inventive in language, coming out with whimsical new words for all sorts of common things. A pipe was stinkysmoke and wine was Papa-milk. I had been telling him bedtime tales from Ovid's *Metamorphoses* which he so much enjoyed that he would ask for more stories by Mr Avid and his Four Seas.

When I regaled Luke Fidelis or Robert Furzey of Hector's word confusions, they rarely found them as entertaining as I did, so that I learned to keep my delight in them between myself and Elizabeth, who fully shared it. I was learning what all parents learn: that, while friends took great pleasure in the general fact of our having a child, they were not in the least curious about the minute particulars of our son's genius.

I had sent an early reply to Joe Pickering's letter in which he'd told me of Captain Garland's release back into society. I had thanked him and said I'd be interested if he could find the time to tell me of any further developments with regard to the Captain. I wrote this without any serious expectations that Pickering – busy with pottery and constabling – would take the trouble to do so. But three weeks later, in the first week of May, I had this from him.

> Dear Mr Cragg,
>
> You may perhaps be interested to know that Captain Garland (as he still calls himself though we all know that it is a soldier-name and he is really Dolland) is staying with Mrs Greenwood, a widow of this town. He has gone about using money that she gives him (for she is rich and marvellously under his spell) to drink in the Squirrel, play at cards, attend the cockpit and just recently the Easter horseraces on

Aughton Moss. At such sporting occasions he is said to make prodigious wagers.

I also have news of Giggleswick's family. His old mother, with her grandchildren, have left Chimneystacks Farm and are settled with her daughter in north Wales. Meantime Mr Parr administered Mr Giggleswick's estate and has published its details. He left property worth five hundred pounds and securities in almost the same amount, but according to Mr Parr's account there were many debts to pay, with the outcome that only a little more than two hundred were left to his heirs. Much of the debt was (so it seems) owed to Mr Parr himself, and as a result the lawyer is now proprietor of the farm and surrounding land.

I will say no more of this matter except that I wonder if it is seemly for a lawyer to take into his own hands the property of one whose estate he administers.

Yours, Joseph Pickering

The letter gave much to ponder on. The first thought was that of the Captain brazenly living the life of a sporting blade in the town whose citizens had branded him a murderer. This was quite surprising in itself, but the more so as he was doing it in the teeth of the Dolland family. They must want him to pack himself off without delay. Keeping him off the gallows was one thing. But to see him gadding about Ormskirk flaunting himself on the money of a rich widow must be bitter gall to his wife and his uncle.

The second question flowed from the first. The Captain had been branded a murderer, and for a reason. The evidence was damning. True the inquest had not been able to say why he did it, because at the time we knew nothing of his interest in the tontine. But was he now going to make another move of the same kind, or had the inquest verdict frightened him off his original plan?

The third question from Pickering's letter was nothing to do with the tontine. It concerned the conduct of Ambrose Parr. Pickering's own doubt about Parr seemed to me entirely justified: was Ambrose Parr's legal practice 'seemly'? Was it even legal?

This third question came up again only a week later, on a warm day in May after breakfast. I entered the front office where Furzey worked, though was not there. Sunshine streamed down from above Market Place and into the east-facing windows, the light animated and dancing from the shadows of swooping birds. It is on such days that my profession is sometimes born anew in me. I crossed to the bookshelves and ran my fingers along the spines of the volumes of Fitzherbert's *Grand Abridgements* and Coke's *Institutes of the Laws*, their gold-leaf titles lit by the sun, and remembered my time as a student at the Inns of Court, when I used to commit whole pages of these volumes to memory. The law had seemed part of a wonderful active adventure then, a suit of shining armour in which to sally forth against error, greed, cruelty and all the other ills of human society. Such emotions were those of a zealous youth, of course. But occasionally even now they returned, and then I forgot the drudgery of contract and conveyance and felt young again.

The street door swung open and my clerk appeared with the leather satchel in which he fetched our mail from the post office each day.

'Has anything good come in?' I said. 'Anything that does not stink of affidavits and deeds? I need something to get my juices flowing on this beautiful day.'

He dumped the post-bag on his writing desk, unlatched it and plunged his hand inside. A small handful of letters came out, from which he picked one.

'You'll want to read this, then, I reckon,' said Furzey, handing it to me.

The address was from Ormskirk, written in the legal hand and sealed in wax. I turned it over and read what was written on the reverse. The sender was Ambrose Parr.

To Mr Cragg Coroner to the Duchy of Lancaster.
　　Sir, I would be glad of your early attendance at the house of Miss Isabella Pettifer at Aughton, near Ormskirk, Miss Pettifer having been found dead, and perhaps deplorably slain as the circumstances are questionable. Your inquisition would therefore seem to be a matter of necessity. The constabulary duties for this parish are united with those of Ormskirk, two miles distant, and I have therefore informed the constable in Ormskirk, one Joseph Pickering, that I have made this

request. I am put up at the Squirrel Inn, where you will find
me for the next two days.
   (signed) Ambrose Parr Attorney-at-Law

'Well, Furzey,' I said, putting the letter down and taking off my
reading glasses. 'You have certainly turned up a trump card. Miss
Pettifer of Aughton is dead and we have a new inquest on our
hands.'

TWELVE

My next act was to send to Luke Fidelis, from whom I
received a reply, in the almost illegible hand of his apprentice Peason, saying that the doctor was attending a
gentleman patient in Blackburn and would be there at least until
tomorrow. He (Peason) was standing ready to join Dr Fidelis, to
assist him if surgery was required. Peason would inform his master
that he might be useful to the coroner in Ormskirk, if subsequently
able to travel there.

   I supposed I could manage the thing without Fidelis. Perhaps
I had become too dependent on my friend's acumen in face of a
dead body. I told Furzey to stand ready to join me in two days
for a possible inquest, packed a valise, kissed Elizabeth and Hector,
and set off once more down the Liverpool road.

Priestley the landlord welcomed me to the Squirrel Inn but told
me he could not offer me, as before, his best room since a gentleman
from Liverpool had already occupied it. Having settled into the
second-best room, I asked Priestley to direct me to the most
popular barber in town. I was told Lloyd's where I would maybe
recognize both barbers, as they were fiddler and percussionist in
the musical band that entertained the drinkers there at the Squirrel.
I set off at once, as I wanted a shave but, even more, I wanted
information, and there is no establishment better at collecting and
spreading news in a town than a barber's shop.

   I found the establishment of Lambert Lloyd and Son facing the old town ducking stool. As the younger Lloyd, Owen by name, settled me in his chair I remarked on this and asked when the stool had last been used.

Owen Lloyd laughed and called out to his father, who was stropping a razor on the other side of the room.

'Dad! Mr Cragg wants to know last time anyone was ducked. Wasn't it old Rosie Grace that lived by the windmill at Scarth Hill?'

'Aye,' said the old man. 'Before you were born.'

'What did she do to deserve it?' I asked.

'Told lies,' growled the old barber, still stropping. 'She gave light weight at market. And worse.'

'What worse?'

Lambert Lloyd merely winked and I turned back to Owen.

'Do you know me, Mr Lloyd?'

'Dad!' said Owen. 'Mr Cragg wants to know if we know him.'

'Course we know him,' said the old man. 'Didn't we shut up shop for his inquest?'

'So we did,' said Owen, throwing a towel across me and tying it behind my neck. 'It made a change from doing this, an' all.'

'So do you think the verdict was correct?' I said.

'Dad!' Owen Lloyd said. 'Mr Cragg wants to know if the verdict in the inquest on Mr Giggleswick was a good un.'

'Oh, aye, it was a good un.' Lambert Lloyd grunted.

'Are there not some here who think this man Charles, that the Captain had in his service, had a hand in it? The fellow scuttled off as soon as his master was arrested and hasn't been seen again.'

'Dad!' shouted Owen, and again referred the question across the room.

'I've the definite answer to that,' said Lambert. 'Owen and me both were in the Squirrel playing music with the man Charles the very same evening, six o'clock, that Dick Giggleswick was killed on. Practising together we were, with him on that whistly flute of his. He can't have shot him, that's for sure.'

'Aye,' said Owen, working up some lather with a brush in his soap bowl. 'It must've been the Captain, like the jury said, that shot him.'

'Well,' I said, 'the jury of Ormskirk is no fool. But I've heard that, for all the judgement against him, Captain Garland, or Dolland, is at large again, and still in town.'

'He's been leading a very quiet life. Mrs Greenwood keeps him inside as best she can. He doesn't even sing except once in a while.'

'Being nephew to the justice goes a long way towards his freedom,' said the old man.

'And son-in-law,' said Owen. 'Old Dolland's never going to see his kinsfolk hanged, whatever sort of sot or murderer he may be. Mr Giggleswick was a good man, mind. There's no one wanted him dead, except him that killed him.'

'How is it that Mr Ambrose Parr has taken possession of Chimneystacks Farm?'

'Dad!' said Owen, applying the lather. 'Mr Cragg's asking why Mr Parr got the farm?'

'Lawyer Parr came in here yesterday, didn't he?' said Lambert 'For a shave. Lawyer Parr says Mr Giggleswick owed a lot of money. Well I never heard that before. The man looked solid. But, now he's dead, Lawyer Parr's taken up the farm himself as a way of calling in the debt it seems.'

I waited until Owen had finished lathering me.

'Having cleared up as best I can the death of Mr Giggleswick,' I said, 'I did not expect to see Ormskirk for many a day. Yet here I am already back. Can you guess why?'

Owen was now towelling residual lather from my face. He turned back to his father.

'Dad! Mr Cragg wants to know if we can guess why he's come back here.'

'That would be for Miss Pettifer,' said his father, 'her being dead, if I'm not much mistaken. To inquest her.'

'No,' I said. 'At this stage I must only find out if an inquest is called for.'

'Find out? Of course you shall find out. There's a good deal of finding out to be done in Miss Pettifer's house.'

'There is that,' said Owen, applying the razor to my chin. 'With all those driggle-draggle wenches living there.'

'Why do you call them that?'

'Dad!'

Owen stood back from his task to appeal again to his father, who had let go of the strop and was eyeing the blade of his razor.

'Mr Cragg's asking why those trubs at Miss Pettifer's 're driggle-draggles.'

'Well she's only taken them off the street, hasn't she? Reforming them. But I don't see any reform when they come to Thursday market buying ribbons and I don't know what.'

'That's right,' said Owen. 'She couldn't rule them, couldn't Miss Pettifer. She had right intentions but she couldn't rule them.'

The talk went on like this. Then two customers came in and contributed the sum of their knowledge about the life and death of Isabella Pettifer. Opinions were exchanged, too, about Ambrose Parr. I hardly asked another question. As I knew it would be, Lambert Lloyd's was more than a barber's shop. It was an information exchange.

I returned to the inn and went to the writing room, where I quickly wrote an entry in my journal, set out in the form of a memorandum of what I had learned.

> *Item: Ambrose Parr is not liked in this town.*
>
> *Item: It is generally agreed that Miss Pettifer gave too much license to the girls she took in.*
>
> *Item: OF CAPITAL IMPORTANCE Nobody here knows anything about the tontine. It was mentioned in the inquest but it is not part of the townspeople's speculation about the recent deaths. Indeed they do not suspect any connection between Mrs Dolland, Mr Giggleswick and Miss Pettifer.*
>
> *Item: The servant Charles has a solid alibi in the murder of Giggleswick.*
>
> *I am persuaded of Captain Garland's guilt in the matter of Giggleswick's death. Except I don't know why he's not run away.*
>
> *As for the death of Miss Pettifer we must see.*

Then I put down my pen and went out of the room. A moment later I was knocking on the door of the room next to mine – the Squirrel Inn's best. A dog yapped until Ambrose Parr himself opened the door. I could see behind him that a young man was there, sitting at the table with writing implements. The young man was dressed in simple but clean clothing. Ambrose Parr was got up as splendidly as ever.

'Come in, Mr Cragg. I have been expecting you. This is Cutts, my clerk. You find my chamber transformed into a place of affairs. We have been drawing up some documents in respect of Chimneystacks Farm. Local business, you see.'

'You have taken personal possession of the farm, so I hear,' I said.

The dog was sniffing around my feet and I tried to fend it off. Parr turned to his clerk.

'Cutts, I would be obliged if you would leave the room to Mr Titus Cragg and myself for half an hour. You may take those letters to the post office, and at the same time exercise the dog.'

Cutts attached a leather lead to the dog's collar, then picked up a low pile of letters, addressed and sealed, and went out.

'We were speaking of . . .' said Parr.

'Chimneystacks Farm. Your taking it over.'

'Ah! Well, Mr Cragg, we are both men of the law, and you know as well as I how the law works. I was asked one day by Mr Giggleswick if I knew of anyone willing to extend him a mortgage on his property. I asked him the amount he required and when he told me I said that I myself was willing. This would be preferable, naturally, to his indebting himself to a stranger. He was grateful.'

'In what amount of money was that mortgage?'

'Oh, you know, it would be indiscreet of me to give the exact amount but let's say it was covered by the full value of the property. That is why after his death the farm fell by necessity into my, albeit unwilling, hands.'

'You will be telling me next you have an interest in Miss Pettifer's estate also.'

I fixed Parr with what I meant to be a piercing look. It is a look I had perfected over the years, though I first copied it from my father, who used it similarly to intimidate witnesses. Parr did indeed flinch and look down.

'Anything of that kind will come out in the proving of her will. We must speak of the manner of Miss Pettifer's death, must we not? I hope we can do so without the voicing of any baseless insinuations.'

'Yes. Let us do so. I intend to go to the house in Aughton in the morning. I must see the first finder of the body. Who is that?'

'I don't know who found her dead. But of the so-called, but in my mind doubtful, accident that killed her the nearest account we have is from one of the maids. Fanny Kirby is her name.'

'What do you know of the circumstances? When did it happen?'

'The day before yesterday, in the afternoon.'

'And why do you consider Fanny's story of her mistress's death doubtful?'

Parr gave out a loud snort, as of contempt.

'Fanny is a girl of very low morals. Probably also a habitual liar. I suspect she is guilty of the murder of Miss Pettifer.'

'That is a very serious allegation, Mr Parr. Can you substantiate it?'

'I can tell you how Miss Pettifer received the fatal injury and you may draw what conclusions you will.'

'Please do so.'

'According to Fanny Kirby, Miss Pettifer went for a walk to the nearby windmill, which was a favourite walk of hers, and she was accompanied by Fanny Kirby and her spaniel. It was a windy day and the windmill sails were turning. Upon reaching the windmill, the spaniel ran up to it and would not return when called, but stood there barking. Miss Pettifer and the maid went forward to fetch the dog and in doing so Miss Pettifer strayed near the path of the sail as it descended and was struck a vicious blow to the head. She was felled and unable to speak. They carried her home and put her to bed. She died in the night.'

'What reason do you have to disbelieve Fanny Kirby? Were there no other witnesses?'

'No, but my point is that Miss Pettifer was a sensible woman, and something of an invalid. She would never be foolish enough to put herself in such danger.'

'So you are saying that the blow to her head was not from the sail, but from a human hand.'

'I believe that is possible, and even likely.'

'Were there other indications of this?'

'You must put that question to Joseph Pickering. As constable he was called to the house next day and I believe he visited the windmill. He is a fool but he must be able to give you some account of it.'

'Do you know who called for the constable?'

'It would have been Anne Field, the housekeeper. It was Mrs Field who wrote to me the same day. I gave up all business to attend, and I have been here ever since.'

He sighed.

'A great sacrifice of business, but it is my duty.'

I left Ambrose Parr and went to the shop of Joe Pickering.

Pickering's account of Isabella Pettifer's death differed from that of Ambrose Parr in a few points. The facts on the surface were the same. The two women took a walk to the windmill. The sail of the mill struck Miss Pettifer a blow on the head. She fell unconscious and was carried home, where later that night she died without waking up. One difference was in how Miss Pettifer was described. Parr said she was an invalid, and weak in body. But not according to Pickering. He told me she was of determined mind, and much less weak in the body than she allowed to appear. She would have been quite capable of chasing after the naughty dog herself, and quite likely to do so.

Second, Pickering was unsure whether Fanny was the sole witness. According to what she herself told him when he questioned her there had been some people in the vicinity who helped attend the injured woman, and who may have earlier seen the accident. Finally Joe saw no reason to doubt Fanny's story. It was true she was a hard case. She'd been a streetwalker, doing most of her trade with sailors. But when Pickering had spoken with her he'd found her helpful and no dullard. She really had no interest in harming Miss Pettifer as she had benefited not only from being removed from the sinful life she had been leading, but also from the training she'd had at Miss Pettifer's. I said that I got the impression from Mr Parr that Fanny was hardly reformed at all. Pickering arched his eyebrows.

'That was not what I thought when I met her, though I'm unwilling to contradict a great man like Mr Parr. But you must talk to Anne Field, Mr Cragg. If there's anyone knows what Fanny Kirby's like it's Mrs Field.'

THIRTEEN

I slept poorly that night. My journal does not record that any particular disturbing dream woke me but, once awake, I was tormented through the wall by loud snoring coming from Parr's room – two different types of snore, which made me think either the dog was a snorer, or that Cutts was in there also.

I found Mr Parr at breakfast with his clerk, both men giving the appearance of having slept a good deal better than I had. Cutts was eating toast and cheese while Parr was engaged with a mound of grilled kidneys.

'On the scent of the murderer, are we?' the lawyer said as soon as he saw me.

The use of 'we' instead of 'you', as a way of implying fellowship, is one I have never liked. It comes across as condescending, and I am sure that is just what Parr intended.

'I do not jump to any such conclusions,' I said. 'It's too soon. But I shall go to Aughton this morning.'

'Will you hold a formal inquest?'

'That is likely, but not certain.'

'I leave here on the day after tomorrow. I return to Liverpool. So it would be best if you hold the hearing tomorrow.'

'Tomorrow would be my own choice, so I hope it will be then.'

'That would be convenient.'

I could not suppress a sarcastic reply.

'And I am servant to your convenience, Mr Parr. But meanwhile I am surprised you do not put up at your new property of Chimneystacks Farm.'

Parr waved my surprise away with his hand.

'I have men in there. There is reconstruction. There is re-decoration. There is refurbishment. It is not yet fit for use.'

'But will you live there when it is done?'

'My business affairs do not allow it, and besides I am no farmer. The place shall be let to someone with agricultural leanings.'

I ended this stiff, barely friendly exchange and took my place at a table across the breakfasting room.

I walked the two miles to Aughton as the air was fresh and rain did not look likely. The road took me down to the windy open space of Aughton Moss, where the races had recently been held, and upwards again by a turning road to Aughton, a small village furnished with a large church and a scattering of respectable houses with a greater number of miserable hovels.

Miss Pettifer's house stood close to the church – she had acquired it perhaps for this very reason – and I found its interior subdued, with none of the activity seen when Fidelis and I had previously been there. Many of the windows were draped so that even in mid-morning the place seemed gloomy as at day's ending.

A woman who wore spectacles of thick glass came to the door in answer to my ring. This was Anne Field, who had been Miss Pettifer's housekeeper. She was, I judged, about thirty-five years of age and had a stiffness of manner that I found forbidding. I told her who I was and why I had come and she brought me inside with scarcely a word before leading me up the stairs. We entered a bedroom in which Miss Pettifer lay dead on the bed, wearing a lace cap and her grave-clothes.

I made no sort of medical examination, as my friend Fidelis would have done. I did however feel the forehead – it was cold as marble – and I lifted the cap to look closely at the crown of her head. The skull had been staved in by what must have been a mighty blow, though the body had been washed now and the wound carefully cleaned out.

I also looked carefully at the face. When my father was coroner before me, there was a fashion in trying to read the faces of the dead, as you would a puzzle or cipher. Certain shapes in the lips or the brow, or casts of colour in the eye, were held to contain messages left for those still living to discover, as in the mode of death, the last things seen by the conscious mind before oblivion came, even (in the case of a murder) the identity of the killer. It is childish nonsense. Yet sometimes when called to a corpse I still tried to read its frozen face, wondering what I could learn there of the living being who once presented those features more or less bravely to the world.

As usual what I saw was more like a snail's empty shell, or an abandoned hat. Miss Pettifer's face was delicately lined, still handsome, unutterably solemn. But all that it told me was that she was dead.

'Come down to my own day-room,' said Mrs Field who had come no further into the room than the door.

She led me to a small room and swept open the curtains, revealing a parlour with two Windsor chairs beside the unlit fireplace, a writing table and cases against two of the walls that were crammed with books.

'Ah! You are a reader, I see, Mrs Field,' I said, pleased at the prospect of some common ground between us.

Without reply she gestured for me to sit in one of the armchairs while she sat in the other, her body upright and her hands resting on her knees.

'How may I help you, Mr Cragg?'

It was clear that small talk was not one of Mrs Field's accomplishments.

'I am Coroner to the Duchy of Lancaster, and it is my duty to determine whether to hold an inquest into the passing of your mistress. The first requirement is that I know who it was that found her dead.'

'That was myself.'

'Would you describe how you did?'

'I went into her bedroom to waken her. I could not do so as she was dead in bed.'

'Where she had lain all night?'

'Yes. She had suffered a head injury on the previous afternoon. She was brought home and put to bed. We left her to sleep it off but, as I say, it took her off instead.'

'But you didn't see the accident yourself?'

'I did not. She was walking out in the air perhaps half a mile away. The first I heard was when a boy came running with a message. Then when she came home we put her to bed.'

'You did not call medical help?'

'What was the point without her being conscious? I intended to call Dr Jackman in the morning, when I considered she would be awake again.'

'Did you make any examination of her wound yourself? Did you not dress it?'

'Yes, of course I did. I saw that she had been struck just to the side of her crown, as by a glancing blow. The skin was broken and there had been much bleeding, which had by then abated. I called for warm water and cleaned the wound, then bound her head with a bandage. She was breathing normally and peacefully. I considered she would recover her senses naturally.'

'And when you found she had not, did you send for your doctor then?'

'Yes. I thought it prudent to have a medical opinion. There are cases where death is apparent, but not real, I believe.'

'And he pronounced her dead?'

'He did.'

'And does the doctor live here in Aughton?'

'Yes. His house is close by.'

'Had you given instructions for somebody to be in attendance on your mistress during the previous night?'

'Yes, and several of the girls volunteered to sit up.'

'Was one of them Fanny Kirby who was with Miss Pettifer when the accident happened?'

'Yes, I think she was.'

'I would like to speak with Fanny. Would you be good enough to call her?'

Mrs Field shook her head.

'I cannot, Mr Cragg. I have sent her away. I have sent all the girls away. There is nothing for them here now, and there is no money to pay their wages besides.'

'I see. That is unfortunate. Tell me then what you can of Fanny's standing in this house.'

'With me, or with Miss Pettifer?'

'With you both.'

'She was, unaccountably, one of Miss Pettifer's special favourites. I found her devious and dishonest, but my opinion no longer counted as once it had.'

'I see. Do you know a Captain Garland?'

'I don't believe I do. I don't know the name.'

'Very well, there is just one last question. It concerns Mr Ambrose Parr, and his part in Miss Pettifer's life?'

'Mr Parr was Miss Pettifer's attorney. That is all.'

'Did he play any role in the life of this house?'

'No, sir, he did not. He wanted to, I know, but Miss Pettifer kept him firmly out.'

I rose.

'I thank you for giving me your time, Mrs Field,' I said. 'I must now go and examine the scene of the accident.'

I crossed to the window. From here I could see the upper part of the windmill, which stood on rising ground some quarter of a mile away. I pointed to it.

'That is the place?'

'Yes, that is the place.'

Lying on the writing table that stood before the window was a book. I picked it up and glanced at the title: *Saintly Secrets, or By-ways of Religion* by Theodore Muggeridge D.D. Oh dear: it was not my sort of fare.

'Then I shall go there directly. I would ask that you keep yourself in readiness to give first-finder's evidence at an inquest, which I may possibly convene tomorrow. Now I shall leave you to your reading. I can see that it is improving matter.'

'It is more than that, Mr Cragg,' she said, suddenly becoming animated, with burning eyes, as she took the book from me. 'It tells of a beautiful young woman in early Christian times walled up by order of her bishop in a cave, to be fed, watered and clothed by her aged parents through a small hatch. After seven years the stone wall was taken away and they found their daughter struck dumb, crippled, and blinded. All her beauty and capacity for life were forever destroyed.'

She looked at me, her eyes strangely enlarged behind the glasses.

'A tragedy,' I said. 'I wonder, though, why it strikes you so forcefully.'

'It is that I have served Miss Pettifer for seven years, and now am released.'

'I'm afraid I fail to see . . .'

'Exactly, Mr Cragg. There will be few that do *not* fail to see.'

The road went down to the church, and then began to climb in a south-westerly direction. As I strode up the hill I thought about what Mrs Field had told me. There had not been the slightest sense of grief in her account of her mistress's death. Instead I could taste between her words a lacing of vinegary disappointment, which her tale of the walled-up prisoner had only made more pronounced.

The road dipped again and I lost sight of the windmill for the time being. This was a broad highway, which stretched all the way to Liverpool, and as it began to climb again I passed a small forge and a few mean cottages. Two hundred yards further on the road levelled out, revealing the whole of the mill at the end of a sweeping curve in the road.

It was an imposing structure and in full operation. Drawing near I could hear the creaking of the four turning sails, and the movement of the machinery that connected them to the grinding-stones inside.

A stringy man came in answer to my shout. His hair and his eyelids, his nose and chin, his shoulders and his shoes were covered in powdery brown flour.

'You are the miller?' I said.

'Am I?' he said. 'Like your aunty Nelly, am I! I'm Jack Binns.'

'But you operate the mill?'

'That's right. I do the lifting, miller counts the money. That's how it works. What do you want?'

'It's about the accident to Miss Isabella Pettifer, that happened here two days back. Can you tell me about it?'

'Aye, of course. I've got my wits. I'm not likely to forget it.'

'Did you see it with your own eyes?'

'No. I heard the chit's screams. I went out and saw Miss Pettifer lying there, with the girl kneeling next to her.'

'Will you show me, please?'

He walked me around to the side of the mill facing the sweep of road that led back to Aughton, from where Miss Pettifer and Fanny Kirby had approached.

'Miss Pettifer used to walk this way every other day, more or less, with her dog. She would take a turn around the mill and go on her way back home again.'

The mill stood on a grassy mound in the shape of an upturned saucer with a broad flat top. We stood close to the turning sails. They swept down to about five and a half feet above the ground before lifting away again.

'Is it usual for a mill's sails to sweep down as low as this?' I said. 'Surely they must present a constant danger to anyone walking below.'

'Happen, people are taller than what they were when this old mill was built. And Miss Pettifer was a tall lady herself. They put up the fence to stop accidents.'

He indicated a fence that encircled the mill, meant as he said to keep people away from the danger of the turning sails. But the fence was not well cared for, and its rails were broken in more than one place.

I looked at the ground below the sail and followed it all the way back to the fence. There were spots on the grass which, so I thought, might be traces of Miss Pettifer's blood. Or they might not. It was impossible to tell.

I bade Jack Binns farewell and strolled across the road, where there was a row of fairly prosperous houses on two floors. The women from two of them were enjoying some chit-chat doorstep-to-doorstep. I stood by their garden gates and interrupted them.

'I wonder if either of you ladies witnessed the terrible accident that happened at the windmill the other day.'

'They oughter mend that fence, says I,' said one of them, a burly woman made for heavy lifting.

'Did you see it as it happened, madam?'

'Did I? Course I did, didn't I tell you, Kate?'

'Aye, Mary Graves, you did, more than once,' said Kate, her smaller, older neighbour.

'I saw that crazy dog run under the fence and up to the windmill,' said Mary, 'and Miss Pettifer and the girl were shouting after it to come back but it wouldn't.'

'What did Miss Pettifer do?'

'She went across the fence to bring it back down. And the sail of the mill came down and fetched such a crack on her head, she went down like a ninepin. So I ran out to help and we carried her back to the fence and I sent my boy running to Aughton to tell them what was what.'

'How did Miss Pettifer seem to you? Was she conscious?'

'She was in a bad way. Her eyes were rolled up so you could see the whites. Then her lids closed. She'd been put into a stupor as a person fast asleep.'

'I want to go back a little, please, and this is important. When Miss Pettifer went over the fence after the dog, what did you see the young girl that was with her do?'

'She went in after her. I reckon she saw the danger from the sail, which Miss Pettifer didn't. She ran up and grabbed Miss Pettifer but it was at the same moment that the sail hit her, see? So she was just too late.'

'And the dog?'

'The dog?'

'Yes, what happened to it?'

Mary shrugged.

'I never saw that.'

'One last thing: where in the village is the residence of Dr Jackman?'

On my way back through Aughton I called at the house Mary had located for me. It had Jackman's brass plate fixed next to its door, which was opened by a maid who told me the doctor was with a mother and baby. But after only five minutes in the waiting room I was admitted to the surgery.

The doctor was a well-fed youngish fellow with an energetic manner, but he had little to add to what I had already heard. When he was called, at about seven-thirty in the morning, Miss Pettifer was quite definitely dead. From her bodily temperature he thought she had died quite early in the night. He had looked at the head-wound and concluded that this had been the inevitable cause of death. After such a wound she would be lucky to have survived long.

'Had you attended Miss Pettifer much in recent times?'

'No, I hardly knew her,' he said. 'I am locum tenens here, Mr Cragg, and I came only six weeks ago. I was engaged at first for three weeks, while Dr McTavish visited relatives at Inverness in the Scottish Highlands. But his return has been delayed on account of the rebellion, and with troops swarming around the vicinity it is dangerous to travel. But I now expect Dr McTavish will be back soon, as I have just had word of a great battle – do you know of it?'

'No. Tell me what happened.'

'I hear the Pretender has suffered a terrible reverse. He has lost all but a remnant of his army. His adventure is over.'

'Is he himself taken, or killed, do you know?'

'I don't. I am sorry.'

'Do not be. It isn't important. I was in Preston when his army passed through last year and various officers and followers were billeted with us, so I take a slight interest.'

I took my hat and prepared to leave him.

'Thank you, Doctor. I'll be grateful if you would be available tomorrow in the morning. I shall hold inquest into Miss Pettifer's death and I would value your evidence.'

After leaving the doctor I looked in at the Stanley Arms, where I found the ale excellent but the rooms small – too small for the purpose of what might be a well-attended inquest. I then knocked once more on the door of the late Miss Pettifer's house.

'You have come back, Mr Cragg,' said Mrs Field. 'How can I help you now?'

'By standing by, if you please, to give evidence at an inquest into Miss Pettifer's death that I will hold at Ormskirk. You will be the first witness. One more thing only. Utterly trivial, and purely to satisfy my curiosity, you know. The dog. I see no sign anywhere of Miss Pettifer's spaniel.'

'I had it shot, sir. It was driving me mad with its whining and pining.'

FOURTEEN

B ack in Ormskirk I called at the pottery to confer with Joe Pickering over the next day's business. Mrs Pickering offered me a place at their dinner table and we settled matters while we ate her tasty forcemeat sausages with cabbage and gravy. Pickering would have no trouble raising a jury in Aughton, he said. Priestley would happily make the Squirrel available again on account of the extra ale and gin he would sell. I asked him to arrange for the removal of the body from Aughton so that the jury could examine it in the morning, then returned to the inn's writing room and wrote Furzey to join me in the morning, which I sent by an express rider.

'It will not be too complicated,' I wrote him. 'The death was an accident, I am sure.'

Here at the Squirrel I also found that the London newspapers had arrived. They contained numerous details of the defeat of Charles Edward Stuárt at a place called Culloden, from which it was clear the rebels had suffered grievous losses, and would not recover. The whereabouts of the Chevalier himself were 'as yet unknown'. Perhaps his adventure was not, as Dr Jackman put it, over.

I went on to read of parliamentary matters, appointments at court, and ships arriving at the Port of London, but now the quiet of the room, the want of rest in the night and the richness of Mrs Pickering's gravy weighed down my eyelids and I fell into a profound sleep in the chair.

'Cragg! Wake up, man! Wake up!'

I opened my eyes drowsily. I knew that voice but it had become mixed into my dream, whatever *that* was. As I broke the surface of wakefulness, I was looking into the face of Luke Fidelis.

'What's the matter?' he said. 'Are you short of rest?'

'If you must know, yes I am.'

I got up and we shook hands. Although I had vowed to do without him, I was glad he had come. Staying away from Elizabeth and Hector held no joys for me, and nor did listening to snoring through the wall all night. But life in Orsmkirk would be more bearable in Luke's company.

What I did not count on was that after I had fully briefed him on the death of Miss Pettifer, my friend would overturn all my ideas about it, and set my enquiries going in quite a different direction.

'There is something in the story the woman Mary Graves told you that sets my antennae twitching,' he said. 'How far is her house from the windmill?'

'Forty yards.'

'And are you reporting her words exactly when she describes how Fanny Kirby ran after Miss Pettifer when the latter tried to fetch the dog back?'

'Yes, more or less, but why does it matter?'

'Because, according to you, the woman Mary said she saw

Fanny take hold of Miss Pettifer to pull her away from the wind-mill sails.'

'That is right. She did, quite naturally. Why is this troubling you, Luke?'

'Because I am thinking of the deception practised by the eye under the direction of the prejudicial mind.'

I laughed.

'You've lost me. If the eye lies, then what use is an inquest, or a trial? They depend on witness of the eye, and the other senses. Does the ear lie also, in your opinion?'

'Yes, it can do. I am speaking of preconception. Something seen or heard, if it takes only an instant to see or hear, calls for equally instant mental interpretation. But that interpretation is informed, even directed, by what the mind may be expecting.'

'But one sees what one sees, and hears what one hears.'

'No. Consider this. You are out on a dark night. You have been told there are robbers abroad. A figure appears suddenly in front of you, who raises his hand. But you strike first, punching him on the nose. Only later do you realize it is your good friend Fidelis and you have bloodied his nose because you saw him raise his hand to doff his hat.'

'Very well. And how does that affect Fanny's action towards Miss Pettifer?'

'Mary expected Fanny to do what she herself would do in the same predicament, which is to try to pull Miss Pettifer out of the way of the sail. But what if Fanny was really pushing her mistress *towards* the sail. I don't think an observer at a distance of forty yards could necessarily tell the difference.'

'Why would Fanny do that?'

'To do Miss Pettifer harm. Perhaps to kill her.'

'This is far-fetched.'

'From what he told you, Ambrose Parr wouldn't agree. What is needed is a connection between Fanny Kirby and Captain Garland. If we could just find that, my idea would be rather near-fetched.'

'You think Garland put Fanny up to it? Incited her murder?'

Fidelis shrugged.

'We know he has an interest in her death, do we not?'

*   *   *

That evening after supper we joined the throng of Ormskirkers in the public room at the Squirrel. The ale flowed into the men and the women drank gin mixed with the juice of fruits. The talk was raucous so that the band of musicians led by Lambert Lloyd could hardly be heard by the dancers who flung about in the little space allowed to them.

Soon after nine the public door swung open and Captain Garland, as he had continued to style himself, came in. He was sporting a woman on his arm, a woman of undoubted physical charms. She was dark, red-lipped, and walked with a swing: a woman with the ability to make men turn and look as she passed. In everything she did she epitomized that paradoxical figure, so well known in the theatre, of the laughing widow – for this could only be the widow Greenwood, of whom I had heard in Joe Pickering's letter.

The Captain gave every sign of being proud to be walking with her, and to see them together made it quite evident that they enjoyed doing a good deal more together than just walking out. He patted her cheek and her behind, and stopped to whisper in her ear once or twice.

Pickering, who was with us, was incensed.

'This is an outrage, do you not think, Mr Cragg?'

He sprang up and caught the Captain by his sleeve.

'Captain, are you not ashamed to be going about brazenly in a town where you are branded a murderer?'

The Captain brushed the constable's hand from his arm as one might brush off a feather.

'Branded, you say, Constable Pickering? Pills, sir! Pure balductum and pills! Show me the indictment. There is none. Show me the conviction. Likewise. Your inquest jury is no more than a Dogberry squad of idiots, Mr Pickering, and I do this to it.'

He snapped his fingers.

'You will not find many in this town willing to see me hanged.'

He walked by, and Pickering sat down, muttering a string of oaths.

'Perhaps he's right,' I said. 'Look at how they greet him.'

For the Captain was evidently still a highly popular figure – his hand shaken, his back clapped, his ear whispered into. It was clear that many Ormskirkers – possibly not all, possibly not most, but

a good proportion – had put it out of their minds that the Captain
had been fingered for the shooting of Richard Giggleswick. Farmer
Giggleswick may have been 'much liked'. He may even have been
loved. But he was gone, and all trace of him was gone. The people
had already turned their attention to other matters.

Well, it happens to all living things once they are extinguished.
It is why we have gravestones. Without them the dead are lost to
common memory in a wink of the eye, or a snap of the fingers.

There was only one who now came up to Captain Garland in
a less than friendly spirit. A portly figure in the middle of middle
age, he wore the coat and wig of a gentleman. Like the Captain
he was drunk, and his dander was very much to the fore. He
pushed his face contorted in anger to within two inches of the
Captain's face. I saw he was also gesturing at the lady.

'Who is that talking to him now?' I said.

'It's Percy Dolland,' said Pickering.

'Frances's brother?'

'The same.'

In the time it would take to count to ten the argument suddenly
reached a critical moment. The Captain pushed Dolland away,
and Dolland replied by swinging his arm at the Captain and
connecting, not very powerfully, with the side of his head.

'He has struck him!' said Pickering.

'It would seem he does not like his cousin.'

'There's plenty of reason for that, Mr Cragg. Mr Dolland has
seen his sister scorned in marriage. And now people are saying
the fellow seeks to return to her in hopes of getting her money,
while possibly doing murder along the way. I should not be
surprised if—'

'There is another reason,' interrupted Fidelis.

My friend had been unusually quiet since the Captain's arrival.
I glanced at him. His face was pale and set. I recognized this as
the expression he wore at moments when his emotional sensibility
was most strained.

'What is it?' I said.

Fidelis kept his eye on the two men, who were jostling each
other now, pushing and prancing and jostling as if preliminary to
a physical contest. As this was going on, the woman let go of
Garland's arm and skipped out of the way. Fidelis pointed to her.

'It is the lady, Mrs Greenwood,' he said. 'Mrs Dolland's brother has feelings for her. Strong ones. However they are not requited.'

'How do you know?'

'Because she has told me.'

I sat back in my chair, and looked at him. So *this* was the woman he had a connection with in Ormskirk. His woman-friend, about whom he was so secretive, and who refused to see him when he had last been in town. The reason for that refusal was beginning to emerge, and could be summed up in two words: Captain Garland.

The room had fallen quiet, the music had stopped, so that the words being said between Garland and Dolland were audible throughout the room.

'There is only one way to settle this,' said Captain Garland in a ringing voice. 'And I suggest it be with pistols, sir, on Aughton Moss.'

It was at this point that we saw Perceval Dolland more clearly. His eyeballs were very prominent. His body was trembling as was his hand as he put it to his lip. The more I studied him the more pronounced I could see this trembling was.

'Great heavens!' I heard Fidelis murmur. 'The man's palsied. He'll never manage a duelling pistol in that state.'

With a loud scrape of his chair on the stone flags he leaped to his feet and strode towards Garland and Dolland, elbowing his way through the throng until he stood between them. He fixed the Captain with a ferocious stare.

'I'll fight you, you damned blackguard!' he shouted. 'And I'll blow your brains out too!'

'The devil you will,' the Captain snarled, looking at him with arched eyebrows. 'Do I know you, sir? I think not, and my quarrel is with this scoundrel who has just struck me.'

'Oh!' said Fidelis. 'Is that what it takes?'

Without any warning he delivered a cracking blow to the Captain's nose, which immediately spurted blood. Mrs Greenwood gave a little cry and bringing out a handkerchief began to dab at the Captain's nose.

'For shame, Doctor,' she said. 'For very shame!'

Garland collected himself. He wiped his nose with the back of his hand.

'You shall rue that, sir. Let it be tomorrow morning, as early as you like.'

'First light, then.'

'Send me the name of your second.'

'You will have it within the hour.'

Fidelis spun around and headed for the stair leading up to the rooms. I sat in my place, too astounded to move or speak as, by degrees, but quickly picking up volume and velocity, the talk in the room resumed. There was only one topic of conversation: the forthcoming duel between Captain Garland and Dr Fidelis.

Taking the arm of the lady once more, the Captain navigated his way to a table. In awe the people in their way began to part. The folk sitting at the table he was moving towards scrambled to get up, gesturing for the couple to take their ease and the Captain threw himself into one of the chairs and ordered a pint of wine. As if responding to a cue, Lambert Lloyd picked up his fiddle and began uncertainly to play. His son rapped a tattoo with a stick on his tambourine, while the third man joined in on his instrument, which was some kind of bagpipe. As the sound of the music swelled there was a whoop from the middle of the room and quite suddenly the dancing resumed.

When I recovered my wits I made my way up to Fidelis's room.

'What insanity is this?' I said. 'How can the woman be worth it, truly?'

'She isn't,' he said. 'But I shall still deal with that preposterous pasteboard soldier.'

'You want to kill him?'

'That won't be necessary. And you'll act as my second, of course.'

First light over Aughton Moss revealed a placid morning. The land was veiled in mist as if by cobwebs, so that grazing beasts and labourers heading to their work appeared as blobs or blurs to the eye. The chimneys of the better homes, and the holes in the roofs of the worse, were sending up lazy streams of smoke. A barking dog from half a mile away and a flock of bleating sheep a little nearer were the loudest sounds.

I have never fought a duel – or studied in any way what was called the Science of Quarrelling by (I think) the *Spectator* – but

I imagine that there is usually much jockeying before the first pistol is fired, and that points may be scored by the duellists for their manner or comportment in face of possible death. To be on the ground first, with a jutting jaw, might show a man's determination. To arrive there at the last minute might betoken an insouciance that is even more intimidating. Of these two courses of action, Fidelis took the former, and Garland the latter.

Fidelis had woken me in the dark, saying he meant to be first on the scene, and we arrived to find the place deserted. Although I regarded the whole idea of duelling with horror, and had all the way been trying to talk Fidelis out of it, I could see that this was an excellent place for the encounter. The ground was flat and covered in soft lush sheep-cropped grass. There were no obstacles to the process either underfoot, or otherwise.

Soon after our arrival Dr Jackman came. He and Fidelis, both carrying their medical bags, took the measure of each other with a touch of suspicion, until I made the introductions.

'It is as well you are here, Doctor,' I said, a little acidly. 'Dr Fidelis may be in no position to practise his skills when this is over.'

The two doctors shook hands and Fidelis began to exchange with Jackman remarks on the strong reviving salts that he had with him, and the styptics to staunch blood flow, and to compare other remedies besides that might prove useful on an occasion like this. Both men were pleased to find that they thought broadly alike on such matters, particularly in the use of brandy or any strong spirit as a medicine, which they agreed to be deleterious in cases of shooting.

'I beg you to reconsider this, Luke,' I said drawing Fidelis away from Jackman. 'Call it off. It is not too late. The Captain is likely an expert marksman. Can you outmatch him?'

'We must see.'

'And I wonder what Mrs Greenwood thinks of this. She cannot approve of you putting your life at hazard.'

'She does not give a ha'penny whether I live or die, that is clear,' he said.

I sighed.

'Well, there is the possibility Garland will not show his face. What's promised in wine is soon regretted.'

No sooner had I said this than we saw two horses coming towards us. A second look told us neither rider was Fidelis's adversary, as one was older and stouter and the other was riding side-saddle. It was Mrs Dolland, coming with her brother to witness this trial of honour.

'We have come to give you our support,' said Dolland to Fidelis, his tremor very visible. 'I wish I could do this myself, but it would be hopeless. It must be you that puts a bullet between that good-for-nothing's eyes.'

I pondered on this. I knew that Fidelis was a fair hand with a pistol, but I also knew that the Captain was in all probability more practised.

Now two more riders came into sight and they were undoubtedly the Captain accompanied by a fellow officer who I did not recognize. Following them was a closed carriage with blinds drawn down. As the two horsemen left the road and cantered the short distance to the duelling ground, the carriage stopped on the verge of the road.

Captain Garland remained on his horse while his companion, a thin, tight-lipped fellow, dismounted and beckoned to me.

'I am Captain Preece,' he said.

'Cragg, Titus Cragg.'

'I am here, Mr Cragg, as Captain Garland's supporter. I take it you act in the same capacity for Dr Fidelis?'

'Yes, although this is an absurdity – honour, satisfaction – do you not agree?'

'That is a civilian opinion. Honour is never absurd to a soldier.'

Preece had with him a flat, rectangular leather case, which he now opened with an attitude of reverence. Two pistols nestled inside. They were, as the rules of duelling insist, an identical pair.

He removed one of them and handed it to me, then took from his pocket a small pouch of powder and a packet containing bullets. These he also gave me. I brought them to Fidelis, who at once began loading the piece.

The Captain now dismounted. He looked around him and puffed out his chest. He was royally drunk so that even from a few yards away one could smell the wine on his breath. Taking the pistol to load it, he swayed on his feet and frowned as he struggled with the task, repeatedly dropping the bullet on the ground. In the end

Preece patiently took the gun from him and completed the loading himself. Now we stood in awkward silence. The Dollands, brother and sister, stood apart with their heads together. Garland and Preece took pulls from a flask. Then Garland said:

'Priestley promised me he'd be here to act as referee. Where the devil is he? We can't get this business over until he comes.'

Another five minutes passed.

'This is intolerable!' shouted the Captain. 'We must have a referee.'

'Oh, I'll do it!'

It was a woman's voice calling from the carriage on the road. The carriage door opened and Mrs Greenwood stepped out.

FIFTEEN

Despite having arrived in a carriage, the lady was wearing riding dress, with her hat at an angle and a riding crop in her hand. She was vastly enjoying herself.

'As this affair concerns me, or so I am led to believe, then it is rather fitting I should see fair play.'

She gave the two principals a stern talking-to about the rules – not firing before time and being sure to take careful aim. Then she walked the two duellists into the centre of the ground, saying a word or two to each of them privately in their ears, and then arranged them back-to-back with their pistols at the ready, pointing upwards. She walked around them in this position like a governess inspecting a pair of recalcitrant pupils. Here and there she poked or tapped them with her crop.

'Now, boys, stand still, backs straight. That's better, Doctor. But I can't say the same for you, Captain. Hold yourself together, man. Stomach in! Are we ready?'

Fidelis stood in what seemed an easy attitude, like a man waiting for a stage-coach or the postman, while Garland, on hearing the word 'ready', drew himself to his full height, though still swaying and with his brows and lips contorted from the effort.

'You will walk away from each other in a straight line,' she commanded, 'and I shall count ten paces. When you hear "ten" you stop but do not turn until I give the word. Is that understood? Now take your first step – one!'

Garland took a step and wobbled a little sideways, then, on 'two' he took another, deviating in the other direction. By the time the number 'ten' was spoken he had arrived at more or less the required spot. Fidelis meanwhile had marched crisply forward to his own mark.

Mrs Greenwood waited to issue her next instruction. When she did she raised her voice to a higher pitch.

'When I say "Now!" you will turn and adopt the firing position. Then you may fire as you choose.'

Still she held us in suspense. I looked at her proud and beautiful face. It wore the suspicion of a smile.

'Now!'

Fidelis swivelled through 180 degrees and raised his pistol to the horizontal but did nothing more, waiting for Garland to be facing him. The Captain was taking considerably longer to achieve the about-face. He almost lost his balance and hopped on one leg for a moment before he, too, was ready to shoot. The two men looked into each other's eyes and for a moment both held fire. The Captain was squinting along the barrel with one eye while trying, and failing, to keep the other eye closed.

At last there came a sharp crack and smoke plumed from Garland's gun's barrel. I had no idea where his ball went, but it was nowhere close to Fidelis. Meanwhile the explosion and recoil of the gun seemed to catch the befuddled Captain by surprise and, at exactly the moment that Fidelis returned his fire, Garland staggered backwards and went down like a felled tree.

All my attention had been on the performance of Captain Garland. Now I looked back at Luke Fidelis. He was holding his spent pistol at forty-five degrees from the horizontal, with the remains of the smoke from the percussion curling out of its muzzle.

Mrs Greenwood was the first at the Captain's side, followed by Captain Preece.

'Is he hit?' she said. 'Doctor! Come and tell us if he's hit.'

I followed Jackman to the side of the spread-out duellist and saw the neatness and method of the doctor's work. He loosened the collar, felt the pulse, put the back of his hand to the nose and finally applied his ear-trumpet to the chest.

'There are signs of life,' he said.

He looked and felt with his hands around Garland's person, especially the chest and belly.

'There is no catastrophic bleeding that I can see. He is insensible but not in my opinion shot.'

'Can you wake him up, then?'

Jackman raised the patient's head with a hand behind his neck and used the other hand to bring a small phial from his bag, unstopping it with his teeth. He waved the open bottle under his patient's nostrils and, with a jerk, Garland came round.

'Jesus!' he said. 'The sulphurs of perdition. I thought I was dead and gone to hell. Have I killed that devil of a doctor, though?'

Preece laughed.

'Not a chance, old fellow. Your shot would've brought down a passing crow before it shot Dr Fidelis.'

Garland struggled up into a sitting posture.

'And he has not hit me, by God!'

'I believe that he deliberately shot into the air,' I said. 'So it would appear that Dr Fidelis had no intention of removing you from this life after all, Captain Garland.'

I looked back to see where Fidelis was. He had walked to where the pistols-case lay open on the grass and placed the gun inside. He glanced for a moment to where Mrs Greenwood knelt beside her lover.

'Did you deliberately shoot over his head?' I asked Fidelis when all was over and we were walking back to Ormskirk. 'I was not looking when you fired.'

'I told you, I had no need to kill him. I do not value him so highly. And besides, the lady asked me not to.'

Back in Ormskirk, I found that Furzey had arrived from Preston and was overseeing the arrangement of the inquest room, exactly as before. As to the hearing itself, there is not much to say except that it was a brisk affair. Only Mrs Field's evidence detained the court for any time. I knew already most of what she would have to say, but I began by asking a more general question about Miss Pettifer herself, and the character of her household in Aughton.

'It was a religious house, with a religious purpose,' she said. 'We took in young girls fallen into immorality and we gave them a new start in life by training them for service. The force behind this was my employer's firm purpose and direction. It was her dream to enlarge what we had already started in a small way. Supposing she could find some rich sponsor to give her the capital, she wanted to build a workhouse for fifty fallen women, not just the five she had room for in her house.'

'Were you strict with the young women? I have heard that they received considerable licence in their recreation.'

'You have heard wrong, sir. There was no licence and strictly controlled recreation. Rules of conduct were enforced. Any young female who did not comply was sent back to where she came from.'

'You're saying the girls were not allowed to go to Ormskirk on market day for their recreation? I have heard differently.'

'A pair of them might be sent to buy cheese, or cured meats. Things we needed in the kitchen. It was not for their enjoyment.'

'Was there resentment that they were so restricted?'

'There were instances of it from time to time. As I told you, those girls who objected were sent away.'

'And the one who was with Miss Pettifer when she went out on her last walk – was she resentful?'

'Fanny Kirby? She was a dutiful and modest person. Her history was unfortunate but she had put it behind her. You would have thought she had nothing but gratitude towards Miss Pettifer: she was one of those who volunteered to sit up with her as she lay wounded on the night following the accident.'

'And would you describe exactly how that accident took place during that walk to the windmill – as far as you understand it?'

Mrs Field's continuation hardly deviated from what she'd told me during my visit to her small parlour at Aughton. I let her go and invited Dr Jackman to give his conclusions and then, there being nothing further of importance to add, the jury brought in the only possible verdict: death by misadventure.

'It stinks,' said Fidelis to me.

We were in the private coffee room, which we had to ourselves.

'What do you mean?' I said. 'Do you still say the death is murder?'

'It is another tontine murder. The coincidence of deaths is too great. We should have heard from the girl, Kirby. You never told me she was one of those who sat up with her mistress the night after the accident, the night during which Miss Pettifer died.'

I was just going to say, in reply, that I agreed it was a pity we'd never had the chance to question Fanny in person. But then – astonishingly and without any warning – that very chance presented itself. There was a loud bang. The door of the room had been thrust open and swung all the way to the wall, and Ambrose Parr stood in the opening with a young girl. He was holding her by the ear.

'Where's the inquest?' he boomed. 'I thought it was to be held here, at the Squirrel.'

'You're too late, Parr,' I said. 'The inquest is done.'

'It cannot be. I've scoured Liverpool to find this minx and to bring her here to give evidence.'

He let go of her and, with a push in her back, propelled her into the room ahead of him.

'Is this Fanny Kirby?' said Fidelis.

'Aye. She'll deny any guilt, of course, because she's a lying trollop, but she caused Miss Pettifer's death and should have been here to tell the inquest all. Then she'd be off to Lancaster Castle and the assize.'

Fanny was a skinny, big-eyed girl, looking younger than in likelihood she was. Her hair was in a tangle but her dress, though the cloth was plain grogram at best, was decent. From the look of her, being arrested by Parr had made Fanny both fearful and angry. With her mouth turned down and her eyes wetted with tears, she appealed to me.

'I came against my will, sir,' she cried. 'I have not done owt to Miss Pettifer only try to save her when she was hit by the windmill.'

I put down my pipe and stood up.

'So why not tell all to us now?' I said. 'Come and sit with us, Fanny. Don't be afraid. I am Titus Cragg, Coroner to the Duchy. I would very much like to hear your side of the story.'

I motioned for her to join us at our table. Evading contact with all our eyes, she sat without a word. I saw Fidelis's eyes on her: they were like a cat's tracking a fly across the window-glass.

'Her side of the story?' growled Parr, taking a seat at the table himself. 'A story would be right, and a fairy story.'

'Do not pre-judge her, Mr Parr,' I said.

I poured out a cup from the coffee pot and held it out to Fanny, but she grimaced at the offer. I gave it to Parr instead and resumed my seat.

'Now, Fanny, will you tell us about yourself? Where were you born?'

'The devil to that!' expostulated Parr. 'We don't want to hear the life-story of a damned blouse. Just ask her what she did to Miss Pettifer.'

I held up my hand.

'Mr Parr, you must allow me to question Miss Kirby as I see fit. So, Fanny. Did you return to Liverpool after Mrs Field sent you away?'

Fanny sat silently, still looking down, as if contemplating my question. Then she awoke, and looked around at us, catching our eyes for the first time. Her voice was light and clear.

'I went with one of the other girls to her mother's home.' She nodded in Parr's direction. 'It's where this . . . where *he* found me.'

'You have no parents, no family, in Liverpool?'

'No, sir. I'm from Preston, me, like yourself.'

'You know that I am from Preston, Fanny?'

'Oh yes, I know you. Me dad's Doddy Kirby of Moor Lane.'

'Good heavens! I know your father, of course. When did you leave home?'

Dodson Kirby was a cartwright and drayman with a brood of (when I'd last counted) fifteen children. He was best known as a lay preacher, the organizer of Preston's Methodist Society, and a man most serious man about theological rules. The rule of his family was another matter. Mrs Kirby had a fondness for gin and his sons were ruffians suspected (but never convicted) of robbing travellers as they crossed the moor to the north of town. Some of his daughters were devout, and helped Doddy with his religious work. Others, of whom Fanny was clearly one, had left town for pastures new – or rather pavements new.

'I left Preston with me sister Babba, two years back or more. There was nowt in Preston for us, with me dad talking about nothing but hell-fire and me mam nazzy from taking her rag-water half the day, and us expected to be for ever chasing after the littluns. So Babba and me came south, thinking about London but never getting forrader than Liverpool. Then we were taken up by a ship's captain – well, he said he was, but I never believed him, nor that he was a single man, neither. He put us in a house with who he said was his mother, which she wasn't of course, and then he started introducing us to his friends. We had as much quality gin as we liked, and were as idle as we liked, with pretty dresses and ices and Indian fruits and all sorts of fun that we were treated to. It was not a bad life even if the men were mostly old and ugly – we put up with that just to get the other things. But then both me and Babba got sick together and days and days went by and we just didn't get better, so the captain so-called threw us out on the street. He said there were plenty more he could bring in that were healthy.'

'Did your sickness not get worse?'

'No, strange to say, it got better once we were out of that house.'

'But how did you get by?'

'Have a guess. Sailors, mostly. You might not think it but they're a girl's best bet. Most of 'em are fairly clean and healthy and they've got ready cash. They don't want to do anything very gross, neither. It's usually just in-and-out in a back alley and here's your money, doll! Not like the gentlemen we'd been entertaining before, who'd be wanting you to do all sorts once the door on the room was shut. So then me and Babba got a lodging, and our money was our own, and it was going well when one fine day Babba died on me. I don't know how or why. One morning I woke up and looked across at her and there she was lying dead in bed.'

As she went on, Fanny's voice was finding a new register. It was not grief, nor was it pity-fishing. It was the voice of someone trying to understand her own story.

'So how did you fetch up at Aughton, Fanny?'

'I wasn't happy with living on me own, you follow me? I hadn't got a man or any friend to look after me. I was moping all the time. Then after about two or three weeks of this I was walking down by the dock looking for business when Miss Pettifer came up to me and said I was made for better, and would I like to come out of Liverpool and be trained up as a maid? Well, I don't really know why but I was feeling that weak and that friendless, I just said yes. And that was a year since.'

'Miss Pettifer approached you in person?'

'Yes. I'd have laughed at her and never given up my independence if I'd had Babba. But without my sister I thought, well, what could be worse?'

'Did you go with her right away?'

'Oh yes. She had this basket of food with her to take to some prisoner in Debtors' Gaol. I carried it for her and after we left it there, we went to where I was living to get a few things I didn't want to leave and so I came with her here.'

'And how was your life in Miss Pettifer's house?'

'If I'm honest, I hated it. I lived twenty year in me dad's house, remember. If I knew anything I knew religious duty. It's what I'd run away from. Now, I'm not saying living at Miss Pettifer's was worse than being a whore; what I am saying is it weren't any better than living with me dad.'

'Of course it was better!' said Ambrose Parr. 'To be a maid in a God-fearing house, and to serve a mistress in every point so admirable, and be trained by her in godly habits and housework: that is the very height of happiness for a reformed doxy, you ungrateful girl.'

'I am not a girl, sir. I am long past the stage of being a girl. I know my mind, I do.'

'What would you like in your life, then?' I said.

'Why, to be married to a handsome lord, of course; with ten thousand a year, of *course*; and have all my children called honourable.'

She laughed bitterly.

Parr had been having difficulty containing himself.

'You are a great fool, Fanny Kirby. You should have been content with your station in life, which is and will always be that of a servant to your betters.'

'Why not a wife, then?'

'With a cod's head for a husband, as only a foolish jobberknoll would marry a self-confessed harlot like you. But now, now . . .'

He shook his finger at her.

'It comes to nothing because now, with this business of Miss

Pettifer you must forget all your midsummer night's dreaming. You have instead set your course for hell, where you shall roast most horribly for all eternity.'

'Mr Parr,' I said. 'You are interfering with our conversation. Please leave us so that we may continue with it in peace. Please leave us *now*.'

Parr leaped from his chair and with a curse left the room.

'That man should guard his words,' said Fanny.

'Fanny, I have another very important question for you. What do you know of Captain Garland, who has been living here in Ormskirk?'

I studied her face. She was thinking, but I felt sure it was just to consult her memory. Then she shook her head.

'No, I've not heard the name. I've not met such a captain. Now, may I tell you something?'

'If it is useful information.'

'It is to me. I'm hungry, Mr Cragg, with being dragged here having no breakfast.'

So I sent for the waiter and ordered food. We were waiting for the meal to come when the door burst open again and Pickering stood before us.

'I am sorry, Mr Cragg, but I must take the young woman up and to gaol, on the warrant of Magistrate Dolland.'

SIXTEEN

The food I'd ordered now came in, all too late for poor hungry Fanny. I paused over this thought for a moment. The law takes its course and justice is blind, as everyone knows. Blind to hunger. Blind also to poverty and misfortune, as often as not. There was nothing a man could do about that, or not in a moment. Not in between breakfast and dinner. So I ate my dinner.

'I shall take Fanny Kirby some food afterwards,' I said. 'And then I shall try old Dolland. I do not think he's cajolable into rescinding the warrant on the poor girl but we must try.'

Fidelis, the slowest eater that ever lived, picked up his knife and surveyed the meat and lid of pie-crust on his plate, without showing any haste to devour it.

'So, she has won you over, Titus.'

'Has she not you? Do you still say she had a hand in her mistress's death?'

'I see no reason to change my mind.'

'But, surely, the girl is intelligent and deliberative. She scorns to be blown around by chance, or by the devices and persuasions of evil men. I don't think she could easily be talked into harming Miss Pettifer unless she wanted to do so. And I see no reason why she should. I think the inquest has found correctly.'

'No, Titus, it has miscarried. I keep to my previous opinion on the case, and that is exactly because, not in spite, of the character you give Fanny Kirby. She is pert enough and resourceful enough to take an opportunity when one is offered. And I believe it was offered by Captain Garland, somehow. Probably during one of Fanny's visits to the market in Ormskirk. Fanny is not shy of men. He would have got into conversation with her, might even have got into bed with her. Then he offered her money for intelligence about Miss Pettifer. They might even have plotted together to get her out of the way.'

'So you think Fanny pushed her mistress into the windmill sail with the aim of removing her from the list of tontine survivors?'

'Possibly,' he said. 'It may have been planned, it may have been improvised. Fanny puts on a good show, but that is her profession, is it not? However, even if there was an accident at the mill, did she not have the opportunity in the night to finish the job?'

That is her profession. My friend had often asserted his violent aversion to prostitution.

'You are against her only because you think of her as a whore,' I said. 'But just remember – she is not one now. She has resigned from the profession.'

'Once a whore, always a liar,' said Fidelis. 'That is my experience.'

I was about to ask him to enlarge on this 'experience' when Robert Furzey whom I had sent for to share our meal came in.

As he filled his plate with pie, he asked what we'd learned from Fanny Kirby.

'One point is, she's from Preston,' I said. 'She's one of Doddy Kirby's lasses.'

'Is she that?' said Furzey. 'It doesn't surprise me. He may be a righteous man but half his children are criminals.'

'Do you incline to Dr Fidelis's view, then, that Fanny is a murderess?'

'I don't say that. But she's a harlot, isn't she?'

'She has been. But Miss Pettifer made her a new girl.'

Fidelis murmured something.

'Luke!' I exclaimed impatiently. 'In time the fox repents, you know.'

'And a wolf must die in its own skin – if we are bandying proverbs about character.'

'I don't think Fanny is bad at heart. I'll give you just one example: her loyalty to her sister. That speaks of a good character.'

'Character, if I may state my own opinion, sir, is twaddle,' butted in Furzey. 'Anyone with any type of character can do any crime, if the time is right and the desire strong. That's not a proverb; that's what I think. Twenty-five years of being clerk to you, and your father before, has taught me it.'

I had the feeling that my clerk had spent the time since the inquest supping tavern ale. He was usually more subtly critical of my handling of affairs. Yet Fidelis backed him up.

'Well said, Furzey,' said Fidelis. 'Instead of marvelling at her character the point is to ask the pertinent question: did she push Miss Pettifer into the windmill sail? Or did she later smother her in her bed while she lay insensible at night?'

'Not the latter, surely,' I said. 'There were two sitting with Miss Pettifer all night.'

'Then the other girl is an accomplice,' said Furzey.

'This is futile,' I said. 'The inquest is done and Fanny is the concern of Mr Dolland now.'

'There's one thing that still piques my interest, though,' said Fidelis. 'Her mention of "what I know about him".'

'Who was "him"?' said Furzey.

'It was Ambrose Parr she referred to,' I said. 'But what it is she knows, she did not say.'

'Something she can use to bend him,' said Fidelis. 'It is a threat. And if Fanny Kirby is not above blackmail, then she might not be above murder.'

I took the remains of the pie to the town gaol. The watchman in charge told me Fanny must have no visitors by Mr Pickering's order, but agreed to give her the food.

'Tell her Mr Cragg wishes her well,' I said, 'and will petition as best he can for her release.'

In truth, the story Fanny had told us touched my heart. But I doubted any petition would succeed, at least not directly. By his own account, Mr Dolland relished nothing more than the chance of her execution. But it was possible I could approach his daughter instead of him. Mrs Dolland might listen to reason, and persuade her father to do so. I put this to Luke Fidelis as we rode away from Ormskirk and towards the Dolland house.

'I think not, Titus,' he said. 'She would not interfere with her father's pleasures. Still, you may try. Mrs Dolland is a strong-minded person. I will not go in with you, however.'

'Can you be shy of her, Luke?' I said teasing him.

'Last time I was expected to examine old Dolland *gratis*. I detest people who ask for a medical opinion in the expectation of having favours as a friend, when they are not friends.'

Arriving at Dolland Hall, Fidelis, Furzey and I, we were surprised to meet Captain Garland, or rather Dolland, coming furiously away just as we were coming near. He gave me a curious look, and Fidelis an angry one, not deigning to speak, but brandishing his fist as he brushed past. Leaving Furzey and Fidelis with the horses, I hammered at the door and a burly fellow came out. He told me Mrs Dolland could be found at the brickworks seeing to business. He gave me directions for the fastest way to walk there.

There was a moment during my visit to Dollands' brickworks when I thought I was peering into a room in hell. The works were spread across an open field, but a field in which vegetation was a long distant memory. Two large domed chimney-topped structures, one emitting belches of thick smoke, stood at each end of the field. In between I saw what appeared to be circular pits, around which horses trudged, harnessed to some kind of machinery that was working inside the pits. Around the edge of the field was a range of roofed shelters in which men laboured at various tasks, and out in the open carts were unloaded of hogshead barrels or loaded with finished bricks.

I found Mrs Dolland dressed in her working clothes, which appeared to be a modified riding habit: sturdy boots, a quilted bodice over a hardwearing skirt and a plain black felt hat. Mud clung to the hem of the skirt while dust coated her hat, shoulders and arms.

'Have you ever visited a brickworks, Mr Cragg?' said Frances Dolland.

I admitted that I had not.

'Then allow me to show you ours. Here we make two thousand bricks a week. As you see, it is not a clean process. My father used to say, you can't make bricks without first making a mess.'

'What is that round pit where the horse is working?'

'That's a tempering pit.'

We walked across to look more closely. The machinery was mounted across the pit by heavy wooden spars, and seemed to consist in great wooden paddles that churned the mud like a huge butter barrel.

'We add water and sand to the clay as it comes in to us, and we put in other things to make the composition we want.'

'What are the other things?'

She smiled and laid a finger on her lips.

'That is a secret that I cannot tell, Mr Cragg. The secret of the trade. We make bricks of a rare hardness by it.'

We walked past the row of thatched shelters in which men and women were using trowels to fill rectangular wooden boxes with the sticky clay mixture. Mrs Dolland greeted them each by name as we passed.

'The boxes are moulds for the bricks,' she said. 'The composition is left to stiffen until it can be turned out. Then it is perfectly dried in the air, as you see, ready for firing.'

I saw great stacks of these uncooked bricks dotting the whole area of the works, the apertures between them allowing the air to circulate inside and around, and all under cover of their straw awnings.

'We must keep them from spoiling in the rain,' said my guide.

'When they are dried enough we stack them in the kilns and fire them.'

She indicated the nearest of the two beehive shaped structures, the one from which smoke rose.

'It is the most efficient method. We emulate the potters but on a bigger scale. Old-fashioned brick-makers always baked in clamps.'

'Clamps?'

'It's the method of firing the bricks in the open. The furnace which cooks your bricks is made of the same bricks that are being fired. But a purpose-made kiln, like our two, is a far superior method.'

We continued around the smoking kiln until we found a couple of red-faced stokers attending to an aperture low down in the kiln, into which they were continuously pushing fuel in the form of faggots or tightly tied bundles of stick, fern, furze and other brittle burnable material. They used long iron plungers with wooden handles to shove the faggots deep into the heart of the kiln. I bent and peered into the kiln. This was my hellish vision: a roaring storm of fire the more furious because it was cribbed in a confined space. It brought to mind the 'combustible and fuelled entrails' of John Milton's volcano in *Paradise Lost*.

I put my face nearer and, feeling the furnace blast my face, jerked back in sudden alarm. The stokers laughed, being themselves inured to the scorching heat.

'How long do you fire them for?' I said, regaining my composure.

'Up to two days,' said Mrs Dolland. 'We know they're done when the colour of the smoke changes from black to white.'

'Oh! Rather as in the election of a pope,' I said.

Mrs Dolland frowned.

'I fail to see the relevance of that,' she said briskly. 'Shall we walk back to the house? I have shown you my business: now, please, tell me what is yours.'

As we walked back I explained in outline about Fanny and her legal predicament, with strong arguments – including the inquest verdict – in favour of her innocence. Then I asked her bluntly to intercede with her father to withdraw the prosecution. She heard me out, sighed, and adopted a kinder tone.

'Mr Cragg, I know that you know about the ridiculous matter

of the tontine, of which Mr Giggleswick, Miss Pettifer and I were unfortunately a part. If there is anything of deliberate intent in either of their deaths then I must take very seriously what you mentioned when you were here last: the possibility that I myself might be a target for foul play.'

'If that is your concern, look, there is nothing that says Fanny Kirby had any interest in the tontine. Do you have any notion of a possible foul player who *does* have? I am quite confident that it is not Kirby. Indeed I am convinced Miss Pettifer's death was as accidental as those of Thomas Hesketh and John Bourke.'

'But the shooting of Mr Giggleswick was no accident.'

'That, I know, is a very different matter. But consider this: should you be the last one of the tontine subscribers to be alive, your husband would then take possession of the whole amount. He is, you will recall, accused of Mr Giggleswick's shooting, with in my opinion the tontine as his probable motive. But far from endangering your life that fact protects you. From his point of view your life must be preserved so that, as your husband, he can take possession of the tontine.'

'Please, Mr Cragg!' she broke in. 'I am aware of all that. And it is the very reason why I will not put this plea of Fanny Kirby's innocence to my father. I think it not unlikely that Kirby is guilty.'

'But what is her motive?'

'The motive of being the dupe of my husband. She is just the type for him, by the way. But more important is the fact that she is young, easy to impress, easy to dominate, and those are things my husband is a dab at.'

'But there is no evidence pointing to her guilt! A contact between her and the Captain is nothing but a supposition. Will you not concede that?'

'It is for jury and judge to decide, not me. The case must be examined, and tried, and I will not be satisfied until it is. In that I am quite as determined as my father – though not on the same grounds – that it go before the assize at Lancaster Castle and be judged as to whether she is guilty or not.'

We were skirting the hall now, which reminded me of how the Captain had burst from the house at the time of our arrival.

'I was surprised to meet your husband just as I arrived,' I said. 'Was he coming away from a visit?'

Her smile might have soured a glass of milk.

'You may be assured that he made no visit, as I do not receive him. He comes here almost daily asking for an interview but I invariably have him turned away. I employ a strong and faithful man solely for that purpose.'

'Do you know why the Captain is so persistent?'

'The fool wants reconciliation, so he says. He has written me many letters asking for it. Ha! And him in and out of the bed of that Greenwood widow. I won't give him the courtesy of a reply. Now, I see your friends are waiting, and I desire to go in. Goodbye, Mr Cragg. I am glad at least to have introduced you to the mysteries of the bricking trade.'

'Alas, madam,' I said, thinking of her coyness beside the tempering pit. 'You have kept the secret of your hardness to yourself.'

'So the lady's mind is the same as mine,' said Fidelis, with undisguised satisfaction.

'And mine too,' said Furzey. 'Taking all known facts into consideration I am persuaded Fanny acted just as Mrs Dolland suggests.'

We were on the road to Preston, and I had told my companions of my visit to the works and my conversation with its proprietor.

'Have you also concluded she's guilty, Furzey?' I said. 'Tell me why.'

'Because that family, the Kirbys, are entirely a disgrace and Fanny must face justice, and receive it too.'

'But how will she receive it? True justice, I mean. The assizes are a chancy business for any defendant. For a poor girl, indeed a former whore, what hope does she have? Eh, Luke?'

'I am sure she killed her mistress, Titus, so I think she should be tried.'

'If Fanny is to be tried,' I said, 'the Captain must go for trial alongside her. Without him in it, there is no case against the girl.'

'That'll change when she peaches on him, Titus,' said Fidelis. 'To save her skin, the truth will out. That is what we all want, isn't it? That is how justice operates.'

'But are you not moved by her story?'

'Why should I be? There are thousands like her.'

SEVENTEEN

And so our lives in Preston returned to their courses, which in my case meant the usual round of legal business. One day not long after I had been revising the will of a bed-ridden client in Fulwood and was returning by a path across the moor to the north of town I came upon a small crowd of people listening to a field sermon. I saw that it was Doddy Kirby, atop one of his own carts, who addressed them. Like many of his kind, as I have noticed, he sounded much more interested in evil than in good.

'You must cast aside the evil in your hearts, my friends. Your heart is a dark wood out of which you must find your way. But the snares and pitfalls of the evil one are laid on every path. You may think by avoiding the path you will evade these traps. But be wise! Do not! For there are many more of the same traps concealed even in the undergrowth and, should any close on you, you shall be held as prey to the beast of eternal damnation. Therefore stay on the path and lay hands on the traps of the evil one and cast them bodily aside as you come to them. It is the only way.'

All deranged twaddle, I was thinking as I moved on. Soon the path joined Moor Lane, and I went along it towards home. After a few minutes I came to the home of the preacher himself, the Kirby house, and saw Mrs Kirby sitting at her door in the sunshine, with a glass that she refreshed from time to time from a stone bottle, and a book in her lap. I greeted her, and said I had been listening to her husband preaching, and asked why she did not attend herself.

'I have no need, dear. I hear all at home. He practises on me. He's been talking for, what? Twenty minutes now? He's only just getting started, then, but I'll wager he's gone past the Dark Wood and the Beast of Damnation by now. They are his invention and he is extremely proud of them. The sin of pride, see? Every preacher commits it, and every preacher is blind to it, my husband being no exception.'

These remarks not being easy to answer, I changed the subject. I asked her what book she was reading.

'It is poetry by Mr Dryden,' she said. 'I am reading it because I enjoy it though it infuriates Doddy. "John Dryden?" he says. "He was a Papist and full of obscenity." But I find him charming. Do you not, Mr Cragg?'

My opinion of Mrs Kirby was being rapidly revised. Never mind the gin, she was a reader, and a discriminating one. I wondered what sort of a hand she might play in literary conversation, so I dismounted and tethered my horse. I would try her.

'What is the poem, Mrs Kirby? I have read much Dryden and I may know it.'

'It is from the *Metamorphoses* put into English from that naughty Roman fellow Ovid.'

'That is a strange coincidence, Mrs Kirby. I have been reading Ovid myself.'

'But you are learned, Mr Cragg, and can read the Latin. I only wish Dryden had got all the books into English, for his lines are quite a delight, but also a canny judgement on society. Listen, I've just read this.'

She held up the book and read aloud.

'Mankind is broken loose from moral bands,
No rights of hospitality remain,
The guest by him who harboured him is slain.
Faith flies, and piety in exile mourns
And Justice here oppressed to heaven returns.'

'They are fine lines,' I agreed.

'Not only that, but they say just what is happening in this country today. Can there be any justice for my poor Fanny? Not according to Mr Ovid, or Mr Dryden, and not according to me neither.'

'Well, Ovid writes about a different kind of justice, I suppose: the way in which miracles or transformations bring about just deserts.'

'Ay, well, those were the days of miracles, Mr Cragg.'

'Yes, the Golden Age, the Silver Age. Such miracles do not happen now.'

'God can do any miracles he likes, can't he? But he seems not to like doing them any more. I've never seen a miracle, unless you count the births of my fifteen children, twelve of 'em living.'

'Ah yes,' I said, thinking of my dearest Hector, 'new life is always a miracle, Mrs Kirby.'

'Well, it'll take a miracle indeed to save my daughter's life. She's been a fair naughty child, there's no denying it. But she's my eldest alive, now her sister's gone, and I cannot bear the thought of losing her.'

Back in Cheapside I told Elizabeth of seeing Dodson Kirby preaching on the Moor, and of my conversation with his wife at Moor Lane.

'I discoursed with Mrs Kirby on miracles, among other things. The miracle she wants now is the saving of her daughter.'

'Poor woman!' Elizabeth said. 'And poor Fanny! I am sure you, and not Luke, are right and the girl is innocent. What can we do for her? I will pray, of course, but what practically can we do?'

'I am determined to let the judge know my opinion of the case. I will get him to read the papers in the inquest at Ormskirk, and give him the reasons why I think it was a just verdict. What more can I do?'

'You? Nothing. I shall make a novena. Nine days of prayer.'

'You and your Papist ideas! But it can do no harm. And as it happens the assizes are nine days away so your campaign of prayer will be fresh in the Almighty's ear just as Fanny Kirby mounts the dock.'

'Here's a letter just come in from our cousin Peppard, at Little Crosby,' I said to Elizabeth next day, as I came through to the house having spent the morning at work in the office.

The Peppards of Little Crosby were Elizabeth's relatives through her mother's cousin old Nicholas Blundell of Crosby Hall, who had left all his estates to his daughter Frances when he had died ten years back. She was married to Henry Peppard, the son of a considerable merchant settled in Liverpool from Ireland. The great antiquity of the Blundells, alongside the Peppards' complete lack of pedigree, led to much comment at the time, but the Blundells were Catholic and impoverished by double taxation. Henry's greatest attraction, in addition to his own Papism, was that he had plenty of money.

Elizabeth came to my side as I broke the seal and unfolded the paper.

'It is a request that I come to look at a body they found washed up on the beach,' I said.

Elizabeth took the letter and examined it.

'He does not even send his greetings. Squire Peppard and his lady – ha! They think they are above us.'

'Peppard has done well for himself, though. How old would he be now?'

'He's almost forty, is cousin Henry. But look, I see no greeting for me in his letter and you are not even addressed by name, but only as "Dear Hon. Coroner".'

'He hardly knows me, after all. I would hardly know him if I bumped into him today. Or her.'

'They were guests at our marriage, Titus. You must remember them.'

'Well, yes, I do. But I can't picture either of them.'

Our wedding was ten years before, and we had not seen the Peppards since. However hard I tried to picture Henry and his wife I could not form a sharp recollection. I did remember that she was fifteen years older than her husband.

'I will go down there first thing tomorrow and bring Luke, if he will come.'

Crosby Beach at low tide was a wide, empty strand endless to the eye and swept by a keen wind. It was bordered on one side by lumpy sandhills, and on the other by a humpy green-grey sea. The body they had found was wrapped tightly like a mummy in sacking, wound around with hemp rope. It had been stored in one of the boat-huts that abutted the dunes. When we came up an old fisherman and a boy were crouching in front of this decrepit structure, carefully examining a net stretched on the sand. Fidelis and I introduced ourselves.

'Come about the stiff 'un, have you?' said the old man.

'Yes. How did you know?'

'I had word from the hall you were a-coming, as it was me that found it.'

He tapped his chest with pride.

'Hold myself in readiness, they said.'

'And you are?'

'John Nutt. This here's my grandson Art.'

'Tell me how you found it, Mr Nutt.'

'Me and Art here, we came down one morning and we found it.'

'Where was it lying when you first saw it?'

The old man waved his hand towards the empty beach.

'Out on the strand.'

'Above or below the tide-line?'

'On the *strand*, man, like I said. Sand was wet under it.'

'What did you do with it?'

'Moved it up here above the tide and wrapped it up and then went to Squire to tell him we found it.'

'Well, Mr Peppard's written to me of it now.'

'So they tell me.'

'It will be my job to try whether the death was lawful.'

The fisherman chuckled, showing a residue of stumpy teeth.

'Lawful? Is that a nice way of saying, was it a murder?'

'What do you think happened?'

'Washed up. Perished in a shipwreck, or swept overboard, or jumped: one of the three, I reckon. Or pushed overboard would be another. Would that be unlawful enough for you?'

He gave a snorting laugh as if I, a landsman, could hardly be expected to understand a seafaring question.

'Did you know the person?'

'Never saw him before.'

'Him? It's male, then. A boy or a man?'

'Man. Not young.'

'How long has it lain in this shed?'

'Four days now.'

'Could not a more suitable place have been found, man? Hungry animals, or seabirds might have got in here.'

'We set a watch.'

'It won't do any more, anyway. We must take the body to the hall, where we shall borrow an outhouse or stable for it.'

'Then it's you must tell Squire. He won't like it.'

I walked ahead of the litter, improvised from a canvas sail, on which the still shrouded body was carried by two fishermen called upon by old Nutt from a nearby boat-hut. Luke Fidelis brought up the rear as we wound our way around the maze of paths between the sandhills. Twenty minutes after we had left the dunes behind us we reached Crosby Hall.

'You mean that you went straight down to the shore without seeing fit to call here first?' said Henry Peppard, with unmistakable belligerence.

We had found the Squire of Crosby in his gun-room. He had come in from a shooting excursion and was tying up the legs of three limp rabbits. He was short of stature and broad of build with blunt fingers that fumbled at the knots.

'I believe in getting straight to the point in cases like this,' I said. 'However, we have now brought the corpse back here with us. It really should not have been left almost in the open.'

Peppard finished his tying and reached up to hang the rabbits from a ceiling hook. He finished the action and turned back to me.

'Do you find fault with me in that, Cragg? I ordered the man to rest where he was found. I see no need to alarm Mrs Peppard.'

'The boathouse is not secure, and Mrs Peppard's feelings, while I sympathize with them, are not the main consideration.'

Peppard reddened, his face appearing to swell from indignation.

'They are to me, sir.'

'I must nevertheless ask that you now harbour the body in a suitable outhouse of your own, and under lock, pending my enquiry.'

'No, Cragg! We don't want it here! That was my motive in sending for you – so that you would dispose of it.'

'I am sorry, Henry, but I'm afraid it must stay here, unless you can obtain some other enclosed place for it – close by, mind.'

He stiffened when I called him Henry. Cousinly feeling was not uppermost in his mind this morning.

'You are a trifle high-handed, Cragg, I must say.'

'I am sorry. But I have to follow the correct procedure,' I said. 'I am legally obliged to see this corpse secured so that I may convene an inquest as close as possible to where it was found. We might do it tomorrow, or the day after at the latest. We must make arrangements. But in the meantime you must care for it.'

'What other arrangements are there?'

'The first of them will be for Dr Fidelis here, under my direction, to make an examination of the body.'

'Very well,' said Peppard expelling a burdened sigh. 'The corpse might go into the stables somewhere.'

He turned to Fidelis, who he seemed to respect more than he did me.

'How may I assist you in this, Doctor? Tell me what you need.'

'Not much,' said Fidelis. 'A six-foot table and a bucket of water will suffice.'

'And I meanwhile must speak to your parish constable,' I said. 'May I have his name, and whereabouts?'

Peppard turned back to me, his face sulking again.

'A man called Speirs. He lives in one of the houses facing the green at Great Crosby. For constabulary purposes there is no difference between Great and Little Crosby. But Speirs is a fellow with whom we have as little commerce as possible.'

I left Peppard with Fidelis and walked a mile or so towards the tower of Crosby's village church, near which lay the green and Speirs's house.

Thomas Speirs was a very different cast of man from the constable of Ormskirk. I judged him to be of the dissenting sort not only in religion but in his view of his fellow men, in whom he all too easily saw the devil at work.

'I heard about the corpse that washed up, but I've not seen it,' he said when I told him of my business. 'We reckoned one of you coroners would be sniffing around soon enough.'

'Was it not your duty as constable to have a look?' I said in surprise. 'It might be a villager, a neighbour.'

'I have as little as I can to do with Little Crosby. I took old John Nutt's word that it was no villager. I've never known John lie. One of the few people around here I can say that of. Besides there's nobody gone missing, or I'd know it myself.'

'We will have to inquest him,' I said. 'Do you know the process?'

'No, there's never been any such business here that I can remember.'

So I explained the procedure, and his part in it. Most constables in my experience relished their role in the drama of inquest but Speirs presented himself as a reluctant though not resistant participant. I told him I would hold the hearing in the morning and, while there was the sense of much effort in his compliance, he agreed to get up a list of jurors and summons the necessary witnesses – primarily John Nutt.

My next call was at the Blundell Arms, where the landlord was Martin Ashby. I told him I needed a chamber in which to hold the inquest and he showed me his public room which though not large was sufficient. I did not think in this little place that many would turn out to see the inquesting of a stranger's corpse. He also showed me two bedrooms in which Fidelis and I could put up for the night.

Ashby then asked me to drink a pot of ale with him, as there was something he wished to tell me. We sat down together in his private parlour.

'Now, Mr Cragg, everyone around the village believed at first that we had the body of a washed-up sailor. But one of the men from the hall has just been in here for a drink and he says a ragged man was at the hall on the day before the body was found, looking for alms. And I believe I also saw that man myself.'

'Tell me about him, Mr Ashby.'

'It was on Monday. I was in the yard taking delivery off the butcher's van and he came up and said to me, where's Little Crosby Hall?'

'Did he indeed? What business did he have at the hall?'

'I asked him that myself. He said he was known to the family. So I said, "You? Known to Squire Peppard!", which I added was a likely story, but he swore he was, though fallen on hard times. Well, I was busy with the butcher so I showed him the road, and off he went.'

'What time was this?'

'About an hour or so before noon.'

'And why didn't you speak to Constable Speirs about this at the time? Why wait until now to report it?'

'Because everyone was saying it was some drowned sailor they'd found.'

I drained my pot.

'Thank you, Mr Ashby. You have done the right thing in telling me this. I will see you later.'

EIGHTEEN

At the hall, Fidelis was at work in one of the stalls in the stable yard. A trestle table had been put up under the roof-light, and he was well on with his examination. It was a process I rarely watched, as I would usually find my gorge misbehaving itself, so I went out for a walk back over the sandhills, saying I'd be back within the hour.

Neither of the Nutts, old or young, was at their boat-shelter, though the boat was still there. I strolled along the beach to see who else I could talk to. Most of the fishing boats were out on the water but I found one fellow applying pitch to a small, shallow-bottomed skiff. Going up to him I learned that his name was Ben Jenkins. I soon got him talking about his trade.

'What do people go after from here?' I said. 'What fish, I mean.'

Jenkins waved his arm towards Crosby Sound.

'Flounder – there's plenty of them to catch out there, but not by me. Not with this boat. I'm a shrimps and cockles man. When you've got a wide beach like this with a shallow slope, you get shrimps when tide's in and cockles when it's out. That's what they call reciprocating economics.'

'Yes, I can see why. You have something to do whatever the state of the tide.'

'It means I can please myself when to work. And I don't have to go deep or weather any storms. Not that I'm afraid of that, mind.'

'Are there many fishing boats overturned? Men drowned?'

'Aye, there's some wash up every year. And some that never wash up.'

'I heard a body came ashore this week.'

'Yes. I didn't see it. John Nutt made out he was its sole proprietor, as it was him that found it. Most of us wasn't let near.'

'What's the word, though? Is it a local man?'

'No, he's not from here, or John would have said. Very tight with information he was, though. Just let it out that he wasn't dressed like a fisherman dresses. He seems to think he'll get money for finding and keeping it. I don't see how he will, myself.'

'Didn't anyone else see the body?'

Jenkins pointed up the beach.

'Billy Threlfall, second boat along there. You won't miss his red hair. He saw it.'

I excused myself and walked on to Billy Threlfall's boat shed. He was a young man with curly ginger hair boiling all over his scalp. He had just brought his day's catch ashore.

'I am the County Coroner, Mr Threlfall,' I told him. 'I am charged with enquiring into the body that was found here four days ago.'

'Oh, aye?'

'Mr Jenkins there tells me you saw it.'

'I did. I came down to the beach not long after John Nutt got here, and there it was.'

'What time was that?'

He raked his fingers through his curls.

'Hour and a bit after dawn, happen.'

'I understand when the body was found the tide was going out.'

'Aye. It went out and left the floater lying on the sand, we reckoned.'

He pointed to a place now fully submerged.

'Just over there.'

'How long before you saw the body would the tide have gone down from the place where it lay?'

'Oh, an hour, hour and a half . . . not more than two, any road.'

'Can you remember the state of the weather?'

'The sea ran high all night. Wind and heavy rain.'

I thanked him and set off back to the hall. I found John Nutt hanging about in the stable yard.

'That's my corpus found, is that,' he said, jerking his thumb in the direction of the stable where Fidelis was working. 'I reckon something is due me for it.'

'What sort of thing, Mr Nutt?'

'The money sort of thing, Mr Cragg. A payment for finding and preserving the remains.'

'Who would pay it, I wonder.'

'His family, of course. He's got to have family somewhere. And they've got to be grateful to them that's found their drowned son, or brother, or whatever it is.'

'We must find out who he is first. I will go in and see how Dr Fidelis is getting along.'

I found my friend had finished and was draping a horse blanket over the body.

'Well?' I said. 'What kind of specimen are we looking at?'

'Superficially I see a man aged about fifty. Malnourished. Signs of infestation such as lice. Ragged dirty nails, unkempt hair. Not an ornament of society.'

'What are your conclusions? Word's already got out that you don't think he drowned.'

'He didn't drown, Titus. He hasn't even been in the sea.'

'How can you tell?'

'The first thing is that he had no water in his lungs. That rules out drowning. But neither was there sea water in his ears. And I scraped his skin – no sign of salt on it. *Ergo*, Titus, he hadn't recently been in the sea.'

'Did he have any injuries?'

'Some cuts, one or two bruises that he could have come by quite naturally. Nothing fatal.'

'What did he die of, then?'

'He had diseased kidneys. Incipient goitre. Fatty heart. Thin bones. Enlarged liver – probably fluke-worms. He was extraordinarily poorly and had many ways in which to die. He had vomited before he died, and fouled his under-drawers. You will see further evidence of that over there.'

Luke pointed into the corner of the stable.

'His clobber. I haven't examined them in detail.'

The piled-up apparel that I now began to sort through was filthy and ragged. Patches had been applied here and there, but an equal number of rips and tatters were unrepaired. With Fidelis's warning about infestation and contagion in my mind, I handled them gingerly. My first impression was that they were damp, which seemed to agree with the idea, contrary to Fidelis's opinion, that the fellow had been in the sea. I squeezed some of the moisture as best I could on to my hand and then – suppressing my revulsion – tasted it. I could detect no salt. I concluded he had not been in the sea, but out in the rain.

One thing I could tell was that this had once been the clothing of respectability. The footwear, to be sure, was the cheapest: a pauper's clogs, with wooden soles and uppers of roughly cured cowhide, secured to the soles by iron nails. But the topcoat had a very different origin, for I found inside it the label of a fashionable Liverpool tailor, though unfortunately with no owner's name inked on to it. The Holland linen of the shirt too was of good quality; the cloth of the breeches and under-linen likewise, though shirt, breeches and drawers were all unutterably filthy and inexpressibly rank, the shirt crusted with vomit and the drawers stained by excrement.

I felt inside the coat pockets. One contained an old crust of mouldy bread. There was nothing else. A man without anything at all in his pockets has either been robbed or is reduced to home-lessness and penury. It was therefore possible to interpret these clothes as belonging to a prosperous man fallen on the hardest of times. But they might just as easily be respectable cast-offs worn by a poor vagrant.

I dropped the coat on top of the clothes pile and returned to Fidelis's side.

'Show me his face,' I said.

With deliberative care Fidelis pulled the blanket away from the dead man's face. We looked down at the illusion of a placid death. The lips were closed, but composed rather than compressed. The eyes were open but did not stare wildly or in horror. The muscles of the face were relaxed.

'Nothing to remark there,' said Fidelis.

'As a matter of fact there is,' I said, bending to look more closely, to make quite sure.

'What, then?'

'That I know this face, Luke. And I know the name that goes with it. In short, my friend, I know this unfortunate man.'

'You do?'

'Yes.'

'Then who?'

'His name is Prenton Smisby, late of Liverpool, where his address for the last several years has been the Debtors' Gaol.'

'By God! You mean Smisby of the tontine?'

'Exactly so. Smisby, the last-but-one surviving name of that ill-fated experiment, is dead.'

'But what was he doing here?'

'I suggest we see if Mr and Mrs Peppard can enlighten us.'

We found the Peppards in the hall's Great Room. The wife made a great show of welcoming me.

'Cousin Titus! This is a very pleasant surprise. I knew that Henry had written to you, but not that you would be coming here in person.'

'That is my duty, Frances. Elizabeth sends her very best. She says I must not fail to bring back all the news of your family – the little ones, you know.'

'They are all well except for little Bettany.'

She sighed almost theatrically.

'Bettany is my precious sickly one.'

'I am very sorry to hear it, indeed I am. May I introduce my friend Doctor Luke Fidelis?'

As a piece of mischief, I admit it was slyly enough done. I remembered Fidelis's resentment at the idea of giving free medical advice as a form of social politeness and I had no doubt the same would be expected of him now.

So, as it happened, did Fidelis, and on an impulse, or perhaps to ease our relations with the Peppards, he decided to anticipate the request. He gave a stiff bow.

'Mrs Peppard, I am at your service. If you will permit me I might have a look at the child. I have some knowledge of childhood diseases. There would be – erm – no consultation fee.'

Frances Peppard was of course delighted. She launched into an account of Bettany's medical history, and the various opinions on it they had had from Doctor Bob and Doctor Jig, not to mention the opinions of Old Mother Hubbard and the Man in the Moon.

With a cough, Peppard interrupted his wife.

'Titus has identified the dead man who was found on the beach on Tuesday, my dear.'

Frances whipped around to face her husband.

'Really, Henry? I thought he was just a . . . an unknown vagrant.'

She turned again to Fidelis and myself.

'It's what John Nutt told us, you see. Filthy clothing, nothing in the man's pockets, no way of knowing who he was.'

'Mr Nutt was telling the truth,' I said. 'There was indeed nothing on him to reveal his name.'

'How, then, have you found it?'

'It happened that I recognized him.'

Frances caught her husband's eye.

'Well! Well!' she said turning back to me. 'That is an extraordinary chance, Titus. Now, I must fetch those flowers in here, indeed I must.'

She bustled out of the room. Henry Peppard appeared to be studying the knots in the floorboards. After a moment he cleared his throat.

'My wife is right, Titus. It is indeed a marvellous coincidence that this man should wash up on my beach and that you find you know him by name.'

'He was not washed up, Henry,' I said. 'He did not come out of the sea at all.'

'Of course he did,' said Henry. 'A shipwreck. There was some particularly filthy weather offshore last week.'

'I can assure you, Mr Peppard, he had not been in the sea,' broke in Fidelis. 'We have performed tests which prove it.'

'Tests?' said Peppard. 'What sort of tests?'

'I have established that the damp in his clothes was not from immersion in sea water. There was no salt in it, Mr Peppard.'

Peppard hesitated, then finding nothing to say on the subject of our tests, turned back to me.

'You say you know his name, Cragg? Tell me what it is?'

'He was called Smisby. I met him in Liverpool. It's where he lived. Does the name mean anything to you, Henry?'

'Me? Ah, no, I don't think so. I've never heard the name, as far as I know.'

'Well, it is strange, because Mr Ashby at the inn in Great Crosby told me a man came through there on Monday last enquiring after you. He claimed to be an acquaintance of yours, or perhaps of Mrs Peppard. This was the same man, I have every reason to believe, as I have now identified as Smisby.'

Peppard's eyes widened, but he showed no other sign of alarm.

'This is the first I've heard of it, Cragg.'

'He did not come to your door, asking for alms perhaps?'

'He may have. The servants deal with such matters.'

Mrs Peppard came in again with a servant, who was carrying a vase of flowers. The maid was directed to place it on a table in the corner of the room, before being dismissed. Frances Peppard tidied up the blooms, then turned back to us with a smile.

'There! That brightens the room up, I think.'

'My dear,' said Peppard, 'the corpse on the beach is that of some unknown vagrant fellow called Smisby, and not a drowned sailor at all.'

His tone of voice alerted me. It sounded as if he was trying to put his wife on her guard. There was a short awkward silence, in which Frances Peppard stood in silence, with compressed lips. Then I said, 'Will you come into the stable yard and have a look at him, Henry? I would just like to be sure you don't know him.'

'Yes, of course. I would be interested.'

Fidelis broke in.

'And in the meantime would you care to introduce me to the patient, Mrs Peppard? I have my medical bag with me.'

While Fidelis was with Bettany I went with Peppard into the stable yard. The body lay covered with a horse blanket. I pulled this aside at the head's end, to reveal the gaunt, yellow visage of the dead man. Peppard leaned towards it much as a man might look at a turd, then immediately straightened and stood back.

'No, sir. I don't believe I know him.'

'Are you certain? Bear in mind that a man's face changes somewhat after it is four days a corpse.'

'I am quite certain. Now, if that is all . . .'

He walked out into the yard and filled his lungs several times with fresh air. I replaced the blanket and followed.

'Dr Fidelis and I must ride into Liverpool,' I said.

'Then you will need your horses,' said Peppard. 'Corrigan!'

Peppard's groom Corrigan, who had earlier brushed and watered our horses, was at this moment crossing the yard with a bucket. He came over and his master gave instructions that the horses be saddled, before excusing himself and returning to the house.

'So, where are we going to?' said Fidelis when he came out of the house at last.

'Liverpool. I want to introduce you to one Muldoon.'

We watched the groom pulling in my mount's girth and latching it. Fidelis said, in a low voice, 'Peppard didn't recognize the corpse, I take it?'

'He did not. Or rather, I think he may have, though he flatly denied it. By the way, how is young Bettany?'

'She has a cough and a fever that comes and goes.'

'And?'

Fidelis took my arm and walked me out of Corrigan's earshot.

'She will die, probably in a few months.'

'Is there nothing to be done?'

'She has consumption, Titus. There is no treatment. The disease has always been with us, dogging us like a shadow. But nobody knows what it is. Nobody knows where or how it starts, and its course is the very devil to predict.'

'If you cannot predict it, why do you pronounce poor Bettany's death sentence so easily?'

'Easily? I don't do it easily. But I know when the disease has taken such a hold that it won't let go until it exacts a life. I could recommend that she be taken abroad to some warmer climate. That may prolong her life. But it would be only a short deferment.'

'What did you tell her mother?'

'That she must have a gentle diet, and should be allowed to sit in the sunlight whenever possible. I told her to cherish her daughter and pray.'

'A novena perhaps?'

'What do you know of novenas, Titus? That is a practice of us Papists.'

'Elizabeth is making one for Fanny Kirby to save her from the gallows.'

The horses were ready by now. We mounted and were soon jogging side by side along the road towards Liverpool. Soon the mastheads of brigs and snows riding in the estuary or discharging cargo at the dock began to appear ahead of us.

'I didn't tell you that while you were cutting that poor fellow open I went back to the beach,' I said. 'I believe I know what time Smisby died. It was about dawn. A fisherman who saw his body lying on the sand told me that part of the beach was still flooded by the receding tide until just before daybreak.'

'You don't mean that was the time he died, Titus. You mean it was when his body was found. There is a significant difference.'

'Very well, whether he dropped dead there, or was placed there, that was when it happened. It was after first light, but not long after.'

'I wonder who placed him there.'

'Why are you ruling out the idea that he died naturally?'

'I am not – or not entirely. The vomiting, the loose bowel – they certainly might have been the result of disease: a colic, or a cholera.'

'And from your examination you knew he was diseased?'

'Oh yes, he was very sick. The question is over the immediate cause of his death. I would say the chances it was disease that killed him are much the same as those of Miss Pettifer having being accidentally smacked in the head by the Aughton windmill's sail. Like her, Smisby was part of the tontine and his death is of considerable significance to the last remaining member of that syndicate. Don't you think it is suspicious, his dying in this strange place, at this moment, and with no known witnesses, whilst vomiting and shitting himself?'

I could not deny it. I kicked the horse into a trot.

'Come on,' I said. 'There's no time to dawdle. Apart from all else I want a tobacconist, as I am out of tobacco.'

Muldoon was sitting at his table under the window in the gaol's porter's lodge, with a ledger open in front of him. He was copying some details from a paper.

'You will remember me, Mr Muldoon,' I said. 'Titus Cragg. This is Dr Fidelis.'

Muldoon looked up, squinting.

'Cragg,' he said. 'Titus Cragg, you say?'

He stood up and examined my face. Recollection came to him slowly.

'Oh yes! Yes, yes. I remember you all right. County Coroner. You had an interview with one of the prisoners.'

'That's correct. Prenton Smisby.'

Muldoon looked suddenly on his guard.

'Smisby, was it?'

'Yes.'

'He's not here.'

'I know. And I know where he went. Do you?'

Muldoon looked uneasy. He raised his hand and dabbed with his fingers at the strings of black hair draped across his scalp.

'Well, I . . . I mean to say he's . . . No, to be exact, I don't know where he's gone to. Only that he was supposed to be back in his room by ten o'clock last Monday night, and he never was. I've not seen him since.'

'Did you not report him as being missing?'

'No. Well, I reckoned he would turn up, of course I did. He had not money enough to live for long out there.'

'Did he escape, or did you let him go?'

'What odds does it make? I'll be in the mayor's black books any way.'

'Which was it?'

'Smisby asked the favour of me, as he wanted to go and visit someone who was dying, a relative. I'm not a cruel tyrant. I said yes.'

'Did he say who this relative was?'

'He did not.'

'Or where he lived?'

'No. But it can't have been far, or he wouldn't have given his solemn word to return at nightfall.'

Fidelis and I exchanged glances.

'I regret to inform you that Prenton Smisby was lying,' I said. 'There was no dying relative and the only person that died is Smisby himself.'

Muldoon sank back into his chair, placed his elbows on the table and rubbed his face with his hands.

'He's died, you say?' he said when he removed them. 'That's a bugger, is that. Where did he die?'

'He was found on Crosby Beach. Have you ever heard of any connection between him and Crosby?'

'I never heard him so much as mention the place.'

'Mr Muldoon,' I said, 'I am finding this hard to understand. You let Smisby out on your own ticket, without even asking him where he was going?'

'That we do often do, sir. Some of our gents do need to go out to earn a few pennies to support themselves, see? And it's well understood that they often give a different reason for going out, just to protect their own dignity. They do come back, I assure you.'

'Not Smisby. Not this time. You took his solemn word that he would return the same day, yet inside his head – on your own say-so to me a few weeks ago, and by my own observation too – he was halfway to drinking dew with the fairies in Cloud Cuckoo Land. When I met Smisby I thought he might even have got lost finding his way back from the jakes.'

'Prenton had his good days and his bad days, Mr Cragg.'

'May I see his cell?'

Muldoon had no objection.

We went straight to the room in which I had previously found Smisby digesting his ragout of mouse. It was not exactly like a cell. He could be locked in, but the door was not studded and iron-bound as in criminal prisons, and the room had some of the conveniences of an ordinary dwelling-room. The bed had sheets and blankets, though filthy ones. There was an old stuffed chair, the horsehair spilling out through splits in the fabric. There were some books on a shelf and stuck between them an untidy sheaf of papers. Fidelis pulled these out and glanced through them.

'Legal papers,' he said. 'It seems they mainly concern Smisby's case in the debtors' court.'

He crossed to the table under the window and spread the papers out. We bent over them. There were a number of letters from people to whom Smisby must have appealed for financial assistance – all refusing help except one. This was Isabella Pettifer, who promised to do what she could by way of sending in food, though she regretted she would not provide him with any money.

The most interesting document, though, was the indictment laid out in legal language and legal script, but with raggedly scrawled notes and exclamations in the margins. The text itself also was marred and with one particular redaction: the name of the plaintiff was rudely inked over wherever it occurred, alongside marginal exclamations of 'Blacken him!' and 'Expunge!' Smisby's crazed but meticulous obliterations meant that the name of the one who had caused his imprisonment was illegible. On the other hand the name of the attorney in the case had not been touched: it was that of Ambrose Parr.

NINETEEN

'Mr Smisby received food from time to time,' I said to Muldoon when we returned to the lodge. 'It was from a charitable lady, a Miss Pettifer.'

'If you say so. I didn't know her name.'

'How often did it come?'

'Every week, Fridays. Except it has not come in recent weeks, to the great distress of Smisby.'

'Did Miss Pettifer bring the food herself?'

'A lady did come once or twice, at first. But lately it's been delivered by a boy from the lawyer's office.'

Fidelis and I exchanged a glance.

'Mr Muldoon,' I went on. 'I would be glad of a look at your register of prisoners during the last year.'

He went to a shelf, brought down a ledger and brought it to me. I opened it and turned the pages. The particulars of prisoners accepted and released were entered on opposite pages, balancing each other like a set of accounts. I turned the pages, running my finger down the column names. At last it stopped at the one I was looking for.

'Here it is, Luke! "Taken in, Garland, Captain. One hundred and two pounds owed. Mr Gerard Poole creditor." And look, the date is just two months ago. Garland was a prisoner in the Debtors' Prison with Smisby.'

I hunted down the lists on the balancing page until I came to another entry: *Released Capt Garland on settlement of debt to Mr Poole.*

'See here, the date, Luke?' I said. 'Just a week or two before Giggleswick was shot.'

At that moment we heard the whistling of a tune and a lanky young man sauntered in from the street. He was about to walk through the arched gateway and into the prison yard when he heard the name of Smisby spoken and it stopped him short. He looked at us through the door of Muldoon's lodge.

'Did I hear you mention Smisby?' he said. 'Has he turned up?'

'No, Mr Holland, I'm afraid not,' said Muldoon.

Muldoon turned to Fidelis and me.

'This is another of our indwellers, sirs. Mr Ferdinand Holland.'

'Ferdy, please,' said the lanky one with a pronounced aristocratic drawl. 'I would like to see the confounded fellow back here. What could be keeping him? He said he might cut me few bob and would certainly bring me back a quarter-pound of bacco.'

'Mr Holland,' I said, 'I am sorry to tell you that Mr Smisby has been found dead. I suppose you knew he was in poor health?'

'Oh, Lord, was he? I've no idea about things like that, though I'll admit he looked none too sprightly when he walked out of the gate. Not like the way I feel when I cross the threshold in the outward direction. I've got the spring in my heels of a bantam cock, I can tell you. But oh Lord! I didn't think it'd be the death of him to go out, indeed I didn't.'

He passed on and we heard the same cheerful tune whistling from his lips. Muldoon tipped his head in the direction of the whistling.

'A gent of the highest class, that Mr Holland. A viscount's son but disinherited. I swear it's true.'

'For God's sake let's eat,' said Fidelis as we entered the street once more. 'I've had nothing for hours.'

'First we go to Ambrose Parr's. His name has cropped up again, but in a new light. You yourself told me Smisby's death could be by poison.'

'And Parr was sending food into the prison. I suppose it is worthy of note.'

'I would expect you to be more excited, Luke.'

'I am hungry, Titus.'

'We will dine, but let us first be the first to tell Parr of Smisby's death. His reaction will be interesting.'

Parr's footman told us his master was not at home, but could be found dining at Masterson's Chop House, a few minutes' walk away. Fidelis was delighted to hear this.

'Thank God,' he said. 'You and I can dine there too.'

Parr was sitting alone at a recessed table, finishing off the last of what, from the bones, must have been a dozen chops. We greeted him very much in the manner of old friends, and he in turn invited us to sit and join him in a glass of wine. As usual his manner was one of glassy geniality and it was impossible to tell what he was truly thinking. I sat down, while Fidelis went to the hatch to discuss victuals with the landlord.

'Mr Parr,' I began. 'There are two matters I would dearly like to discuss with you. The first is a piece of news I have discovered today.'

'Oh, yes?'

'In truth, it is four days old but the fullness of it has only just come to light. I wonder if you have heard of the thing. I believe you are very much attuned to the life of Liverpool.'

Parr had been mopping up gravy with a piece of bread. He now forked it into his mouth.

'You flatter me, sir,' he said. 'This is a teeming town and no one can keep abreast of all that goes on here. What is your news?'

'It is sad news, I'm sorry to say. Prenton Smisby was found dead on Crosby Beach four days ago. I am holding an inquest.'

While still chewing his bread, Parr gazed for a moment into the space above my head, then swallowed. He said slowly:

'I am grieved to hear it, with that particular kind of grief that attaches to the death of an associate from one's youth.'

'Do you confirm that you acted for Miss Pettifer in providing Smisby with baskets of food from time to time?'

'Weekly, it was. We sent in a pie or some cheese or some such on Fridays without fail. On her account, of course.'

'You must be distressed that this associate of your youth has died so soon after Miss Pettifer herself. You knew them both for many years, as you did another recently deceased person, this time one that lived in Ormskirk.'

Parr sighed.

'Yes, indeed. These are heavy matters to bear.'

'May I remind you of a certain matter that has come up between us with unnatural regularity, and in which Smisby, Miss Pettifer and Mr Giggleswick were all equally concerned?'

'Ah! Yes! The tontine! Good Lord! You are right. The tontine states that the money devolves upon on the last member standing. With Smisby's sad death Mrs Dolland is the last member. Therefore the contract is satisfied and the principal should, of course, be paid across.'

'Will it now be your part as the original administrator of the tontine to release the sum?'

Parr sighed.

'I suppose it will. But with a heavy heart. That wastrel who calls himself Garland will get his hands on it.'

'So it would seem. And that brings me to the second thing I want to mention, Parr – the prosecution of Fanny Kirby for the death of Miss Pettifer. She maintains that you are persecuting her, and for a single reason. She will not tell me what that reason is but she is certain that if revealed in court it will bring you discredit, and will also bring off her own release. May I ask what that revelation is, Mr Parr?'

Parr gave an exaggerated shrug, and a smile.

'Who knows what she might have thought up? Nothing that is true, you may be sure of it.'

'Perhaps you had business with her, not in your own profession, but in hers? And I don't mean that of housemaid.'

'No, no, Mr Cragg. I? Consort with streetwalkers? That is an absurdity.'

Although Parr had registered this protest, he retained his composure.

'No, sir,' he went on, that ingratiating smile fixed on his face. 'I prosecute the girl because she has taken the life of a lady very precious to me, a most religious and charitable lady, and that is all.'

'Then my question is, why would Fanny do that?'

'It is a speculative question, Cragg, and I am interested in fact not speculation.'

'Let me put it to you that your real murderer is the same Captain Garland who, as you have just regretfully stated, will be the final beneficiary of the tontine.'

'The killer certainly wasn't Garland. I hold no brief for him but he was nowhere near that windmill. There were witnesses.'

'Have you not considered the possibility that Fanny was his agent? Think about it, Mr Parr. You can satisfy your desire to see Fanny tried while also prosecuting the real villain, the Captain. And by the way if you can prove him a murderer, it will prevent him seeing a farthing of the tontine money.'

Parr held up an index finger.

'It will also disqualify his wife from having the money. Remember that. The principal will go direct into the Treasury. Only a villain would do that to her.'

'Yet, as you have yourself mentioned, with Garland her husband alive and a free man she would not get it anyway.'

Fidelis now joined us.

'Ham hock in caper sauce, Titus, coming in ten minutes. Thank you, Mr Parr. A glass of wine would answer very nicely.'

Parr took Fidelis's arrival as a useful juncture and handing across the bottle he stood up. He was as unperturbed as ever.

'Please finish the wine between you, gentlemen. I must be on my way, but it has been a pleasure talking to you.'

And, with a bow, he left us.

I gave Fidelis an account of what had passed between us.

'He has been treating you like an idiot, Titus,' he said, 'which is unwise of him, I think.'

'So it is, very. But he is the damnedest fellow and impossible to pin down.'

Our dinner arrived and for the next half an hour Fidelis had little to say, as his attention was on his food.

'Good heavens! Over there. Isn't that Ferdy Holland?' said Fidelis outside the tobacconist. We had finished dinner and he had been waiting for me to emerge with my purchase.

The disgraced son of a viscount was standing on the pavement in the throng of passers-by, with a wooden tray suspended by means of string around his neck. He was calling out in a high-pitched voice, hardly able to make himself heard over the clatter of clogs and the rumble of iron-rimmed cartwheels.

'Clay pipes two a ha'penny! Two a ha'penny clays! Buy my pipes, two a ha'penny!'

He was displaying on his tray a jumble of various pipes, mostly stub-stemmed sailors' clays, but with a few of the longer variety that shoremen more usually smoke in taverns and coffee houses. They were by no means new and most had been broken. But Holland had collected, repaired and roughly cleaned them for sale at second-hand.

I took out a ha'penny and went up to him.

'Pick me out two of the cleanest you have, Mr Holland, and I shall be delighted to buy.'

'Mr Cragg, ain't it? You are a Christian gent, sir.'

He picked out a couple of pipes and put them into my hand.

'By the way,' I said. 'I was wondering about something ever since we talked about poor Mr Smisby: he promised you the loan of a few bob, but I wonder how. He evidently had no money himself. Did he tell you how he proposed to get your few bob?'

'From a man that owed him some rhino and a good turn, that's what he said.'

'This man's name?'

Holland screwed up his face, trying to remember.

'He didn't tell me. He only said where he was going: Little Crosby Hall, he said.'

I felt in my pocket and brought out one of the two puddings of American tobacco that I had just bought.

'Mr Holland, may I present this to you with my sincere compliments? You have been very helpful, sir. Very helpful indeed.'

'Have I, by God?' said Ferdy Holland, looking perplexed. He pocketed the tobacco. 'Thank you very sincerely, sir. Poor old Smisby. More to him, you know, than appeared. Now he's gone. Well, well!'

'Smisby *did* go to see Henry Peppard, by God,' said Fidelis as we left Holland plying his wayside trade.

'Or someone else at the hall.'

'No, I had a suspicion it was Peppard from the behaviour of your cousins earlier. This is the proof of it.'

'Why did the Peppards deny knowing Smisby, then?'

'Smisby had claimed he was owed money, presumably that would be by Peppard.'

'It can hardly have been a large enough sum to embarrass Peppard. If it were it might have sprung Smisby from the Debtors' Prison.'

'A trivial sum, then?'

'Or an imaginary one. Remember Smisby's unhinged mind.'

'We must ask the Peppards then, must we not?'

As soon as we retrieved and remounted our horses, Fidelis was back in the saddle and kicking on in his impatience. I kept up

with him and so, by cantering most of the way, we were back
at Crosby Hall less than an hour later. The Peppards, though,
were not at home. Or to describe it more exactly, Henry Peppard
was out with his gun and his game-bag, while Frances sent word
that she was unable to see us, as she was caring for her sick
daughter.

We went instead to Great Crosby and to the Blundell Arms,
where we settled into the rooms Ashby had set aside. After that,
leaving Fidelis to his own devices, I went to Speirs's house.

'How do, Mr Cragg?' he said. 'I've got a jury together. Not an
easy job, but I've done it. And I've sent the summons to John Nutt
to appear as your first finder.'

'Good. I will myself send one across to the hall for Mr and
Mrs Peppard. Now there is one further thing I would like to talk
over. Mr Ashby has told me that a ragged fellow answering to the
description of the dead man had been seen coming through Great
Crosby on Monday. He enquired at the inn for the road to the
Peppards' house. Have you heard anything of this?'

'We have vagabonds through here regularly. They don't come
to my notice unless they show signs of dropping anchor, if you
follow my meaning.'

'I can understand that.'

'The parish will not support them, you see. So we make sure
they get on their way. In the last three months I've marched half
a dozen of the kind to the parish boundary and given them a kick
in the backside to send them off.'

'So did this man get the same treatment on Monday?'

'No. I never heard of him. Happen this is the dead man?'

'Yes, I'm afraid it is.'

'And he was going to Squire's house?'

'As I've said.'

'Then why? Hasn't the Squire told you his connection with
him?'

'No. I have not had the chance to ask him – yet.'

TWENTY

A Thursday evening at a country inn is not lively, although Fidelis found enough company to interest him. I left him deep in conversation with some local men and went up to my room, where I brought my journal up to date. Then having my copy of *Metamorphoses* with me, I worked on my Englishing of the lines on Cephalus's love for Procris, which I intended as a present for Elizabeth. More beautiful lines on the happiness of marriage cannot be imagined.

Next morning I broke my fast alone – Fidelis is an inveterate lier-in of a morning – and went out to walk the dunes and sands of Crosby Beach. I walked far enough to greet John Nutt and remind him to be at the Blundell Arms by ten to give his evidence. I greeted Ben Jenkins, and together we watched Billy Threlfall roll his boat on poles down to the sea's edge, and launch it on to the surf.

'Man called Smisby, the stiff, so they're saying,' Jenkins said.

'Yes,' I said. 'And didn't the word on that get around quickly enough?'

'Word does, here. Do you reckon he was killed or died natural?'

'Is that what local people are asking?'

'Aye. It's got to be one or the other, though, hasn't it?'

I let the question hang.

When I got back to the inn Furzey had arrived from Preston with the accoutrements we would need – primarily the register, a bound book in which the case details and the verdict of every inquest are recorded, and the handbell that I used to bring the room to attention.

'Another victim of the tontine, is it?' he asked me drily. 'Rich feed for the coroner's court is that legal invention, and no mistake.'

I opened the proceedings at ten by the church clock. Fidelis was in line to be the second witness though he had still not appeared. I knew of his propensity for last-minute-ness and was not concerned. The Peppards both came in, causing a stir as they made their way up the room and took their places at the front, rather as if they were coming to church. Like them, though in a humbler conveyance, the corpse had been brought down from Crosby Hall and lodged in one of the inn's outhouses. Following the jury's swearing they reviewed the body, then filed back to their form to my left in the makeshift courtroom. I sat with Furzey behind a table in the middle. The witness chair stood on my right opposite the jury.

John Nutt came up and spoke of how he saw the body humped on the sand in the early morning of the previous Monday, how he turned it over and found it was a stranger, concluding that this was a drowned sailor or perhaps a passenger fallen off an Irish packet-ship. Before he left the chair Nutt could not restrain himself from appealing for the fee that he thought was due to him.

'And will not his kin reward an honest man who finds their brother or son, or happen their father, lying dead on the foreshore?'

'That is unlikely, Mr Nutt, but thank you for your evidence.'

It was almost at the end of Nutt's evidence that I saw Fidelis enter the room, at the same time as a woman with yellow hair and large blue eyes. He seemed to be in charge of her, as he carefully saw her into a place in the audience before coming forward to give his own testimony.

In the witness chair he explained his idea of Smisby's death. He had died in essence because his body was severely disordered but the immediate cause was something in the food he had recently eaten. He noticed a great excess of bile in the stomach, which made him conclude that he was suffering from a cholera or had eaten something that gave similar effects. He could not explain how the dead man came to the beach where he was found.

Fidelis returned to the audience, where he sat next to the yellow-haired woman. I then spoke directly to the jury. I told them how, when the doctor had finished his examination, I had myself looked for the first time on the dead man's face. By a strange coincidence, I said, I immediately recognized him as being Prenton Smisby, a merchant of Liverpool, formerly prosperous but recently confined in miserable circumstances to the Debtors' Prison. I had then made enquiries in Liverpool, I said, and learned that Smisby had left the prison with the intention of getting some money that was owed to him.

'I can't produce the necessary witness for you, as he too is a prisoner,' I told them. 'So you should treat the information as hearsay, though you may take it into account.'

I then called landlord Ashby to the chair and we heard how Smisby had approached him in the inn yard on Monday and asked for directions to Crosby Hall.

'Please try carefully to remember that conversation, Mr Ashby,' I said, 'and then answer me this. Did Smisby particularly say that he was visiting the Squire, or his lady, or indeed mention anyone else at Crosby Hall that he might have been visiting?'

'No, sir. He did not.'

'He merely asked the way to the hall itself?'

'That is right.'

'Thank you. You may get down. I now call Mr Henry Peppard to come up to the chair.'

Henry Peppard looked acutely uncomfortable. Perhaps it was sitting before a panel of men that he must have regarded as his social inferiors, but who in these proceedings were his legal superiors. Or perhaps there was another reason. He took the oath almost in a whisper and I warned him that he must answer my questions loudly enough for all to hear him.

'We have heard that Mr Smisby had asked directions to your house,' I said. 'Do you know why he was going there?'

'I do not.'

'He was not going in particular to see you, or Mrs Peppard?'

'As I just told you, I have no idea.'

'You have no idea. Again I must ask you kindly to speak up, Mr Peppard, so that everyone present can hear. Did you know Mr Smisby at all?'

'I did not.'

'Had you ever heard his name?'

'No.'

'Maybe someone in your household knew him.'

'I could not say.'

'Has it surprised you to hear that Smisby was allegedly coming to Little Crosby to get some money that was owed to him?'

'How could it surprise me when I know nothing of the man?'

'Have you not asked your servants whether any of them knew Smisby, or expected his visit?'

'Mrs Peppard has, and none of them was expecting anyone.'

'Very well. But can we establish for a fact whether Smisby did or did not appear at Crosby Hall last Monday?'

Peppard straightened his back.

'Yes he did.'

It was the first crack in his defence.

'He *did*?'

'Yes.'

'This is the first I have heard of it. Please tell the court what happened.'

'My head groom Corrigan saw him lurking near the stable gates. He challenged him. The man merely said he was a wayfarer and was hungry, or perhaps he said thirsty.'

'What did Corrigan do? Did he give the man anything? Food? Drink? Money?'

'I don't know.'

I leaned across to Furzey.

'Go and get someone to fetch Corrigan here as fast as possible.'

I rang the handbell.

'These proceedings are briefly suspended,' I said. 'I have sent for Mr Corrigan and we must await his arrival. You jurymen may stretch your legs but please do not wander far. Mr Peppard, the same applies to you.'

Many of the audience stayed in their places. Others laid their hats on their seats to keep them from being taken and went outside to stroll around, smoking and gossiping. Luke Fidelis was one of those, accompanied by the fair-haired woman, but before they left he caught my eye and, with an almost imperceptible twitch of his head, invited me to join them. I followed them out into the air and saw my friend and the woman setting off towards the centre of the green in close conversation. They were talking together with much enjoyment. He was animated, gesturing and joking, while she laughed at his jokes and was not shy in answering him back.

I caught them up.

'Ah! Titus,' he said. 'You won't get anything useful out of Corrigan, you know. You might as well question the kitchen sideboard. He won't say anything that might lose him his job.'

'He might let something slip.'

'You should speak to Miss Benson, here. Rosie, may I introduce my friend the coroner, Mr Titus Cragg?'

We nodded at each other.

'Rosie serves at the inn, at the bar,' Fidelis went on. 'We became acquainted yesterday evening after you had retired to your bed.'

'How d'ye do, miss?' I said, looking more closely at her. She was very pretty indeed and with a sharpness about her eyes that told me she was far from empty-headed. I fancied the two of them had spent the night together. She was exactly the type of woman that appealed to Fidelis, and she had obviously taken a fancy to him.

'How do *you* do, Mr Cragg?' she said. 'Luke tells me that you shall be interested in my history and that I must tell it you.'

'Must you? I wonder why that is. Luke?'

Luke wore the wooden face that he liked to adopt when teasing me by withholding information.

'Because it bears on certain enquiries you and I have recently been making,' he said.

I turned back to Rosie Benson.

'Miss Benson, please elaborate without delay.'

We had come to a bench long enough for three, and there we sat down.

'I am an orphaned girl,' she began when she had settled herself. 'But you mustn't feel sorry for me. My mother was a whore and my father – well, I suppose he was one of her customers. When I got old enough I went into my mother's profession. Oh! Don't misunderstand, Mr Cragg. My eyes were wide open and I knew what I was doing. I considered whoring to be my destiny.'

'You were happy then?'

'Of course not. I was miserable most of the time, not the least reason being that a whore has to play at being happy. It's why Nell Gwynn made such a good whore, you know. Actresses do. But when acting don't come natural, playing at being in ecstasy day in, day out, just to please men for a half-crown a time: that's a hard tug, a very hard tug.'

'You told me not to pity you, but I'm afraid I do, Miss Benson. How were you saved?'

'By a certain lady of Ormskirk.'

'You went into the establishment of Miss Isabella Pettifer?'

'Yes. She took me off the street and Mrs Field taught me house-maiding and a lot of religion besides.'

'Ah! The redoubtable Mrs Field. Did you also know poor Fanny Kirby, by any chance?'

'That's what Luke wanted to know. Well, if she was there at Ormskirk it was after I left, which was three year ago.'

'And how long had you been there?'

'Two year. Then I came to work for Mrs Peppard at Crosby Hall. After two more year I came to an agreement with Mr Ashby and started work for him at the inn.'

'So, you heard that the inquest this morning is into the death of Prenton Smisby, who was a stranger to this neighbourhood. Does that name mean anything to you from your time at Crosby Hall? I would dearly like to establish that Smisby and the Peppards were acquainted.'

'I beg pardon,' she said, 'but I've never heard of anyone by that name.'

Fidelis broke in.

'It isn't Smisby who is the point here, Titus. Rosie, tell him about who brought you to Miss Pettifer's in the first place, and later took you away. I mean, tell him about who arranged the job for you here at Crosby, and who arranged jobs for all Miss Pettifer's young women.'

'Oh?' I said. 'Who was that, Rosie?'

'That was Mr Parr, sir. Mr Ambrose Parr.'

I felt a sensation flood over me that might be described as the happiness, in rather the way that listening to an aria by Mr Handel does. Of course it was Parr! It made beautiful sense.

'Tell me about Mr Parr, Rosie.'

'Mr Parr had professed to be in love with Miss Pettifer and wanted to marry her. He acted for her in all sorts of business. He would do anything for her it seems.'

'Is that so? Mrs Field said nothing of the kind when I questioned her. So were Parr and Miss Pettifer lovers? I mean in a bodily way.'

'Lovers? Them two? Don't make me laugh. Oh, Miss Pettifer liked plenty of the other all right, but not with a man. If she wanted a bedfellow she could have any of us girls, couldn't she? In the finish that was why she had us there, Mr Cragg. You said she was charitable, but that wasn't the half of it.'

I looked at Fidelis.

'My God, Luke! I am suddenly seeing life at Miss Pettifer's house in a different light.'

Fidelis's face radiated satisfaction.

'Life *and* death at Miss Pettifer's house, Titus.'

Looking back towards the inn I saw Furzey hurrying towards us gesturing impatiently.

'Your witness is here,' he called out from thirty yards. 'Hurry up, man. We've an inquest to get done.'

Corrigan was a former jockey but he was sinewy as a greyhound, which he also resembled in having a markedly pointed sort of face, the nose forward and the mouth and chin receding.

'No, sir,' he replied to my opening question. 'I didn't know this Smisby until I saw him on Monday coming into my stable yard.'

'What did you make of him?'

Corrigan shrugged.

'I took him for the tramp that he looked like.'

'What did he want?'

'Food. That's all it was in the end.'

'Not to speak to Squire Peppard or Mrs Peppard?'

'No.'

'What reply did you give him?'

'I gave him some bread.'

'Was that the crust I found in his coat pocket?'

'Happen.'

'What else did he want?'

'Somewhere to sleep. I told him no, and that he must be on his way.'

'What did he do?'

'He left.'

'Without a word?'

'Aye. Without a word.'

'What time was that?'

'Afternoon.'

'And how did he look to you in general?'

'He was sweating and breathing heavy, with eyes popping, like.'

'Was he ill?'

'Happen.'

'So if you thought he was ill why did you not give him more help?'

'I didn't say I thought he was ill. I only told you what he looked like.'

'Do you have an explanation for his ending up on the beach?'

'Aye. I reckon he went down there to sleep in one of the boat shelters. Got took poorly down there, nobody to help. Probably didn't know where he was at the finish.'

There was nothing more to be had from the groom. It was exactly as Fidelis had predicted. Useless. I called Peppard to the chair again and found him coming at my questions now with a new arrogance.

'I have told you all I know about this man. I cannot tell you more,' he said.

'How do you account for what I heard from his fellow debtor at the prison? That he was looking for you and expecting some money?'

'I don't account for it. I have not heard this as sworn testimony. Therefore it means nothing. You said it was hearsay, and that is all it is.'

For another five minutes, like a wily batsman frustrating the bowler at cricket, he blocked my every question. I let him go and feeling ill-temper stealing over me, I addressed the room.

'We have heard the evidence of Mr Nutt who found the dead man, Dr Fidelis who examined the body and Mr Ashby who spoke to him the day before he was found. Finally we heard from Mr Peppard, who said nothing of interest although it was his house that we know the dead man was looking for. And we heard from Mr Corrigan the groom, who spoke with Smisby and sent him packing with a crust of bread as you might pack off a beggar. I say this is not enough, indeed it isn't. We must know why Prenton Smisby was asking for Crosby Hall. Surely it was for more than a crust of bread. If anyone present can tell us this reason, I ask them to make themselves known and come forward now.'

The room was almost silent. A few whispered to each other, creaked their seats and craned their necks to see if anyone was volunteering to speak. No one was.

And so I brought matters to a head, asking the jury to deliberate and give me a verdict. They argued together for quite some time, though my notes and Furzey's more formal record do not go into the detail. Finally the foreman stood up and told me they had made up their minds.

'And what have you decided?' I asked.

'We reckon Mr Smisby has come here for a reason of his own which we cannot tell you, not for sure. He was turned away from Crosby Hall and going down to the beach was overcome by a fatal illness which, being beyond the reach of medical help, made him unfortunately die.'

'Very well, let that be your verdict,' I said, turning to Furzey. 'Write "Death by natural causes", Mr Furzey, if you please.'

My feeling was that the jurymen were pleased with the result, and with themselves. Any other conclusion, especially one embarrassing to the Squire, would have caused all manner of troubles to them, and to the rest of Crosby. It was as if they had come across a large dog asleep in the road. They did not want their throats torn out and so, prudently, they had tip-toed around the dog and gone on their way.

'Remind me, Titus,' said Fidelis. 'What exactly is the good of Rosie's information unless you put it to use?'

He had been aggrieved from the moment the inquest ended, and severely taxed me about the verdict. He continued to do so as we rode back towards Preston that afternoon.

'I couldn't see a way of doing so,' I said. 'Rosie knows nothing of Smisby. And she knows nothing of Captain Garland. I relied instead on the groom but he would or could not help us. Nobody in Crosby would willingly ruffle Peppard's feathers, including the jury. They are all in his thrall. So there are no witnesses who might tie Smisby to the Peppards.'

'So we still do not know if Peppard did owe Smisby money.'

'If anything, it was surely a trivial amount, which Smisby because of his circumstance magnified into a large sum. He probably had dealings with the Peppards years ago, in Liverpool or in Dublin. Henry may never have known about it.'

'At all events, you should have asked him about his dealings with Ambrose Parr.'

'Why is that?'

'Because you are forgetting what this is about, Titus. The tontine. Parr is the constant element in all the matters surrounding that fatal experiment.'

But on this matter I was growing impatient with my friend.

'I know that, Luke! But what are you suggesting? That Smisby was murdered by Ambrose Parr? That there is a conspiracy between Parr and Garland? The idea is ridiculous and you know it.'

'No, Titus. I am not suggesting a conspiracy but a contest. A contest between Parr and Garland to profit from the tontine.'

'If that's the case, Parr's hopes have been dashed by the death of Isabella Pettifer. He may indeed have hoped to marry her and stand in line as her husband for the money, but he cannot do that now. He has nothing to gain from Smisby's death.'

'Although Garland does.'

'We have no evidence that he ever came near Crosby, or had any knowledge of it.'

'I still consider Parr to be a factor in this, Titus. He controls the money, remember. We shall see if he now pays it over to Frances Dolland and allow the Captain's ultimate triumph.'

TWENTY-ONE

News often raises a strong wind, and runs like fire through a town; then even those not directly burned are scorched and they skitter to and fro blabbing about it. So it was next day in Preston when we heard that Fanny Kirby was to be prosecuted for murder by Ambrose Parr and was set to face the grand jury at Lancaster and, when found to have a case to answer, would face the judge in the court of assize. First there was the gale of talk that swirled up and down Church Gate and Fisher Gate. Coming into the market, the turbulence swung a few times around the cross and the Fish Stones before flying away down Friar Gate, past the Bar and, for all I know, away across the moor. And then came the second draught of news: Fanny herself would be passing through Preston on her way to Lancaster the very next morning.

Indicted felons of the common people are not given the luxury of a travelling coach, so Fanny was brought through town in a four-wheeled ox-drawn cart, for all to see. Already at the old bridge at Walton below Preston there was a small welcoming party, mostly quiet and sober although not all of them bemoaning the fate of their one-time neighbour. Fanny's reputation had preceded her so that on her first visit to her birthplace since deserting it two years before her history as a whore was on everybody's lips.

'No one talks about her living blameless at Ormskirk and reformed,' Elizabeth said when she brought me the news that the cart had been seen. 'She is reviled as a harlot and therefore must be a murderer too, I suppose. It is just as her mother said to you, Titus. What chance does she have of justice if even her old neighbours condemn her?'

'You are right, wife. She has little. But I am determined to do what I can for her.'

The gallows at Lancaster stand on a hill outside the city because, it was said, the angel of death has less far to fly down. Plenty of women have been folded into that angel's arms on Gallows Hill: nine all on the same charge in 1612, after the famous Lancashire witches' trial. Poor Fanny.

The window of my private business room looks out on to the side-alley, whereas Furzey in the front office has a full view of the marketplace from two windows, one on either side of the door. I knew that Fanny's cart would come up Church Gate and turn into Cheap Side, passing right in front of those windows. I told him to call me when she came into sight.

In the event there was no need: I heard her approach. There is usually a clamour of sound from the marketplace, but the progress of the prison cart through town gave an extra incentive for a racket. Hooting and whistling, cries and hollers came to me in my inner sanctum and I knew that the cart must have turned the corner of the Moot Hall and was broaching Cheap Side. It was followed by a rout of Prestonians. I did not know precisely what their mood was but it was a decided one. They had decided on not the slightest grain of evidence that she was guilty, or at least that she would be found guilty, and would hang.

In the front office Furzey had gone to the window. I crossed the room, opened the door and stood on the step to see her pass by. The oxen that pulled Fanny were less than noble beasts, and the cart was ill-repaired, the front half of it having a patched and dirty sailcloth covering over a rickety framework. Yet she stood outside in the air upright, riding like Boadicea. Her ankles were shackled but with her arms free she was able to keep a firm hold of the side rails to left and right. Her face was angled towards the rooftops, chin jutting out, but I could see her eyes were looking down at the baying mob. It was a scornful look. She was saying with her body that if they hoped for penitence they would be disappointed but if they were hungry for defiance they could have their fill.

I followed the progress of the cart with my eyes as it trundled past me and along the side of the marketplace before turning into the head of Friar Gate. On the box-seat alongside the driver sat Constable Pickering, who was in charge of delivering the prisoner to the gaol at Lancaster Castle. I did not catch his eye: he was occupied watching for any mischief coming from the besieging crowd.

I stepped back inside and shut the door, ashamed that I had been tempted to join the throng following the wagon as it trundled its way towards the town bar. No, I would not run with a mob of idlers, moralists and sensation-seekers, on the chance something should happen. I went into my inner room and sat down reflecting on the image of Fanny Kirby as I had just seen her, standing so tall and brave. I did not believe she had done anything to deserve this. It had been done to her first of all by Ambrose Parr, the one pressing the charge of murder. But although he remained the prosecutor, the business had now passed out of his control and into that of the magistrates and at last the assize judge. It had never been, and never would be, in Fanny's control.

I think of myself as a sensible man. I am not an idler. I have a moral sense all right, but I try not to moralize. Yet in most of us there is something of the sensation-seeker and I am no different. So now, in a sudden impulse impossible to suppress, I jumped to my feet. I *would* go down and see her on her way.

I hurried into the front office and from there to the front door which I once again pulled open.

'Mind the office, Furzey,' I said over my shoulder as the door slammed behind me.

I leaped down the steps into Cheap Side and hurried to the top of Friar Gate. I could see the back of the crowd dancing along, shouting and singing, as they followed after Fanny Kirby's progress towards the town bar and the northern road. Quickening my step I soon caught them up.

There was a place in the surface of the street, close to the top end of Friar Gate, where the paving had sunk in, making a sharp-edged hole. The oxen passed over this without difficulty but then I watched as one of the front wagon wheels smash down into it, striking hard against the edge of the paving, breaking its spokes and splitting apart. With that the wagon lurched forward and to one side and with a crack the front axle broke.

The wagoner and constable climbed down and looked doubtfully at the damage. It was clear that they would not be going on to Lancaster until the axle and broken wheel were replaced. Pickering picked out a proper-looking person among the spectators.

'We'll need a cartwright,' he told her. 'Can you tell me the nearest?'

'Aye, sir, that'd be Mr Kirby a few minutes along there, up Moor Lane.'

'Is his work good?'

'He's the best in town, so they say.'

It was not until she said this that the woman made the connection between the girl in the wagon and the cartwright. As soon as she did she quickly put her hand to her mouth, but had no time to mention it to Constable Pickering for he had already turned away. Having ordered the carter to guard the prisoner, he was striding away towards Dodson Kirby's house and yard.

I went into the Swan Inn which stood on Friar Gate just at the point where the wrecked wagon lay. I climbed the stairs to the common room on the first floor and, ordering some ale, sat in the window immediately overlooking the scene. The bed of the wagon was so tilted and askew that Fanny was brought forward by the wagoner to the box, where at least she could sit. She remained very contained and quiet, though the crowd shouted many taunts, lascivious suggestions and other provocative things at her.

Ten minutes passed before Pickering returned with Dodson Kirby, neither yet knowing that the wagon's cargo was Dodson Kirby's daughter. Without taking any notice of her, Kirby knelt to inspect the damage. But he lifted his head with a jerk when he heard his daughter's voice above his head. With the window open I could hear every word.

'Dad, for shame!' she said. 'Shall you mend the cart that is carrying your daughter happen to her death?'

Dodson Kirby stood up and looked at her, perplexed.

'What? Is it you, daughter?'

'Aye, it's me. They take me to Lancaster Castle to be trialled for what I never did.'

Kirby took off his cap and scratched the back of his neck.

'Well I'll be oystered! Fanny, love!'

He turned to the constable.

'It's my daughter, Mr Constable. What a bad chance is this, and a pickle! My own daughter.'

Pickering looked from Dodson to Fanny and back again as if to verify the family resemblance for himself.

'Oh, aye,' he said, 'she's Fanny Kirby all right, but I never—'

'My daughter!' said Dodson Kirby. 'Where are you taking her all shackled up like this?'

'To Lancaster Gaol, Mr Kirby, on the charge of a murder, and the law demands you must help us by fettling up this wagon-wheel and axle, so we may get on our way.'

Kirby had still not shaken off his profound perplexity.

'I don't know, I—'

'Dad! You'll never help them, will you?' said Fanny loudly. She wanted everybody to hear. 'You'll never do all they want, so they can take me away to die.'

Doddy now scratched his forehead. He frowned.

'Fanny,' he said, 'you and your sister so we've heard've gone to live in the proper Babylon which is Liverpool. And in that city of perdition you gave yourselves over to nothing but sin and ungodliness.'

'That was before,' she said. 'I'm not the same now. I am not a whore no more.'

Her tone was not pleading. She spoke as someone stating a fact.

'I am a respectable maid and house-servant. And innocent.'

'Innocent? Did your actions in that hellish city sit well with that beautiful word? No, say I. You were a whore, daughter, as was your sister. There is no getting away from that. Confession of sin and repentance – them's the only way.'

As happens with self-important people, what begins as a private word turns into a public announcement. A word of advice becomes a sermon. And so, though he had begun quietly, his voice gathered strength and resonance. He mounted an imaginary pulpit. He could be heard right across the street and beyond.

'And have we not also heard that poor Barbara your sister's since paid the devil's price, to her mother's and my great pain. Shall you, then, not suffer the same? Shall you not perish on the word of an earthly judge for your undoubted sins that you owe repentance for to a higher judge?'

At any moment words carved from biblical stone would be falling from his tongue. But now Fanny's mother came bustling up. Pushing through the throng she reached up and began to stroke Fanny's cheek, and pat her hand whispering to her, the sight of which entirely dried up her husband's discourse. Doddy Kirby's granite heart melted to the softness of wet putty and tears came to his eyes.

'Nay, lass,' he said. 'Nay. Family is family. I couldn't find it in my heart to mend this broken wagon, whatever trouble you've come into.'

I had drained my mug and headed for the stair. I was just at the bottom step when Constable Pickering entered the inn.

'Mr Pickering,' I said. 'I hear you may be delayed here in Preston.'

'Mr Cragg! How are you?'

We shook hands.

'You've seen the state of the wagon?' he said. 'I have sent for another cartwright and Lord knows how long it will all take, though it's a certainty we can't reach Lancaster before dark. So we're here for the night. I must ask the landlord for a boy to bring me a message to the mayor. We have to make arrangements for the safe disposal of the prisoner, not to mention the oxen.'

'The House of Correction is a few minutes' walk away. Let me show you where. If there is an empty cell Arnold Limb who keeps it will hardly refuse you the use. Then you must allow me to give you dinner, and a bed for yourself tonight.'

So it was arranged. We left the wagoner to wait for the cart-wright and took Fanny down to the House of Correction, which was partly built out of the ruins of the old friary. Limb was obliging and a dry if not remarkably comfortable cell was found for the prisoner. She was still holding herself proudly as she went in. Limb promised to victual her and give her water.

'Make it ale,' I said, handing him some pennies. 'And give her warm bedding besides.'

Pickering returned to the broken wagon and I hurried back to the office. There was no time to spare. It was past three and I had work for myself and Furzey to be done by the day's end. First, I made Furzey do me a copy of the records of the hearing into Miss Pettifer's death, which from habit he grumbled about.

'What are we doing this for?'

'To help poor Fanny Kirby,' I said. 'She will stay the night at the House of Correction and I aim to see her before she leaves in the morning. I want her to have something for her defence.'

'I don't know why you take the trouble,' said Furzey. 'She's as good as hung already, with Judge Lacey sitting. When a woman's in the dock, there's no man with a harder nose.'

This was true. It was well known on the Northern Circuit that Jethro Lacey's nose was hard as granite.

'He's low-born, of course,' Furzey went on. 'That makes him resemble the elder Cato even more. His father was no better than a Leicestershire butcher.'

'A butcher's son, is he?' I said, marvelling at my clerk's know-ledge of judicial genealogy. 'Well, I must do what I can for Fanny anyway.'

I sat down to write a memorandum about the case. I gave an account of the inquest into Miss Pettifer's death at Ormskirk, and stated my opinion that the jury's verdict of accidental death had been a true one, making me firmly convinced that Fanny Kirby had no guilty part in her mistress's death. I offered myself as a witness in the trial, and said if there happened to be anything more I could do to assist in the conduct of the case I would be very willing.

There was little chance that my offer to give evidence would be taken up. Some readers may not be familiar with the criminal assizes, so I should explain that all witnesses are for the prosecution. The only voice to be heard on behalf of the accused is that of the accused herself, when she gives a statement and may be questioned by the judge. She is not allowed to call on any witnesses in her defence. Therefore, though it was possible, if the judge was looking for mitigation, that he might want to question me, it only would be as part of the prosecution process. Judge Lacey was not one who often applied mitigation. Yet with these papers I was determined to try. When the memorandum and Furzey's copy were ready I signed, sealed and bundled them up and took them directly to the House of Correction to present to Fanny Kirby.

'Mr Cragg, I won't say I'm not grateful. I do believe in myself, yet it is a comfort to know there is someone else who does.'

'These papers are important because they tell of a previous legal process about Miss Pettifer's death, an inquest. There was no suspicion of murder in it. Can you read, Fanny?'

'Yes, of course. Do you not think my mother didn't make sure of that?'

'Ah yes, I spoke to your mother quite recently. I know she is an avid reader. So Fanny, this is what you must do: read these papers, and remember the details. You can mention them in your statement to the court. But you must also make sure the judge has them, so that when you talk about them, he knows what you are talking about. There will be very little time, and you must be concise. Most trials are finished and done with in less than half an hour. You will need to try to explain why Mr Ambrose Parr has so much wanted to prosecute you. If you can impute a bad motive to him, that will help you a lot.'

'Well, he knows all about me, and my past way of living. He thinks he can make people believe anything about me. But then there is what I know about him. So he's not to be hasty of what he says about me.'

'What is it you know, Fanny?'

'No, I have told nobody of it and I won't tell you. But in time I will, if I have to. I'll tell the judge.'

'Well, Fanny, your case must be considered by the grand jury first, you know. They may release you without any need for the judge. I intend to try to persuade them to do so.'

'Thank you kindly. Will you also speak to Mr Parr for me? Ask him to come and see me in private. Perhaps we may reach an agreement.'

'That Mr Parr will withdraw his prosecution?'

'Yes.'

'It is worth trying. I shall write to him. But in the meantime I urge you—'

I tried to press the papers on her once again but she was adamant in her refusal to take them. So I gave her some money and got up to leave.

'Will you be there, Mr Cragg? If my try with Mr Parr doesn't work, I mean.'

'Would you like that, Fanny?'

'I would. You and your clever doctor friend. It will be good to get myself off in open court and prove him wrong and a villain.'

TWENTY-TWO

A fortnight before the assizes at Lancaster I was forced to take to my bed with an ague, for which I was given a milk diet and a bitter-tasting draught made up by Luke Fidelis. Whether either of these did me any good I couldn't say, but the fever took its course and by the time Fanny Kirby's trial in Lancaster was a week away I was up and about, though by no means fully restored.

On my first visit to the office after my recovery I asked Furzey if we had heard from Ambrose Parr.

'He has answered your letter – here.'

Furzey produced a letter with the seal broken.

'You've read it, I see.'

'Of course. While you were upstairs between life and death I had to, as best I could, manage your affairs.'

I had written to Parr to remind him of the inquest's verdict on Miss Pettifer, and to tell him that I considered his prosecution of Fanny to be both unjustified and unlikely to succeed.

I happened to see the girl here at Preston when she was being brought on her way to Lancaster. I must tell you that she stoutly maintains her innocence and she feels that should you be prepared to meet her she might persuade you to withdraw the prosecution even at this late stage . . .

I had thought carefully how to word the rest of this sentence. My idea was to convey to Parr the possibility that Fanny might make public something that would embarrass him – something that of course I myself didn't know the import of.

. . . and she feels that you persecute her, for a reason only you yourself can know. I urge you to reconsider the action, if only to prevent any untoward matters being spoken of in open court that you may not wish to be spoken of.

I looked quickly through Parr's answer, and then sat down to read it again, brief though it was.

Dear Cragg,
I am grateful for your care in the matter of Fanny Kirby. Having spoken to her I am surprised you have not formed the conclusion that she is a vixen full of lying and deceit. Anything she may say about me will proceed from childish malice and will be refuted with ease. She has no credit, being a harlot, and no judge will believe any word of hers. I am, Sir, &c. Ambrose Parr.

'What do you think, Furzey? Whatever information Fanny has concerning Mr Parr, he is not afraid of it.'

'He is not,' said Furzey, 'the reason being in the closing words of his letter. And I don't mean "I am, Sir, &c."'

I read the words aloud.

'*No judge will believe any word of hers.* That depends on the judge, in the end. Though I admit Fanny's history will not tell in her favour.'

'You should not go to Lancaster, Titus,' said Elizabeth, the same day. 'You are still not well enough.'

'But I must. I've promised. And Luke assures me I'll be safe in another few days and won't relapse. Besides he will be there himself, and can advise me.'

'But you are still weak. You must certainly not ride. If you insist on going, *I* insist you take the mail coach.'

'If I agree to that, will you come with me?'

'Good Lord, no! I find nothing entertaining in a trial. It's all pomp and prejudice.'

'Then come for a change of scene. Lancaster is lively during assizes week. There is no need to attend any trial, as there will be assemblies and society to enjoy.'

'Yes. I don't know. Shall I, after all?'

Elizabeth rarely dithered but, for a few more minutes, she did so now. Questions for and against were weighed, and finally she made up her mind.

'I must call upon Mr Talboys, then, as I shall need a new dress if we are to go to assemblies. There is just enough time for him to make something up if I see him today.'

'If that is the price of your company at Lancaster,' I said, 'you shall have the dress, and a hat to go with it.'

So it was arranged. She went out immediately to Friar Gate to order the dress at Talboys' shop. Meanwhile I walked over to the coaching office. I found that I could get two inside seats to Lancaster on the day before the opening of the assize. They were in the midday coach that departed the White Bull Inn every day except Sunday. I also sent ahead to secure accommodation at an inn and I felt lucky to be found a bedroom. During the assizes week Lancaster would be full to bursting with visitors.

The mail coach was a six-seater, so that Elizabeth and I had four travelling companions. Two of these were sisters from Rochdale. Mrs Adcock was about thirty-five, plump and talkative, while her sister, Alicia Simpson, with a very much longer and narrower nose, was younger, bonier, and almost silent. Elizabeth chatted with them – in effect, with Mrs Adcock – and soon established that Miss Alicia was attending the assizes in the hope of netting a husband, with her sister whistling for her cause. Their prey was to be some clever but penniless young man sufficiently desperate for money that he'd take the bait the Rochdale ladies were casting on the water. That bait was not Miss Alicia's physical charms.

'She's got her portion from our late father,' said Mrs Adcock, 'and it's quite a tidy sum, is it not, dear?'

The pair were veterans of many a marriage market, having plied their wares without success at regimental musters, Oxford's degree days, Buxton spa, assemblies in the excellent Rooms at York and the instalment of that city's latest archbishop.

'The ideal would be to get a bright young man in one of the professions, you see. One who may rise high in the ranks but who is at present rather short of funds. In this case, a likely young barrister who might be carried – who knows? – all the way to the bench at the Royal Court of Justice in due time. All he needs is a little ready money just to get him into a good set of chambers and help him on his way. We see it as an investment.'

One of the two gentlemen completing the coach's half dozen spent his time studying a printed sheet, which he had just bought off a hawker in the Preston marketplace. When I asked what it was, he thrust his paper under my nose.

'It is the calendar, sir, for the assizes, in trial-order. Have a look for yourself. I am surprised you do not have one of your own.'

The paper had been run up by an enterprising printer for the use of the public. It pointed out how much of interest each assize case held, with the celebrity of the accused and the sensational nature of the crime being the two greatest indicators. The outstanding trial, placed first in order and taking up as much space on the sheet as the rest put together, was to be that of the celebrated highwayman Shamus Fingal O'Higgins, also known as Jim Fingers, or the Lancashire Turpin, who had been finally taken after eluding capture during a bout of crime that lasted two or more years. Having had my own past dealings with O'Higgins, I read with interest the tale of his criminal career. The final arrest was given as follows.

> O'Higgins at last overplayed his Hand when he robbed the Coach of the Countess of Derby, for he did take not only Her Ladyship's Gold and Jewels, but also with great effrontery her Carriage Horses, whereupon he said he was loath to see a Countess a-walking home so he sat her Ladyship on to the

Rump of his own Mount and himself rode her to the Gate of
her Hall at Knowsley, where he took her down with much
False Chivalry such as Highwaymen are often wont to employ.
Unfortunately for Fingers a party of His Lordship's Men were
gathered nearby and upon hearing their Mistress crying out
did run to her Aid and quickly overwhelmed the Dog, though
two were wounded when O'Higgins discharged his weapons.
It is fully expected he will hang.

The author's choice of words – *rump* for example, and *rode* – gave
scope for ribaldry and this (from what I knew of O'Higgins) would
have only delighted the man. Looking further down the list of
malefactors I soon located the name of Fanny Kirby, under which
I read the following brief note.

Arraigned for Petty-treason viz. the horrid Murder of her
Employer and Benefactrix this Servant girl is a former Harlot
from the notorious streets of Liverpool and has had the
Knowledge of Sailors, Rakes and Gamesters in those Parts
from whom she no doubt learned the Arts of Homicide and
other wicked Practices.

I showed this to Elizabeth.

'What did I say about the assizes, husband?' she whispered
when she'd read it. 'The prejudice starts before one even reaches
Lancaster.'

She looked over the sheet as a whole.

'Oh!' she said, seeing the leading article. 'I had forgot Jim
Fingers was taken. A merry dance he led us last year!'

'Well, he has had his day now, so it seems.'

'I wonder if that woman is with him still. Perhaps we shall see
her at Lancaster.'

That woman! She had near bewitched me, with her red hair and
white skin.

'Perhaps we shall,' was all I said.

The owner of the sheet was impatient to have it back and,
yielding it up, I turned my attention to the other gentleman who
was with us. He said not a word to anyone, and seemed enclosed
behind his thick beard. He looked out of the window for some

time but caught my eye momentarily while glancing briefly around inside.

'Are you going to Lancaster to attend the trials, sir?' I said.

'No.'

'You are perhaps a citizen of the town, then?'

'No.'

'Ah! So what does bring you there, if I may ask?'

'Cricket,' he said.

I thought I had misheard.

'Cricket, you say?'

'Yes. I go only to play at cricket.'

And he shut his eyes and composed himself to sleep.

'That other fellow in the coach,' I said to Elizabeth when we stopped at Garstang, and had all gone into the inn for refreshment. 'Either I have seen him somewhere, or else he looks like someone I've seen. I cannot think who.'

'I don't know him.'

We resumed the journey and as we bumped along I thought about the likely fate of O'Higgins, and the possibility of seeing again the woman who had risked all to follow the highwayman. How would she manage, I wondered, if her man swung? My thoughts then circled back to the case of Fanny Kirby. I had had no notification that my testimony would be required in court, so I had decided on a different strategy during my time in Lancaster: I would beard old Lacey at the judge's lodgings. He would have to listen to me.

We trundled into Lancaster at half-past five in the evening and stopped in the yard of our inn. As we gathered our boxes from the roof of the coach, I noticed that as the cricketer stooped to pick up his valise, a flute protruded from his inside coat pocket – and suddenly I knew who he was.

Lancaster was not then a modernized town. True there was a fairly new hospital but many of the buildings were in need of attention, if not demolition. And yet a new breed of Lancastrian was emerging in the shadow of King John's great castle: traders sailing in and out of the River Lune estuary to the Indies with woollens and hardware, and bringing back sugar and tobacco. It was these men who led the way in Lancaster's society, and to them was owed the conversion of a house into a set of quite serviceable assembly rooms a short walk from the castle.

Elizabeth and I walked there, having purchased tickets from the landlord of the Golden Anchor, where we lodged. House martins darted around above our heads, and the encroaching stillness of evening still retained a residue of the day's warmth. We had just presented the tickets at the entrance and gone in when I caught sight of a lawyer I knew, by the name of Stephen Dinkin. He was standing with his wife just inside the entrance.

'Titus Cragg!' he exclaimed, coming towards us with a broad smile. 'This is a pleasant surprise. You know my wife, Anne?'

Dinkin was a man of my own age, a popular attorney with a successful practice in Lancaster, who also happened to be my counterpart as coroner in the northern duchy.

'What brings you to our assizes week, Cragg?'

'The interest of a young woman, Fanny Kirby. She is from a Preston family and is arraigned for petty treason.'

'Oh!' said Anne Dinkin, clapping her hand to her mouth. 'Did she murder her husband?'

'No, she is accused of killing her employer,' I said. 'But it is very doubtful, in my opinion. She is prosecuted by Ambrose Parr of Liverpool.'

'I know the man,' said Dinkin. 'An unusual fellow but clever enough, it seems.'

'He was attorney to the dead lady, and is determined to convict the girl for his client's death. It does not hold water and I'm doing what I can to see it defeated.'

'One fine day,' said Dinkin, 'defendants will win the right to have their attorney speak for them in court. We all know it must come.'

'All except our law-makers, it seems. As it stands Fanny must match her wits against a learned counsel.'

'With your sage advice she may come through, Cragg. Shall we go into the dancing room?'

We moved from the ante-room into the much larger ballroom. Most of the throng was found, either dancing or chatting beside the walls while tapping their toes to the music, which was produced by a small string band energetically sawing at their instruments but making only a thin and reedy sound against the steady rumble and trill of talk that filled the room. These assemblies had become in my own lifetime marks of how far society in a town or city advances. It is not I find a matter only of indoor social pleasures, to be had at any season. The price of tickets means poor people are excluded, so that assemblies are the preserve, and the glue, of the polite world.

Almost immediately Dinkin and his lady joined the dance, I looked along the wall and touched Elizabeth's arm.

'Elizabeth, do you see the overdressed fellow down there talking to the bored-looking clergyman? That's Ambrose Parr.'

'The one prosecuting poor Fanny?'

'The same. Now notice the ladies just behind him.'

'It's Mrs Adcock and her sister. I wonder how goes their quest for a young man to suit Miss Alicia.'

'I propose we nudge her in a different direction. You remember that I told you how anxious Mr Parr is to find himself a wife?'

'Oh! Mr Parr and Alicia Simpson? She won't be interested, surely. She is set on the notion of a likely young lawyer – as an investment, she said.'

'It doesn't look as if she has found any. This is worth trying. Anything that might distract Parr from Fanny's case is worth trying.'

Elizabeth was game. She said she would go by herself to speak to the ladies.

'I will prime them with some information about Mr Parr. Then after a minute you come up to him, and on your signal I'll bring the ladies up for an introduction.'

I let her go ahead and then went up to Ambrose Parr. He greeted me not warmly, but warmly enough to allow the clergyman to make his relieved excuses.

'How do you progress in your search for a wife?' I said when the reverend had gone.

'Not well. Not well. I continue to offer my wares, but without generating any business. I proposed marriage to a lady only last night but she wouldn't have me.'

I commiserated with all appearance of sincerity.

'Tell me, how many times have you asked for a lady's hand since we met last?'

'A dozen, at least. Yet I persist. My old father used to tell me that he put the question to forty-nine women until he found one willing. My mother. They were exceedingly happy together so I follow the same system.'

I glanced towards Elizabeth and caught her eye. She touched Alicia's forearm and gently shepherded them towards us.

'Mr Parr, may I present my wife, Elizabeth?' I said. 'And Mrs Adcock and Miss Alicia Simpson of Rochdale?'

Parr's eyes lit up.

'Ah! Miss Simpson!' he said. 'Delighted. Quite delighted.'

He took her hand and bowed low over it, his lips stopping just short of a kiss. Then he gave Mrs Adcock a perfunctory nod before returning his attention to the younger sister.

Elizabeth and I chatted to Mrs Adcock, enquiring whether she had found suitable accommodation, and such matters. I kept half an ear on how Parr was progressing with Alicia Simpson. He was speaking earnestly, with an ingratiating smile, his face pushed forward towards hers. She was saying very little, and did not seem much gratified by the attention.

The rest of the evening took its course. Parr danced with Miss Alicia. I danced with Mrs Adcock. Elizabeth danced with Parr. By the end I had had quite enough of their company.

As we walked home Elizabeth was quiet, thinking. Finally she said, 'I believe I have got to the bottom of Ambrose Parr.'

'In what way?'

'In what he likes most in the world. In what drives him.'

'Very well. How did you get to the bottom of him?'

'Oh, just by talking, and listening.'

'It's not too hard, then, as all he talks about is the female sex. And his love of marriage. He has a monomania for it. He told me he would like to be a Mussulman in order to have half a dozen wives.'

'No, that isn't it. I admit he talks about them a good deal but still, it isn't women and it isn't marriage that drives Mr Parr.'

'What, then?'

'It is money, Titus. Secretly, that is what he worships. That is what he thinks about from morning until night. That is what drives him.'

TWENTY-THREE

Next morning, the Tuesday, and with still twenty-four hours to go before the trials would start, I set off to carry out my stratagem of seeing the judge in his lodgings in Church Street. The lodgings, a house reserved entirely for the comfort of the visiting judiciary, is a fine building, six windows wide with its front door behind a gate that I approached up double steps from the street. Judge Lacey received me in the salon, a sizeable panelled room warmed by a fire of aromatic logs.

The judge was sallow and sunken-cheeked, but with a lively gleaming eye. He made no attempt to play the host but, with a sigh, went straight to the point.

'I suppose you are petitioning. Are you petitioning? I have scores of petitioners daily, all of whom I turn away. I have made an exception of you, Mr Clegg, because you hold a public office. I believe, that of coroner?'

He said it in such a way as to suggest it was a word that rarely crossed his lips, so low did it rank in the legal hierarchy.

'It's Cragg, my lord. Titus Cragg.'

'Oh yes? Who is your suit in favour of?'

'Her name is Fanny Kirby. She comes before your lordship on Thursday.'

'What of her?'

'If your lordship has cast an eye over the papers in the case—'

'Papers? Why the devil would I look at any papers beforehand? I have a prosecuting attorney to do that for me.'

'So you have, my lord. However may I give you a short summary? The case is over the death of a Miss Pettifer of Aughton near Ormskirk in Lancashire. When Miss Pettifer died I conducted the formal inquest, and—'

I was interrupted by the double doors being swung open by a footman. A lady sailed in, a large lady swathed in silk with pearls and feathers. Having looked me up and down with an air of utmost disapproval, she addressed the judge.

'Husband, have I discovered you in the act of interviewing petitioners? Shame on you, sir! A petitioner is in general a very low species. They will only muddle you. Have nothing to do with them.'

Lacey, already lean enough, seemed to shrink even further, to deflate indeed, under the penetration of his wife's gaze.

'This gentleman is from Ormskirk, my dear,' he said. 'Mr Clough.'

Lady Lacey turned towards me again.

'Ormskirk, is he? About that case of petty treason that my brother sent up to us, I suppose.'

'Your brother, Lady Lacey?' I said.

'Yes of course! My brother Arthur Dolland. He has sent us some grubby housemaid to be tried for killing the good lady that she worked for in one of the nearby villages. Don't look so stupid, man! You must know brother Dolland, if you come from Ormskirk.'

'Yes, as it happens I do know him, though I'm not—'

'Then you will know of his probity and good sense. I suggest therefore that you go on your way. There is really no profit in petitioning on behalf of any case sent up by my brother, as the parties are invariably guilty.'

I realized then that to persist in this line would do more harm than good. The judge, while he ruled the court, was himself ruled by his wife. I did not even bring the papers I had prepared out of their linen bag. I merely stood up and bowed at the judge and his lady.

'I am very much obliged to your lordship for seeing me. And to you also, my lady.'

I found myself walking backwards whilst bowing, as one does (I am told) at a royal court. Mr Justice Lacey may have been the son of a Leicestershire butcher, but there were few practical limits to the pretensions of a judge who stood as eminent as Lacey, not excluding the expectation of being treated as a prince. When I was in arm's reach of the doors I straightened up. I heard voices on the other side, which were evidently approaching, one the voice of a lady and the other the gruff tones of an elderly man, accompanied by a rhythmical squeaking sound which I could not account for.

'No, daughter, no! Don't lead us in there, it is the dining room.

That is the salon. Don't you know your way around this house yet?'

'I am sorry, father. I remember now.'

Both doors now swung wide simultaneously, by the action of a footman stationed outside, and I saw the reason for the squeaking. The mountainous form of Arthur Dolland in his Bath chair was bearing down on me, pushed by another footman. His daughter Frances caught him up in time for them both to enter the room together. I stepped smartly to one side to avoid being run over.

At this point neither of the Dollands were taking any notice of me. Arthur Dolland greeted the Laceys with much warmth and, having been rolled up to the fire, allowed himself to be kissed on both bag-like cheeks by his sister Lady Lacey. At the same time Mrs Dolland accepted the desiccated compliments of Judge Lacey, and the four of them began to exchange pleasantries about bedroom accommodation and washing facilities, as hosts and newly arrived house-guests generally do. But after a few moments, as I was still standing there waiting to take my leave, Frances Dolland turned and looked at me.

'Why, it is the coroner! This is a surprise. What brings you to the judge's lodgings, Mr Cragg?'

I stepped forward and gave her a slight bow but before I could say anything Lacey butted in.

'Do you know this fellow, Frances? He's the devil of a petitioner. Wants to change the course of the trial Arthur sent up to us. Pettifer. Killed by a tart by the name of Kirby.'

Hearing these names, Arthur Dolland turned his head.

'Well, I hope you're not entertaining it, Lacey. She must burn, you know. As she deserves. I haven't come all this way to see her acquitted.'

'Do not worry, brother,' said Lady Lacey. 'We are all agreed on that. Your judgement in the case will not be impugned and the whore's petty treason will be punished to the fullest extent of the law.'

Lacey now rubbed his hands in a gesture of relish.

'Certainly it will, Arthur. I haven't known you for forty years to impugn you now. By God I haven't.'

'Have you come to Lancaster on purpose to see Fanny Kirby tried?' I said to Mrs Dolland.

'Oh yes,' she said. 'My father insists on seeing the cases he sends up to the assizes through to their conclusion. But of course we enjoy the round also, you know. Assemblies, dinners, the cricket and of course the Assizes Ball on Saturday.'

Lady Lacey took her arm and swung her around to face the men at the fireplace. With another bow, which only the footmen saw, I took my leave.

Reaching the inn I found that Luke Fidelis had at last arrived. I sat with him in the parlour and told him of my interview with the judge and his lady.

'I suppose that means Fanny Kirby will die,' he said. 'It is a sorry thing when a judge makes up his mind in advance, without taking so much as a glance at the papers.'

'I thought you wanted her executed.'

'No, I want a true trial,' he said. 'Not a predetermined theatrical presentation.'

'That is a good description, Luke. It will be like a play with the words already written and the end inevitable.'

I felt plunged into gloom. My faith in the law had never sunk so low. I could not even raise a smile when Elizabeth came in from the street, carrying a few purchases that she had made in the marketplace.

'That's a long face you're showing the world, Titus,' she said.

'Arthur Dolland is here, Lizzie. He means to see Fanny Kirby's conviction in person.'

'The wicked old man. We must be thankful he will not conduct the trial.'

'He might as well. He stays at the judge's lodgings with the Laceys, because the judge's wife Lady Lacey is Arthur Dolland's sister and she rules Judge Lacey in everything, including it seems his rulings. She is the power behind the bench.'

Elizabeth placed her packages on the table and touched my arm with a tender gesture. I grasped her hand.

'Poor Fanny,' she said.

I sighed.

'Poor Fanny indeed. Her only real hope will be before she comes before Lacey, if the grand jury decide there is no case against her. That's remote. They almost never dismiss a capital case.'

She let go of my hand and gathered up her purchases.

'Well, we must hope. I will take these upstairs I think.'

When she had gone, I said, 'I must tell you, Luke, that we had an interesting companion on the road coming here. I was sure I'd seen him somewhere but it was not until I noticed he had a flute in his pocket that I placed him.'

Quick as a cat, Fidelis read the clue.

'Did he have a thick black beard?'

'He did.'

'Well, well. So Garland's servant is in town. I wonder why.'

'To play at cricket, he told me. He had walked away into the crowd before I could speak to him again. I wonder what really brought him here.'

'Being Garland's man is what brought him.'

'Well, he *used* to be Garland's man. Is he still?'

'He must be. Garland himself will not risk leaving the jurisdiction of Orsmkirk, so he has sent the man as his eyes and ears: Charles Watt is his spy.'

'But why does he need one?'

'Remember, Titus, now that Smisby is dead nothing remains between Garland's wife – and therefore Garland himself – and the tontine money.'

He held up his hand with thumb and index finger half an inch apart.

'Garland is this close to getting his hands on it. As he put Fanny Kirby up to killing Miss Pettifer, he knows she may peach on him in return for her life. So he has sent Watt here to stop that happening.'

'How can he? Fanny is secure in the castle gaol.'

'There is much he can do. She's allowed visitors. He can come at her that way.'

'And say what? Offer her what?'

'Oh, persuade her that she will receive a pardon and be transported to America. There she can start her life up again.'

'No, Luke, it will not do. That is the feeblest of ploys. You cannot be sure she would be pardoned, not unless she peaches, which would be the one thing Garland doesn't want to happen – that is, if your hypothesis is true, which as you know I don't think it is.'

'We will see. If Charles does visit the girl in gaol, that would prove me right and you wrong, Titus. And I cannot see why he is here, except to do that.'

'But Fanny has nothing to say of the kind that you suggest. I saw her in Preston. She passed the night in the House of Correction on her way here and we talked about her defence. She told me nothing about being suborned by Garland, and nothing about peaching on him. She relies entirely on attacking Parr for falsely prosecuting her.'

Fidelis smiled.

'We must await the verdict of time, Titus. Father Time knows all and will judge between us.'

'Speaking of judges, there's something else I haven't told you,' I said. 'Arthur Dolland is accompanied on his visit to the Laceys by his daughter. The last remaining name in the tontine is here in Lancaster.'

'And so, of course, is the man who drew it up,' said Fidelis, and smiled happily.

The assembly in the evening was a less jolly affair than the previous one, the dampener being the presence of Mr Justice Lacey and his lady wife. The orchestra played patriotic marches while the assembly awaited the judge's arrival. In due course and in stately fashion the couple made their entrance. People shuffled out of their way, bowing and applauding while the judge and Lady Lacey looked to left and right with imperious disdain.

Lacey had that afternoon carried out his first duties of the assize, the empanelling of the juries. There were two of these, the grand jury, whose job was to decide which cases were to be answered, and the petty jury, who would try them in front of the judge. Both juries had to be sworn in and given instructions as to their duties and powers, whereupon the grand jury was sent away to decide on the cases listed in the calendar for trial the next morning. Lacey's business was then done for the day. That was when the serious business of trial and retribution would begin.

Remembering what Furzey had said of Lacey being a common butcher's son, and seeing him walk around now like Roman emperor, I thought about the judicial mystique. It derives not from a man's birth, like a king, nor from any quality of his soul, like a preacher or holy man. A judge is an ordinary man appointed to extraordinary power: the power indeed to hand out extreme legalized suffering; and ultimately to ordain someone's torture and death. That is why people talk about him in awe, and why they try to know and understand him. And the more they do this, the more the judge reserves himself and practises aloofness.

'I have just run into a fellow from Liverpool who leads one of the cricket teams,' said Fidelis, as we watched these proceedings. 'He has asked me to turn out with them. One of their players was hit between the eyes by a ball and is seeing double.'

I knew how much Fidelis loved the game, and had heard something of his skill with bat and ball – mainly from his own mouth.

'Who is the captain?'

'Charles Turnbull, a wine importer. We are to play Sir William Lowther's men on Saturday afternoon at Johnson's Field close by the town.'

'It must be the game in which Charles Watt plays.'

'On the other team, I fancy.'

'Elizabeth and I will certainly not miss the chance of applauding as you knock down each fielder with timely hits from your bat, Luke.'

'I wonder if you have grasped how the game is played, Titus. You hit the ball and run. You aim to miss the fielders, not hit them.'

'I suppose there is money at stake.'

'A hundred guineas – and side betting, of course.'

Elizabeth joined us.

'Judge Lacey is not an impressive figure, to my mind,' she said, 'He makes me think of a hen, while Lady Lacey has the look of a prize-fighter. She is much the older of the two.'

'He is a butcher's son, according to Furzey.'

'I wonder how he ever beguiled a rich older woman. He cannot have been much to look at even as a young man.'

We watched them process around the room, receiving the homage of the entire assembly. Elizabeth shook my arm.

'Well, I believe I have it, Titus. Remember the mission of Mrs Adcock and Miss Alicia? I shouldn't be surprised if the Laceys first met at an assize. If Lacey was a young man with promise but no family, and Miss Dolland was like Miss Alicia, an unfavoured rich girl, she could have proposed with enough money for young Lacey to get himself into a prime set of chambers.'

'And made herself a stock-holder in him, with the dividend of directing his judgements as she chooses.'

She turned to Fidelis.

'It is very much what this woman in our coach wants to do, Luke. Find a poor but promising young lawyer and do a marriage deal with him.'

'Unless she falls prey to Ambrose Parr first,' I said.

The assembly broke up at ten o'clock. Many of the guests stood around in the street as it was a warm night, the men smoking and all of them feeling a little looser now that the judge and his lady had retired to the lodgings.

Fidelis, Elizabeth and I chatted for a while to the Dinkins although Elizabeth detached herself for a few moments to speak to Miss Alicia. Finally we said our goodnights and set off to make our way to the inn, by the longer route past the lodgings.

'She says she has refused Mr Parr,' Elizabeth told me in a whisper. 'He came straight out with it in the middle of a gavotte. When they joined up again one or two brangles later she told him no.'

We were on Church Street, with the judge's lodgings about fifty yards ahead, when there was a commotion among the party walking in front of us. Looking more carefully I saw that a Bath chair had been upset and Fidelis and I ran forward to see what had happened. The figure of a man ran away into the darkness of a side street as we arrived. The chair was Arthur Dolland's conveyance and it was lying on its side with a free wheel revolving uselessly in the air. Arthur himself lay dazed on the ground, attended by the servant who had been pushing him. Beyond lay the form of a lady, senseless, unattended and unmoving on the cobbles. Fidelis knelt beside her, then looked up at me.

'This is Frances Dolland,' he said. 'And I would say she has been bludgeoned.'

TWENTY-FOUR

On Wednesday morning the sky was cornflower-blue, with clouds scudding high and white before a warm wind. Drawing open the bedroom curtains for the first time I wondered how the eye of the highwayman Jim 'Fingers' O'Higgins would be viewing this new day so pleasantly framed – supposing his cell at the castle had a window. Today the criminal trials would begin and O'Higgins was first on the list. On the previous day the grand jury had found no reason why he should not stand in the dock and today his ultimate fate would be pronounced.

The timing of O'Higgins's trial was not accidental. His crimes were so notorious that Lacey wanted to get the case out of the way early, before the fickle public could act on its feelings. As he knew quite well, riots surrounding the arraignment of a popular highwayman are not rare during assizes week, and O'Higgins had for some time been a hero to the herd.

Many people, among whom are the whole of the clergy, deplore the heroizing of criminals by the common people, but for my part I perfectly understood it. I didn't mean violent urban blackguards such as the presumed thief who had attacked the Dollands the night before. I meant highway robbers, who the common people are quite safe from, as they never travel between towns carrying their valuables (assuming they have any). So O'Higgins and his kind rob only the rich, which the commons, if anything, rather approve. Few think the rich deserve their wealth and most enjoy seeing it, or some of it, taken off them from time to time. Highway robbery is usually quite a peaceful crime – the theft of a horse, a few jewels, watches and silver snuffboxes. It does not upset the natural order of society, but the common people think it salutary to discomfort the wealthy from time to time.

I was thinking about this alone, having come down to breakfast ahead of Elizabeth, when Fidelis joined me from outside.

'I have been at the judge's lodgings all night sitting with Mrs

Dolland,' he said. 'She was within a hair's breadth of dying two or three times but I think she is saved now, or for the moment at least.'

'How is old Arthur Dolland?'

'He is unhurt. His fluent curses and calls for vengeance have convinced me of that. But her skull is cracked and she has not properly awoken. We may find out more about what happened when she does. Well, I am going to bed. What are you doing this morning? Have you tickets for O'Higgins?'

'No. I have other business.'

The assizes trials were for ticket-holders only. I did not have one for O'Higgins, unlike my clerk Furzey, whom I'd already seen in Lancaster this morning. He had come to the inn wearing a greatcoat and long-distance boots, having walked from Preston overnight with a friend, another clerk, with the intention of watching the trial. He told me he would come back when judgement was given and I'd have a full account.

Having met O'Higgins during the rebels' incursion into Lancashire the previous winter, I did want to know how the case would end. As readers of my memoir of that time will know I was also interested in O'Higgins's beautiful red-headed mistress, who was bound to be present in court. I hoped Furzey would tell me how she looked and conducted herself, but the truth was I did not myself want to look on her again.

It was the case of Fanny Kirby that pressed on me more than O'Higgins, and the grand jury was due to consider the bill of her indictment this same morning. Their job was simply to examine the bill and decide if it were a true bill, in which case Fanny would go to trial, or no true bill, in which case she would be set free. They would not be examining Fanny in person, which was unfortunate because they would surely not hold the same prejudice against her as Judge Lacey, and Judge Lacey would not be in the room to sway them.

Fidelis had left and I was getting ready to go across to the castle when I found Elizabeth standing before me.

'Titus, my dearest, don't you go.'

'But I must see Fanny.'

'No, I mean let me go to Fanny instead of you. She will listen to another woman better than to a man. You men bluster so about knowing better that even when you do know better, we find it impossible to believe you.'

I laughed because I knew I did bluster sometimes, though I tried not to do so with her.

'I must admit I'm stuck for anything new to tell her,' I said. 'But will you go in my place, truly? The cells in the castle are not for faint hearts. There is standing water, buckets of excrement, and rats.'

'Shame on you, Titus Cragg!' she said. 'Have you lived with me all these years thinking I have a faint heart?'

I kissed her.

'No, never, Lizzie. You are more stout-hearted than I am. You are more stout-hearted than King Richard the Lionheart.'

'Then tell me what I must say.'

So Elizabeth ate eggs and drank tea while I took her through my argument that Fanny's best line of defence was a legal one. She must play up the decision of the Ormskirk coroner's court that Miss Pettifer's death was an accident. She must further emphasize that her action of moving towards Miss Pettifer near the windmill sail was to get her out of its way, not to push her under it. Finally she must insist there was no evidence of her wanting Miss Pettifer dead.

'Tell her she won't get the chance to state her case to the grand jury today, but she must make these points tomorrow before Judge Lacey. Oh, and one thing more. Keep an eye out when you go down to her for a fellow with a black beard. He would be likely to try to harm her and you must warn her to be on her guard. His name is Charles Watt.'

I walked with Elizabeth to the castle and saw her inside. A moment later I noticed Philip Porter, the chief clerk of the court, bustling towards the gate carrying a bundle of legal papers from which dangled many seals and coloured ribbons. I greeted him and we chatted about lawyers that we both knew. Then I slipped in a casual question about the membership of the grand jury, and how they are chosen.

'Oh, they are generally the same people for every assize,' he said. 'With Joshua James the print-seller in the chair, as usual.'

He had given me just what I wanted to know. I told him farewell, and hurried away to James's shop, which I had noticed when walking down Penny Street the previous evening. I knew the grand jury was meeting at ten o'clock. I might have just enough time to find its foreman still in his shop.

The door displayed a card saying 'Closed' but I pushed, and it yielded. Inside were numerous tables piled with paper in various sizes, every one an engraving or etching.

'I'm closed,' Joshua James said without turning to look. He was absorbed in adjusting his collar, stock and wig in a mirror.

I did not retreat but stopped by a heap of prints, of which the topmost was entitled *Marriage-à-la-Mode*. I paused to study it, as a customer would. It showed two fathers with a lawyer, all engrossed in doing the deal that will lead to their children's miserable union. On the other side of the room the young couple themselves are seen, showing little interest in one another. The youth preens himself in the glass while the girl turns away and sulks. Another lawyer, whose name if I remembered right is Silvertongue, whispers in her ear. He will soon become her lover and before long her downfall.

'This is not a very flattering view of the legal profession,' I said.

Joshua James turned to see what I was looking at.

'Ah yes, Hogarth!' he said. 'He regards lawyers as parasites upon society.'

He put on a pair of spectacles and came to my side to peer at the picture.

'Lawyers like these feed on the stupidity and cupidity of men, do they not? And of women, which I take it is the point the artist makes in this picture.'

'And yet I am told you are foreman of the grand jury, Mr James, and have much to do with the legal world. It must be hard if you believe this of lawyers.'

'I do the job in spite of the lawyers, sir. The jury is a body of respectable laymen, gentlemen for the most part, that check on the lawyers. I am punctilious. I read all the indictments before our meeting and I expect the other jurors to do the same.'

'There's a girl up today from Preston. Fanny Kirby. What do you make of her case?'

'It's a poor look-out for her.'

'Why is that?'

'His Honour is dead set on convicting her. Told us so at our swearing-in yesterday, when he gave us our charge and reviewed the calendar for our benefit.'

'He took you through the list of prisoners?'

'Oh yes. Not every judge does it but this one – Lacey – he insists on it. We say our oaths and then he lectures us on our duties and tells us what he thinks of each case, one by one. In that of Fanny Kirby he says there is no doubt she must burn.'

'I am surprised that he seeks to direct you, Mr James. It sounds as if Judge Lacey would undermine the independence of the grand jury. Do you always follow his direction?'

James was back at the glass, planting his hat on top of his wig.

'I don't know that it is a direction,' he said. 'More like an opinion. A legal one.'

'Which may always be overridden by common sense, I hope.'

'Oh yes. You may rely on the common sense of the grand jury. Now, I must be on my way to the castle. Our proceedings begin at ten sharp.'

He ushered me outside and, as he locked up, I said, 'Mr James, I am acquainted with Fanny Kirby's family at Preston and they are religious people. Her father is a preacher. Well, I am sure she is innocent. I appeal to you to look dispassionately at her case.'

James turned to me with a look of indignation.

'It is improper of me to listen to a petition on a defendant's behalf, just as it is improper of you to press one on me. If you have a petition there is only one procedure: you must go to the judge. Now I should leave you. If you wish to have the print, please return in the afternoon. I offer special terms for assizes week so it will only cost you five shillings. Good-day, sir.'

He touched his hat and strode away.

I went back to the inn to await Elizabeth's return. Fidelis was there reading the London news.

'I see they have hanged Colonel Townley and his officers,' he said.

Townley had been the leading Lancastrian supporter of Charles Stuart and his rebel Highlanders, and had raised a Jacobite regiment in Manchester during the rebellion. He was made prisoner after failing to hold Carlisle against the Duke of Cumberland after the Prince's retreat into Scotland. Fidelis showed me the account of the traitors' executions, with the awful details of hanging, disembowelment and quartering.

'Pure barbarism,' he said. 'It makes me ashamed.'

Elizabeth returned from her visit to the Castle. She looked pale and troubled. I showed her the newspaper report and she read a few lines before handing it back to me.

'I cannot read this. Those poor men.'

Her face looked shocked.

'Elizabeth, my dearest, are you unwell?' I said.

'I have felt more well, shall I put it that way? You know, there are still rebel prisoners held in the castle here. Not men like Colonel Townley, but common soldiers. I asked if they were up before the assizes for treason, but they're not because they'll never be tried at all, it seems. They'll only be shipped off as slaves to the West Indies, if they don't die first of gaol fever. They are held in unspeakable conditions, conditions of horror, and deliberately so. My stomach is quite turned over from what I saw and heard. And smelled.'

'What of Fanny? Did you see her?'

'Oh, yes. I forget myself. Yes. Fanny received me kindly. She has a dirty cell but not one of the worst.' Elizabeth shuddered. 'Not a dungeon, such as the rebel prisoners are in.'

'Did you speak of her defence at trial?'

'We did. She told me her secret. Ambrose Parr is quite disgraceful. Indeed he is.'

'In what way?'

'She made me promise not to tell anyone, even you. Besides I should find it hard to repeat it. But she believes when the judge and jury hear it from her own lips they will dismiss her case. She is adamant on this point.'

'There must be real thunder in it if it sways Judge Lacey. From everything I hear – and not only from his own mouth – he is quite determined to execute her.'

I described my conversation with Joshua James.

'And will the grand jury comply with Lacey?'

'From what Mr James told me they would be strongly influenced, but he maintains they would also apply the light of common sense.'

'Common sense?' said Fidelis. 'It is a muddy light at best.'

*   *   *

At eleven o'clock we heard the sounds of a crowd up and down Castle Hill. Until now they did not make much noise, but waited in quiet suspense for news of Jim Fingers's trial. Now it seemed that news had come, for they were shouting, clapping and stamping their feet. Here and there a drum or a blown horn was heard.

'What is all that?' I said.

Fidelis sprang from his chair and went out into the street. He came back five minutes later.

'The Lancashire Turpin has been convicted,' he said. 'Lacey has sentenced him to hang.'

'That is much as expected. Why all the rackjack?'

'It seems his supporters, which is most of the common people, had some vain hopes for him and are showing their disappointment.'

'It will not stop them flocking to see him swing on Saturday.'

Lacey still had some seven further cases to hear today, and he ran through them in short order, finishing up by one o'clock, when he meant to eat his dinner and take an afternoon nap. In those two hours Elizabeth Huntley, a dairymaid, was convicted of stealing a butter-churn worth forty-five shillings and two rounds of cheese from her employer, and sentenced to death. John Kenny, guilty of fraud, was given seven years' transportation. Michael Jones, a seasoned horse-thief, received death. Christopher Nicholson, who killed his brother in a brawl, pleaded 'clergy' and was sentenced to transportation to America. Ann Pleasance and Peter Thompson, a pair of bigamists, were ordered to be branded in the hand. And John Morton, a boy of twelve, was sentenced to hang for his incurable habit of housebreaking. The judge had had a very productive and (as I am sure he thought) satisfactory morning.

Then came through some other intelligence, directly from the castle. It was as startling as it was delightful. Furzey and his friend had sat through the morning's business in court, heard the final sentence pronounced, seen the wretched Morton led sobbing down to the cells, and watched Lacey's clerk tucking the black cap away in its velvet bag. All that remained was for the returns from the grand jury on the calendar of next day's business to be announced. The clerk of the court read the indictments out in order and they were each along the expected lines – one true bill after another – until he came to the case of Fanny Kirby. Here, to Furzey's astonishment, the indictment was dismissed. It had been no true bill.

So, with his companion in tow, he had scampered out of court and down the hill to our inn as fast as he could to bring us the news that Fanny was not to be tried after all.

'It's "no true bill"!' Furzey cried struggling to catch his breath. 'She's to be set free. Her ma and pa are there at the gate to meet her and half the gaggle of their family an' all.'

'Did the grand jury hear her after all, then? Was it her story about Parr that swayed them?'

'No, they never examine defendants. They came to the conclusion after questioning one of the prosecution's witnesses, Jack Binns.'

'I don't know him. Oh! Yes I do. He keeps the windmill at Aughton. But this is very strange. Binns didn't see anything of Miss Pettifer's injury. Why did they not question Mary Graves, who did?'

I ordered drinks all round so we could raise our glasses to the wisdom of the grand jury. Even Furzey and Fidelis joined in the toast, though both had previously believed in Fanny's guilt. In Furzey's case this was to be expected: a free drink was a free drink. In Fidelis's I wondered if he had changed his opinion and was glad the girl was set free.

'If you want to know, I am disappointed,' he said. 'We won't now find out if she was planning to peach on Garland.'

'Or on Ambrose Parr.'

'She may still do that. But I can see that in truth the evidence against Fanny was thin as a spider's leg. I am sure for the prosecution to succeed Parr would need the Graves woman to say she saw Isabella Pettifer deliberately pushed. The court won't hear that now.'

'I wonder what Jack Binns can have said to sway them.'

After we had drunk up I proposed we go to the castle and welcome Fanny into freedom. On the way up the hill I took Furzey's elbow and slowed him until we were a little way out of Elizabeth's and Fidelis's earshot.

'By the way, Furzey,' I said. 'Did you happen to see O'Higgins's woman in court?'

'La Sultana, you mean? Oh yes. She was there all right. Lacey kept ogling her and leering at her.'

'How did she take his delivery of the sentence?'

'Without emotion. She was like . . .'

He thought for a moment.

'Like a blank page. I could read nothing there.'

I increased my pace again and reached the edge of the crowd gathered around the castle gate. They were quiet. The news of Fanny's release had put them in an expectant mood.

Fanny came out smiling and they cheered. She was greeted by her parents, who embraced her, the mother swinging her daughter around in delight. The crowd then parted to form a passage through which the family party could come away. But, before they did, the constable appeared in the gate attended by members of the castle guard. Two of these rushed forward and barred the path of the Kirbys by crossing the antique pikes they carried in front of Fanny. The constable caught up with them, brandishing a paper.

'What is he saying?' I said.

'Something about a new indictment,' said Elizabeth, who had sharper ears than mine. 'Oh! I believe she is being re-arrested, Titus.'

A few moments later, it was all undone. The guards had surrounded Fanny and, followed at a stately pace by the constable, they took her back through the gate and into the gaol.

TWENTY-FIVE

We heard shortly afterwards that the grand jury had approved a revised bill against Fanny and that she would be tried on the new charges on Friday morning. The last thing I did on Wednesday night was to draw up a legal letter, which I was obliged to write in full myself as Furzey and his friend had by now set off to walk it back to Preston. This letter was a formal application to be allowed to see Fanny in gaol. Early on Thursday morning I went up to the castle to present it.

There were several other applicants waiting, many in a great state of sorrow or agitation, and some that had been waiting there

all night. I saw that they were relatives of men and women who
had been tried and sentenced to death during the week. These
death sentences were to be carried out on Saturday morning and
the families were applying for stays of execution. The Governor
of the Castle had the right to grant these pending a decision in
London over a royal pardon. But the governor was dining at two
in the afternoon with Lord Strange and the Laceys and would see
no petitioners until later – if he would see them at all.

My own pass could be obtained from the deputy governor but
even he kept me waiting. So I sat with the families of the
condemned in a damp and anxious gatehouse room. The woman
on the bench next to me was snivelling into a handkerchief. I asked
her what was the matter.

'It's my son, sir. John Morton. They've condemned him to hang.
He's a thief I know but he's only a boy and if only they'll let him
off he'll mend his ways, specially after this. He hadn't a dad to
leather him when he did wrong, see? I was too easy with him, I
know I was. But I loved him. And I do love him now, even though
he's brought me such heartache.'

'Now, now,' I said. 'There's such a thing as mercy and there's
few people so hard-hearted that they'd willingly hang a boy.'

'But is the governor one such? Judge Lacey hasn't recommended
him for mercy, I do know that.'

Judges often endorse their death sentences with recommendations for a royal pardon, and many pardons are indeed issued. So
many crimes are punishable by death that, if all were carried out,
there would not be enough hangmen in England.

'You must hope the governor is a reasonable man and even a
compassionate one,' I said.

The deputy governor at last sent for me and I was brought to
his office. In the outer room two clerks sat writing at their desks.
One got up and dived into the inner room to fetch out the deputy,
who emerged with a handkerchief and a smelling bottle in one
hand and my letter in the other. His nose was red and he gave a
volley of sneezes as he approached me.

'Please excuse me, sir,' he said. 'It is the hay fever. Now, you
wish to see the prisoner Kirby?'

He looked through my letter of application.

'Yes,' I said. 'But first her indictment, if you please – the new one whereby she was taken up again after the grand jury sent back the first as no true bill.'

He sighed.

'I will see what I can do.'

He left the room and after about ten minutes returned with a piece of parchment, which he handed to me.

'You may read it here but not take it away. And please be quick as I have much to do.'

After telling his clerk to write a pass for me to go into the cells to see Fanny Kirby he retired to an inner room. I sat down to read the indictment – not a long document – to the accompaniment of the deputy governor's muffled sneezes, but I could find no difference between it and the original indictment. I approached the desk of the deputy governor's senior clerk.

'Excuse me,' I said. 'I wonder if you know this document?'

I showed it to him.

'Oh aye,' he said. 'I wrote it. Judge Lacey came up here straight from the courtroom and he gave me the job.'

'It seems to me just the same as the previous indictment, the one the grand jury threw out.'

'Well yes, it is exactly the same except in one detail. But that one makes all the difference, see?'

He pulled open a drawer and withdrew another parchment sheet.

'I still have the original here. So you see, it says the sails of the windmill turned in the direction of a clock's hands, while here, in the new version, it is stated, more correctly, that they turned counter to that direction.'

'Why does that matter?'

He gave me a withering look and turned back to his writing.

'I'm sure you can answer that yourself. You just have to think it out. I'm busy.'

Clerks! It was the sort of answer Furzey gives me when he himself doesn't have an answer. I had hardly begun to give the matter any thought, however, when the deputy governor came out again. He signed the pass that the clerk had written out and handed it to me in exchange for the parchment.

'You may have ten minutes with the prisoner. Good day, Mr Cragg.'

He returned to his room, where he was heard giving another

thunderous sneeze. I made my way downstairs to the bowels of the castle, where I had to avoid treading in the puddles of filthy water on the passage floor. I passed many stairwells, studded doors, grilles and barred windows from which emanated smells so foul they were impossible to describe, and the sounds of men and women calling out in anger and despair, in hunger, or far gone in disease.

Compared to these I found Fanny, though fettered and wearing a dingy grey dress, sitting in relative comfort. She was with two other women whose cases would be heard next day. I took her away from them into a corner of the cell, and we conferred in low voices.

'I have read the new indictment,' I said, 'and it is exactly the same as the first one, except where it talks about how the windmill sails turned. I cannot explain the significance of this.'

'Don't be fretting, Mr Cragg,' she said. 'I know Ambrose Parr is set on burning me. But I am ready for him. I offered him to meet me and to give him the chance to drop the case. He wouldn't come near. So right you are. I will destroy him first and he will be so surprised. He has no idea of the damage I can do to him.'

'I wish you would tell me, Fanny! You told my wife after all.'

'I know *she* will not tell. It must be a surprise when I speak out in public.'

'So be it,' I said. 'I wonder, by the way, have you heard of a heavily bearded fellow who calls himself Charles Watt?'

She shook her head.

'The name does not mean anything to you? He has come to Lancaster in the last few days.'

'No, I have not heard of him. Why do you ask?'

I examined her face. I did not think she was concerned by the news.

'Only in case his being here was something to do with your case, Fanny. He is the servant of the Captain Garland that I mentioned to you once. Do you remember?'

'Yes, and I told you I didn't know a Captain Garland.'

'So you did. Well, I have brought you this loaf of bread, and this also.'

Having put the bread into her hand I brought a bottle of rum from my coat pocket.

'Eat the bread now. Save the rum for . . . well, in case the verdict goes against you.'

She laughed.

'So if I do go to the stake I will burn brighter?'

'No, so that . . .'

She grasped my hand, her manacle clanking.

'No, I understand, I do. Thank you, Mr Cragg. You are a good man.'

On my way out I asked a gaoler where O'Higgins was lying. He directed me to a cell door, through whose peephole I could see the highwayman attended by a clergyman. The reverend gentleman had not, however, gone there to give spiritual comfort to the condemned man. Instead he sat at a table with pen in hand, and a lit candle and a sheaf of paper in front of him. O'Higgins was striding up and down the cell declaiming like an actor.

'And then it was,' I heard him say, 'that I got a mighty haul for the robbing of the coach of Lord Jedborough, by a cunning stratagem which I shall now relate . . .'

Leaning over the paper the clergyman was writing down every word.

Over dinner I told Elizabeth about my visit to the castle.

'How can it matter which way the sails of the windmill turned?' she said.

'It matters because an indictment must be true in every particular – on any matter of fact. If it isn't it fails. That is the law. Some sharp-eyed grand juror must have noticed that the windmill's sails were said on the first indictment to turn in an unusual direction, so they sent for the mill operator, who is on the list of witnesses, to tell them if that was true. He confirmed that the description was wrong – that his mill in fact turns the other way. So they sent back the verdict of no true bill.'

'It is ridiculous and it isn't much help as it has only delayed Fanny's trial. Is there any hope for her?'

'Well, my meeting with her strengthened my belief in her inno-cence. I find it hard to see how Ambrose Parr is going to argue his case. Will he produce some evidence at the last minute of a conspiracy to kill Miss Pettifer between Garland and Fanny? Unless

I am very much mistaken – I mean, unless Fanny is a consummate liar – she really does not know either Captain Garland or Charles Watt. And if she doesn't what possible reason would she have to push her mistress into the windmill's sail?'

'But we suspected Charles Watt might be here to stop her peaching on Garland.'

'She cannot peach on someone she does not know.'

'What, then, is Watt's business here in Lancaster?'

'I cannot imagine.'

Later we walked to the Dinkins' house, where we were invited to take tea. We already knew that Fanny Kirby's case had become the subject of much speculation among the assize-watchers. Mrs Dinkin was very voluble on the subject.

'If she is convicted, they are saying she will be burned alive, you know,' she said. 'Dinkin says it is the proper penalty for a woman convicted of petty treason.'

Dinkin nodded sagely but, before he could speak, his wife's tongue surged onwards.

'This has made people – certain people, not oneself, you know – *so* excited. Not that we are morbid here in Lancaster, far from it. But you know we haven't had such an execution here for, oh, fifteen years, wouldn't you say, Dinkin?'

'1732,' he said. 'Woman from Oldham that killed her husband. Don't you agree the whole idea of petty treason is unreasonable, Cragg?'

'It is traditional, Dinkin. But if I had charge of the law I would certainly be happy to see it off.'

'I am with you. Burning alive is a barbarous form of punishment.'

Mrs Dinkin however did not agree.

'Oh! No, no, Dinkin! It was brought in to lessen the punishment, did you not know? It is a merciful thing.'

'How is that my dear?'

Mrs Dinkin smiled.

'Because it does not involve the – ahem! – bloody desecrations of the body carried out on male traitors.'

The woman had a particularly grim way of smiling.

*   *   *

'Mary-Anne Dinkin can't wait to see poor Fanny burned,' said
Elizabeth as we walked back to the inn. 'In her mind it is nothing
to do with justice. It is just the excitement of the thing.'

'The only recommendation for that way of putting someone to
death is that it attracts attention. The sight of it, and the terror of
it, may turn others against doing murder.'

'But reason should enlighten our age. Burning is for witches
and we don't believe in witchcraft.'

'There are many that do.'

Back at the inn we found Fidelis. He had news of Frances
Dolland, whom he had been attending at the judge's lodgings.

'She is awake with a bad headache and a little mental confusion. She will live, I think.'

'Was she robbed?'

'Yes, a rope of pearls was ripped from her neck. I am guessing
it was only done to spoil the scent.'

'What scent, Luke? What do you mean?'

'I mean I do not think Mrs Dolland was attacked by a mere
robber.'

'Then why?'

'I cannot answer that – yet. Let us have supper together, when
we can examine this in more detail. Now, I must go out again.'

Upon which he was gone.

Elizabeth and I took a turn around town. We visited the church
and read the monuments. We saw the old bridge across the Lune,
from which the parapets had been removed to allow traffic to pass
in either direction, though not without danger of toppling over the
edge and into the water below. We inspected the old quay where
seagoing ships unloaded, which were very primitive wharves but
held much promise of the improvement many townspeople spoke
of. Finally we returned to the inn, where Fidelis joined us after
only a few minutes. He was holding something hidden under his
coat.

'I have found something highly significant,' he said.

He drew the concealed object from his coat. It was a cricket
bat. He laid it carefully, almost reverentially, on the table.

'Look at this bat. What do you see?'

It was carved of ash wood, about a yard long and darkened by age and whatever polish or oils had been rubbed into it. It was divided between a handle, tightly wound around with twine, and a blade which was planed flat on one surface, that which faced the bowler and against which the ball was struck. At its lower end the bat was slightly curved and then finished off squarely. It had several small dints and many stains on it, especially around the bottom edge of the curved section. I could see the extent to which the bat had been played with by the tiny cracks showing in the dints on the blade, both on the outer surface and on the edges, and by the small amount of caked mud on its end.

'I see a well-used cricket bat,' I said. 'What does it mean? How did you get it?'

'I stole it.'

'*Stole* it?'

'Yes. I mean to take it back before its absence is noticed, but I wanted to show you first.'

'Well, now you have done. I don't know why, though.'

'Don't you see anything else about this bat? Pick it up.'

I did so, weighing the bat in my hands. It was no more than two or three pounds in weight. I swished it this way and that. I put it down again.

'I find nothing unusual,' I said.

'Nevertheless there are things about this bat that make it significant evidence, and that is why I have brought it to you. I want you to witness them. Look here. Look very closely.'

He pointed with his finger at the bottom edge of the curve. I took my spectacles from my waistcoat pocket and put them on, then bent to look more closely. At first I still saw nothing.

'Look more carefully,' instructed Fidelis.

Now I saw it: a hair stuck in one of the tiny cracks.

'Ah! A hair.'

'Exactly. I think it is a hair from Frances Dolland's head. And look again. Do you see? There are a few brown stains around the hair – well, hardly stains, but traces. Blood, I think. Frances Dolland's blood.'

'My God! So you think this belongs to her attacker?'

'I do. I think it was the weapon of assault.'

'Where on earth did you obtain it?'

Fidelis picked up the bat and turned it so that I was looking at the back of the blade. There were a number of marks and scratches all across the wood but he indicated a place close to the base of the handle.

'That looks like ink,' I said. 'It looks like writing.'

'Can you read it?'

'It's indistinct.'

I looked more closely.

'My God!' I said, then read it out. 'It says "Charles Watt".'

TWENTY-SIX

Luke Fidelis went off once more with the purloined cricket bat while Elizabeth and I talked about Watt and his activities. I had been sure he was here to deal with Fanny, so why had he – if Luke was right – attacked Mrs Dolland instead?

'If he was acting for Captain Garland, it makes no sense,' I said in one of the inn's private parlours, as we waited for Fidelis to return. 'The last person Captain Garland wants dead is his wife.'

'Watt might not be acting for Garland. Suppose all the time he has been Smisby's agent, who went on acting in his interest all unaware of Smisby's death.'

'That is possible. We must then suppose Smisby was part of the scheme to have Garland do the dirty work of removing Richard Giggleswick from the scene.'

'But in that case we are still left with the problem of who killed Smisby.'

'And Miss Pettifer, don't forget.'

I sighed. 'How can I?'

'Put her aside for the moment,' said Elizabeth. 'Should not Watt be arrested for attempted murder of Mrs Dolland? The weapon he used can now be produced.'

As she spoke the parlour door swung open and Luke Fidelis came in.

'No, I'm afraid we cannot do that,' he said. 'We lack evidence. That hair on the bat could be anybody's. That blood might not be blood.'

'What to do then?'

'We must hope he shows his hand and in the meantime not alert him.'

'We are waiting for him to try again?'

'It is Watt who is waiting. He is waiting for Mrs Dolland to die. And in the meantime he has to justify his presence in this town.'

'Justify? How can he do that?'

'By using that bat for its proper purpose. Cricket. He is a member of Lowther's team in Saturday's match – on the opposite side to me.'

'That we must not miss,' said Elizabeth.

Immediately after our arrival in Lancaster I had taken the precaution of obtaining tickets for Fanny's trial. The next morning I discovered how well I'd done. With O'Higgins's fate now decided, the only important question remaining in the public mind was whether the Preston girl would burn. Public seats at her trial were therefore changing hands for large sums, and as I took my seat in court next morning the gallery was packed.

Fanny held herself straight in the dock, with her chin out. Her mother had passed her a bunch of wild flowers – had she been out and picked them by dawn light? – and these Fanny held close to her bosom for a while, before placing them on top of the dock rail. As was the custom Lacey also carried a posy of flowers, supposedly to mitigate the stink from the cells beneath. Everyone stood as he came in and waited for him to sit. He placed his flowers on the table in front of his throne-like chair and scowled across the court at the defendant. She looked back at him over her own bouquet without flinching. Her strength was extraordinary.

The dress Fanny wore was different today, and much brighter. Evidently her family had smuggled it into her cell for the purpose, and the colourful material stood out clean and vivid in the gloom of the court.

'Now, we have no business left over from yesterday so the first today is the case of Frances Kirby,' said Lacey, plumping into his seat. 'Is this person present in court?'

The clerk, Philip Porter, said she was.

'Read the indictment, then.'

Porter did so and when he had finished he addressed the accused.

'How do you plead to the charge against you, Frances Kirby?'

'I am not guilty,' she said firmly.

Porter sat down and Lacey paused a moment before saying, 'We have Mr Parr prosecuting. Is that so?'

'Yes, my lord,' said Parr from the lawyers' benches as he stood up.

'Well, get on with it, sir. I haven't all day. I have until one o'clock, and there are five more cases after this. Proceed with expedition if you please.'

Parr cleared his throat and began. From the start he divided his attention between the judge and the jury. His technique could not be faulted. To speak only to the jury might be deemed disrespectful to the bench by some judges. To speak only to the bench on the other hand risked losing the jury's attention.

Parr gave a rapid account of Fanny Kirby's previous life as a whore and then of events on the afternoon at Aughton windmill when Isabella Pettifer, in the company of the accused, had been struck by – or in Parr's terms, pushed into the path of – the windmill sail, and what later happened in the night when Miss Pettifer died, at a time when the accused was sitting by her bed. He produced his witness Mrs Graves, who had a clear view of what happened. I had a clear memory of what the woman had told me when we'd met: that Miss Pettifer appeared to walk unawares into the path of the descending sail while Fanny had tried to pull her back. Now she spoke very differently.

'It was right before my eyes, your honour. Right before. The dog ran under the turning sails. Miss Pettifer tried to catch it up the slope but it was too quick for her, was the dog. So she went up after it and the girl went up behind her and gave her a great shove in the . . . well in the rear end, and that was how Miss Pettifer got under the sail, and it hit her on the head, it did. Smack on the head. And she went down like a skittle.'

'And you are quite sure that the girl did this deliberately, this fatal push?' asked the judge.

'Oh yes, that's what I saw.'

Parr was about to ask a further question but Lacey had not finished.

'Good. That is very clear, Mr Parr. Very clear. And this is all your witnesses, I trust?'

'Well I, er, I have—'

I had seen Mrs Field in court and I supposed now that Parr intended to produce her to say that Fanny had volunteered to be one of those who sat up with their stricken mistress overnight – and no doubt the lawyer would make much of this. I had not been looking forward to the moment because one way the facts could be interpreted was that Fanny had wanted to ensure Miss Pettifer would not live until morning. But in the event Lacey did not want to hear Mrs Field.

'No more witnesses?' he said. 'Excellent. Be kind enough to sit down, Mr Parr, and let us hear from the accused, Kirby.'

He glowered again at Fanny in the dock.

'You have maintained your innocence, young woman, and you have now heard what Mr Parr has said about you and about the wicked thing you have done, and which Mrs Graves saw you do. Will you not now admit your lie? Be brief, if you please.'

Fanny rested her hands on the dock rail, either side of her mother's posy.

'I was a prostitute in Liverpool, a professional one, I admit that,' she said. 'But I didn't try to kill Miss Pettifer. I was trying to pull her back not push her. That woman there that says I pushed her was yards and yards away. She couldn't have told the difference between pushing and pulling. This charge is nothing but a malicious charge by a wicked man, Mr Ambrose Parr.'

Lacey thumped the table in front of him.

'How *dare* you an admitted whore call your honourable prosecutor wicked?' he thundered.

'I dare because he once did buy me, and used me for his pleasure,' she said. 'So I know what he is like.'

A buzz of murmurings arose in the public seats. Drama was in the air as Fanny extended her arm in a gesture worthy of Peg Woffington herself and pointed at Parr.

'I know that Mr Parr is a foul stinking pervert who does love to copulate with animals in the presence of women wearing animal masks and this I know because I have been one of those women and I was paid to take off my clothes and put on a piggy mask and caress him while he was a-going at a nanny goat, so help me this is true.'

She stopped again. The court sat for a moment in shocked silence. Their mouths were open in disbelief, not least that of Judge Lacey. He looked at Fanny, and then at Ambrose Parr, and back at Fanny. He was for once lost for words. Parr, meanwhile, had gone the colour of a custard, clutching his papers under bloodless knuckles, his eyes darted to right and left as if seeking a route of escape.

Fanny had not finished.

'So what I say is,' she said, lowering her finger until it was levelled at her accuser, 'Ambrose Parr there wants me dead because of me knowing this, and he heard I was there when Miss Pettifer had her accident, and thought it was a chance to get me out of the way. He didn't think I would have the guts to say all of it openly in court. But I've said it and I'm not sorry because it is the truth and I won't burn for something I never did, just because of his shame at being a goat-fucker.'

Lacey's face was flaming now, and his eyes bulging with fury.

'Enough!' he shouted. 'I have never in my life—'

'No! Listen!' Fanny shouted back. 'It is all true, on my life. He did that! And I was there, with my boobs hanging out wearing a porker's face over my own!'

'Drivel! Filthy drivel!' screamed the judge. 'I have never in all my time in the law heard such stuff spoken from the dock. You will cease mouthing these loathsome derogations forthwith, or I shall hold you in the most serious contempt.'

'Hold me in contempt?' said Fanny. 'I'll hold you in contempt, you old cuff.'

The court was in uproar now. Some of the audience were laughing, others shouting out, and many were jostling and making leaps in the air to see better what was happening, wanting in particular to see how Ambrose Parr had taken Fanny's accusation. I caught sight of Alicia Simpson sitting in the midst of the public benches. Her face was the very picture of someone shocked by a bolt of lightning.

'Prepare to take her down, warder!' shouted Lacey above the din. 'I will not have this! The chit must be silent or be taken away to be tried in her absence. Order! Silence in this court! Order!'

It took more than a minute for the room to become quiet again. Fanny had stopped calling out and now stood in the dock, flushed and with the same look of jutting defiance I had seen that day when she rode through Preston in her prison cart.

My heart softened at the pathetic faith she had had in this line of defence. I did not doubt that what she said might be true. Nothing, not the vilest, and not the most laughable in the whole range of men's physical tastes was unknown to a seasoned harlot. But to believe that the power of sexual outrage could turn a courtroom in her favour was likely to be a fatal mistake. Lacey's rage alone meant that the trial was unlikely to end in her favour. Of course it depended finally on the jury. I looked at them, upright citizens, some of them gentry. I guessed they would likely just shut their eyes to such images as Fanny had just put before them. And I guessed, too, that before they believed the word of a former Liverpool strumpet they would listen to the instructions of Judge Lacey.

Lacey was satisfied at last that order had been restored, and now those instructions were about to be issued.

'I now declare that the argument and evidence stages of this trial are completed and I shall move to my summation. As I have already said I have never heard such a catalogue, such a tissue, such a contemptible farrago of lies and deceit laid before me as I have this day by the prisoner at the bar. She is charged with petty treason after killing her employer Miss Pettifer by pushing her into the path of a descending windmill sail, sustaining injuries from which the good lady later died. I will leave you the jury to decide whether a foul-mouthed hoyden such as you see before you, formerly a public prostitute that has sold herself on the very streets, can in any way be believed when she makes filthy, spiteful and unsubstantiated accusations against a man that lawfully prosecutes her. I will leave you to decide whether to set such a woman free to go out into the world and murdering, and repeating wicked and appalling libels, and committing other felonious deeds to the detriment of the commonwealth, or whether – as Mr Parr has so admirably argued – she is guilty of murdering the lady she owed her duty to and is the foulest petty traitor who deserves the extreme penalty prescribed by the law.'

He made a tidy pile of the papers before him and nodded at the jury foreman.

'Consider therefore your verdict, Mr Foreman, and don't dawdle about it, if you please. We have much business ahead of us.'

Fanny sat on a stool in the dock while the jury's conference took place. Her only hope it seemed, after such a judge's summary, would be a thorough revolt against Lacey by the dozen jurors. But my heart was heavy as I watched them moving into the corner of the courtroom set aside for the purpose. They formed a huddle, their words protected by the buzz of general conversation in the room. I looked up at Lacey. His face was an epitome of impatience, tapping his fingers on his table and fixing the jury group with aquiline ferocity.

There was apparently one juror at odds with the others. He was young, and it was not impossible that he was affected by Fanny Kirby's pretty appearance and forthright manner. Was it in her favour that he was making his passionate appeals? If so none of the others was impressed. I saw the foreman interrupt, take him by the elbow and speak into his ear. The young man immediately wilted, his brief revolt snuffed out. The foreman smiled in satisfaction and began to work his way from juror to juror, putting a question and in every case getting a nod for an answer from each of them. Then the twelve returned as a body to the jury box.

'Have you reached a verdict on which you all are agreed?' said Philip Porter, rising to his feet.

'We have,' the foreman said.

'And on the charge of petty treason do you find the defendant guilty, or not guilty?'

'We find her guilty.'

The clerk swivelled to face Lacey, who lifted his hand and snapped his fingers. Seizing the velvet bag that contained the black cap, his clerk extracted the cap and sprang up. He stood behind Lacey and, with a flourish such as one crowning a king might make, he draped it over Lacey's wig.

The judge wasted no time.

'I will therefore proceed,' he intoned, 'to pronounce the appropriate sentence according to the law. Frances Kirby, please stand.'

Fanny rose with a look of bewilderment on her face. Events were now moving faster than her understanding could catch them.

'You have been found guilty of the crime of petty treason,' Lacey was saying, 'and must suffer the penalty of death in the manner laid down.'

Fanny did not seem to be taking this in. She was turning her head this way and that in distraction, as if searching for someone that she knew, or for some kind face. Most of the faces, however, were staring at her in stern fascination. Lacey continued.

'You shall be taken, therefore, to prison and from there to the place of execution where you shall be burned at the stake until you be dead. And may God have mercy on your soul. Take her down.'

TWENTY-SEVEN

I stood at the window of our inn room, looking out into the street. Elizabeth sat behind me at the writing table, working on a letter to our girl Matty in Preston. I felt a mixture of impotence and anger. After Fanny's trial I had left the courtroom and immediately gone to the business room of the Governor of the Castle. There I waited, pacing from wall to wall, going over and over what I would say. This barbarity must not go forward. Fanny must receive clemency, yes, a better word than mercy. She should by right be pardoned, and there were grounds. The judge's summation had been an outrage of prejudice. Even more significant, the usual standard of proof required in cases of petty treason should be the evidence of no less than two witnesses. In this case, there had only been one – the short-sighted Mary Graves.

But time was short and it was more expedient to ask for a recommendation of clemency in the hope her sentence would be commuted to transportation. Only the king could do this, but he only did so on advice. This usually came (when it did) from the trial judge, but there was no prospect of that in this case, as Lacey had clearly relished pronouncing the death of Fanny in this terrible way. The only other officials in town who could make the correct representations were the high sheriff of the duchy, who was Lord Derby's son, Lord Strange, and the Governor of the Castle. In my opinion the governor was far the more likely of these to oblige.

After a full morning of frustration I was told by the head clerk that the governor was fulfilling another engagement and would not return until evening.

'What engagement?' I asked.

'I believe a cricket match, sir. The governor has a playful side to him, you know. He has accepted the office of umpire.'

'Where is this match?'

'Upper Lune Meadow. You will find it bordering the far bank of the river above the bridge. They have already begun play, I believe.'

Now, as I looked out of the window, it was just after midday. I had gone back to the inn and found Elizabeth writing letters.

'Will you come with me this afternoon to the cricket?' I said.

She sanded the wet ink and folded the page, then came over to join me.

'Of course. We cannot miss Luke's performance.'

'To watch the cricket is not my main reason for going. The governor is umpiring and I mean to appeal to him on Fanny's behalf. Look, Elizabeth.'

I pointed through the window glass.

'Look out there. That is why.'

'What am I looking at, Titus?'

'Those carts.'

I pointed at a file of three donkey carts coming along the street, attended by mounted men in castle livery.

'What are they carrying?' said Elizabeth, peering through the glass.

The leading cart was now passing directly below the window, but I had already seen the answer.

'Faggots and sticks,' I said. 'Firewood. On its way to Gallows Hill.'

'Oh, Titus!'

Elizabeth took my hand and gripped tightly, but said nothing more. We watched the carts until they had gone up the street and out of sight.

From the crown of the bridge we saw the flat water meadow, and the place where the ground, encircled by a long ring of rope, had been marked out for cricket, with a wooden hut standing beside it. Men in white shirts and breeches, caps on their heads, were disposed around the green and in the middle a pair of batsmen were stationed at each end of a strip of mown grass. I saw a ball bowled at the batsman in front of the stumps. He struck it far enough to allow him to gallop to the other end, crossing with his colleague who did the same in the other direction, reaching the stumps before the ball was returned to the wicket and receiving a small round of hand-clapping from the watchers.

I am not very knowledgeable about the game but Elizabeth's brothers had been cricketers in boyhood. She had explained during our walk across the bridge that a batsman is out in one of three ways: if he lofts the ball so that it's caught before it reaches the ground; if he misses it and either (or both) of the stumps is knocked over; or if the ball is hurled at the stumps and hits while the batsmen are running. We came up to find Luke Fidelis sitting on the ground near the hut, waiting his turn to bat.

'When will that be?' I enquired.

'I am next,' said Fidelis. 'Lowther's men made one hundred and seventeen, which is not insurmountable. Turnbull is batting well. He has thirty.'

'Where is Charles Watt?' I said.

Fidelis pointed to one of the stoppers on the far side, his black beard conspicuous even at that distance.

'I have not had a chance to speak with him yet,' he said. 'He made most of their score with that bat of his – forty-eight.'

'I've heard that the Governor of the Castle is standing as one of the umpires.'

'Yes, and Lord Strange is the other. We are extraordinarily honoured.'

I shaded my eyes with a hand and looked. The players were moving around so that the bowling could be switched from one end to the other. I recognized Lord Strange as the young man taking up his position behind the stumps at the bowler's end. At his signal play resumed, and we watched four bowls sent down, before his lordship called 'Over' and play switched ends once again. Now and for the next four bowls a portly gentleman adopted the position of presiding umpire – the governor himself. I studied him. He looked a mild sort of fellow, ruddy of complexion and unhurried in his movements.

I looked around at the watchers. Some sat on the ground, others had brought folding stools. Several clustered around a man holding a long ashen staff and a knife who made, with each successfully completed run, a notch in the staff. At the end of the contest the team with the most notches would be the winner.

'Catch it!'

The shout from the field accompanied a lot of scurrying by the stoppers and running by the batsmen. I saw Charles Watt jump in the air with his arm raised. The ball smacked into his palm and he held it safe before throwing it triumphantly into the air.

'Out!' shouted the governor.

The batsman swung his bat angrily and began to trudge off the field, to be replaced by a jaunty Luke Fidelis bustling out into the centre while swinging his bat. 'Over' had been called and Charles Watt was appointed as the new bowler, possibly as a reward for catching the opposing captain out. Luke took up position to receive his first bowl from him.

'This will be interesting,' said Elizabeth.

The first bowl was sent down and making little effort with it, Fidelis flicked it back down the wicket where the bowler picked it up. I studied Watt's style over the next two bowls. My own favourite ball game is crown green bowling, where the bowls are the size of those large yellow oranges they call in the West Indies pample-mouses. In cricket the ball is more like an ordinary orange in size and made of leather not wood. However the method of bowling, I noticed, is very much like in bowls: the bowler steps up to the line by the wicket with the ball in hand. He draws the same arm back and, as he swings it forwards again, goes down on one knee to send the ball as fast as he likes along the ground. The difficulty for the batsman is that the surface, though flat enough, is not so completely even as a bowling green is. The ball may hop up or deviate from its path so he may miss it or nip it in an unintended direction.

Watt seemed to be good at bowling and Fidelis treated him with caution. The first over was uneventful until the fourth and last bowl, from which Fidelis managed a single run. The spectators gave some restrained handclaps but for many of them this was a social occasion before it was a sporting contest, a chance to converse, drink and eat pies, particularly as the sport was not at this point very exciting.

I walked over towards a group of men who were talking excitedly together, around one who sat at a collapsible table writing. These men had a different reason for finding excitement in the cricket.

'I'll give you ten guineas to your twenty,' I heard one man saying.

'Done,' said another, turning to the writer. 'Put it down, George, and don't forget to time it. The Preston doctor to be out within the next ten minutes.'

Coming nearer I heard other bets being struck, not only on who would win the game, but on the total number of notches by the batting team, the form or time of the next dismissal, or the number of dismissals a bowler would claim. After I had been observing this activity for a minute or so a slightly drunken, fair-haired young gentleman came up to me.

'Now, kind sir, will you take odds? Four guineas to one that the doctor will not get to two dozen notches.'

'Which is four, and which is one?' I asked, unsure how this worked.

'If he's out with twenty-three or less I take your guinea. If he gets more you take my four. It's simple.'

I looked over towards the game. Fidelis was breathing hard at the passive end of the wicket. Turnbull had just made four notches off a single hit and passed three dozen. If Turnbull could do it, I thought, why not Fidelis?

'Done,' I said.

'Put your money on the table,' said the young fellow.

We both laid our money down and the clerk wrote the wager in his book. I returned to Elizabeth.

'I have just bet a guinea that Luke will pass two dozen notches,' I said.

'How extravagant,' she said. 'He has a long way to go. He still has only one. Look, he's facing Charles Watt again.'

Watt was just releasing his first bowl. Fidelis took a mighty swipe and missed. The ball rolled past him, through the gate and into the hands of the wicket-keeper. But the cross-piece forming the top of the wicket had not been dislodged: not out.

'Hit it, Luke,' I shouted in encouragement.

The second bowl bobbed up just in front of him and he met it perfectly with his bat so that it sped away between two stoppers while each batsman ran there and back: two notches and a rattle of applause. The third bowl brought Fidelis cautiously forward, prodding at it. But it curled around the edge of his bat and continued towards the wicket. My heart was in my throat, but the ball did not hit. The fourth bowl sent down by Watt was whacked hard, but straight to a stopper: just one more notch.

When Fidelis had eleven notches, Turnbull batted a ball high in the sky and it plopped into the hands of a waiting stopper.

'Mr Turnbull, with regret, you are dismissed, sir,' said the governor.

Turnbull quitted the field with forty-one notches against his name. His successor nipped a swerving bobbing bowl from Watt straight into the hands of the wicket-keeper and was out immediately. The performance of the next three batsmen, against the same bowler, were almost as disastrous, with notches that could be counted on one hand. So now, with four more batsmen to come, Luke Fidelis had twelve notches and the total for Turnbull's team was only halfway to the target with six men out. Meanwhile Watt was bowling with ferocious skill.

The new batsman brought new hope. He was a giant of a man called Matteson, a farmer, and he immediately set about striking gigantic blows. In short time Matteson and Fidelis had added another thirty-one notches, all but a couple to the farmer. But a man of his size has a lumbering gait and this resulted in his downfall. He made a firm strike and called for Fidelis to run, but the ball was intercepted and the wicket that Matteson was striving to reach was thrown down when he was five paces short of safety. Turnbull's team now needed twenty-one notches to win.

Watt had been having a rest, but now he came back to bowl again. Fidelis was playing him carefully, getting two runs from nips off his bat's edge and three more from a neat sweep that sent the ball away behind him. But meanwhile two more batsman fell at the other end adding only one to the score. The Turnbull side now needed sixteen more to win; the Lowther side needed to get just one man out. It all depended on Fidelis.

Slowly his score increased: fifteen, sixteen and, with a glorious swipe that almost sent the ball to the boundary rope, nineteen. The score of the team was a hundred and twelve.

'Five runs to win,' I said, now entirely engrossed in the game.

'Yes, and Luke has nineteen notches,' said Elizabeth. 'You know what that means, my love?'

I had completely forgotten my bet.

'My God! If he gets the five runs I win my bet too!'

Watt began a new over with Fidelis facing him. He sent his first bowl down, and it ran true and straight. Fidelis helped himself to two runs by striking it away into a gap between two stoppers. The second ball bobbed up at the perfect moment to meet Fidelis's bat and he found another gap, and another two runs.

One run to win.

The third of Watt's bowls was a snaking delivery that deliberately exploited an uneven place on the ground, so that the ball moved two inches off its line at just the point when Fidelis expected to hit it. He aimed for a hefty swat but the ball took the edge of his bat and nipped up in the air.

'Catch it!' yelled Watt, flinging his arms high.

The nearest stopper flung himself forward. For a moment he had it in his hand, but a moment later it was rolling away from him. We all breathed again. Watt had one more bowl in his over, with one run to win. He should have played safe by sending down a delivery from which Fidelis would find it impossible to score. The bowling would then have switched to the other end, where the number eleven batsman was a spindly, hollow-chested youth, who looked scared out of his wits.

But Watt didn't play safe. He wanted Fidelis out, and he wanted to do it himself. So he tried something different. He didn't roll, or bowl the ball; he tossed it, hoping it would bounce between bat and body and go through to strike the wicket. Or, if not, glance off the bat and go for a catch. Fidelis's response to this unusual delivery was instinctual. He jumped forward to meet the ball and with a mighty swing smacked it as hard as he could back towards the bowler. It hurtled the length of the wicket at head height and struck Charles Watt square on the forehead. For a moment he stood as if thunderstruck, and then went down in a heap.

Both batsmen, the umpires and the entire field of stoppers were immobilized for a moment in horror. Then somebody called out.

'Is he hurt?'

The call seemed to awaken Fidelis. He raced down the twenty-two yards of the wicket and dropped to one knee by Watt's side. He felt his wrist and listened to his heart. I heard him shout for water and bandages and then he was lost to sight as players and umpires clustered around the fallen bowler. After another five minutes the cluster parted and four men carried Watt across the field of play. They took him into the hut beside the boundary.

Fidelis was following this group and I intercepted him.

'This is very unfortunate, Luke,' I said. 'I was about to win five guineas in a bet when that happened.'

He looked at me in astonishment.

'A bet? I might have killed that man, and you're thinking of a bet?'

'Yes, but I suppose you haven't killed him, have you?'

'He is alive at the moment. But since we are speaking of bets, I wouldn't wager on his life being much longer.'

He collected his medical bag and went into the hut. I looked around and saw that the betting men around the table were surrounding the two umpires, arguing and shouting. The question was, what was the result of the match? I pushed through the crowd, and as I did I bumped into the man with whom I had struck my bet. I stuck out my hand for a shake.

'I believe the game is abandoned and I congratulate you, sir. The doctor made only twenty-three notches.'

He smiled happily.

'It was a close-run thing.'

But as it turned out the game had not been abandoned. The reason for the turmoil around the umpires was that, on the contrary, it been declared completed.

'It is quite clear,' the governor was saying, 'and I am sure my colleague Lord Strange will second me. The doctor at the last ran the full length between wickets, while no one broke the wicket at the end to which he was running. I therefore declare the match won by Mr Turnbull's team.'

'But he wasn't running!' shouted one impassioned gambler. 'Or rather, he was running, but not in the cricket sense. He was going to the assistance of the injured fellow.'

The governor shook his head.

'It makes no difference, no difference at all, why he made the run. He *did* make it, and that is all that counts.'

Some of the men, who all had money riding on the outcome, were angry at this ruling while others were naturally delighted. I went back to the fair-headed young man.

'It seems we were mistaken,' I said. 'The doctor completed the winning notch, even though he did not intend to, which means he scored twenty-four and I fear your four guineas are mine.'

He was gnashing his teeth but he could do nothing about it. The umpires' decision, just as irrevocably as that of Judge Lacey, was final.

Pocketing my money I went into the hut, where I saw that cushions had been arranged on the floor as a makeshift bed for the patient. He was lying motionless with his eyes shut until Fidelis produced a phial of volatile liquid, which he opened and wafted under the patient's nose. With a start, accompanied by a loud coughing grunt, Watt came to himself. His eyes opened and he looked around in alarm.

'Where am I? My head hurts.'

'You have received an injury at cricket, Mr Watt,' said Fidelis.

'You have been unconscious, Mr Watt,' said another man. 'You are being tended to by a doctor.'

Watt looked from face to face, confused.

'Why are you all calling me Mr Watt?' he said.

'Because that is your name, isn't it?' said Fidelis. 'Charles Watt.'

'Charles Watt? No of course it isn't. I know the man, of course. A complete rapscallion, he is. You're playing a joke on me. However do you mistake me for him?'

He still looked around the company, as if searching for a face that he knew.

'Charles Watt,' said Fidelis, 'is the name under which you have been playing this game of cricket. If it is not your true name, tell us what that is.'

'My true name, sir? You mean my *own* name.'

He frowned and seemed to be making an effort of memory.

'I don't know my name.'

At that moment one of the cricketers pushed through to look at the invalid. It was the captain of Fidelis's team, Turnbull.

'*He* may not know his name,' he said. 'but I can tell you who he resembles. A man I knew years ago in Liverpool, but I thought he was dead.'

Fidelis's face had changed. For a moment he was still, then he broke into a beautiful smile. He grabbed Turnbull's forearm.

'Yes, of course! Of *course*! And I'll bet he had no beard then.'

'He hadn't, you are right. Do you know him too?'

Fidelis turned back to the man lying prone on the cushions.

'I do. You desire to know your name, sir? You are John Bourke, formerly a trader in wine, whom everybody believes was drowned while attempting to cross the Menai Straits. Am I not right, Mr Turnbull?'

TWENTY-EIGHT

Luke now jumped to his feet and pushed back the inquisitive throng.

'This hut must be cleared. Everybody go out. This man is to be kept quiet and calm. In the meantime will someone fetch a litter so he may be carried to his lodging?'

The mixture of cricketers and spectators that had crowded into the hut began to withdraw and I went with them. Elizabeth met me outside.

'Is he still insensible?' she said.

'No, he has woken, and talking but making little sense. He says he is not Charles Watt.'

'Who is he, then?'

'That's what doesn't make sense. *He* doesn't know but Mr Turnbull our team captain confirms he knows him and he is John Bourke.'

'John Bourke? I seem to know that name.'

'He was the wine merchant who was one of the names on the tontine. Turnbull is in the same line of business.'

'But Bourke drowned, didn't he?'

'He was reported to have.'

'How extraordinary.'

I put my hand on Elizabeth's shoulder and kissed her surprised mouth.

'You are not alone, my love,' I said. 'I don't understand it either, though I have reason to believe that Luke does.'

'Mind your back there,' said a voice behind me. 'His lordship's and the governor's horses coming up.'

We turned. Two riding horses had been brought up by their grooms and were now awaiting our two umpires to mount up. Suddenly with a stab of guilt at my carelessness I remembered why we had come to the match in the first place. I looked for the governor. He and Lord Strange were bustling towards us, ready to take their leave.

I was about to speak to him but Elizabeth forestalled me just as they reached us.

'Governor,' she said, standing in his path. 'I wonder if I may speak. It is about one of the prisoners in your cells who has this morning been condemned to death.'

Lord Strange appeared to have just made some witty remark, and the governor's face still had a laugh on it.

'Oh yes, madam?' he said. 'And what's this dolly's name?'

'Fanny Kirby. She was found guilty of petty treason and Judge Lacey condemned her to burn at the stake. But my husband is a lawyer, sir, and he believes it was done on extremely bad evidence.'

'I suppose you want a recommendation?'

'We do.'

'Kirby, you say?'

'Yes. And she is—'

Lord Strange interrupted.

'Come on, Harry! We must not be late for the dancing. I'll race you to the bridge.'

Strange was already in the saddle. The governor immediately turned away and got a leg-up from his groom.

'Governor,' I called up as he turned his horse. 'I am Titus Cragg, stopping at the sign of the Golden Anchor. Please send word of your decision.'

He gave no indication of having heard, but looked down at Elizabeth. He showed her his teeth.

'I will send it to this pretty lady,' he said. 'And only to her.'
He kicked the horse again and set off in pursuit of his friend.

Elizabeth and I parted ways with Fidelis at the bridgehead, he
going along with the litter that carried the injured man to his
lodging, and we returning to our inn. I had told Fidelis I wanted
to speak to his patient as soon as he was making sense and we
returned to the Golden Anchor to wait for news – whether from
Fidelis on the patient's progress, or from the governor on our
petition for Fanny. It was Fidelis that we heard from first, though
not for some time. We knew that the hour was too late for any
news from the castle so Elizabeth had gone to bed while I sat up
to write my journal.
    The note that came, by hand of a boy, read as follows:

> *Titus – You said you wanted to speak to the man, and now
> is your chance. Come over to the sign of the Deerhound
> where Charles Watt (or is it John Bourke?) lies. You will
> be most interested to speak to him. It is something remark-
> able. L.F.*

The Deerhound was a half-squalid alehouse with rooms above that
they let cheap. I found Luke sitting in an attic alongside his patient,
who lay in bed fully awake up against a hill of grubby pillows.
He sported a head-bandage like a turban.
    'Now, sir,' said Fidelis as I came in, 'here is my friend Mr Titus
Cragg, who would like to know what you know about Charles Watt.'
    'I am happy to oblige him,' said the patient, gingerly nodding
his head at me. 'Charles Watt is a man who has much to answer
to. He is a disgrace to society. Indeed I think he is hardly a civil-
ized person himself. A kind of savage, so he is.'
    He spoke with a marked Irish accent.
    'But by your leave, sir, you yourself are Charles Watt,' I said.
'It is the name you have been going by.'
    'I don't know how you make that out,' he said. 'I know I had
a blow on the head and certain things are obscure in my mind.
But many other things are perfectly clear, and one is that my name
is John Bourke, as my old friend Mr Turnbull of Liverpool earlier
agreed. Charles Watt, now. He is another fellow altogether.'

Fidelis winked and nodded at me. He meant 'humour him', so I did.

'Very well,' I said, drawing up a rickety chair and sitting down alongside Fidelis. 'Tell me how you know Mr Watt.'

'Well, I know him from Dublin, d'you see? We became friends and we saw much of each other. It was only when I told him about certain matters that he began to pester and annoy me. Now of course I realize that he did so because he is a rascal, no, he's worse than that. He's a villain. And a greedy one.'

'What were the matters that you told him about?'

'That I'd sunk five hundred guineas into a tontine with some Liverpool people I knew when I was in business there. The payback is mighty high, but you have to outlive all the others to get it. Watt kept whispering in my contcha – you know, my ear – that all I had to do – because I had some debts I wanted to clear, see? – was to hasten the departure of the others and then I'd get the money.'

'What did you say to that idea?'

'Of course I said no. It would be unconscionable. I could never entertain the murder of my former friends. But Watt kept on at me, day after day, week after week, until it was driving me wild. He made me tell him the names of everybody that signed the tontine. Then he made plans for how they could be got out of the way, one by one, in every detail.'

'Was this when you were in Dublin?'

'Oh yes, here in Dublin. But Charles went away to England—'

'*Here* in Dublin? You think you're in Dublin now?'

'Of course, where else would I be? As I was saying, Watt left me to go to Liverpool where he made enquiries and soon he'd found where they all were. One was already disposed of on the hunting field. Man by the name of Tom Hesketh. And he found that another was dead by the normal action of Death himself.'

'Was that Isaac Jones?'

'Yes! How did you know that? The clockmaker. Died of . . . of . . . something-or-other. So that left only four more alive, Watt said.'

'"Said"? How did he tell you all this if you were in Dublin?'

'He wrote to me, I expect. That is the normal way we communicate across a distance, is it not? Let me continue. I heard that

Watt had hooked up with a certain captain of the Fusiliers, Garland. The fellow had been locked up in Liverpool for some debt or other. Locked up with Smisby, indeed, so he knew him. Watt became the Captain's manservant because he knew he was the husband of one of the living tontine members. So by that means Watt was able to whisper into *his* contcha and tell him the fortune that could be his if he did this and that. So the Captain never saw he was being used, d'you see? That was Watt's cunning. So Garland just went into action and killed poor Dick Giggles, a terrible thing. Everyone was so fond of Dick.'

'So you can confirm that Captain Garland did murder Mr Giggleswick?'

'Certainly he did. Shot him.'

'And it was at the instigation of Charles Watt that he did this?'

'Well, he gave Garland the idea. Like I said. And he was going to do in Miss Isabella next, a very nice girl she used to be, and religious too, but then they found out she'd been killed by the accident of a windmill sail smashing into her head. So now as far as the Captain and Charles Watt thought the only one left was the clever Mr Smisby, though he wasn't so clever latterly, because he owed a ton of money and was in gaol for it. Watt gave the Captain some medicine to take to Smisby and tell him it was a preservative against gaol fever. The instruction was that he must take before every meal.'

'And did he do this? How do you know? Did Watt tell you?'

'Watt confided in me. He told me all.'

'So would you tell me something else? Why did Watt personally attack Mrs Dolland with his cricket bat last night?'

'Because now Captain Garland couldn't leave Ormskirk. Some fool of a coroner had made an inquest into Dick's death and branded the Captain as the murderer. So now, you see, Watt had no one else to do it for him.'

'Did you know of this plan to attack Mrs Dolland?'

'Yes, and I argued with him to stop him, of course. But Watt is impossible to stop once his mind is made up.'

'So you knew it was wrong?'

'Of course I knew it was wrong, man! But I could do nothing to stop him, being here in far-off Dublin. Now, gentlemen, I am gratified by your company but I am mightily tired. I believe I must sleep. We can perhaps continue this pleasant conversation in the morning.'

'Yes, it will be good for you to sleep, Mr Bourke,' said Fidelis. 'But there is just one more thing I would like to know. How did Tom Hesketh meet his end? Did you see it?'

'I was near at hand right enough. I never saw what happened but I have my suspicions. See, we were searching a covert. Hesketh was found later on the ground, dead. He had the wound of a gun shot.'

'You think he was shot dead?'

'Well, there was a fellow there who bore a marked resemblance to Charles Watt, very marked, though it was years before I ever met him. Thinking about it now, I am quite sure it was Watt himself that was there, and that he shot Tom. But it was many years ago, so it was.'

Fidelis now made Bourke as comfortable as possible and, blowing out the light, we went downstairs where I proposed a glass of something from the bar. The landlady who served us asked after her injured guest.

'He is asleep,' said Fidelis. 'I advise that in the morning you look in and tell him to stay in bed by my orders until I come.'

We ordered a jug of bumbo and sat in a corner at the only free table. The small room was full of drinkers, most of them outdoing each other in loud conversation, not to mention songs and roaring laughter.

'Well, Titus,' Fidelis said. 'What do you make of that as a confession?'

'The strangest I ever heard. While pretending to accuse another man, he openly accused himself.'

'You don't believe him?'

'Not for a moment. My first thought was that he is a most daring liar. But now I see that it doesn't make sense. He invented Charles Watt so he would not be recognized as John Bourke. So why now admit that he is Bourke, with the preposterous lie that Watt is someone else?'

'I don't think he is lying.'

'Of course he is!'

'Not if you define a lie, which you must, as a deliberate falsehood. In his own mind he believes Charles Watt really is someone else.'

'But Charles Watt isn't someone else!' I insisted. *'He's* Charles Watt.'

'We know he is, but *he* doesn't. Not any more. The injury by the cricket ball has had a very strange effect on his mind. Previously he was, and I assume knew he was, John Bourke playing the part of Charles Watt. But he was playing it so well, and at such length, that by degrees Charles Watt became a whole and complete person distinct from himself.'

'Can all that be done by a blow from a cricket ball?'

'The sudden injury must have finally divided Watt from Bourke. It returned Bourke to being Bourke and made Watt, not just a whole person, but now also a separate one, another man. The rest of it, about the letters Watt wrote, and about Bourke being in Dublin, are necessary false beliefs.'

'Why are they necessary?'

'Because otherwise none of this would be intelligible.'

'Intelligible, ha! None of it is!'

I shook my head and drained my glass of bumbo.

'We shall learn more when Bourke wakes up in the morning,' Fidelis said. 'Here, let me fill your glass. You really should be pleased, Titus, I mean about Fanny. All this proves you right, and me wrong, does it not? You are vindicated. Isabella Pettifer died by chance just as your inquest found.'

I shook my head.

'That,' I said, 'will not make it any easier to watch Fanny burning at the stake for her murder.'

Saturday morning presaged an overcast day, the sky full of iron-grey clouds chased by a fitful breeze. Elizabeth woke me from my bumbo-slumber at seven and I came down to breakfast with a heavy head.

'Titus, this is no time to be sorry for yourself,' said Elizabeth sharply. 'You have to see the governor, and I am coming with you. Time is short if we are to save poor Fanny's life.'

Half an hour later we were once more at the gatehouse. I asked if the governor was at home. He was.

'What time are the hangings?'

'Midday.'

'Then I request an immediate interview with the governor.'

The gatekeeper gave a scoffing laugh.

'You may forget it, sir. The governor was out dancing until one in the morning. We shall not see him these two hours.'

'On executions day?' cried Elizabeth. 'This is not to be borne. Come on, Titus. We are going in.'

Lancaster Castle contains many internal parts. There are prison cells, below and above ground, and such buildings as the Guardhouse, Crown Hall, Emperor's Tower, and various apartments for residents other than the prisoners, the finest being those of the governor in the gatehouse itself. Elizabeth took no notice of the cries from the guards and marched through and up the stairs that led to those apartments, with me following. On the first floor we were confronted with a heavy nailed door, but Elizabeth seized the latch and pushed. The door opened and in a moment we were inside the governor's quarters.

A large and brawny liveried manservant in the ante-chamber tried to stop us, but he was too slow and we circumvented him. We did the same to a startled housemaid carrying a bucket and brush in the passage beyond. After looking quickly into three rooms along the way we arrived at last at a personal dining room where the governor himself was sitting over a breakfast of eggs in their shells with buttered bread. In a house-cap and a slovenly shirt and breeches he had clearly not yet fully dressed himself for the day.

Seeing Elizabeth he rose to his feet.

'Ah! The pretty lady from yesterday's cricket match! How may I—?'

His lubricious smile only faded when he noticed me coming in behind her. Elizabeth started in on him without ceremony.

'I am disappointed in you, sir,' she declared. 'You promised to send an answer to my request for a petition of clemency for Fanny Kirby, and you have not done so.'

'May I remind you, madam—'

'May I remind *you*, sir, that the poor girl is unjustly convicted on the eye-witness of just one person, which any lawyer will tell you is one witness short of the required standard of proof in such cases.'

The governor lifted an eyebrow, and cocked a look at me.

'Your wife, sir?' he said.

I nodded.

'She is spirited as well as a pretty, I'll say that. But far too late, I'm afraid. You both are. The wheels of justice must turn, which it is my duty to supervise and see that there are no last-minute stones in the road. I remind you I am no lawyer, so it is useless to throw legal arguments at me. I can only yield to practical considerations, of which there are none in this case that I can see. There is ample firewood, I do know that.'

He chuckled and fed the last eggy crust into his mouth. Then he rose.

'Now, if you will excuse me, I must dress in preparation for the dread task. Wilkinson!'

The burly footman appeared at the door.

'Show them out, will you?' said the governor.

TWENTY-NINE

Assize towns are hanging towns: the people who live there, and in the country around, grow used to the rituals of judicial death enacted twice a year before their eyes. At Lancaster the people had seen the presentation of many famous executions. The hanging and butchery of rebels and traitors after the Jacobite rebellion of 1715; the celebrated coven of Lancashire witches hanged up in a row a hundred years before; and between them child-killers and horse-thieves, defrauders and coiners, rapists and housebreakers and other felons aplenty had been suffocated out of life at the end of Lancaster's best nautical ropes.

Now, in the middle of 1746 two elements made these hangings more exciting than usual. One was the expectation around the death of the highwayman Shamus Fingal O'Higgins, popularly known as Jim Fingers. What would he say from the scaffold, the people wanted to know, and how bravely would he die? The other was the burning of Fanny Kirby. Burnings, though once common enough, had now become something of a rarity and many younger people had never seen one. On this day the question men and women were asking was, how would the executioner do it? There was a rumour that old Stonecross was about to retire, after thirty years as Lancaster's death-dealer. It was said that his practice, when called upon to burn someone in the old days, had been always to let the fire do the work. He had no truck with the kinder sort of hangman you found down south, who would strangle the condemned female before setting the flames. But it was some years since Stonecross had last burned a woman. Had his heart perhaps softened in old age?

Midday was the hour at which the first cart would begin its journey to Gallows Hill, coming out of the castle gate and lurching down Church Street. It was led by Stonecross on his horse, flanked by two armed outriders. His three assistants came on foot behind him and at the tail of the cart rode two more armed riders and any of the people who chose to join the parade. By tradition they would stop for refreshment at the Golden Lion on the corner of Brewery Lane, then continue along Moor Lane until the town was behind them. All that lay ahead after that was the steep and stony track that led up to the gallows.

By decision of the governor, the carts this day were to be released at half-hourly intervals. There were four of them, each carrying two or three of the condemned. I had seen it all many years earlier from a prominent viewpoint above the gallows. My father wanted to show me the whole procedure because, he said, 'You'll never be a good attorney if you haven't seen a criminal's death, so the sooner the better.'

The spot he chose was popular with families. It was near enough to see and hear what was happening, but not the worst details – the purple extended tongues, the bursting eyeballs, the sudden expulsion of fluids – that might cause horrid nightmares in a child. I was about seven years old. What I remember of it now is the jerking legs of the people as they dangled, and that it was like a dance.

At the Golden Anchor, Elizabeth and I debated with Luke Fidelis what we would do.

'I won't go up on the moor,' she said. She had wept for Fanny but now her eyes were dry, and they were determined. 'I won't see Fanny die, but I should like to see her pass on her way.'

'The carts don't go down this street,' I said. 'We must venture out into Church Street to see her.'

'Let's go to the Golden Lion, where they stop,' said Fidelis. 'We may even be able to have a word.'

There was something in his voice that, knowing him as long as I had, alerted me. He was excited, or in some way expectant, while I was sunk in gloom.

'No word can comfort her now,' I said.

But we followed Fidelis's suggestion and soon after the clock of St Mary's had struck twelve we were there in the crowd, opposite the inn which stands halfway along Moor Lane. There was no going inside as it was crammed with drinkers, singing and hollering. The street too was in the carnival mood. We stood with our backs to a house on the opposite side of the street to the inn and I was heavy in my heart. Elizabeth was pale as marble.

We had lost sight of Fidelis when more cheers and shouts were heard from the direction of Church Street. The first cartload of the condemned had evidently arrived at the top of Moor Lane, but it was a few minutes more before we could hear the rumble of its wheels, and the rattling horses' hooves. When the grim-faced Stonecross with his escort came into view at last we saw that he wore a gold-braided tricorn hat, and a coat with golden threads on its facings, and rode an imposing black gelding. Beside him rode his armed escort, and behind came his assistants. As they halted they all got a cheer, and so did the prisoners who then came up. There were three of them riding in the open cart. They wore shackles and held pathetically on to each other for comfort.

The voice of the inn's landlord could be heard at the front door of his establishment.

'Make way! Make way, you ruffians!'

He led out a train of three inn servants who carried trays high above their heads. These trays bobbed and tilted as their bearers were jostled by the crowd, but the men were expert at their job and none of the glasses and tankards they carried were spilled.

These vessels held different drinks. First the landlord served the executioner with a stirrup-cup of wine. Next came the other riders, who had the same, and then the walking men, who were given pewter tankards of strong ale. Finally the three prisoners were presented with tankards filled with their courage, which by tradition was a fearsome mixture of ale, rum and wine to make a potent dose to soften their approaching ordeal.

The trio of miserable men on the cart drank their courage in different ways. One took it in a few greedy gulps. The next tried to drink with a show of normality, even of nonchalance, while the last took nothing but small sips, either because he didn't like the taste or was intent on drawing the moment out for as long as possible. Finally Stonecross lost patience and ordered two of his assistants on to the cart. One held the slow drinker's head while the other tilted the cup to pour the drink forcibly down his throat. He coughed and retched, and half of the courage was wasted down his chin and chest and across the bed of the cart. But the cup was emptied and it was time to march on.

When this first parade had left, the remaining crowd ceased for a while its singing and raucousness. They fell to murmuring and whispering, suddenly thinking of the fate of the three men they had just been toasting and carousing to. But as soon they heard the second cart with its own armed and equipped escort rumbling down Moor Lane, the excitement mounted again. When they reached the inn the four weeping female prisoners that the cart contained were roundly cheered for each swallow of courage they took.

The third cart came along in due time, also with four prisoners. One of these men was a rapist and he received a volley of catcalls, whistles and shrill curses from the women of Lancaster as he drank his allowance with sullen contempt. The other three men were palsied with fear, one shaking so badly he had spilled a good half of his liquor by the time his cart set off again towards the moor.

The crowd's murmuring expectation following this cart's departure had more intensity than before. Everyone knew the next and last cart must carry not only the popular hero Jim Fingers, but also Fanny Kirby as well as the unfortunate condemned boy, whose mother I had spoken to at the castle. Indeed the air was so quiet that at one moment we could clearly hear the volley of whistles and cheers from half a mile away as spectators around the gallows showed their appreciation as another batch of condemned were strung up and turned off the tail of the cart.

The sense of expectation around the Golden Lion was near palpable, with everybody listening for the approaching fourth cart. Then it came, the iron-rimmed cartwheels on cobblestones, the clatter of hooves and the ragged shouts and cheers of the following mob. Jim Fingers stood in the centre of the cart, with legs apart to brace and steady himself and a smile on his face that had nothing of fear or penitence in it. He was certainly a handsome man and had won the hearts of Lancashire and Cheshire lasses wherever his pillaging took him. Now he won more, from men as well as women, for this display of devil-may-care.

Fanny, wearing a sack dress stained with dirt, cut a very different figure. She was diminished compared to the defiant young woman I had seen riding that day into Preston, and yesterday standing in the dock. Although I saw no tears, her features had grown softer, her eyes milder, as she had her arms around the terrified child. Trying to calm his howls that rang out above the hubbub that surrounded them, she stroked his head, but it was an awkward caress because of the shackles, and it did not seem to be doing much good.

As before, the beverages were brought. Jim Fingers raised his cup in the air and showed it north, south, east and west.

'Here's to the road!' he shouted. 'And here's to plunder!'

He drained the drink in a single draught and then to the frantic delight of the people gave a loud belch.

Meanwhile Fanny and the boy were taking their own measures of courage more slowly. The boy disliked the taste but Fanny helped him take as much as he could. Then she began to drink her own portion in small but rapid draughts.

She was about halfway done when there was a violent sound of explosion, a burst of flame and a puff of smoke from one of the upper windows of the inn. All at once three fellows with knives clasped in their teeth leaped down from the inn's other upper windows. Two landed on the ground while the third, with infinitely more agility, plumped on to the back of one of the escorting horses. He simply elbowed the surprised rider to the ground and urged the animal into position at the rear of the cart.

The other two men worked together, pulling down one of the remaining riders and using their knives to cut the girths of the other two, causing their saddles to slip sideways to the ground, and the riders with them. With each man that fell the crowd gave a cheer, and another when the two attackers leaped on to the now bareback horses. The fifth and last remaining guard, seeing what was happening, kicked his horse and took flight. The carter also leaped down and ran for his life.

One of the attackers was now beside Jim Fingers with a mallet and a spike, striking at the shackles to break them off. With this done, Fingers wrung his wrists, each in turn, to ease their bruises, and was about to launch himself on to the rear of his comrade's purloined horse when one of the crowd caught his attention. He knelt on one knee and bent his head to hear whoever had called up to him from the heart of the mob. He listened and then gave an order to the one with the mallet, who immediately turned to Fanny and the boy. In seconds he had struck the shackles from them both.

The boy instantly forgot his terror: he slipped to the ground and simply disappeared into the crowd. Fanny stood looking around, uncertain what to do. Jim Fingers took her arm, pulled her to the edge of the cart and pointed to the rump of the horse that was still waiting there. Half lifted by Jim Fingers, half jumping for herself, she landed astride and wrapped her arms around the rider's waist. Now, using his pal's knife, Fingers began cutting the draught horse from the shafts. When it was loose he jumped on the horse's back. Then the five horsemen came together, circling in a cluster.

The throng was now in an uproar of cheers and hoots of laughter and at this moment of greatest confusion a sixth horse came into view at the entrance of the Golden Lion's coachyard. This rider wore breeches and a man's coat, yet it was undoubtedly a woman, with a fire of red hair flowing down her back, and a thunder-flash in her eye.

'Is that—?' I said.

'Yes,' said Elizabeth. 'It's Madame Lachatte.'

'So it is, by God,' I said.

She kicked her horse, forcing it through the mob until she had joined Fingers and the others. I saw the look between Fingers and his mistress, a look of triumph and love. They all circled their horses once more and I heard the chief shout.

'Yah!'

As one they turned their horses' heads in the direction out of Lancaster and kicked their flanks. A few seconds later they were all gone in a whirl of dust.

I looked back at the cart, now with its empty shafts on the ground and its tail in the air. Standing by it, in the middle of the uproar, was Luke Fidelis. I fought my way through the hubbub to join him.

'Was that you who spoke to the highwayman?' I said.

'I begged him to oblige me by freeing the boy and Fanny, and by taking Fanny with him.'

'That was marvellously well done.'

'It was the only thing to do. Now, I must go back to my deluded patient.'

He hurried off in the direction of Church Street while I re-joined Elizabeth, clasped her hand and together we navigated our way through the mob towards the Golden Anchor.

There was a hue and cry of course but Jim Fingers was long gone, into the moorland and away. The execution party, robbed of its final three victims, had trailed back into town with bodies piled on the very carts that had been used as their hanging-platforms. Stonecross's face, I was told, was a study in gathering thunder. Most of the respectable folk had withdrawn in fear to their houses, so that the mob now consisted mostly in ruffians and drunken idlers. Being no friends to the law they jeered and hooted, but the executioner rode back into Lancaster with his eyes fixed rigidly ahead.

Fidelis returned to the inn about six in the evening with a very long face.

'Bourke died,' he said shortly. 'He cut his own throat in the alehouse. I got there in time to staunch the blood and he lived for a few hours, but I couldn't save him. He has spared Mr Stonecross the trouble of killing him, I suppose. But I am sorry.'

'It is always very sad when someone takes their own life, even if it's a very bad someone,' said Elizabeth.

'Sad? I suppose so,' said Fidelis. 'But what I mean is that I'd like to have studied the case more. It might have made a paper for the Royal Society: "A Case of a Man Split in Two".'

Elizabeth looked at me and gave an almost imperceptible shake of her head.

'What of Mrs Dolland?' she said.

'I called at the judge's lodging,' said Fidelis. 'She is healing. I am sure she will live long enough to collect the tontine.'

'If Ambrose Parr will let go of it,' I said.

'Parr!' scoffed Fidelis. 'If I were him I wouldn't show my face in public this side of Christmas.'

Since Fanny Kirby's trial, her revelations about Ambrose Parr had become the talk of the alehouses while Parr it seemed had skulked off under cover of darkness back to Liverpool. The tale of his sexual peccadillos would of course catch up with him. Liverpool is a heathen town of grimy enough morals, but even there it was doubtful he could find his level again in polite society.

Going out next day to call on the Dinkins and bid them goodbye, we met Miss Simpson and her sister walking in Market Street. It seemed indelicate to mention Miss Alicia's suitor, but she was not at all shy about him.

'Your friend Parr is a low, dirty exhibit,' she said. 'I wonder that an upright man like you would know him, Mr Cragg.'

'He is not a friend, madam, but a fellow lawyer merely.'

She took my disavowal with a sniff and there was an awkward moment until Elizabeth changed the subject.

'I wonder, has your sister made the acquaintance of any possible young legal men during the assize, Mrs Adcock?'

'One or two, one or two that are promising,' said Mrs Adcock airily. 'Nothing is certain in the early stages, of course. But we have our hopes. Now, we must make haste, Mrs Cragg: we take the ten o'clock coach. Will you be on that one?'

But Elizabeth and I were travelling by the midday departure. We made our farewells and went on to the Dinkins' house.

No sooner had we got there than Dinkins drew me aside.

'The death of this fellow at the Deerhound is a plaguy thing, Titus,' he said. 'I can't decide whether, as coroner, to inquest him. He was struck by a cricket ball which points to accidental death but then I hear he injured himself with a knife. I also hear he is suspected of attacking the judge's relation Mrs Dolland. There must be more to this than one sees at first.'

'There is much, much more than you can imagine, Stephen,' I said.

So I told him as best I could, in the short time I had, the story of the tontine and the involvements caused by John Bourke's sham death at the Menai Straits and his subsequent attempt to solve his financial difficulties by winning the tontine with a campaign of murder.

'He adopted a black beard, and a new name, and came back to Liverpool,' I said. 'There he made the acquaintance of Captain Garland just as he emerged from a short spell in the Debtors' Prison. Garland had known Prenton Smisby there. Bourke must have felt he was being guided by fate.'

'So did he die here in Lancaster in an inquestable way?'

'That's for you to judge, but I think so. The cricket ball did not kill him immediately. In itself it was an incalculable accident, well witnessed. But you have to take into account that he took a knife to himself.'

Dinkin grasped my hand and shook it.

'Thank you, Cragg. I will follow your advice. Have a pleasant journey.'

Later as our coach bumped and shook its way along the Preston road Elizabeth told me of her conversation with Mrs Dinkin.

'Her mind is like a grasshopper, Titus.' she said. 'It jumps from subject to subject, twittering all the while. We talked of Alicia Simpson.'

'What does Mrs Dinkin say of her?'

'Would you believe it she admires the silly girl? She is agog to know when she will find a husband. Ha! If you ask me, Miss Alicia does not really want to marry. She and her sister enjoy the pursuit too much to want to bring down the prey.'

I leaned towards her and murmured into her ear.

'I know one thing,' I said. 'She will not find a man to love her as well as I do you.'

Two weeks later I received a letter from Mr Pickering at Ormskirk.

> *Mr Cragg,*
>
> *You would perhaps like to know that Captain Garland (Dolland as he really is) has suffered an apoplexy and can neither speak nor walk. Mrs Greenwood has taken him into her house and cares for him. The case of Mrs Dolland is very different. After returning from Lancaster she has regained her health and is suing Mr Parr for the payment of the tontine money, which is a matter I know you are curious about. As*

for Mr Parr, to everybody's great surprise he has come to
Ormskirk and lives reclusively at Chimneystacks Farm, which
as you remember he acquired from Mr Giggleswick's estate.
He hardly goes about but keeps to himself there. When you
are next in Ormskirk, I do beg you to come and visit the
house of your friend, Joseph Pickering.

That evening I met Fidelis at the Turk's Head. I gave him
Pickering's letter.

'Will Mrs Dolland's suit succeed?' he asked when he had read
it through.

'She has the law of contract on her side. Parr will have to
pay up.'

'It is a crazy sort of scheme but perhaps of all the names on
the tontine, Mrs Dolland is the most deserving.'

'She is an exceptional woman of business. Mrs Greenwood,
now, is another exceptional woman but she has been burdened
with the care of the Captain.'

'Mrs Greenwood is a forceful person. I cannot understand what
drew her to a drunken and feckless boor.'

'Yet she was drawn to you, Luke.'

'I may be feckless and drunken sometimes, but not both at
the same time. Anyway my intrigue with Mrs Greenwood was
a flash in the pan, while she truly likes this fellow, can you
believe it?'

'Perhaps she hopes he will recover his wits.'

'That is unlikely. Apoplexy gets worse, not better. It ends in
death as a rule.'

'You notice the news of Ambrose Parr?' I said. 'What still
puzzles me looking back is why he pursued Fanny so zealously.
She knew of his sexual secrets and he surely wasn't relying on
the girl's modesty to keep her quiet.'

'He didn't think he needed to. He had no idea that Fanny knew
about the goats.'

'But she was there to see, Luke! She even took part in that act.'

'It was her part to be masked, Titus, remember? She showed
Parr everything except her face.'

'Then why ever did he pursue Fanny for Miss Pettifer's death?
It was always a devilish weak case.'

Fidelis held up a finger in objection.

'I believed it.'

'But not because you had any evidence. Parr only won it with the backing of the Ormskirk bench and the assize judge. He could not have relied on them in advance.'

Fidelis applied fire to his pipe, then said, 'Remember what you said to Constable Pickering about the roots of murder being in love, money or pride? In this case Parr's prosecution of Fanny Kirby, which we might conceivably call her attempted murder, came from a combination of all three.'

'Go on.'

Fidelis counted on his fingers. 'One, love: Parr loved or professed love for Isabella Pettifer. But remember what Rosie Benson told us. Miss Pettifer preferred the company of young women. And remember too what Mrs Field said: that Fanny was her employer's favourite.'

'So Parr was jealous of Fanny?'

'Mortally. But money and pride came into it too. Parr might have secured the tontine money for himself if Miss Pettifer had agreed to marry him, but the women represented by Fanny had always stood in his way. I am sure he hated Fanny for that too, and longed to see her burn.'

'Well, his pride has led to his fall now. He has been forced out of Liverpool and has had to take up farming.'

Fidelis took a long pull of smoke from his pipe.

'That will suit him tolerably well, I think,' he said.

'How is that?'

'Well, we can say at least that there will be a ready supply of goats, Titus.'

EPILOGUE

The Seven Brave Gamesters

I'll sing you seven gamesters
of friends they were the best,
and each made bets
that they would yet
live longer than the rest, my boys,
live longer than the rest.

I'll sing you seven gamesters
when going out to ride.
Then one was tossed,
his balance lost,
he broke his neck and died, my boys,
he broke his neck and died.

I'll sing you six brave gamesters,
merchants in the offing.
Five got rich,
but not the sixth,
he came home in his coffin, boys,
he came home in his coffin.

I'll sing you five brave gamesters,
drinking pot for pot.
But dash my wig,
one took a swig
and piked off on the spot, my boys,
and piked off on the spot.

I'll sing you four brave gamesters,
a-sharpening a knife.
The stone it tips,

the blade it slips,
and another one's quit this life, my boys,
another one's quit this life.

I'll sing you three brave gamesters,
who strolled atop a cliff.
But one fellow tripped
and down he slipped
and now he's cold and stiff, my boys,
so now he's cold and stiff.

I'll sing you two brave gamesters
with business at the docks.
One falls in
but saves his skin,
and the other one dies of pox, my boys,
the other one dies of pox.

I'll sing you one brave gamester,
so happy with his lot.
His comrades six
have snuffed their wicks
and he takes home the pot, my boys,
and he takes home the pot.

Words by Capt. Garland of the Welsh Fusiliers, to be sung to a traditional air.